By Tyler Sehn

Copyright © Tyler Sehn 2015

Tyler Sehn asserts the moral right to be identified as the author of this work.

All rights reserved. No part of this publication may be reproduced or transmitted in any form or by any means, electronic, mechanical, photocopying, recording or otherwise, without the prior permission of the author.

This novel is entirely a work of fiction. The names, characters and incidents portrayed in it are the work of the author's imagination. Any resemblance to actual persons, living or dead, events or localities is entirely coincidental.

## Acknowledgments

I've been looking forward to this part for a long time, since the first draft was completed and I thought I was an author. Little did I know that a first draft is far from a finished product.

First off: Derek, Cole, and Will. Derek, you read everything I sent to you, even the roughest of drafts. Without you, the story would be half as long and wrapped in a neat little package. Cole, you are always willing to hash out ideas and make sure I push the action as far as possible. Wilhelm III, you insisted on being the first reader and made me believe that I actually might have a story worth telling.

Thanks to James Scott-Marryat for the content edit, and Morgan Smith for the copy edit. Your insight was invaluable.

Thanks Dad for keeping news of my attempt to write a novel quiet until you were sure I wanted people to know. Thanks Mom for telling family, friends, and strangers alike (everyone, seriously, absolutely everyone) about my writing from the moment you learned of it.

Carter, you challenged practically everything regarding this book but that only made me work harder to try and convince you that I knew what I was doing, which helped more than you might guess.

Jeff, Blair and the rest of Curbside, you were more inspiring than you know.

Many thanks to those who volunteered as beta readers and took the time to read manuscript versions of varying quality (mostly bad).

Big ups to Jeff Merkel and Danny Jose of Rolling Dice Studios for creating some amazing artwork.

To Laura, Curtis, Amit, Bev, and Kelley for working along with me to figure out this writing game.

Thanks to everyone (there are many of you) who listened to me talk about "the book" in varying degrees of sobriety.

Gerrit and Ute, you took me in (my dog as well) and treated me like family even though I like fantasy stories more than horses.

Beke, thank you for believing in me when I told you that I wanted to be a writer and all I had was a pocketful of Post-it notes that became this novel.

Lastly, I dedicate this novel to my grandparents: E. J. & Joanna, George & Denise. You're all characters in your own right and showed me that if one speaks their opinion honestly (and loudly) that some might confuse it with wisdom.

**The Shining Empire**
Melea, Champion of the Shining Empire, adopted by Martinus Anathasius
Emperor Anathasius, Lord of Light, Shining Lord, god and ruler of the Shining Empire
Belenus Wicket, Beacon of Azra, priest of the Sanctuary
Morokko Kachina, Teeth in the Darkness, assassin
Mandrikos, Melea's tutor at the Palace of Light, known for philosophical quotes
Goldwin, map maker and geographer at the Palace of Light
Kronus Pompae, High Priest of the Sanctuary, of noble birth
Andran Derclerq, Captain of Chosen, Melea's sword master
General Cathair, highest ranking Chosen, military strategist
Lieutenant Osgood, a Chosen from Kannark
Hector, attendant at the Palace of Light
Gern, personal guard to the Beacon
Rendyll, personal guard to the Beacon
Jerome Bogan, Big Bo, overseer of the Pompae estate
Daymon, priest of the Sanctuary
Trinn, street liaison and informant
Gerboa, thief in Azra
Arnul Aderat, inexperienced priest of the Sanctuary
Barroc Wicket, head armorer of the Chosen, brother to Belenus
Mariam Wicket, wife to Barroc, mother of three

**Rhezaria**
Queen Ritika Dracarion, former Tehlos in training, Queen of the Clans
Draggar Vol, Remori General, advisor to the Queen
Reyner Vol, Champion of Verangor's Ring, son of Draggar
Koacachoa O'kanhana'etim, Chief of the Uzanaki
Luka O'kanhana'etim, Uzanaki prince
Soren Daro, Chief of the Nataga
Borus Akklad, Chief of the Remori
Xi Xoatal, Chief of the Sando
Abi'Ragaz Dracarion, Chief of the Rhezi, Uncle to the Queen
Hekäli Mu'godis, priestess of Mar'Edo Kon
Trangdon Wulfstom, Remori ship captain and merchant
Ulaar Tremana, Rhezi warrior
Garret Tumino, Champion of the Standing Prayer, Rhezi warrior
Helgernon, Captain of the guard at Anselmbao
Zlakos, Rhezi merchant
Kianna Dracarion, former Queen, nun to Mar'Edo Kon
Velibor Dracarion, deceased King
Damacles Dracarion, briefly ruled as King, missing and presumed dead, brother to Ritika

**Frozen Tribes**
Kerak, shaman, leader of Cuolocano
Nal-Farrah, wife to Kerak, mother of two, rumored to be a syla
Katano, warrior, called the bear-man

Sixthrok, warrior, called Ta-kal

**Other Players**
Taisto Salero, bandit and smuggler from the Outskirts
Dacre Salero, bandit and smuggler from the Outskirts
Lucius Vand, crime lord in Marikal, proprietor of the Dirty Penny
Jai Alvarros, Chancellor of the Six Isle Republic
Grimbaldi, advisor to Chancellor Alvarros
Forever Boy, street urchin with a proclivity for rhyming
Dreamer, elderly singer and meddler
Mattias Horvkild, King of Strakos
Fitzroy Jenks, crime lord in Marikal
Iribi, step-daughter to Jenks
Elgarth Karracus, Duke of Asyrith
Scar, mercenary
One Eye, mercenary
Skittish, mercenary
Luger, captain of the Bethuna
Zheng Ja'hoth, pirate captain of the Blind Lady
Dago, smuggler

## Prologue: The Age of Blood

*How could I have been so foolish?*

He listened to the screams of his Brothers, knowing there was nowhere to run to. He stood with his back to the ironwood tree and waited for the boy to come.

*I loved him like a son. How could love reap something such as this?*

Flames from the monastery reflected on the canopy of the ironwood above, cloying smoke swirled into the sanctum, coiling around him, mocking him. The screams died away.

"Master? Holiest and most wise of all men, why do you run from me? Where has my beloved Master gone?"

He leaned back against the tree, his failure immense, his betrayal the ultimate foolishness, and waited for the boy to enter the sanctum.

"Master, why do you run from me?"

The boy had discarded the golden robes and now wore the clothes he'd arrived in, all that time ago. His hair was singed and anger shone from his eyes, threatening violence.

"Am I still your favorite pupil?" The boy came closer. "Answer me, old man. Am I still heir to the profound truth? I have killed them all—you showed me the way. The knowledge that you guarded so stoically is mine now; it's with someone who knows how to use it. Is this it? The deepest mystery of the Brotherhood, the secret so carefully guarded by you and your forefathers?"

"There is no secret," the Master said.

"I took it from you, from all of you! Now tell me where to find the Bloodless."

"There is only truth and its preservation. This is all I have given you."

"You did not give me anything, you old fool. I took it. Everything! And I will use it."

"Then finish this, so that I may seek absolution for my weakness in the next life."

The young man produced a blood-stained knife. "Anything for my Master."

## The Emperor's Champion

*Power makes a man a fool.* Melea knew this to be true from a single glance at the Captain. *Men grow comfortable from the feel of power and will react aggressively to keep it.*

Captain Gallo stood formally in his crisp blue uniform. The silver trim along his shoulders and the sigil of an open eye sewn to his right breast signified his status as an officer. Melea wore no symbol as a proxy for the Emperor. She was no leader of men.

Melea gazed across the hardy tundra grass at the last remaining fortress of the Frozen Tribes. The enemy had constructed a huge fortification of rock and other debris around an ocean inlet situated between two large cliff faces. This wall effectively blocked the Chosen from mounting an all-out offensive, turning the battle into a siege. With the sea at their back the northerners had an easy escape route as well as access to food. Melea hadn't known that Rua extended this far north. She'd seen the region on a map but never realized that people actually lived in the section painted an icy blue.

"The bastards chose the location well. We'll lose a lot of men trying to take them here," said Captain Gallo. "Who knows what other tricks that blasted shaman has waiting for us?"

A gust of sea air pushed long strands of hair across her face. The Captain was trying to rationalize his failure and she would not placate him. Instead she surveyed the holdfast; something about it was wrong. Melea concentrated harder, peering at the barricade as if she could will herself into understanding the sensation she felt when looking at it. To her right, Captain Gallo grew tired of waiting.

"Doertsen! Sound the—"

"Hold that order," Melea snapped. "I will have your tongue if you try that again."

"What is it, your Excellence?" he managed through gritted teeth.

*Your Excellence?* The title made Melea cringe. They never knew how to address her.

"Your incompetence has required my presence," Melea kept her voice calm, making sure the Captain understood what was now required of him. "You pushed the army too quickly to the location, resulting in a host of exhausted men forced to face the ambush of a waiting enemy. You walked into trap after trap until the enemy became untouchable within their fortress."

"How was I supposed to know their shaman could raise blinding ice storms? That he could freeze an entire lake and sink my cavalry on the thin ice? That they have a warrior who—"

Melea took a step closer. "Too many casualties under your command." She looked him up and down like a sickly animal not fit for slaughter. "I will end this today."

Gallo broke from the stare down first.

She looked back at the organized ranks of Chosen in identical blue uniforms and bronze armor. The sight of so many men dressed exactly the same always made Melea think of insects. Ants preparing for conquest. Melea wrapped the cloak tight around her thin body and started toward the barricade. The wavering boom of a war horn spread across the valley.

A familiar tingle of anxiety in the belly greeted Melea as she approached the looming wall. Blood was about to be spilled by her hand on the hard tundra soil. Melea knew some had difficulty remaining calm in these situations, but she felt at ease in moments of danger, aware of the options available to her, and therefore able to react quicker, able to stand over the slower, the dead.

Melea stopped beneath the walls, outside of striking distance, as numerous spear points poked above the perimeter.

"Shaman!"

A large figure stepped on top of the wall. "Southerner, I am Kerak, leader of the Frozen Tribes. What would you say to me?"

Melea studied Kerak. His accented Simanu was rough, but the shaman spoke the language of his enemies well enough. He was a big man who looked to be past his prime years. His face was smooth and deeply tanned from the sun and wind. Streaks of grey were beginning to show in his long, jet-black hair. In his right hand he held a driftwood staff adorned with crow feathers, and a black wolf pelt cloak was slung across his shoulders.

More than anything else, Melea searched Kerak's eyes—two bits of stone that refused to be worn down. He would die before yielding. The solid foundation of his people had been shattered but the debris still had sharp edges.

"My name is Melea, and I speak for Emperor Martinus Anathasius, the Lord of Light." She waved at hand at the fortifications. "You have built a strong wall here, but it cannot hold forever. The army behind me will break it and your people will suffer for their effort. Some of you may escape to the sea, but where will you go? The rest of the North has joined with the Emperor and I am sure you have heard how unbelievers are viewed. I offer you a proposition: to do as the rest of your people have, and follow the Shining Empire." Melea paused to let the words sink in.

After a moment, Kerak stated in a clear voice for all to hear. "This wall will last until winter, and then your thin skins will freeze with the first snowfall. You waste your words and my time."

As the shaman finished speaking, Melea heard the unmistakeable sound of a bowstring being released. Melea's training took command as she threw her left arm up in a guard position.

A force smashed into the metal gauntlet on her forearm. The impact spun Melea into a crouch, but she managed to reverse the momentum by bracing her right hand on the ground and pushing off. She ripped the arrow out of the gauntlet in one fluid motion, energy emanating from her palms, spreading over the arrow to make the wood malleable. She used the new consistency of the wood to stretch the arrow three times its original length.

Melea exploded out of her low stance and hurled the makeshift spear back in the direction it had come. A shocked cry of pain sounded from the wall. The lengthened arrow had impaled an archer who stumbled and fell from his perch, landing with a thud on Melea's side of the wall.

"Is this how you negotiate? By firing arrows from the shadows like a coward?" Melea glared at the shaman.

"I needed to see if I was truly dealing with the Emperor's child of death. He must be very concerned about the Frozen Tribes to send you here."

"You look tired Kerak. It seems you have overextended yourself with these elaborate rituals. The storm, the lake, and I'm guessing you also reinforced this wall?" Melea lowered her voice, but it still retained the power of her anger. "I offer a way out of this self-imposed cage. Defeat me in single combat and the army at my back will leave you in peace. To continue is to doom your people."

Kerak's smirk disappeared, his mouth settling into a hard line, grey eyes locking onto Melea's green. "I do not wish to speak with a courtesan pretending to be a warrior. I will not give honor to an Emperor too cowardly to say his own words. This wall is strengthened with glacial ice; your army will not be getting through it any time soon. We will wait until the winter cold makes it even stronger. You may smash your iron against northern ice and die."

She bared her teeth, snarling a response instead of speaking one. She was giving him a chance. An offer like this was not something Melea tossed around lightly or often.

Or was she just rephrasing the Emperor's commands? He had ordered her to attempt diplomacy, and if necessary, to defeat the leader of the Frozen Tribes. Melea found that she was more upset with the shaman's accusation of being a courtesan than at his direct insult to the Emperor. The bastard would lose his head for that insult. Her mission was clear and Melea was a warrior. When things got complicated, it was easiest to cut her way out.

Melea scowled at Kerak's departing figure. "Don't turn your back on me!"

Melea raised her left arm in front of her face as she had done to block the arrow, this time hitting a release on the backside of the gauntlet, causing four small darts to shoot in Kerak's direction. Kerak ducked but two tribesmen were slower to react.

The stunned men clutched at their throats. The poison spread quickly and the men made gurgling noises as they choked from internal swelling. Looks of horror were clear in the wide eyes of the companions who helped the poisoned men down.

"It appears we both have our tricks," Kerak said as he resurfaced above the wall. "I still see no reason to give in to your demands."

Melea forced herself to take a couple of deep breaths. She disliked giving long speeches, particularly when she had to give them to someone who had just tried to kill her.

"You have been given an opportunity that will not last beyond this moment. An offer given by the Emperor himself, an order only I may enforce. You may think you can outlast the Emperor behind your wall but you are wrong. He will make it past your wall and kill you. How long will your people survive without their shaman? The Emperor does not accept failure. Are you willing to fail your people?"

Kerak stared at Melea. "How do I know that your Emperor will honor his word if I defeat you?"

Melea set her shoulders, her face an expressionless mask. "I have not lost a fight yet. You'll have to walk that path if you come to it."

Warriors were prideful by nature and in Melea's experience they always rose to the challenge. Kerak grunted what might have been laugh.

"You are bold, I will give you that. Such fierceness from someone so young. Are you sure that you are not of the Tribes?"

"Your answer, shaman." Melea had tired of this discussion. The message was delivered, it was now up to the leader of the Frozen Tribes to decide how he would die.

"I accept your challenge but my son will fight in my stead. The last ritual I performed was for him."

An immense figure wearing an enormous white bear pelt appeared beside Kerak. The man looked more animal than human. Kerak removed the bear pelt.

"Katano, kill the child of death."

Katano leapt off the wall and Melea felt the ground tremble as he landed.

Melea read reports of the bear-man's rampages amongst the lines of the Chosen in the previous skirmishes, killing men with a single blow of his huge hands when his massive spear broke. He would be trained as a warrior no doubt, and raised as a prince, adding skill and intelligence to his monstrous strength. The shaman tossed an impossibly large spear down to his son and the battle began.

Katano swung the spear, roared at Melea, and charged. He was the biggest man Melea had ever seen, which would make him freakishly strong even without being supernaturally empowered.

Two daggers flitted out from inside Melea's cloak as she rolled out of the path of the charge. Katano managed to deflect one dagger with his spear but the other lodged into his left shoulder. The imbedded blade did not slow him in the slightest as he turned the attack, swinging the spear in Melea's direction in a low sweeping arc.

Melea had foreseen this maneuver and was well out of harm's way when the deadly blade ripped past. The speed of the gigantic man was impressive, but it was no match for Melea's quickness. Most troubling was the shocking disparity in strength.

A feeling of white-hot energy was brewing within Melea's chest and she felt her movements quickening in accordance with it. She palmed a small iron ball from one of the inner pockets of her cloak as she turned to face the bear-man.

Katano was faster than he ought to be, and was almost on top of her again. He lashed out with a powerful spear thrust. Melea took one quick step, leapt onto the shaft of the plunging spear, and used the flex to spring towards Katano.

The iron ball grasped in her palm spread outward and over her entire fist like water. She raised a hand to strike. Melea smashed a fist of solid iron into Katano's nose, splattering blood everywhere as if he had been hit with a mace. Katano raged, roaring as he swung the spear in all directions.

Melea backed out of range, tucking away the iron ball. The length of the huge spear rendered her short sword ineffective so she knelt down, placing her hand flat on a sandy patch of soil.

The feeling of energy within her chest scorched her breath as she focused on the sand. The heat entered the sand, fusing the grains together, shaping them by the force of her will. Melea could feel the rough grains sliding over one another, becoming smoother as they transformed into one mass.

Katano had recovered from the initial encounter. Smears of blood streaked his face. Melea rose for the next attack, now with a long blade of sparkling glass in hand. This time she brought the attack to Katano, racing toward him with the glittering sword held low at her side.

Katano lunged at the onrushing girl with his spear, the glass blade flashed out and a third of his spear fell to the ground. Melea spun on her heel, slashing at the back of Katano's leg, and using her momentum to carry her past. Katano howled in pain as he went down to one knee. Melea turned to slash the other leg and barely got her blade up in time as Katano pivoted on his good leg to deliver a roundhouse fist.

The glass blade shattered into a thousand pieces and Melea was sent hurtling through the air. For a moment she lay stunned on the ground, unable to breath. A huge shadow appeared above her. Katano had covered the distance between them incredibly quickly, hobbled as he was, and swung an open palm covered in glass shards down at Melea.

She rolled out of the way of the oncoming swipe. A large rift of earth was torn out of the ground as Katano's curved fingers missed their target. Melea dove between the giant's legs and raced away while still trying to catch her breath. Katano heaved a large rock that skimmed overhead to smash against the fortress wall behind her. She drew the short sword and circled the bear-man.

He still held the remaining shaft of the spear and waved it in front. A dark look crossed his face as he gestured for Melea to come to him. Melea approached methodically, eyeing the trickle of blood streaming down his injured leg. She attacked in quick lunges and retreats, attempting to put Katano off kilter. The huge warrior blocked all of her strikes, doing well to remain balanced.

"Not good enough," he growled in a deep, accented voice. "I pity any who calls you their champion."

His contempt incited rage; cold, dark, churning.

"I bring death," Melea whispered. "I am a catalyst to the vision of a living god. My every action is victory. Some trade blood for power and believe themselves strong." Melea scoffed at the bear-man's hulking figure. "My blood is power. Your sacrifice is meaningless."

The mixture of rage and pride was toxic, blinding Melea to her training as she threw herself at the huge warrior with a ferocious attack. Katano struggled to block the lightning fast slashes. What remained of his spear was reduced to even less. He dropped the useless piece of wood and grasped Melea's sword with a huge palm.

Blood spouted from his hand but Melea could not remove her sword from Katano's grip. She was too slow letting go of the sword and Katano's free fist smashed into her left side. Pain exploded into her body and she did not even see the next blow. Katano delivered a massive punch that sent her spiraling through the air before crashing into the wall.

Her body was racked with pain, consciousness flickering in and out as she lay on a heap of shattered stones. Katano turned to the Chosen and bellowed a roar of victory.

Melea's mind would not work, the only sensation that managed to make its way through was the firmness of the ground, the stones calling out for her to remain. The energy within her chest was still warm and seemed to answer the call as it swirled throughout her limbs like smoke from a glowing ember.

A spark flared in Melea's mind as she felt the energy make its way to her fingertips, slowly leaking out into the stones below. She could feel the solidity of the stones merging with the tendrils of energy, the firmness attaching to her bones. Melea flexed her hand, hearing the sound of rolling rocks in her mind. Strength once again filtered throughout her body.

Katano approached her confidently. His eyes opened wide in shock as Melea pushed herself up from the ground; the pile of rocks that lain beneath her were gone. He took a step back as she stood.

Her mouth tasted of chalk and her teeth seemed intent on grinding themselves into oblivion. She spit out a wad of blood but a muddy substance came out instead. The skin on her arms looked pebbled—the stones pushing against the skin from the inside.

"Looks like I will have to break you again, witch." He removed the throwing knife from his shoulder, hefting it as he dropped into a crouch.

Melea rushed the northern warrior, her body feeling heavy and cumbersome. She blocked the dagger with her left forearm, only the tip piercing her flesh. More of the muddy substance oozed out. Melea aimed for Katano's groin and threw all of her weight behind her right hand. Her punch missed its mark and landed in his lower abdomen, causing a large puff of dust to be released out of her fist. Katano winced and returned a partial punch. Another puff of dust escaped from where it connected on Melea's shoulder. A cloud of dust enveloped the fighters as Melea delivered a flurry of strikes that brought Katano to his knees. She finished by ramming her forehead into his chin, feeling his jaw crack.

Melea stepped away, her teeth raw and her arms like dead weights. Her skin was no longer pebbled and the solidity of the stones was quickly leaving her body. She retrieved the lead ball from her pocket and it spread out over her hand, the liquid material restructuring into a needle-like blade on her forefinger. She approached once more, intending to finish the fight.

Katano appeared dazed but he still clutched the dagger. He made no move to stop Melea as she angled her hand to deliver the killing thrust. She plunged the needle into Katano's neck, the sharp point coming out the back. The image of an enraged bear flashed in front of her; the beast was inside the warrior, she could feel it. But there was something else.

In her mind's eye, Melea watched a shadow emerge between the warring spirits of Katano and the bear. The shadow oozed forward, sliding over the bronze encasing Melea's finger. She sensed intention within the shadow, could feel it stitching together the killing wound she had inflicted. The shadow transformed into a hand with long, wicked talons—reaching for her. Melea knew this shadow, somehow, and she knew it recognized her as well. It grasped for her and she withdrew.

Katano growled, lifting his dagger. Melea's needle blade lowered; each combatant going for their final strike.

A sudden squall of squawking filled the air as a wall of blackness slammed into Melea and Katano before either could deliver a deathblow. Both were sent sprawling to the ground, separated by a swirling cloud darker than any moonless night.

Melea looked to the wall and saw Kerak, a black feather dangling from the driftwood staff clenched in his hand. Fresh blood tickled down from his fist. Her attention returned to the shrieking tornado in front of her, which she now recognized as a flock of crows. The shaman's voice boomed down to the combatants.

"Enough. Nothing is decided if you both die. I do not trust your Emperor to keep his word."

Melea groaned, her muscles strained to capacity, legs shaky as she stood. Kerak cut her short before she could speak.

"I will go to meet this Emperor with you," a finger jutted out at Melea. "While I am gone, Katano will lead in my stead."

Melea nodded. "So be it. You may accompany me as an ambassador or as a hostage, whichever title you prefer. We leave tomorrow at dawn." Melea turned from the shaman and began walking toward the Chosen without looking back.

The watching army was silent as she approached.

Captain Gallo stepped forward. "And what are my men supposed to do while you take the shaman on a tour of Azra?"

Melea shrugged. "I don't care. Send a physician to my tent and have two carriages ready to depart for tomorrow."

She passed the fuming captain, and spotted a thick-necked lieutenant.

"What is your name?"

"Osgood, your Grace, er uh, your Excellence." The Lieutenant's eyes were the size of dinner plates.

"Osgood! Food!"

The man jumped and swiftly moved through the lines of men back toward the camp. Melea's smile was grim, a flash of white teeth through smears of dirt and blood. She marched to the tent, a ragged black speck beneath an endless blue sky. Exhaustion claimed her the moment she lay down on the cot. There would be no dreams this night.

## New Light

The Emperor watched dusk settle over his city. He plucked a pear from a nearby tree and took a small bite. His thoughts were concentrated on places far beyond the scenery below. Everything north of the Eternal Forest would soon be under the enlightenment of the Shining Empire. *Everything except for the Outskirts*, he mused as he tossed the pear over the ledge.

That windswept territory of deserts, canyons, and steppes was only inhabited by bandits and wandering nomads. The raiding on his lands by these people was irksome, as was their lack of faith in his divinity. The Outskirts would bow to him, or they would be annihilated. At the moment he did not care which outcome came to pass.

Emperor Anathasius watched shadows crawl across rooftops and imagined the view of the palace from below. As the sun set, the people in the streets would see a white palace of slender towers radiating golden sunlight, slowly fading into an orange and purple glow as the last light of the day draped over the domes. The domes should appear flaming red just about now. A bonfire to fend off the fears that came with the sightlessness of dark.

A soft rustle stirred behind, perhaps a dried leaf pushed about by a silent wind, but Anathasius felt no breeze. He knew who joined him within the lush garden terrace of the Sun's Perch.

"If I did not know any better I'd think you were trying to creep up on me," said Anathasius, as he turned to face the assassin.

Anathasius approved of this level of stealth—nobody moved through the shadows like Morokko Kachina. A black scarf covered Morokko's mouth and nose. The assassin bowed in respect and pulled the scarf below his chin, serrated fangs glittering like unholy gems.

"Ah now where did you find those?" asked Anathasius.

"Shark; caught it in the Gulf with my own hands," whispered the assassin.

"The Teeth in the Darkness," said Anathasius. "I have heard that name whispered in fear."

"Yes."

"It appears that you have learned well the lesson I wished to impart."

Morokko dropped to a knee. "My body is yours, my Lord. Loyalty must be earned."

Anathasius nodded. "By now I am sure that you have heard of Melea's victory. Now we turn our full attention to Calanthia. It is vital that you make contact with the established sources and gather as much information about the ongoing politics as possible. Use this information to create unrest, set neighbor against neighbor, weaken bonds to deride their fragile unity."

Morokko interjected, his raspy voice hissing between the fangs. "My Lord, my methods..."

"Use whatever approach you deem necessary. I appoint you with this task because of your unique skill set."

Morokko gave a small nod of the head.

"You have two months to set the pieces in motion. You will leave immediately. Send reports of all noteworthy progress."

Morokko melted into the quickening darkness.

"Oh, and Morokko, take pride in becoming an instrument of your own design. The fine teeth that your mother so adored are nothing compared to these acquired by your own strength and skill."

"Yes."

Anathasius clasped his hands behind his back as he turned to face the city. Lamps and torches were now being lit to fend off the twilight. The moon made its first appearance.

The huge and misshapen mountain adjacent to the palace shimmered in the pale moonlight. The river Choisis wound its way around the far side of the black mountain to empty into the Gateway Gulf. Anathasius stared at the ominous mountain and then to his newly built factory whose smokestacks no longer produced the soot they did during the day.

Azra was the beating heart of his empire and the inhabitants were the lifeblood that powered it. He could feel its pulse more intimately than the heart in his chest. Soon, the veins of this city would extend further than ever before, carrying his blood across Rua to tie this broken and disjointed world together.

Anathasius' thoughts turned reflective as he stared across the city to the glittering waves in the wide expanse of the Gulf. Rua, *the remains*, in the old tongue, was a fitting title for this world. A legacy of the Bloodless.

He had instilled Azra with new energy and was proud to give the people direction and purpose. Anathasius knew that a man would gladly give up his soul in exchange for truth.

Azra was an old city that covered the hills ringing the mouth of the Gateway Gulf. Direct access to the Shallow Sea afforded by the Gulf and the many tributary rivers flowing into this body of water had helped to make Azra a vital trading post for everything north of the Eternal Forest.

Anathasius was the one who had pulled this city out of the rubble when the Age of Stone collapsed, the only person capable of erasing the consequences inflicted by the War of the Gods. But that was in past and the delectable possibilities of the future laced the air tonight. He could taste it. Anathasius left the terrace for the warmth of his chambers.

The vaulted ceilings were tiled to display a colorful representation of the city below. A soft glow produced by many lamps threw warmth on the smooth marble floors, which were covered in finely crafted rugs. A large desk of fossilized ironwood, as immovable as a boulder, was pressed against one wall. The Emperor's spacious bed was against the near wall, laden with exquisite linens.

On the edge of the bed sat a young girl in a milk-white dress. She ran her bare toes through the thick carpet at her feet, clearly enjoying the sensation.

"That carpet is made from a certain breed of sheep in Calanthia. There is no wool softer in all the world," said Anathasius.

The girl looked at the Emperor with glassy eyes, in awe of his presence. She dropped to her knees, forehead pressed to the carpet.

"Do not worry. I asked for you to join me here this evening, you are an honored guest. Please grace me with the pleasure of knowing your name." Anathasius smoothly crossed the distance between them. "Please, rise."

The girl looked up at Anathasius and offered a shy smile. "Shining Lord, Savior of Rua, I am your servant, Shamara."

Anathasius nodded approvingly. "A beautiful name for a beautiful girl."

Shamara smiled and Anathasius noticed that some of the tension left her shoulders but she still would not look him in the eye.

"You have been training with the Flames for some time now and I have heard your skills are progressing along quite well."

Shamara nodded.

"Your progress is why I have called you here tonight. I would like to see you perform the ceremony that you have recently perfected."

"Shining Lord, I do not have the required tools. I am unprepared and unworthy to perform this task for you." Shamara bowed her head in piety, folding her hands on the front of her gown.

Anathasius smiled comfortingly. "Shamara, you have not displeased me, nor will you. The necessary tools are in the desk. Please retrieve them." Shamara walked swiftly to the ochre desk and looked back at Anathasius questioningly. "There, in the main compartment."

She swung open the heavy door and pulled out a black stone box from inside. The box was large for her small hands and heavy enough to cause her to strain in effort as she carried it. Anathasius moved to sit on the edge of the bed as Shamara set the box in front of him. She carefully removed the lid and withdrew the items, placing them neatly in front of the box.

"You see," said Anathasius. "These are the same instruments that you practice with."

Shamara calmed at this and sat cross-legged on the floor with a bowl of cream colored clay, a small thin blade, a thick white candle, and a large goblet before her.

"You may begin." His voice was filled with fatherly approval, reassuring the young priestess that she had his full support. "I assure you that this will be your finest achievement, Shamara. You are a blessed priestess of Light, a Flame to ward off Darkness, a gift to the Shining Empire."

Shamara looked around the room. "Shining Lord, I have only performed the ceremony by the light of a single candle. I am unsure if I will be able to complete it in this bright room."

He looked into her eyes, there was fear there, but only the fear of causing disappointment. "Of course," he said, raising his right hand and slowly curling outstretched fingers into his palm. The many lamps on the walls dimmed before sputtering and going out completely. The room plunged into complete darkness. Anathasius snapped his fingers, the sharp crack echoing in the vast room, and the white candle on the floor flared to life, creating a small ring of illumination.

"Acceptable?"

Shamara gasped. "Yes, my Lord, I will begin."

The burning candle produced a pungent smell that stung the nostrils and made every breath feel like a deep pull of glacial air. Shamara began a low hum in the back of her throat while staring intently at the candle. The young priestess continued this process until her eyes achieved an unfocused stare, appearing to see through the flame.

Her eyes never wavered in their focus as her hands reached for the bowl and the blade. Shamara placed the bowl in her lap and then made a thin cut across her left palm, allowing a stream of blood to drip into the bowl. She put the knife down, slowly closed her eyes, and began to knead the clay.

Her humming, that had began as a steady trance, gradually increased in volume. Shamara's hands moved surely and swiftly as they molded the clay into the form of a child's head and face. Her delicate hands molded the sculpture into fine detail until the clay looked exactly like that of a child with eyes closed and an open, crying mouth.

The priestess opened her eyes, carefully placing the clay creation into the goblet, then set the goblet into the box. Her humming changed in octave as she returned her gaze to the flame. The sound of the hum rose in pitch as Shamara wove it towards an inevitable crescendo, but before this conclusion could be reached, she abruptly stopped humming and closed the lid of the box.

Her eyes closed and she slowly drew her hand past her throat three times in succession. Sea green eyes snapped open, her right hand snatched up the blade, she drew it quickly across her throat. Anathasius leaned forward into the ring of light, his eyes watching every subtle movement. He saw a single drop of blood roll down Shamara's neck and stain the white dress. The wailing cry of a child could be heard from inside the box; the unmistakable squall of an infant searching for comfort. The Emperor and priestess paid no attention to this sound and it ceased. Shamara opened the box, removed the goblet, and swallowed the contents in one swift gulp.

The bed chambers burst into illumination and the goblet fell out of Shamara's hands, clanging across the floor before stopping against the bed. Pale blue light emanated from her entire body. Excitement flickered in the Emperor's eyes as he watched the soft glow build in magnitude.

The ethereal light was infused with swirling grey tendrils of smoke that stretched on their own accord. They moved like conscious vines, slowly elevating Shamara's small body into the air. She rose a meter off the ground and appeared to begin her descent when Anathasius leapt towards her, forcefully clasping his hands around her head.

Blue light seeped between his fingers as he hunched over her incapacitated figure, his white robes radiant in the eerie light. Smoky tendrils wrapped themselves around his forearms and bubbles of blue light traveled into his arms, following the current of his bloodstream.

Anathasius was a streaming vision as Shamara's iridescence rapidly entered his body. His eyes no longer held their natural color of warm honey, instead flashing a brilliant indigo.

The Emperor's jaw clenched and his nostrils flared in concentration. The transfer of light slowed to a trickle and then stopped completely. Anathasius gently laid Shamara down on the marble floor. Her face had a sickly pallor, eyes twitching in distress beneath closed lids. Shamara feebly rocked her head slowly from side to side and her chest struggled to rise.

Anathasius placed an open palm on her chest, causing her body once again to be consumed by light. The powerful white light reaching the farthest corners of the large room. Anathasius lifted his hand and the room sank back into darkness, save for the lone flicker of the ceremonial candle.

The Emperor stretched his arms wide and neck from side to side, letting the energy course through him. *Such power!* He felt invigorated, fuller, invincible. He looked down at the spot where Shamara's body had been only a moment before, then snuffed out the flame.

Not for the first time he wondered what Melea's power would taste like. The girl had a chance to become great but still needed to pass certain tests of loyalty. Her usefulness in the upcoming war could prove invaluable. The conflict might even further cultivate her abilities. Anathasius smiled; he could always take her spirit if she failed.

## The Beacon

Belenus waited in the open doorway of the palace, protected from elements. The rain fell heavy and straight. The priest's knees ached, each raindrop hammering old age into his awareness like nails sealing a coffin shut. Two carriages came to a stop in front of the Palace of Light.

Eight of the palace guard in maroon uniforms arranged themselves on either side of the second carriage. The shaman exited, ignoring the armed guards, pausing to cast a long look into the night sky as the rain splashed down.

"Barbarian," Belenus grumbled, entering the palace.

He crossed his hands inside the roomy sleeves of his white robe. A golden sun was emblazoned across his chest, curving rays of light creeping over the shoulders. Four soaked guards entered, followed by an equally wet shaman, and four more guards.

"Honored shaman of the Frozen Tribes, welcome to the Palace of Light. My name is Belenus Wicket and I am the Emperor's Beacon to the people of Azra and beyond."

Kerak did not look at Belenus, instead studying the grand entry room, glancing upward at the detailed tiled artwork on the large dome above them. The priest of Shining Empire was as tall as the northern shaman, but he lacked the man's commanding physical presence. The shaman sniffed loudly then shook himself like a dog, sending water droplets spraying in all directions.

Belenus wiped the water off his face, a few drops glistening on the fringes of his bushy eyebrows. "A pity the rain obscures the lights. Azra is truly a sight to behold; no other city glows like it."

"Brighter even than Marikal?"

Belenus was surprised at how well the shaman spoke Simanu; a gruff accent blunted by a guttural language, but proficient nonetheless.

"You are well traveled, Kerak. Azra cannot match the sheer size of the golden city, but Azra is unparalleled in its ability to illuminate, as you will find. Gold is only an illusion of power, a frantic hoarding of momentary wealth—what we have here in Azra is more...enduring."

Kerak's eyes swept the hall once again and Belenus followed his gaze. "All of these lamps and yet they do not flicker or produce smoke? A ritual?"

"All of the lamps within the palace are kept alight by the will of Emperor Anathasius. This is not done by any ritual but through the presence of his divine being."

Kerak's eyebrows arched. "I think it is time to meet the Emperor."

"Your endurance is admirable, but would you not care to rest after the long voyage? I can show you to your room."

Kerak shook his head. "I did not come here to rest. I came to speak with the Emperor."

Belenus retrieved a small razor blade hidden in the sleeve of his robe, using it to make a small cut on the meat of his thumb—a maneuver he had perfected over the years. Power surged within his veins. Belenus focused his thoughts on Kerak, sensing the subtle vibration projected by the shaman's body.

This energy hung around the shaman like loose threads floating on a breeze. Each thread was a different note and together they created a harmony that Belenus could sense on the periphery of his awareness. The sound was right in front of him but it seemed as distant as the gleam of the stars in the night sky.

Belenus teased one strand toward himself, feeling it attach to his own vocal cords. His throat immediately felt thicker and the words vibrated in the priest's mind as he spoke to the shaman.

"Surely you would like to rest, enjoy a warm meal and regain your strength. The Emperor will see you in the morning."

Belenus sent his words down the strand, pushing them into the shaman. He felt resistance, the energy blocked by an unexpected barrier.

A flicker of recognition flashed across Kerak's face. "A Beacon that professes words rather than light. Your words do not move me; I will see the Emperor now."

Belenus signaled one of the guards with a wave of his hand. This shaman was well trained. There seemed to be more to this barbarian than met the eye. He spoke as though he'd spent time in Marikal, capital of Calanthia. That likely meant he was schooled in Ba-rük as well as his own pagan witchcraft.

"Notify Emperor Anathasius that his guest has arrived."

The Captain turned on his heel, the echo of his boots filling the silence as Belenus and Kerak scrutinized one another. Attentive guards ringed the edges of the circular room.

The shaman's hair was long and straight and dark, whereas the priest's grey shot out in all directions and was going thin on top. A pang of jealousy stirred in the priest as he realized that he was more portly than the shaman. He had assumed that those from such a frigid region would need more insulation to combat the cold. Belenus could not recall when he had acquired this additional weight around his midsection. He'd always been naturally fit. He was just older, that was it. Wisdom came with age—*so what if a little extra weight accompanied it?*

Belenus observed the driftwood staff gripped firmly in the shaman's right hand, water dripping from the crow feathers to create a small puddle on the floor. A single drop of crimson blood swirled in the puddle.

The priest gestured with his right hand, watching to see if Kerak recognized the tattoo—a lasting gift from Clan Uzanaki of Rhezaria. "You are truly talented my friend, there are very few who can enact a ritual within my presence without my noticing, and even fewer who can detect when I enact my own. You must have started the process before you entered the palace."

Kerak gave a knowing nod. "While I stood beneath the rain. A barrier against unwanted intrusions."

Belenus looked harder at the shaman. Perhaps he had underestimated this long haired man in pelts. "Do you intend to keep the Light out as well?"

Kerak's weathered face was unflinching. "My intentions are for the good of my people."

The Captain returned before Belenus could respond. He started down the hall with Kerak at his side. Guards fell in behind, and they passed many more, standing at attention along the hall. Kerak matched the Beacon's stride, the tapping of his staff on the floor punctuating their travel.

A mural of the Emperor's liberation of Azra and his triumph over the former Steward adorned the long hall. The mural culminated in a showdown where Anathasius stood alone before the Steward's army—a vibrant explosion of orange and yellow swirls to create an indistinct face on a pair large wooden doors painted gold. Belenus pulled open the doors and strode inside.

Thick vegetation dominated the majority of the high-arcing expanse. The wooded area had the look of a small forest, complete with a stone pathway leading through the center. A radiant golden shine highlighted the far end of the forest trail. Soft ferns waved leafy fronds between miniature versions of the massive ironwood trees. The trees nearest to the entrance soared to scrape the vaulted ceiling. Belenus breathed in the crisp scent of fresh leaves and rich soil as he led Kerak along the trail.

The trees gradually lowered in size until they reached the height of a man. The edge of the forest ended at an open area in front of a short granite staircase. Belenus stopped at the bottom of the stairs, squinting slightly against the undulating golden waves washing down from above.

A magnificent sun disk was inlaid into the rock wall above the stairs. Long rays extended from center of the disk to cover the ceiling and walls in their embrace, carrying light with them throughout the room. Emperor Anathasius sat cross-legged on a large purple cushion in front of the sun disk, his white robes made iridescent by the radiance at his back. Straight golden-brown hair fell to the Emperor's shoulders, his face smooth, displaying a strong jaw and high cheekbones.

Belenus shot a glance at the shaman but the shaman's stony expression masked his thoughts. The Emperor remained impassive, the picture of serenity. Belenus addressed the Emperor, his powerful voice muffled by the trees.

"Emperor Anathasius, Lord of Light, and Savior of Azra, I present Kerak, shaman of the Frozen Tribes. He speaks for the people of the North and wishes to share in your divine counsel." Belenus bowed and stepped back, allowing Kerak to move to the fore.

The Emperor opened his eyes, they swirled with the same light of the sun disk. Belenus could feel the Emperor's power even at this distance—a thrum of energy like the reverberation from the impact of a colossal hammer and anvil.

"Kerak, you have done something that most are never able to accomplish. Melea must think highly of you to grant this opportunity. I give you the floor, honored shaman; speak the words you journeyed to say."

Kerak's eyes never left the Emperor.

"The Frozen Tribes have no desire to join the Shining Empire and we wish to keep living as our ancestors have: by the skill of our hands, the sharpness of our minds, and the strength of our hearts. Your child of death made it quite clear that the Empire will not stop until the Tribes swear fealty and I must accept this fact. I am no fool, I know we lack the power to resist forever. The Tribes will enter the Shining Empire under one condition; leave us to remain in the land of our fathers. Do not rob mothers of their sons to bolster your army."

Belenus raised an eyebrow at the boldness of the shaman. Apparently he was hiding brass balls beneath those wolf pelts. The shaman was in no position to propose conditions, but Belenus found himself acknowledging the bravery of Kerak's words. The newcomer still refused to acknowledge the Emperor as a God, but he would. Belenus had seen this play out before.

Anathasius seemed to be considering Kerak's proposal as he looked into the ironwood forest. "The grove behind you is the largest such stand of trees left in existence. The ageless and indomitable ironwoods that used to cover all of this land are all but extinct, the stuff of legends like the Calanthian leviathan and the Green Time. But why? No wind could push them over, no axe could level them, and time is but a minor nuisance to their existence.

"Their doom arrived from the most unlikely of sources; a sickness struck them and the mighty ironwoods of Rua rotted from the inside-out before finally crumbling into dust. They could not protect against what was already within them, what had seeped between their links of armor to leech onto their life force." The Emperor turned his luminous gaze to Kerak. "Humans are much like the ironwoods. They are sick, Kerak, they are rotting and do not even know it. Wise men like yourself may sense this, but what is one to do about such a rampant disorder? To fight what one cannot see? I scoured Rua to gather the remaining ironwoods, making it my goal to keep this noble race alive. They were powerless to change their fate but I am not. I will do the same for humanity."

Kerak looked around the room, at nothing and at everything. "I have sensed this sickness for some time. For this reason I went to Calanthia to study, so that I could better protect my people."

"In your study, did you find a cure?"

Kerak's eyes narrowed to slits but he remained tight lipped.

The Emperor nodded. "I think not. That is because you cannot find such a thing in any Ba-rük text, particularly in Calanthia where the sickness is most deeply rooted. You have done well to lead your people, to lead them to me."

Kerak's emotions boiled to the surface. "Priests and soldiers, followed by threats and death, this is all you have offered the Tribes."

Belenus openly watched the shaman, shocked by the audacious display. One did not address a God in such a manner. Despite the insolence, Belenus found he was clasping and unclasping his hands in excitement.

"Not so fast, Kerak," said the Emperor, always the teacher, a father to querulous children. "You brusquely turned aside the many ambassadors of the Shining Empire that were sent to be a balm for the spirit. These good men traveled to your lands in an attempt to warn you of the sickness, so that its presence might be made known. I believe it was the Frozen Tribes who started the hostilities by returning my disciples without their heads."

"The actions of young warriors who did not take a moment to consider the consequences," grunted the shaman.

"Be that as it may, those actions have brought us here. Actions are the final results of the decisions made in our hearts." The Emperor rose from the cushion and started down the stairs. "It is time to show you how dangerous this sickness will become." The glow of the sun disk dimmed at the Emperor's every step and the room noticeably darkened once he reached the bottom.

The Emperor walked calmly toward the forest trail. "Come." The ease of command in his voice was as natural as drawing breath. Belenus followed, with Kerak behind him.

The ironwood forest took on an imposing presence in the gloom, and the seemingly increased size of the trees smothered the trail. The Emperor stopped near the entrance, beside one of the largest trees.

"Come forward, shaman, and place your hand on the tree." Kerak paused for a moment but complied. "Feel the change as I withdraw my protection."

An offshoot from the gold rays in the ceiling above the tree suddenly went dark, plunging the trio into darkness. For several long moments there was complete silence. A loud sniff broke the stillness.

"Something stinks like curdled milk or rancid butter," said Belenus.

"The tree," Kerak said, quietly. "It does not feel as solid as a moment ago."

The smell intensified and soon violent cracking resounded as smaller branches began to fall from the canopy.

"I know you can feel it coursing within," said Emperor Anathasius. "A man with your abilities can sense the truth of what is occurring."

Kerak moved even closer to the ironwood. A sharp crack and the rustle of branches preluded a heavy thud as a larger branch fell to the ground. The formerly unyielding ironwood bark began to slough off in the shaman's hands.

"Cynaal protect me," Kerak whispered.

"The sickness sleeps within the ironwood, waiting for a moment of weakness to strike," said the Emperor. "It does not care that the tree is needed for its continued existence, only knowing the desire to devour."

The trunk of the ironwood shed its bark in large chunks that were rapidly piling at the shaman's feet. The gold ray above the tree flared to light, causing

Belenus and Kerak to shield their eyes. Belenus lowered his arm to see the Emperor standing beneath the blighted ironwood. The hideous odor was fading and the falling branches had ceased.

"All who stay within my embrace will never wilt."

Kerak stared at the rotted bark. "Do your people know of this?"

"They know enough. Best not to trouble them with the severity of the situation," said the Emperor.

Belenus searched the shaman's posture but the man was a mystery. This pagan was slippery as the black stone of Mt. Skarskaard.

"I ask that you hold an assembly to announce the joining of the Frozen Tribes with the Shining Empire," said Kerak.

"A splendid idea. Belenus, I leave this to you."

"Yes, Shining Lord." Belenus felt a stab of disappointment. He'd almost wanted the shaman to put up more of a fight.

The Emperor left without another word. Belenus raised his hands in a sign of peace. "I humbly ask this time. Let me show you to your room."

"First answer this: have you ever seen these ironwoods bloom?"

The question caught him off guard. He stared into the canopy. "No."

Kerak was watching him so intently that Belenus found it unsettling. He turned to leave and could feel the shaman's eyes on his back.

"This way, I'll have some dinner sent to your room."

The shaman's question churned in Belenus' mind as they made their way through the halls. Surely he had seen the ironwood in bloom, he must have, and had just forgotten. Perhaps, they could not because they were indoors. Maybe it was irrelevant. *They were alive, was that not good enough?*

"Welcome to the Shining Empire, fearless leader of the Frozen Tribes. It's not as bad as you believe it to be. The food has to be better at any rate."

Kerak grunted what might have been a laugh and followed Belenus through the halls of the Palace of Light.

## One Foot in Darkness

Death was coming for Melea.

She had felt it, steady as a pulse, during the return to Azra. This was a known sensation, coinciding with her arrival in the Shining Empire, and hated for just as long.

A pounding in her temple had started when the first lights of Azra appeared through the slits in the carriage window. Melea clenched her jaw and clutched the pommel of her sword. But she could not cut her way out of this situation.

The carriage stopped and Melea stepped into the rain, trying to ignore the creeping feeling taking over inside. A fat-bodied moth collided with the hood of her cloak, bouncing inside to flutter against Melea's face. She batted it aside and entered the palace.

Her headache raged—the presence inside was getting stronger. Melea placed her hand back on the sword, wanting to cut out this part of her. *But how to kill something that was inside?*

She stormed into the kitchen, flinging open the meat locker. Melea snatched up a handful of cured meats and shoved them into her mouth. The meat tasted of ash. She spat it out and slammed the side of her fist against the wall.

The dead did not have to eat, but she still had to try to hold back death somehow.

Melea left the kitchen for her room, legs and arms going stiff and then numb. She made it to the edge of the bed, sending water droplets spraying across the room as she ripped off the cloak. With the last of the feeling in her hand, Melea dragged a throwing knife across her forearm. No blood emerged from the pierced skin.

*Here it comes.* Never had death been this aggressive. She wondered when—if—she would return. All the light drained from the world and Melea collapsed onto the bed.

She was dead and hated everything about it. Darkness, an endless void. Melea seethed at the sensation of drifting, raging with her non-existent limbs against the futility of it all. Then she noticed the space was not empty, felt watching eyes prick hairs on the back of her neck. There was movement within the ether. A voice.

Melea floated above her corpse, noting the pale skin and unblinking eyes. The room spun and she crashed into her body. She blinked rapidly, careful to let in the light. Sun spots blotted her vision, bright enough to be the sun hanging in the canopy of the room before disappearing in a blinding flash to plunge the enclosure into night.

Movement was not an option—not yet. Not while an uncanny vibration still made her a prisoner of her own body. Her teeth rattled together and she hoped they weren't being chipped or broken. The vibration agitated her organs, they jostled for position like warring nations. Her skin itched so terribly that she half hoped it was an animal that might peel itself off and crawl away. A few deep breaths pushed through grinding teeth seemed to help and in time the powerful sensations faded.

She sat upright, twisting her neck back and forth to break the last grip of confinement. Melea clenched her fists so tightly that the skin began to turn white around the knuckles. She was falling into the void of death with regularity now, slipping off the path and into a shadowy realm despite having greater control in her abilities.

Her reflection in the mirror against the opposite wall looked tired and skittish. "Just smother it, push it all down until the squirming stops," said her reflection. Melea set her jaw. "But it wasn't even this bad in the Sanctuary."

*When was the last time she had thought about that place?*

"Pull yourself together," she said, halting the recollection before it could disturb the buried sediment of memories.

A small crack near the edge of the mirror caught Melea's eye. She walked over on shaky legs and reached out to touch the blemish, but the glass felt smooth. She scraped a nail across the section to find the seam but was unable to discern a break in the material. Were her eyes playing tricks?

It didn't matter.

Death was winning the battle for Melea's body and she grudgingly acknowledged this condition. This constant foe was gaining strength with each passing day and she needed a way to defeat it.

## The Skar

The priest's words washed over the crowd like a crashing sea, pushing and pulling their emotions with his every gesture and carefully placed inflection. His booming voice held the throng enraptured as he spoke of the glorious Shining Empire.

"People of Azra, the Chosen have sent word that they will return! These righteous bearers of the vision given to us by Emperor Anathasius, Lord of Light, now march toward the safety and warmth of their homes. Your husbands, sons, brothers, fathers, and friends, have brought the faith into the cold reaches of the North. They have undertaken this dangerous and difficult cause so that the unenlightened Frozen Tribes may be brought into the bounty of the Shining Empire. The Frozen Tribes have accepted the truth of the Binding Doctrine and the Shining Empire burns brighter than ever because of it!" The crowd roared at the proclamation.

When the word had gone out that the Emperor was to make an address the people had quickly congregated in front of the ancient stone steps that stood before Mt. Skarskaard. Flags bearing the standard of the Shining Empire—a hand cradling the sun—were attached to two huge posts standing on each side of the stairs. The flags flapped in the breeze, but the sound of their movement was no match for the power in the priest's voice.

The citizens of Azra had assembled to hear proclamations from the Emperor but it was Belenus who first worked them into a frenzy. That morning Belenus had urged Kerak to join him before the assembly but the shaman adamantly refused, saying that he did not yet have the words to address the citizens of Azra.

Kerak could be an exceedingly stubborn man when he made his mind up about something and eventually Belenus acquiesced to the shaman's refusal, leaving him in the palace garden when the shaman abruptly sat down to meditate. The Emperor would not be shamed into canceling his address to the people on account of an uncooperative outsider. Belenus would deal with that mule of a shaman when he returned to the palace. Such disrespect could not be allowed to continue.

Bright summer sunshine and a warm sea breeze caressed the crowd of men, women, and children that stretched far out before the faded steps and towering black mountain. Sunlight cast numerous reflections from the odd angles of the Skar.

"We are locked into a battle that we did not choose to enter, a struggle that began before we were born, one that stretches back to the very beginning of time. Light against Darkness; goodness struggling to resist the forces of evil. It pains me to tell you this, but the truth must be spoken. Darkness has sunk deep into the fabric of this world and will not stop encroaching on us until everything has been swallowed.

"Darkness is confident, it is without fear, and why should its strength be doubted? The earth along with the human spirit is devoured. Nothing has opposed Darkness, nothing has slowed the tide of encroachment—until now.

"We are the brave few who stand united against this enemy, pushing it back with our strength of will. We say no more! A line has been drawn in the sand and that line is Azra. Darkness will not be allowed to advance any further. The reign of fear and death is ending. The countdown to our triumph began with the return of our champion, of our savior, Rua's one true God. It is not enough to wall ourselves up behind Light, to become besieged on all sides, instead we must take the fight to the enemy, to strike now and show Darkness that we are not afraid. I ask you Azra, are you afraid?"

A communal roar surged back at Belenus. Men raised their hands in exultation, children hopped with excitement, and women wept for joy—all were caught up in the emotional fervor.

"Your strength gives me strength. United, we are unstoppable!"

The crowd roared and Belenus let them feel the power of their own voices.

"Darkness has never met an adversary the like of Emperor Anathasius: a God who cares for the people, who will stand before them and provide protection, who has the courage to march out with us, the vision to save us from destruction, and the compassion to extend enlightenment to the entire world. But Emperor Anathasius cannot be victorious alone; our faith is needed to establish a new foundation, one that is solid and free of cracks where Darkness might hide. Your help is needed. I ask you Azra, will you fight for Light, for all that is good, will you fight for your God?"

Belenus was inundated with sound as the cheering mass swayed like a single gigantic organism. The energy of the crowd continued to rise and Belenus felt his spirit rise with it. He smiled, savoring the moment.

"Now bow your heads my brothers and sisters, in a sign of reverence for the Lord of Light. Take this moment to be thankful for the grace of Emperor Anathasius, and feel the power of his words, as you stand witness to all-encompassing truth."

The priest's throat hummed with energy, making his body feel stronger than it ever had in his youth. Belenus felt in a state of bliss, one that he hoped would last forever.

Silence fell over the crowd as they bowed. Within moments, the attention of the crowd was once again directed to the steps as a pulsating orange-yellow glow flared to life. Belenus held a lit torch and was joined by Emperor Anathasius who wore a white robe that flowed down to obscure his feet. A thin golden cape was attached to his shoulders by links of gold chain.

"My disciples! Generations ago I returned from the emptiness of the interminable abyss to bring your salvation!" At the Emperor's words the flame appeared to flare brighter and extend in his direction. "I returned with a vision of greatness for you, my chosen people, and the power to create the Shining Empire so that we may share this vision with the rest of the world!" A cheer rose from the masses at this declaration. "Together we shall convey this vision of peace and unity. The Frozen Tribes have accepted the truth within the Binding Doctrine and journey with us on the Illuminated Path as fellow disciples. Soon it will be our duty to help those in Calanthia to see the life-giving power of Light." Anathasius reached his fingers to the lit torch that Belenus held and pulled the flame into his hand.

A wisp of smoke went up from the end of the torch and the crowd gasped as Anathasius molded the fire into a ball. The fire danced between his fingers to become the real life depiction of the symbol represented on the flags. The Emperor's eyes appeared as two swirling orbs of molten ore as he worked the fire like a ball of clay. The flame brightened and Belenus felt the heat.

"Approach, young disciple," Anathasius called to a figure in the front row.

A small boy, his face showing the marks of pox, slowly walked up the stairs. His thin frame trembled in the presence of his Lord. The fire within the Emperor's hands continued to build in intensity until its constant swirling movement abruptly stopped. Anathasius took a step toward the boy while cradling the unmoving flame. A collective gasp escaped from the crowd as Anathasius placed the flame across the boy's face and held it in position.

The boy's face was entirely consumed by the fire for several tremulous heartbeats before dissipating into wispy streams of smoke. A heavy silence weighted down the crowd while they watched in rapt anticipation. The boy turned towards the crowd, running his hands across a smooth, unmarred face.

The crowd released its excitement in a massive exhale; cheering bounced off the Skar and back onto the square. Belenus thought the echo sounded like that of an enclosed cathedral rather than under the open air.

A peasant woman raced up the steps with tears streaming down her face, falling to her knees and wrapping her arms around the boy. Belenus stood behind Emperor Anathasius, the priest struggling to ignore the itch of the fire still felt on his face.

A great cheer erupted out of the crowd as the boy and his mother made their way back into the mass, those nearby reaching out to touch the blessed young boy. The cheering continued as Anathasius stood with arms upraised in his resplendent white finery.

"Light gives life and we must give this gift of life to the less fortunate. Calanthia wallows in Darkness and we must help them find the truth!" Anathasius paused. "You have all heard the story of how Calanthia sent the leviathan against this great city and how your valiant ancestors sent it back to the ocean from whence it came." A look of sorrow passed over the Emperor's face. "Sadly, Calanthia has not changed its perverse relationship with the natural world in all the years since the War of the Gods. They take the natural and transform it in their twisted image. Every manner of animal and plant are worshipped as totems of their non-existent God." Anathasius kept his tone measured but the doubt he felt was clearly transferred by his words. "Their God of nature may have once walked the ground they so revere but no sign of his presence has been made apparent for generations."

The Emperor turned serious. "He is gone. Their god saw Calanthia for what it is and severed all ties with these beasts masquerading as men." His speech slowly built in passion, rising in intensity until his voice boomed large as the mountain at his back. "Their insistence for clinging to a decaying and distorted faith clouds their minds, obscuring the truth of the Shining Empire. Our faith banishes all doubt but they refuse to walk the Illuminated Path. We will bring them our vision of life and unity to save them from the despair of ignorance! Light and life for eternity!"

The crowd echoed the last sentiment. "Light and life for eternity!"

In that moment the Emperor was the God all in attendance knew him to be—his white robes shining, gold cloak streaming out behind, and the reverberation of his voice still impossibly cascading over the crowd. A loud, cackling laughter splintered the euphoria. The laughter built in volume as the confused congregation continued to look for the source.

"On the mountain!"

Belenus and Anathasius turned to look up at the Skar behind them. On one of the odd outcroppings unique to this particular mountain stood Kerak, shaman of the Frozen Tribes. Kerak's hair billowed out behind him in the breeze as he looked down at the Emperor, some ten meters below. The shaman addressed the incredulous crowd.

"People of Azra, do you find it surprising that I have climbed this strange mountain? I find it surprising that so many of you are ready to believe the lies of your leader and his minion. How can you swallow their deceit as they rip the heart out of the Frozen Tribes and now aim to do the same to Calanthia?"

Belenus was about to shout that minion was the best title a defeated warlord like Kerak could hope to be called but the Emperor raised a hand.

"Why do you speak to my people with such disrespect?"

"I am Kerak and was leader of the Frozen Tribes until your army marched in and forced us into the Shining Empire. Now I am a man who has come here to speak the truth of your actions and the horror of your vision."

Belenus moved to intercede but was again impeded by the Emperor.

"Kerak, I ask that you come down from this sacred mount to discuss your grievances in a manner befitting a leader of your status."

The shaman smiled a wolfish grin. "No, I think I shall remain here where the people can hear my words. The walls of a prison cell would likely silence them."

"I ask you once more to show respect for this city and its people. Come down so that we may speak."

Kerak's flinty eyes held the Emperor's gaze as he sat down and crossed his legs. "People of Azra! Your Emperor is a deceiver, he cares only that you die for his cause. The song of the Ancestors is one of death, they see despair in the future he ushers in. He hides the depth of the sickness from you—"

Belenus watched as the Emperor strode up to Mt. Skarskaard and placed his palms on the smooth, black rock. A white glow flared around the Emperor's hands as he pushed against the mountain. Kerak's confidence changed to anxiety as a low rumble shook through the Skar. The Emperor's hands became so bright that Belenus had to shield his eyes from the glare.

Shouting rang out from the crowd as some ran for cover, but the majority remained where they stood to watch the divine display. A deafening crack was followed by the sound of grating stone as the ledge supporting Kerak slid earthward.

Kerak tried to rise but it was too late for escape. He bounced down from his perch to land heavily. The guards rushed over to subdue the malcontent but his body was limp and unmoving. One guard knelt to feel for a pulse and proclaimed the shaman alive but unconscious. The Emperor motioned to gain the Beacon's attention, making a quick gesture to the crowd with his eyes. Belenus understood the silent communication and turned to address the crowd.

"Brothers and sisters, did you see how Darkness can affect the mind of an unenlightened soul? What you witnessed today was a fall from dark heights so that a man may rise to walk the Illuminated Path. The shadows gather so deeply in the heart and mind that tremendous forces of Light are needed break through the wall of lies and deceit.

"Our misguided disciple was so shocked by the blinding truth given by Emperor Anathasius that his mind could not help but be momentarily overwhelmed. It has been difficult for this man to recognize the truth of the Shining Empire's vision after a lifetime of practicing pagan arts. I will personally work with this leader of our newest disciples to show him that Light does not abandon you even when it appears all is dark." Belenus paused to sense the emotion of the crowd.

"Execute the blasphemer!" More voices echoed the outcry.

Belenus placed his hands together before him in the stance of his order, the sleeves of his robe hiding his hands from sight. He flicked the hidden blade against his left thumb and drew it all the way across his palm. Divine power thrummed in his veins, making his blood feel like it was boiling.

Death would not be the outcome, not while he could influence the hearts of the crowd. Belenus would soothe the angry spirits here, he would show them there was nothing to fear.

If the energy Belenus had felt around the shaman could be compared to strings on a breeze, then the flow he felt from the crowd was a massive corded braid. The braid was not seamless as Belenus could detect loose strands drifting on their own. His heartbeat entered a manic, staccato rhythm as he reached for these strings. Belenus felt the strings connect to his throat, causing the world to become a shimmering landscape.

"Light heals all wounds, an indisputable fact that was shown to you by Emperor Anathasius," the energy of the Beacon's words spread over the crowd with the effect of a choir. "Now is not the time for punishment. It is the time for mercy. The Shining Empire does not turn on its disciples in their moments of weakness. Once our newest disciple regains his wits he will recognize the undeniable truth that we have all witnessed. As it says in the Binding Doctrine: Judge not your fellow man as all are susceptible to the workings of Darkness, instead lend the spark of your faith."

The muttering stopped. "Go now and revel in this beautiful day. Remember the miracle of life that was witnessed here." Belenus scanned the crowd for the pox-ridden boy, spotting him a few rows in. He motioned for others to lift him up. "Rejoice in this boy's healthy life! Delight in the renewal of one of our youngest disciples and hold fast to the life-giving power of Light!"

The Emperor's gilded carriage began the slow procession up the road of cobbled stone that led to the palace. Kerak was placed on the floor of an open carriage meant to transport the guards, with two of them standing beside his unconscious body. The guard carriage followed closely behind the Emperor's, leaving only the modest carriage that Belenus had arrived in. Belenus waved off the driver and returned to the slowly departing crowd that was carrying the healed boy.

The priest's awareness dimmed as the landscape returned to normal, the shimmering glare fading back to a duller reality. Belenus paused and turned to inspect the fallen section of Mt. Skarskaard. The stone was about the size of a large traveling trunk and looked like it had been sheared cleanly off the mountain in one long swipe. A moment of curiosity overtook the priest as he reached forward to touch the jet-black stone. Belenus extended one finger to the rock and immediately pulled it back in pain.

"Hot as a roaring hearth."

A humming started in his head, as if a hornet had flown into his ear and could not escape. Belenus backed away from stone, shaking his head to quiet the humming. He made his way down the ancient steps without looking back.

He blended into the mass of people, offering personal comments to those he passed by. He spoke of the miracle of the pox-ridden child and his new health as well as the glorious future they could provide for themselves. He plucked on strands of energy floating amongst the crowd, having to make several additional cuts to his palm. Belenus clutched a cloth in his wounded hand to stem the bleeding.

The mood of all those he encountered improved as he gently altered them like a current of warm water from the bay pushing out into cold deep of the open ocean. Belenus considered himself to be a man of the people and tried to interact with them as often as possible. He had joined himself with his faith in order to help the citizens of Azra, finding that his spirit seemed most tangible when speaking with those who could use some of his passion. Belenus was the Beacon—it was his duty to shine as a devout example.

Yet he could not shake the feeling that had crept into him while watching the Emperor's exit. His finger still throbbed from where it touched the Skar stone. Waves of anxiety simmered in his mind while he played the part of the confident and jovial Beacon. His faith was not shaken by Kerak's words but by some unnamable worry. The sun was on its descent by the time Belenus made his rounds from one end of the crowd to the other.

The square was now far behind as Belenus stood with his back to the wharf, observing the clusters of people that had formed after the assembly's exit. Many of the crowd had taken the day off from their normal tasks so they could attend the Emperor's speech. They now headed to the taverns. Belenus held no false illusions about what would dominate conversation tonight. While in the crowd he had heard the words, *Kerak*, and, *shaman*, mentioned often, but those conversations had quieted as he approached.

Most of the conversations he overheard were about the powerful display given by Emperor Anathasius. Belenus could not and did not expect to stop people from talking about the words of the shaman and it seemed that the interruption was mostly overshadowed by talk of Emperor. Kerak's arrival might actually work to strengthen the faith of people. The Emperor's last address to the city had been some time ago and the shaman's challenge helped to provide a spark of the divine.

But the whole incident with Kerak remained unsettling for Belenus, causing questions to crop up in his mind. He watched the ships gliding across the water for a few moments before beginning the long walk to the palace. His personal guard, two stern soldiers in maroon and gold silently followed.

Fatigue was setting in, one that would root Belenus in place if he remained still. The closing speech and conversations with the crowd had necessitated that he use more of the Emperor's Gift than expected. The extra effort was taxing on his body.

Belenus took the shortest route back to the palace, a wide road that bordered the waterway before cutting through the center of Azra. His personal guard, two soldiers, Gern and Ryndell, fell in on either side.

This road by the water was one of the busiest in the city and was always bustling with traders, sailors, fishermen and vendors. Many people offered greetings to the priest as he passed.

His height and the snowy robes of his order clearly distinguished Belenus from the common person. Walking among the people often caused Belenus to lose himself in thought, moving through the busy walkways like a shrouded spirit. At other times, Belenus was quite sociable and would talk to the vendors, merchants, and beggars about their day and the goings-on of the city. This day was more of the former rather than the latter, as Belenus acknowledged those around him but did not pursue conversation.

Small shrines dedicated to Emperor Anathasius were constructed along the streets of Azra. The smallest were erected from wood scraps and draped with cloth to hide the poor quality of craftsmanship, while the grandest were elegantly carved into the sides of stone buildings. All were filled with rows of lit candles placed around a pair of upraised hands cradling a glowing orb of shine glass that cast an otherworldly gleam over those who knelt before the shrines. Many reached out to touch the hands while saying the prayer, "Light fill me up."

Belenus noticed there was a steady stream of activity around the shrines, but soon his eyes clouded over and the prayers of others disappeared from his awareness. His ears pricked at the occasional half-heard criticism and mention of Kerak, but he was too weary to investigate. As his mind wandered, Belenus failed to notice the big alley cat that had claimed a location on the street. The cat's shrill squeal caused Belenus jump backwards in panic.

Belenus retreated a step as the one-eyed tomcat arched its back and hissed vehemently. The grimy cat gave Belenus a wicked look with its one good eye before scurrying away from a swing of the priest's foot. The cat offered one more derisive hiss before continuing on its way.

He looked to his personal guard. "Gern, aren't you supposed to alert me of danger? What's the point of having you around, Ryndell?"

The soldiers exchanged a look, trying to suppress their laughter.

"Go," said Belenus. "Off with you. I'll do the rest on my own."

Gern placed a mailed hand on the priest's shoulder. "Beacon, we—"

"Go!"

Gern and Ryndell exchanged another look, shrugged, and departed.

The road took Belenus toward the city center, his shadow stretching out before him. Merchants were beginning to close their shops for the night on either side of the street. Taverns were lighting lamps to fend off the burgeoning shadows. Belenus continued on past the market where the last buyers of the day were bargaining for a sale. He stopped to watch a spirited back and forth over the price of iron ore.

An Azran merchant stood straight backed with arms folded across his chest, slowly shaking his head as a small, dark skinned man gesticulated wildly with his hands at the iron in front of him. The small man was dressed in a scarlet toga and wore a bright blue turban on his head. This man appeared to be the leader of an entourage of four other men wearing similarly colorful garb. One of the men was clearly a bodyguard as he was much larger than the others and sported a cudgel-like weapon tucked into his waistband.

The trader's brown facial hair wagged as he attempted to make a profitable deal, the many gold and silver bands on his hands and forearms glittered with the motions of his emphasis. Belenus guessed the group to be from Nefara, which was just about as far away from Azra as one could get.

The Nefaran trader spoke quickly, the tone and fluidity of his language almost made it seem like he was singing. Finally, he raised his hands to stop the meaningless exchange, indicating to one of his comrades to open the large crate they had brought with them. The small Nefaran pulled out a glass vial of the most vibrant green that Belenus had ever seen. Next, a vial of burnt orange, and then a sapphire blue.

The iron merchant was clearly interested in the offering but remained unwilling to make a deal. The Nefaran trader pointed to the crate, counted his fingers from one to ten, then pointed at the Azran merchant. The merchant gave a brisk head shake and walked away. Belenus whistled softly, a small fortune had just been denied for both sides.

He was now passing by the guild section and had often raced along these streets as a boy but the memories of that time brought more heartache than joy. The thought of running made his old hip injury flare up. Belenus winced, he had meant to get his hip cared for, but had become distracted by the discovery of new variations to his ritual technique. His ability to access the Emperor's Gift was still improving and nothing thrilled Belenus more than the thought of perfecting his craft. Nefara created the world's greatest artists but the Shining Empire possessed the greatest priests.

Belenus wandered off the main road, taking a narrower path that led to Stone Park, the original town center, which was now abandoned and overgrown with vegetation. He had spent hours here as a boy, scrambling across the debris on imagined adventures.

The charred and petrified remains of a gigantic elm stood in the center. Lightning had blasted it some untold age ago and cracked it in half, leaving a shattered token from the ancient inhabitants of Azra. The layout of the debris implied that the structure had been built around the elm. This notion piqued Belenus' curiosity as to why the citizens of Cambor would have done this.

Belenus thought it odd that he had never heard the tale of the tree's demise, the telling of this story had somehow eluded his ears. Some searching amongst the scrolls in the palace library was required. He found himself growing more curious as the years passed by, sensing that there were many things he would never come to know. This realization troubled his tired mind at night. Lately, he needed a special sleeping tonic in order to get a decent rest.

Sudden movement in the shrubbery to the left caught the priest's attention. The peacefulness afforded by the solitude of this forgotten place suddenly seemed more dangerous than comforting. Imperial law forbade anyone from raising a hand against a priest, but Belenus brought the razor blade to his thumb and forefinger anyway as he started to make his way back toward the main street.

He was not about to investigate as to what sort of person or creature would creep around Stone Park at night. The rustling stopped and Belenus listened but could only hear the pounding of his own frightened heart. There was a scrape of boots on stone and then the cool nick of a blade at his throat. A large presence pressed against his back.

"You did a lot of shouting today," said the presence, "but raise your voice now and it'll be the last thing you ever do, understand?"

"Yes," Belenus whispered.

"Good."

Another person stepped out of the greenery on the left but Belenus was unable to see his face.

"You'll be taking us to the palace."

Belenus attempted to make an incision in this thumb but his captor shook his wrist in a firm grip, sending the razor into the grass below.

"Palace is invitation only," Belenus squeaked out.

Belenus gasped as the knife at his throat pressed tight. His vision blurred and he felt his knees go weak. Belenus dropped to the ground.

He did not know how long he was out but he kept his eyes shut when he came around. The two captors traded harsh whispers. Dirty fingers pressed his nose shut. Belenus held his breath as long as he could but was soon struggling for air.

His captors chuckled and hoisted Belenus to his feet. The knife was once again at his throat.

"The palace," the man behind him growled.

"I can't get you in," Belenus huffed. "The palace is swarming with guards who would love nothing more than to skewer you and your comrade on sight."

"There is another way. You have been seen exiting the palace through a secret passage."

"Preposterous."

"That's not what Kerak says."

Belenus felt the air stir above him. A shadow dropped from the sky to land on a nearby stone. The harsh squawk of a crow ruptured the darkness. The old priest's heart leapt—was the shaman a shapeshifter? *No, such things could not exist.*

"A bird," Belenus scoffed. "Nothing more."

"He speaks for Kerak, and he has seen your secret. He will lead us there and you will grant us access."

Belenus sighed. His captor must have sensed the defeat, because he pushed Belenus forward. The Beacon of Azra lifted one leaden foot after the other, his mind numb. Something brushed up against his leg causing the priest's heart to leap into his throat.

The rumble of a contented purr floated around his ankles. Belenus looked down to see one yellow eye floating in the darkness. He kicked at the tomcat, but his captor took the motion for an attempt at escape and shook him violently by the shoulders. The cat hopped out of range, strutting into the darkness with its tail upright.

"Somebody kick that cat," he gasped.

Rough hands shoved him up the hill toward the palace. An odd sensation pricked against his skin, one Belenus had not felt since his time in Rhezaria. The understanding that his life could end at any moment. Belenus felt alive.

In this moment, as in his past, Belenus felt no fear in his heart. He had supreme confidence in his faith, an unshakeable certainty that Light would dispel the flock of shadows gathering at his back. Darkness was walking him directly into the Emperor's domain, a realm in which it could not hope to survive.

## Ghosts

Smile, she must remember to smile. Melea knew that people liked others who smiled, even strangers. Something about the gesture intimated trust, calling for mirroring. Melea wiped sweaty palms against her trousers and approached the boys sparring in the training yard.

Their wooden swords clacked together as if in the midst of a great battle. Melea's lip curled, distorting her carefully practiced smile. She'd never been allowed to train with a wooden sword, not once. The boys took a break and guzzled from a jug of water.

A slow burn of embarrassment tickled at the base of her throat. A gag response at her own weakness. She shouldn't need these boys or their help.

*Not good enough. I pity any who call you their champion.* Katano's words cut deeper than any of the injuries he caused. The accusation would not leave her mind because the giant was right. If she was better trained, she would have scored a decisive victory and not just an unsatisfactory draw. This is why she needed the boys; to remain undefeated.

The boys were watching her, she could feel their judgement. *Smile, just smile and go from there.*

The boys said nothing. They looked to be several years younger than she was. Awkward silence filled the mostly empty training yard.

"You two look strong enough."

The boys smirked, the larger one puffing up his chest. "Strong enough for what, beautiful?" He flexed the arm holding the wooden sword and sauntered closer.

Melea used every ounce of restraint in her body to refrain from wiping the smug look off his face. "I need you boys to carry something."

"Boys?" questioned the larger one. "I don't see any boys around here, only a couple of Chosen."

"Right, right," she said. "Infamous warriors, no doubt."

The boy gripped the wooden pommel tighter. "Watch your mouth, you—"

The smaller one stepped forward, placing a hand on the other's shoulder, whispering. The confident boy suddenly lost all of his boldness and stepped back. A sliver of fear flashed in his eyes as he looked at Melea, truly looked, for the first time since she'd approached. Melea smiled again and this time it was genuine.

"I need you two to carry something for me."

The big one saluted.

"This way."

The Chosen in training followed like whipped dogs.

A block of wood chiseled into the basic shape of a person lay on the ground. Melea had requested it made into the approximate size of Katano. The heavy item had an awkward shape, so much so that Melea had been unable to transport it by herself. She could summon great strength in the heat of battle yet could not access this power for more mundane tasks. Years of physical training and numerous battles had hardened her body and strengthened her muscles, but these experiences had their limitations.

"Lift this," Melea ordered.

The boys grunted with effort to lift the wooden mannequin. Melea entered a side door on the ground floor of the palace, taking a few seldom used hallways, until reaching a set of descending stairs. The stairway was dimly lit and looked to disappear into the bowels of the earth. She caught the frightened look that passed between the boys.

Melea continued and the boys followed, slipping and sliding their way down, struggling to support the weight. Several breaks were needed for the boys to catch their breath; Melea avoiding eye contact until they were ready to continue.

They passed the level that housed the dungeon and one of the boys whimpered. Melea grabbed a torch from a wall sconce and continued into the ancient foundations of the palace. Strange depictions of half-man, half-beasts decorated the walls on these lower levels—forgotten vestiges of the palace's former inhabitants. The images were barely visible and seemed to disappear completely when Melea moved the torch closer. The air turned colder the lower they went and condensation dripped down the stone walls.

Finally the stairs ended, opening into a small arena whose circular structure indicated that it was designed for ritual ceremonies. The air was musty and stagnant, the walls covered in dust where they were free from condensation. The arena felt more like a cave than a human-built structure as most of the walls displayed the rough surface of natural rock interspersed with a sickly grey moss.

"Over there," Melea pointed to a pile of other materials.

The boys hurried to deposit the mannequin and quickly left, practically running up the stairs. *Cowards*, thought Melea.

She went around the room clearing out cobwebs and lighting additional torches. As far as Melea knew, this was the only section of the palace that was not continuously lit. Thin streams of water seeped down the walls to disappear into the earth and unknown depths below.

She set to piecing together the design she had imagined on the carriage ride back from her mission in the North. The return journey to Azra had been a blur. Melea had mostly slept, letting her injuries heal as she rested in the carriage. Kerak had his own carriage and she had not spoken to the shaman since that day at the fortress. Her duty was to eliminate or retrieve, not play at being a diplomat, and certainly not to entertain guests.

Melea realized that she had never practiced throwing at men of Katano's size. One of her throwing knives had been blocked but the other made it through Katano's defenses to strike his shoulder.

During the fight she had thrown her knives out of reflex at the level where an average man's head would be. A good place to target, since the majority of men were nowhere near the size of the northern warrior, but she had not been in a mortal struggle with a normal man. The shadow creature inside of the bear-man was evidence of that; Melea knew the final strike to have been a killing blow but Katano still lived.

Some tinkering with the setup was required to get her design working correctly but soon she had the pulley system moving just right. Several hours later and Melea was still training. A creaking of spinning wheels attached to a pulley system disturbed the silence.

Melea sprinted a few steps, tucked into a shoulder roll, then sprang up to face a large onrushing figure. With her right hand she hooked her fingers around the loops of two knives strapped to her left hip. Melea's left hand parted the cloak as she snapped the knives through a small opening with a flick of the wrist. One knife stabbed into the eye of the wooden dummy and the other was buried where a mouth would be.

"That's more like it," she said, grabbing the rope and pulling the dummy back into its starting position. She retrieved the knives before leaning against the cold stone wall.

She was dressed in a loose fitting tunic and a light cloak, her black trousers were covered in dirt from rolling around on the ground. Melea often found herself wearing the same outfit for days on end, only changing into fresh clothes when the current attire acquired an unpleasant smell or when holes in the fabric started to appear. Only her boots were given a great deal of attention, the well-worn leather oiled each night so that it gleamed like new. Melea pulled on the same boots every morning no matter the occasion.

She wondered what the boys were telling their comrades, how they would describe their encounter with Death's Daughter. Melea pushed off the wall, looped her forefinger and middle finger around one knife handle and her ring finger and pinky around the second. She raised the knives overhead, sighted the line, and hurled them at the wooden replica. The knives hit within a fraction of each other and sunk deep into the replica's groin. Enough thinking about boys. Time to call it a night and get out of the dankness of the arena. Melea grabbed the knives, along with a torch, and started up the long flight of stairs.

Perhaps she should have done something to put a real fear into the young Chosen. Really give them something to talk about.

Most people didn't dare speak to her. Nobody asked her opinion, as they did not view her as a person. All they saw was her status and reputation. Sometimes she felt like a ghost, no ties to anyone or anything, drifting through the world, trapped in her own existence, and avoided by everyone. Maybe this restlessness was part of the curse of being dead and alive.

Nobody was truly honest, everyone used each other to reach their own goals. Others might paint this self-deception into a pretty picture but she saw it for the grease-smeared canvas that it was. If there was one thing she had learned in her life it was that strength and conviction produced the victorious. The rest perished.

*One good man with a sword is better than ten without.* Those were Andran Derclerq's words during a training session after knocking Melea's blade to the ground. *But you are not a man so what good are you?* The arrogant swordmaster always made sure that Melea knew he was superior but at least he wasn't afraid to speak with her.

Melea almost missed the muddy boot print on the stair. Another print on the following stair, and the next. She was sure she had not passed any bootprints during the ascent but looked behind to make certain. Nothing but the dust moved by her own smaller feet. She was halfway up the stairway and had yet to pass the dungeons so it was impossible for someone to start walking from this point. Someone had walked right through the walls. The hairs on the back of her neck stood on end. Spirits were said to be able to pass through walls. This section was old, there could be spirits wandering about, but Melea had never heard of any spirit leaving muddy bootprints.

She cast out her senses into the darkness like a net. Somebody was in the palace and their access to the rest of it would be completely unknown to those above. She needed to find out who, or what, was with her in the lower levels.

To her right was a small alcove cut into the wall, not unlike many others that lined the stairway. The alcove made a small arch that supported the structure. She pushed the torch into the enclosure and inspected the tight space.

Dust and cobwebs were firmly entrenched and there was no apparent sign of entry. Melea paused. Something was different than on the stairway, she just could not see it. She stilled her movements and inhaled deeply. A small breeze pressed the cold against her skin, but this cold lacked the stale mustiness of the stairwell. The breeze was coming from the back of the alcove, near a carving of a goat-legged man. Melea leaned in for closer examination.

A small, vertical gap of blackness split two stones in this section of the wall. A handful of sand and crumbled mortar littered the area underneath the stone. Melea wedged her fingertips into the opening and pushed. The stone block slid sideways with surprising ease to display a groove cut in the stone beneath it. Melea pushed the lower block and it moved as smoothly as the first. A gust of fresh air greeted her face like the whisper of a departed spirit. She wedged the space open wider to view glittering stars overhead.

Someone was in the castle and had not properly restored their entry, or they had deliberately left it slightly ajar as an exit. Melea was now on full alert. An intruder had slipped into the Palace of Light and was skulking around uncontested. She stepped out of the alcove and swiftly followed the footprints, moving as quietly as possible.

The footprints continued for several more steps until the last of the mud crumbled off the intruders boot. Melea followed the bare stone, arriving at a level platform extending to become the entrance of the dungeon.

Where was the sentry that had stood at the entrance of the dungeon? His figure had barely been perceptible on her descent but Melea remembered seeing him standing in front of the gate with a spear in hand. She cautiously approached the dungeon entryway, creeping tight against the wall, her hand on the pommel at her hip.

The front gate was only locked when prisoners were brought to the entrance so that visitors did not have to enter the dungeon proper. Melea doubted that it would be locked now. The main gate was further within, around a slight corner and should have a jailor posted there. No guard was present at the main gate but there was no sign of a struggle. The apparent calmness did not alleviate her suspicions.

Melea continued forward, lifting the gate latch and slowly swinging it open. A horrible grating reverberated throughout the corridor. Abandoning all stealth, Melea shoved the door open and drew her sword, but neither guard nor intruder raced out. She listened intently, her breathing the only noise in the corridor.

Somebody should have come to investigate the noise of her entry. The narrow hall extended for a few meters before making a right turn to give access to the heavy iron of the second gate. Melea paused in the entrance of the first gate to survey the situation—a tight area and a blind turn. She would be in a difficult position if the intruder was laying in wait for her around the corner. Melea took a deep breath. The stagnant dungeon air did not inspire confidence.

She dashed forward with her sword raised in a guard position. A spearpoint flashed out at her head, deflecting off the blade of the sword. Melea transferred the block into a quick retaliation strike but her opponent jumped back out of range and lunged again. Melea relied on instinct to counter the rapid thrusts and slashes delivered by the unknown assailant.

Melea withstood the barrage until a break in the attack appeared, which she immediately used to close the distance and press her adversary, attempting to negate the length of the spear. Her furious attack succeeded in moving her opponent backward, but the intruder was skilled and Melea could not land a clean strike.

He was tall and thin, appearing to be past the prime of life but the speed of his hands had not slowed with age. The older warrior redoubled his efforts, trying to end this fight with the next attack. Melea predicted this maneuver and sidestepped a powerful lunge, dropping her sword to grab the shaft of the spear with both hands.

A white-hot fire pulsated within Melea's body, moving from her hands and into the spear, binding her to it and it to her. The intruder tried to wrest the spear away but Melea's grip was like iron. Her green eyes glowed as she stared intently at the spear. With a blink, her focus ended and a sharp crack of snapping wood filled the hallway.

In each hand Melea held a section of the spear, the ends cleanly severed. Shocked disbelief painted the warrior's face as he now only held the handle of the spear. He dropped the handle to the floor and surged forward howling with a knife in hand.

Melea used one spear segment to block the knife while plunging the spear point into the intruder's thigh. His angry howl morphed into to a painful outcry but he did not collapse like she expected. Instead, his left hand shot forward and strong fingers clamp around her throat.

Drawing air was impossible. The fingers of her free hand scrabbled across her midsection, searching for the throwing knives. Melea's vision grew dim and she could feel her defense against the knife weakening. Her frantic fingers finally found the familiar loops of the throwing knives. A snap of her wrist sent the knives into her attacker's chest and his death grip released. Gasping and coughing, she backed away as black spots danced in her vision.

The intruder slumped against the wall, one hand still holding his knife and the other draped across those in his chest. He tried to throw his knife but collapsed to the floor with a ragged wheeze. His eyes glazed over and his hand released its hold on the knife. Melea snatched up her sword and stalked through the open door.

She could make out several forms just beyond threshold and none were moving. The nearest body was that of the missing guard who had blood congealing from a large wound in his chest. The next body was that of the jailor who was sprawled haphazardly on his stomach. Last was a tall man in a white robe; the Beacon. Melea did not concern herself with the jailer or the priest, instead pausing for a moment to consider which direction the other intruder had gone.

She was willing to bet that the spearman was keeping watch for someone who had continued inside. Two torches on each wall illuminated the immediate section before sinking into darkness as the dungeon branched off in either direction. Melea considered waiting at the crossroads as the intruder would have to pass by this way and she might be able to catch him unawares. On the other hand, she could creep up on him in the darkness and subdue him without being seen.

Her pulse was racing now and she could not stand to remain in one place. She looked left and then right. Every aspect of her body screamed for action. Melea started down the corridor on the right. Waiting in the darkness for something to happen was too similar to being dead.

The dungeon darkness was pervasive, occasionally disturbed by the furtive movement of rats along the walls. Melea walked a fair distance, yet there was still no sign of the intruder. The dungeon might extend forever, it was impossible to discern. She paused, hesitant to continue. An orange glow appeared in the distance, from the direction she had come. A bobbing torch was moving speedily towards the intersection.

"Bloedeth!" Melea sprinted in the direction of the flame.

The outline of the intruder continued to increase. The big man appeared to have a prisoner slung over his shoulder as he jogged back to the entrance. He saw Melea before she reached the intersection and carefully placed his load down on the ground. She leapt across the junction while slashing at the intruder's throat. The man was quick to duck the attack as he turned to fight. Melea spun on her heel as she landed, her face blanching at the sight of her adversary.

Katano rumbled toward her swinging a vicious blade. Melea countered the blow but the force of the impact knocked her sideways into the wall. Katano swung again, sending chips flying from where her head was a moment before. She retreated a few steps and reached for the throwing knives. The space was empty, she had forgotten to remove the knives from the chest of the other intruder.

"Luck of the dead," she mumbled.

Katano's brutish shoulders dominated the passageway and he showed no signs of his injuries. Melea was dumbfounded. Perhaps the crafty shaman had conducted a ritual to heal his son but it was almost unheard of for someone to have such diverse abilities. Anathasius did, but he was as beyond Kerak as a man is to a dog. Katano charged, and Melea stepped forward to meet him.

The clang of metal on metal rang out. Katano held a torch in one hand and a sword in the other. His strikes were savagely powerful and Melea tried to avoid countering them because of the mismatch in strength. Katano was fast for a man of his size but his speed was overmatched by hers. She skittered across the corridor on the balls of her feet, flicking out attacks when an opening was presented. Several streaks of blood shone on Katano's sword arm from glancing strikes made by Melea's blade.

Their swords clashed in another bout and this time Melea scored a solid hit to Katano's wrist. His sword dropped to the floor and Melea kicked it away. The northern warrior did not hesitate, throwing the torch at Melea while charging. Melea sliced the torch in two and slashed at the onrushing figure before rolling out of the way. A painful grunt from the shadows indicated a direct strike. She edged backward toward the torchlight at the gate.

Melea nearly tripped over the body of the prisoner that Katano had come to retrieve. She felt around, finding an arm and dragging the body into the light—Kerak, shaman of the Frozen Tribes. His face was badly bruised and he labored to breath.

Katano walked slowly out of the corridor, one arm held tight to his midsection where Melea's sword had cut through the leather jerkin. His dark eyes looked sad.

"You have doomed my people and now you have captured my father, you truly are a child of death."

Melea was taken aback. This was not the guttural voice of the bear-man and the otherworldly presence of the shadow was absent. This was not Katano after all. Melea peered at his face and she did notice some different features. The man's nose had never been broken whereas Katano's had looked like it had been reset several times. His eyes had a more thoughtful look and lacked the fierce wildness of the bear-man's.

"Who are you?"

"I am Sixthrok, second son of Kerak, warrior of the Frozen Tribes."

Melea thought he might charge after this announcement but instead he looked forlornly at his father. This man was definitely not Katano.

"What is Kerak doing here in the dungeon? He was to meet Emperor Anathasius," said Melea.

Sixthrok looked up from his father and spat. "He did not want his words to be silenced. Your Emperor did not like my father's choice of location to speak."

Melea was confused, but not at all surprised that the shaman had changed the rules of the meeting. He had seemed too eager to come to Azra. "Why are you here?"

Sixthrok's face contorted in bitterness. "I came to save my father from your treachery."

"My part in this venture is over, it is between Kerak and Anathasius now."

Sixthrok pounded a fist against the wall and spittle flew from his lips. "Already your priests travel to our communities! We passed more groups going north on our journey. Already our captured warriors are being added to your armies!" He bit back a further outburst and looked at his father once again. "My father came here to talk to the people of the Shining Empire, he believes the future of the Frozen Tribes resides in them. I do not. He will return to the Tribes with me."

As Melea looked at the warrior he seemed to grow younger before her eyes. All of his strength and hardness melted away, leaving a young man trying to make sense of the world as it crumbled around him.

An unexpected burst of emotion passed through Melea, distorting her thoughts and weakening her resolve for what must be done. Sixthrok looked at her as if he was also aware of her inner thoughts.

"I can't let you take him," Melea warned.

"I will not become a prisoner and I cannot leave my father to die as one."

Melea braced to fight. Sixthrok took a step towards Melea but a wheezing breath stopped him in his tracks.

Kerak gasped on the ground and weakly flailed an arm in his son's direction. Sixthrok rushed over to kneel beside his father.

"Live, my son, you must live." Kerak broke into a coughing fit before starting again. "Leave me, I am not finished here. You must help Katano lead the Tribes. Keep them together, play the Emperor's games if you must, but do not let the Tribes forget that they are unbreakable ice. Protect your mother."

Melea watched Sixthrok intently as Kerak spoke; the young warrior's face as grim as a death mask. He nodded his head and clasped his father's shoulder before rising.

"I will do this for you, father. The Tribes will not become the Emperor's play things, the song of Cynaal will remain in our hearts."

Melea recalled the strength in Kerak's face as he stood defiantly on his wall. She saw it now in Sixthrok's determination, a look that was not there a moment ago. She sheathed her sword and stepped to the side.

"You managed to get yourself into the palace, I will give you a chance to get yourself out, but he," she pointed to Kerak, "remains here. I will count a span before I alarm the guards that an intruder has broken in."

Sixthrok did not say another word as he jogged past Melea toward the exit. At the gate he turned to face her. "You have taken much from us but not all, not yet."

"One...two...three," Melea counted.

"This is not finished," Sixthrok promised.

Melea looked to see Kerak's reaction but he had lost consciousness once more. She sat beside the shaman and counted silently. While counting, she tied Kerak's hands and feet together with strips of cloth cut from the white robes of the unconscious priest near the gate. She would have liked to cut a little deeper for payback to how the priesthood had treated her as a child but this was not a night for revenge. If Sixthrok could wait, then so could she.

After informing the guards of the intruder Melea sidled into the kitchen to make herself a plate.

Melea returned to her room on weary legs, ready for sleep, but found an unexpected message waiting on the bed. A note, written in the Emperor's own hand. She was to meet him on the upper balcony at dawn.

She slipped into the kitchen long before dawn, moving swiftly through the massive room of bustling people.

There were few instances when Melea liked to blend in, but sneaking into the kitchen for a bite of food served with a side of gossip was one of them. Common folk seemed to live for the successes and misfortunes of others, spreading hearsay as fact and turning fact into scandal in a never ending exchange of rumors.

Melea casually grabbed an apron from the wall and scooped up a small mixing bowl filled with an unknown concoction. Most of the people who worked in the kitchen never saw any other section of the palace so they would have no cause to recognize her. She absently worked the mixture with a wooden spoon and started toward the bread makers. The women who pounded the dough into all forms of delicious creations were a great source of information. Melea wondered how the bakers got so large; it was difficult to imagine them having time to eat anything as they never stopped talking.

The apron, and her young appearance, made Melea look like any other servant girl in the large kitchen. A middle aged man called out to her.

"You there. Have that ready for me in two minutes."

Melea was careful not to make direct eye contact and nodded meekly. This response satisfied the man and he turned to bark orders in another direction. Humility was not her strong suit but it had its uses.

She navigated her way smoothly through the kitchen until she was in proximity to three heavyset women kneading balls of dough. Flour covered every surface in sight, even the foreheads of the women as they periodically raised their forearms to wipe sweaty brows.

She had to wait longer than she wanted until the conversation came round to the shaman.

"...this Kerak fellow, they say he can look into your chest and turn your heart to ice so that you freeze solid. He tried to use his dark power to escape last night."

"I heard the Emperor smote him with a powerful blinding at the Skar."

"Aye, I heard that too, pagan witchcraft is no match for the Light."

"Well of course Emperor Anathasius is the stronger of the two, he is a living God after all, but it chills my bones thinking about that shaman on the loose. I'm glad the North is part of the Empire now, who knows what dark plots they were up to?" The other women nodded in agreement.

"Did you hear about Calanthia? Rumor has it that they're preparing to blockade the Chuku Bartha Pass, so you know what that means." The other women nodded again.

"Trade has slowed to a trickle anyhow. Without Strakos I don't know what my husband would do."

Melea sensed a presence behind her. She turned to find the middle aged man with his hands on his hips, face screwed into a scowl.

"Are we just about done eavesdropping?" He extended a meaty palm. "The bowl, if it's not too much trouble."

Melea handed over the mixing bowl, muttering something that might pass as an apology, and briskly left. On the way out she grabbed a warm bread-roll and a few apples.

What if Anathasius knew of Melea's part in allowing Sixthrok to escape? There had been no word of the northerner's capture even though search teams had been sent out after him. Anathasius punished dishonesty severely but even so she did not feel responsible to always tell him the whole truth involving her doings. His tangible power put her on edge, stirring an instinct to preserve part of herself. Melea did not have it within herself to capitulate. Survival had been her sole focus for too long to give her trust fully.

"Melea." The call came from a side room. She glanced inside to see Mandrikos waving.

The tutor's room was little more than a closet and filled to the ceiling with scrolls and manuscripts. Mandrikos was wedged behind a small desk in the corner, poring over what looked to be a map of the western mountains. He was a short man of average build, completely bald and always clean shaven. Melea stood in the entryway, but Mandrikos beckoned her to join him in the cramped room.

"What?" she grumped, angling beside a teetering shelf vomiting stacks of paper.

He jabbed a finger into the map. "Does this region look familiar to you?"

Melea looked away. She knew the region, it was in those mountains where she had been sent on her first mission.

"A quiet place, not much in the way of communities," said Mandrikos. He drew his finger over to the city of Kannark. "A capable people, eh?"

"I suppose," said Melea. Her swordmaster was from Kannark, a member of the renowned Amparo Tannoi. A former militia, widely regarded as the best swordsmen in Rua.

"Kannark swore allegiance to Emperor Anathasius several generations ago, when he first came to power in Azra," said Mandrikos. "But the arrangement has not always been peaceful—surely you remember the stirrings of revolt several years back?"

"I don't have time for a lecture."

"A charismatic warrior of some repute was the instigator of the uprising, but he disappeared before a true rebellion took hold."

"What are you getting at?" Melea glared at her tutor's bald head as he chattered away to the map.

"There are rumblings, rumors, hearsay really," Mandrikos mumbled.

Melea hated the way Mandrikos skirted around a topic. He drummed his fingers on the map, knuckles dancing across mountain ridges from west to east. She knew full well what he was implying, he could only be referring to one thing by mentioning this event. Melea would not solve his dilemma by voicing what he did not want to say.

Mandrikos finally looked to her, his blue eyes questioning. "The truth is a slippery substance, capable of being a leash or a bridge."

"Is that all, or are there more pearls of wisdom?"

He offered a wan smile. "Never underestimate how the past will affect the future. We tend to forget what shapes us when it disappears from sight."

Melea left her tutor staring at the barren region of the Outskirts in the East.

How much did the prattling Mandrikos know? Certainly he was not privy to the details of her first mission. How an inexperienced Melea allowed a certain warrior of some repute to flee into the mountains with his pregnant wife.

Melea cursed herself for being unable to kill the man. That damn wife. She with the bulging stomach and desperate, pleading eyes.

Anathasius never discovered the truth and she had stopped the rebellion. There was no reason to believe this instance would be any different. She might be a killer, but she was no creeping assassin.

She rounded a corner to see Andran Derclerq, the Tannoi swordmaster, strutting down the hall toward her. His brown hair was fading and seemed to be thinner each time she saw him yet it was always slicked back with an oily sheen. He kept a swooping brown mustache and constantly walked with his chin up in the air. His blue uniform was marked with the Emperor's Eye and gold shoulder pads to signify his ranking as Captain of Chosen.

"I told the Emperor it was madness to train a girl in the way of the sword, but I assured him if it was possible that I was the only one who could do it." Derclerq always spoke as though he was satisfied to hear the sound of his own voice. "Perhaps I was too lenient on you, being the fairer sex and all, and that is why you failed against the barbarian."

Melea didn't bother to explain that she had fought a giant who was empowered by a supernatural ritual, making him an uncanny mixture of strength and skill. Derclerq would bend these facts into excuses. *You should have been more patient. You never focus enough on the counterattack.*

"The bear-man would have crushed you like a grape," she said.

Derclerq stared impassively through half lidded eyes. "If you were serving tables like a girl your age should be, then you would know that crushed grapes turn into wine which becomes better with age. You haven't even ripened yet, much too soon to be plucked from the vine."

"And yet I was sent while my esteemed swordmaster remained in Azra."

"There are many more who require my expertise. This war will be won by men, not skinny girls waiting for their tits to come in."

"I'm not a child." Melea smirked. "At least I don't have to pay to see tits."

Derclerq lifted his nose even higher and brushed past Melea. Rumor had it that the sword on Derclerq's hip was rusty when compared to how often his other, smaller sword was wielded. He was more famous for his conquests in the brothels than for any on the battlefield.

Melea reached the walkway leading to the garden terrace and tossed her apple core into a nearby bush. The colorful foliage running alongside the winding path was perfectly cropped, not a blade of grass out of place or a shriveled flower in sight. Many of the plants looked exotic, with only a few recognizable to the area around Azra. Melea wrinkled her nose in distaste. It all seemed so fraudulent, a beautifully staged depiction, like a living tapestry.

*This is not how nature is supposed to look*, she thought. The realization struck her—*how was it supposed to look?* She had spent time in the wilderness on several missions but nature was an obstacle to overcome or a tool used to conceal her presence.

Melea paused at the edge of the garden as her imagination spiked—she saw herself racing through a thick forest like an animal, running through tall grass, scaling towering trees with branches as wide as roads, and biting into fruit so sweet that juices dribbled down her chin. She was momentarily lost in this forest of her mind's eye, until the nagging requirements of reality tugged at her awareness. She was sensitive to the subtle signals of her intuition, an acquired skill that made her an expert at survival—despite that fact that she temporarily died on occasion.

Her hair pricked up at the feeling of being watched. Melea slowly turned and found Emperor Anathasius standing in her blind spot.

"Daydreaming? That is not like you. Walk with me."

Melea joined the Emperor as he entered one of the larger gardens. He wore white garments fringed with crimson thread. His brown hair had a luminous sheen to it and he smelled of some fresh fragrance that Melea could not quite identify. Lilac, perhaps.

"You did well to stop the attempted escape last night. What were you doing in the dungeon anyhow?" Anathasius did not look at her as he spoke but instead examined a nearby begonia as if it was of the most pressing importance.

"I was on my way up from the lower levels when I noticed boot prints that seemed out of place. I had been training in an abandoned arena."

The Emperor watched the irregular flight path of a bumblebee. "All the way down there? A lonely place for training but it appears that your determination to improve yourself has once again aided the Shining Empire."

Anathasius looked squarely at her, his golden eyes radiant in the soft morning light. She had to actively focus on not being overpowered by their magnetic pull.

"As you know from experience, this shaman is an unpredictable man, and I'm sure you have heard about the commotion at the assembly yesterday." Melea nodded, and Anathasius continued. "The shaman's words have placed doubt in the hearts of some of the disciples. My informants tell me only vague rumors of the usual superficial discontent griped about in bars when one has had too many drinks, but my intuition tells me that this disaffection runs deeper.

"Several months ago it came to my attention that there is a desire to remove me as the leader of the Shining Empire. Have you heard any such news?"

"I have not. You know that I do not concern myself with rumors and hearsay."

Anathasius left the garden for the balcony. "I ask only in passing. My dependable Melea; so uncomplicated and immune to the troubles of others. I remember when you first arrived in Azra, such a wild and untrusting creature, but you have changed tremendously in your time here."

"You have given me purpose and direction. I barely remember a time before the Palace of Light."

This last statement was only a half truth. Melea had buried her memories, leaving the bones of the past to decompose until nothing remained.

They reached the balcony and looked over the edge at the sprawl of Azra. The Gateway Gulf glittered in the distance, with many ships traversing the harbor front. Sunlight streamed through the arches, slowly creeping across the city toward the water. Anathasius waved his hand over the city.

"Somewhere inside this home I have built there are people plotting against my vision and the Shining Empire. Humor me for a moment, Melea. What is the first tenet of our faith?"

"The Light of truth shall eradicate the wickedness of ignorance in the hearts of mankind."

She could dictate all of the tenets verbatim but that was about as far as Melea intended to go. She fought for the Emperor, not for his vision. Leave the piety and preening to the priests in their white robes.

Anathasius nodded. "Precisely, and what does this mean?"

"We all enter from Oblivion and come screaming into the world, unaccustomed to Light. This transformation is confusing and humans often want to revert back to the Darkness from whence they came. We must find the courage to step into the Light and accept its full brilliance to understand its truth."

Anathasius looked pleased with this response. "It is a difficult task for one to embrace truth with one's entirety, which is why I am needed to guide my people along the way. I have walked the Illuminated Path and navigated Oblivion and have seen a wondrous vision for those willing to follow." Anathasius paused and glanced down at Melea, searching for something in her countenance. "Humor me one last time. What is the vision of the Shining Empire?"

Melea had not discussed these topics for some time. She spent little effort listening to sermons or reading scrolls anymore. She looked out across Azra as she considered which words to use.

"To bring Light to all corners of Rua and unite all of humanity under the banner of truth."

This answer produced a captivating smile from Anathasius, his flawless teeth sparkling. "I could not have said it better myself. I knew when I first saw you that you were a key piece to this vision. There was no doubt in my mind that you would help me bring this future to fruition."

"Your help is needed now. Our glorious vision, the very same you so eloquently described, cannot be allowed to rot from within due to germs of doubt spread by misinterpretation. Our newest disciples have not purged the Darkness from their hearts."

Melea recalled that Sixthrok had promised to keep the song of Cynaal in the hearts of his people. She wasn't sure what, or who, Cynaal was but it definitely was not part of the Binding Doctrine.

"These unfaithful citizens that I spoke of, I need you to uncover more of their machinations. I worry that Darkness has claimed the hearts of these confused souls and drives them to commit wicked acts."

Melea was shocked, she had never been given a mission like this before. Tending the flock was better left to a shepherd than a wolf.

"Surely there is someone more suitable for this task. I have no experience in such things."

The Emperor shook his head and looked at Melea. "Morokko Kachina has other duties to fulfill and the priests lack the fortitude—you are the perfect person for this task. You are becoming a beautiful young woman and I suspect that you can be quite charming when you are not bristling with weaponry."

Melea's mind swarmed with so many thoughts that none were able to make their way to her mouth. She felt nervous, her apprehension was magnified tenfold. Using her fists came naturally, not her words. Talking to secretive strangers and gaining their trust seemed impossible. Anathasius continued before she could respond.

"You have unparalleled skills; I would feel more comfortable knowing that you are on this mission. I have arranged a meeting for you with one of my street agents who will provide aid through his established resources. You are to meet him at the Hog's Ear Tavern near the wharf at sundown tonight. Dress in plain clothes befitting a common girl of your age."

Melea was still recovering from the unexpected mission details and could only swallow the lump in her throat as a response. Anathasius moved to leave the terrace and she instinctively followed his lead.

"You have never failed me before and you will not fail me now."

"Yes, of course, I am honored."

Melea turned to leave when Anathasius unexpectedly stopped her. "You have baking flour on your shoulder."

She brushed it off and gave a wan smile before exiting through the garden. Her mind reeled from the thought of leaving her sword behind for a skirt. An image of her skipping carefree through the streets in a frilly dress popped into her head. *Is that what women wore?* She would feel naked no matter how many layers of clothes if she was without a blade. Melea almost wished that Anathasius had interrogated her about Sixthrok's escape instead of this unexpected horror.

She did not have to decide on what to wear. A full outfit was perfectly arranged on her bed.

Thankfully, it was not a dress.

A tan blouse of indiscriminate style, dark leggings, brown ankle height leather boots, and a rough spun wool coat. Melea sat on the bed beside the clothes and looked at the disguise quizzically, trying to determine which weapons could be concealed within. She sighed and rubbed her face with both hands.

She began removing the outfit she wore almost every day. First to come off were the tailored boots made from the finest leather. She looked longingly at the water resistant cloak lying on the other side of bed, its pockets filled with various tools that were commonly used during a mission: the small lead ball, a lock pick, leather gloves, healing herbs, bandages, and matches. A common girl would never wear such a thing. Maybe she could keep her boots though, they were not so new anymore as to draw attention.

Melea went to the mirror and looked at herself in her small clothes. In her mind she looked completely unimpressive. Perhaps no one would notice her innate difference. Recalling the Emperor's compliment about her features caused an involuntary blush to rise to her cheeks and she quickly got dressed in her new clothes. She noticed a slip of paper on the floor, it was a note written in the Emperor's hand that must have fallen off the bed as she had gotten dressed.

> *Melea,*
> *I know that I ask the unexpected of you and without proper preparation but I ask that you trust in my belief in your abilities. You are capable of much and I expect the Shining Empire will need even more from you in the future. Your name is to be 'Shamara' for this mission and you are to play the part of an orphan and to remain away from the palace during this time.*
> 
> *The breadth of this plot against the Shining Empire is unknown, as is the level of organization. They have evaded the attempts of previous informants. You will be unknown to them as you are a fresh face to the streets. I have provided enough coin to last two weeks. Do not doubt yourself, follow your instincts.*
> *M.*

Melea did not remember seeing any coin but eventually found a leather purse wedged under a wrinkle in the blanket. The letter lessened her anxiety a little. The Emperor allowed her to call him Martinus in private and the letter was an even rarer and more intimate gesture. She looked into the mirror once more, her reflection a sneering impostor.

The doubt in her eyes unsettled her more than she wanted to admit. *It doesn't matter. Martinus needs me. I will complete this task for him.*

Time to embrace the game she only occasionally played in the palace kitchen. She stared into her own green eyes, ignoring the doubt lurking around the edges, and actively avoiding the thin, vein-like cracks reaching up from the bottom corner of the mirror.

## Myths of the Green Time

Belenus detested the smell of dungeon air. He took short, rapid breaths in an attempt to keep the smell out. The process succeeded in making him feel nauseas. *This air could change a man*, thought Belenus, *makes one forget sunshine.*

The jailor, shockingly rat-like in appearance, offered Belenus a torch as he passed through the iron doorway. He looked at the spot where they had both had lain unconscious only a few days ago. Strange that the men did not feel the need to talk to each other after going through such an ordeal. Embarrassment warmed the priest's face as he remembered the state he had woken in, after leading the northerners to the dungeon.

The Emperor's favorite instrument had halted the escape. Belenus unconsciously rubbed his backside where she had cut strips of cloth to bind the shaman. He did not particularly care for the cold, hard girl that the Emperor employed and these actions did nothing to endear her to his heart. Belenus had walked throughout the palace with his undergarments showing without noticing until returning to his chambers. No one had mentioned his appearance, out of respect, but he was sure they were snickering about it. *The sycophantic cowards.* Sometimes showing respect meant telling someone a truth about themselves they might not want to hear. At least he thought so.

This evening Belenus was on a visit and had arrived at the gloomy destination. A pitch-black opening extended away from the priest into a rough hewn cave. His torch did little to banish the darkness on the other side of the bars.

"Beacon." The voice emanated as a disembodied aspect of the cell. "I thought you would have come sooner."

"I figured you weren't going anywhere."

Laughter came from the back of the cell. "I could have left if I wanted to. You wouldn't happen to have brought any seal meat would you? It's been weeks since I've had some."

The shaman's irrational confidence never ceased to astound Belenus. The man's grip on reality was permanently disturbed by his pride; he still fancied himself able to make demands.

"What were you thinking? Your actions at the Skar was the most foolish thing I've ever seen committed and I once saw an idiot smother himself in honey and roll around on an ant hill. I honored your wishes and let you remain at the palace and you returned this kindness with an act of betrayal propelled by that slanderous tongue of yours. Fool me once, shaman."

"Bold—yes—honest—yes, but foolish? I do not think so. Your people need to know the truth. Do not patronize me, there was no trust given."

"The people of Azra witnessed the truth when Emperor Anathasius placed his hands on the sick boy, healing him so that he may live a full life. You saw the Emperor's conviction and loyalty to his people when you defied his requests for civility."

Kerak scoffed. "He saved that boy so that he may grow into another soldier to spill blood in the Emperor's name. How many more will rush to join the ranks now?"

Belenus grew hot. "Watch your words, shaman. Your son kidnapped me and killed several people to get to you. He is no innocent child, his hands are stained with the blood of the Empire, as are many others in the North. You know as well as I do how this game is played."

Silence filled the dungeon. *Good*, thought Belenus, *maybe Kerak will learn some humility*. The shaman's face appeared between the bars, the firelight dancing on his pupils.

"Light protect me! You startled me."

"Why does your Emperor not heal all of the sick? Why will other children die horrible deaths in the arms of their weeping mothers?"

"The Emperor has saved many lives and will save many more. Death is unavoidable but the faithful walk the Illuminated Path and those unfortunate few who die before the vision of the Shining Empire is realized will reach a far more beautiful existence just a little bit sooner than the rest of us. Do not pretend to think that you know anything about him or the Shining Empire."

Kerak faded back from the bars, the darkness of the cell wrapping around him like a demonic cloak. "I do not pretend to. It is amusing that you do."

"You braying jackass. I am older and wiser than you can ever hope to be, particularly if that tongue persists on tightening the noose around your neck. Remember that I am all that stands between you being sent somewhere less luxurious, somewhere so small that there won't be enough room to fit all of you inside."

"Only threaten a man if you are willing to follow through." Kerak's calm rebuttal smacked Belenus like a back-handed slap. "You could have me chopped into bits but then who will tell you what you came to find out? You came to see me and I doubt that it was just to check on my health."

The priest's anger momentarily stopped his tongue, which was a rare occurrence. Kerak continued. "Do you know how I made my way atop the mountain?"

Belenus did not, and he hated to admit that he was quite curious to find out how the shaman managed that feat. As a boy, Belenus had tried to climb the black mountain of Azra, but had scarcely been able to even lift himself off the ground.

"Through the use of impure rituals, by actions that bring more Darkness into the world?" queried the priest.

"My methods are that much different than yours?"

"You do not use the purifying source of the Emperor's Gift and thereby, knowingly or unknowingly, contaminate your own blood and any power drawn from it."

"Cynaal sings through me. What is more pure than that?"

"Where does Cynaal come from, do you know for certain? I'm sure there are stories passed down through the Frozen Tribes, but how have they changed through the years? How many of them have been altered by ambitious shaman? Emperor Anathasius is a living testament to the truth, he has taught the priesthood the correct way to draw directly from the source, to change the world without tainting it."

"You did not journey with the Emperor," said Kerak, his voice as cold as a frozen river. "You believe his claims because he stands before you. I trust in Cynaal because she is all around us."

"I'll take what I can see over what I can't."

"Can you see his vision?" asked Kerak. "I can. He is not content with conquest, even if all territory and peoples are under the banner of the Shining Empire. No, he wants more, something that most do not realize they should be unwilling to give."

Belenus jabbed a finger at the shaman. "You witnessed the ironwood sickness, how it will lay waste to all if left unchecked. The Emperor endeavors to save humanity before such a level of affliction occurs. Malcontents like yourself only hinder the process."

"I did not climb it, or not much of it. I asked for help and my request was granted."

Belenus needed to blink several times to process the change in topic. "The Skar."

"I was carried by a flock of crows, they carried me as high as their wings could take us, and I made the rest of the way on my own. Ask what you came to ask."

Belenus was bothered by how Kerak was directing the conversation but he had come to the dungeon with a purpose. He spoke grudgingly, each word further wounding his pride. "During your studies in Calanthia, did you come across anything that referred to the elm in Stone Park here in Azra?"

He heard Kerak pacing. "I have not. But I have read about a certain forest that this tree might belong to."

Belenus shook his head. "One tree is not an entire forest. I know one tree might seem like a lot where you're from but they are exceedingly common around here."

"Every forest is made up of individual trees. This particular forest is spread out further than most, it reaches all corners of Rua, even though there are only few members that belong to it. The trees are the last vestiges of the Green Time."

Belenus snorted. The Green Time was a children's story, a myth of an era before the Age of Stone. For all of the shaman's wisdom he remained a barbarian wrapped in superstition like swaddling around a babe.

"Are you trying to tell me that the people of the Green Time planted elms across the entire world? How many elms can withstand harsh northern winters or the monsoons along the southern coast? Besides, do you have any idea how old that would make the tree in Stone Park?"

Kerak's appeared between the bars, his face solemn. "Not only elm. A different tree for each region was planted and worshipped. The trees were believed to have great power."

"You expect me to believe this nonsense? You must have hit your head harder than I thought. I'll leave you be, shaman." Belenus turned and started down the corridor.

Kerak called out after Belenus. "How high do you want to go, Beacon?"

He kept walking; some people were beyond saving. "Crows eat the dead. I don't trust them."

As he walked, Belenus felt his anger diffusing, dissipating completely once he was free of the dungeon air. Anger was an emotion he could never hold onto for long. His faith empowered Belenus to strive toward the Emperor's vision, and anger would muddle his mind in these matters.

*The trees*. Kerak's mention of the Green Time forest might be a tool he could use to keep hearts along the Illuminated Path. Barely able to contain his excitement, Belenus hurried to the library, cursing his knee as it prevented him from running.

The library was located in its own wing, adjacent to the palace, and was primarily used as a storage area for the recordings of taxes and other such administrative matters, but it did have a substantial collection of historical scrolls. A special denomination of priests occupied the library and it was their responsibility to record the accomplishments of the Shining Empire.

Belenus slowed his pace, his knee aching. "Librarian! I need your aid and that of your assistants for an important task."

The scratching of quills on parchment ceased as robed men and women looked up from their desks.

"I am looking for information about the Green Time. Where have you tucked this away?" asked Belenus.

The head librarian blinked rapidly as he scanned the floor. "Green Time, not sure about that," he muttered. He gestured and several librarians left their desks to search the many shelves. Belenus waited but each librarian returned empty handed.

"Nothing?" Belenus asked, his frustration obvious.

"Maybe in the cave, don't know for certain, haven't been down there since I was initiated."

"The cave?"

"Sorry, librarian slang for what we call the oldest section of the library, it might very well be the original library. Right this way."

"Nobody tells me anything in this blasted place," Belenus grumbled.

The librarian squeezed beside a tottering stack, descending down a spiral staircase carved into the floor. The staircase continued, growing increasingly dark.

"Should we get a torch?" asked Belenus.

"Fire in a library?" admonished the librarian.

Belenus rolled his eyes but supposed the librarian had a point. Images of the stacks catching fire, of flames leaping onto Belenus' hair as he rushed out of the smoke sprang to mind. A fire would tear through the dried out stacks like a hog left alone at a banquet. The thought of losing his hair was equally troubling. The staircase opened into a chamber the size of a small hall.

A strange blueish hue emanated from the walls. Belenus, examining the source of the light, was surprised to find that it was produced by a form of phosphorescent moss lacing the walls and gave off no heat whatsoever.

The librarian waved a hand at the few stacks of scrolls and documents ordered neatly against the walls. "If there is any mention of the Green Time it will be in here. Do you wish for assistance?"

"No, that will be all."

Cobwebs crisscrossed the corners of the cave like gloomy decorations and a revoltingly hairy spider scuttled away as Belenus reached for a scroll.

"You better run," he mumbled.

The scroll crumbled against the pressure of his grip. This material was old, very old. The hair on the back the priest's neck stood up; the room suddenly felt like a place hidden outside of time, a forgotten crevice that did not tolerate the intrusion of outsiders.

He stepped cautiously as if walking on ice that might crack at any moment, carefully brushing the dust on top of documents so that he could spy their topic without having to rummage through them. The extreme patience finally paid off as Belenus carefully pulled a thin manuscript titled "Legends of the Green Time" from a stack.

The manuscript was made of what Belenus thought was tree bark, even though it had the feel of tough leather. The ink was red and the words were sunk into the smooth material. No author or date was given to offer context. Frayed strings looped through small holes on one edge to tie the pages together. Belenus sat on the cold stone floor, cradling the manuscript in his lap. The opening page read as such:

*The Green Time is a title used to designate an era before time, an age before ages, one that might be compared to the sense of everlasting perceived by youth. This is not to say that time did not exist but time was a concept of little use for the people of this epoch, making for markedly difficult* categorization. The tales within these pages are written as they were passed down to me and may have never before been recorded.

A measured account, the prose read as that of a scholar, leading Belenus to infer that it must have been written far removed from the Green Time. The next page was titled, "The Giving Moon." Belenus skimmed through the narrative but there was no mention of a global forest. Next came an outlandish story about the origin of mankind called, "Children of Earth & Water." No forests were involved, so Belenus flipped through to the third legend, "Man the Beast."

An inventive tale describing how an apparently insatiable man devoured every animal in the forest by swallowing it whole. The man grew larger and stronger and seemed quite pleased with himself. Once all of the animals were inside of the man he turned to the vegetation and soon had consumed an entire forest. Eventually, the man had devoured everything and laid down to rest for a moment but his short nap turned into a deep slumber that he could not wake from. Some time later—the specifics were vague—a star fell from the sky and punctured the man's belly. All that he had eaten burst forth from his stomach, forever changed by their confinement. The story did not elaborate on how exactly, but things were different than they had been before ingestion. For one, the animals no longer trusted the man and the story ended with him wandering alone for eternity.

Belenus found the tale curious but the forest mentioned did not seem to match the one he was after. The last entry was titled, "Root & Leaf." Belenus felt his pulse quicken as he read—this story was about a forest, a forest full of important trees.

*Man traveled the world so that he might know his limitations as a map without borders is incomplete. He planted seeds along the path to find his way back. The journey took many years as man ranged far and wide, he grew weary but could not return until his task was completed. The seeds he planted grew into tall and graceful trees while he journeyed and he was surprised to find other people living underneath them. "Thank you for showing us the way!" the people would call out to him but he did not respond as his task remained unfinished. Great settlements formed around the trees and the man began to feel crowded as he journeyed. The people shouted from the settlements, "Come, stay with us, this is your home." Man was tired and longed to join them but he knew he could not as seeds still remained in his palm. He continued to stitch the borders together and eventually the last seed slipped between his fingers. The people called to him from under their different trees saying, "Ours is the way, it is the first, see how it suits us?" Man was confused as the seeds were only markers so that he may find his way home. With his task nearly completed, man continued his journey. He spoke to the people, "I am returning home, you may join me if you wish, the path is laid out before you." The people were confused and said, "We are home, see how our trees' branches hold up the sky? See how its roots reach into the soil to hold the land in place?" To this the man always replied, "I see." Man continued home and eventually some of the people followed after him but they never found him or the home he spoke of.*

Belenus wrinkled his brow at the abrupt ending. He was not one who read deeply into symbolism, he preferred straightforward messages imbued with clear meaning. The Binding Doctrine was structured in this way, leaving little room for debate about the intended meaning of the lessons within. Tenets were laid down with steadfast conviction. The man who brought them into existence was still living and his presence acted as confirmation.

He tried to fathom how someone could live their life by such a story, but was quickly lost in his musings as they turned in on themselves until becoming indistinct. It was time to speak with the Emperor.

Belenus arrived before the massive, rounded doors that barred entry to the Emperor's chambers. The guards gave nods of respect and granted access.

The Emperor was not expecting him and a result the greeting room was empty. There was no wife to occupy the space with her handmaids nor were there children running about; the Shining Empire did not have an empress or heirs. Emperor Anathasius had no need for such trivial mortal trappings; he was a God, all powerful and immortal. His legacy would live on in the faith of his disciples, in the divine conquest of Darkness that would usher in an unprecedented era of prosperity.

Belenus bypassed the stairs to the upper terraces and bedchamber, opting to try the main garden first. The echo of his footsteps made Belenus feel like he was trespassing and he gratefully stepped out into the open air of the garden. He followed a gently curving path of interlocking stone blocks that led through the garden to the balcony. There was no sign of the Emperor so he took a side path he knew ended at a staircase providing access to the upper terraces.

Vegetation packed the sides of the path, the quiet evening air pushed waving branches across him as he walked. The thick growth gave way to a small grassy clearing occupied by a single peach tree. Heavy fruit dragged the branches down and a sweet scent wafted when the air ruffled through the leaves. Belenus thought the tree looked beautiful but tired, like a pregnant woman who was ready to bring her child into the world. The Emperor sat beneath the peach tree so quietly that Belenus almost missed him. His eyes remained closed, yet the Emperor knew who walked through the garden.

"Belenus my friend, come join me." He turned a palm to offer a spot beside him. "You seem anxious. What is it that troubles you?"

Belenus sat in the same cross-legged manner as the Emperor, his hip popping as he made himself comfortable. The priest thought he could hear the peach tree breathing, gentle and sweet. Such extraordinary perceptions were possible when in the presence of the Emperor.

"Shining Lord, I thank you for your kindness. I am not troubled but I do have something of fairly pressing importance to discuss." Belenus meant to bring up his newly formed plan and was shocked by the question that came out of his mouth. "What do you intend to do with Kerak the shaman?" He immediately attempted to retract the question. "I am sorry, that is not my concern. I spoke out of turn."

The Emperor opened his green-gold eyes, amused by the Beacon's distress. "No harm done, a valid question considering the circumstances. The shaman will remain here for now. His purpose has not yet presented itself."

Belenus changed the topic. "I know I am no strategist but I have stumbled across some information that might work well for the upcoming endeavor in Calanthia."

"Interesting. Go ahead."

"Odd as it may be, my plan centers around trees."

The Emperor looked up at the branch above his head. "Fitting."

"Yes, I suppose so." Belenus grew more confident as he spoke. "Calanthia, as you know, is obsessed with trees and animals and ridiculous legends. Their revered pines are the symbols which hold their past firmly in place. Their religious leaders find strength in this as it proclaims their difference from the Shining Empire. I propose we use this perceived strength against them."

"Very devious of you Belenus, I must say this is unexpected. How would you go about turning strength into weakness?"

Belenus felt jittery, he didn't know how the Emperor would respond to mention of the Green Time. He still felt like an awed young boy when in the presence of his Lord. How could one not when the sight of the Emperor warmed the skin like that of the sun?

"I discovered a text claiming that a forest of special trees connected the people of Rua during the Green Time. The trees were planted by a single man who wanted to show all people the way to their true home—as the tale goes. These kinds of myths are ingrained in the spirit of Calanthia so they would not be able to rebuff such a tale. I would elaborate connections between the ancient elm in Stone Park and Calanthia's pines."

The Emperor finished the plan. "But you would need their sacred grove to die, to crumble their faith, so they might believe I am the one to lead them to their glorious new home."

"You could heal the trees as you have done for the ironwood here in the palace, they would be unable to deny your divine power."

"A beautifully subtle plan that could prove effective if given enough time and the right influences. Your abilities would work wonders in such a situation."

Belenus gulped. He was going to Calanthia. He knew it.

"Unfortunately this will not be the case. Actions have already been set in motion. It will be my army, not my priests who will march into Calanthia."

Belenus felt a wave of relief but it lacked any calming influence. The Emperor had already decided to take Calanthia by force, which meant that a great deal of death was on the way.

"You said this plan was inspired by a text?"

Belenus produce the manuscript from his robes. Recognition reflected in the Emperor's eyes. "Where did this ragged thing turn up?"

"In the Library, the cave, actually."

"May I keep this?"

"Of course. I'll take my leave. Thank you for your patience."

Belenus bowed and left the Emperor. He had tried, he told the Emperor his plan, and the Emperor even agreed that it could work. Nothing more could be expected of him. But why did feelings of unease twist in his gut?

He was no strategist, he was no soldier. Belenus had chosen the path of peace by becoming a priest. Kerak's laughter rang out in his head. *He saved that boy so that he may grow into another soldier.*

The world needed saving, Calanthia more than most and soldiers were necessary for now. Belenus hoped there would come a time when strength of spirit was required more than strength of arms, even if he never saw that day.

His eyes drooped, weary from reading in the dim light of the cave. Belenus returned to his chambers and made a tonic, carefully grinding up the ingredients that would ease him into sleep.

## Moon Song

Shadows crisscrossed the busy street, stretching out from multileveled buildings. The hurried movements of pedestrians in the deepening twilight created a sense of urgency. Melea felt as if she walked in two different worlds—one of imposing structures made of human design, and another that was hidden within the created habitat.

Glimpses of this other world appeared, then escaped her grasp, slipping away the moment she turned her attention in its direction. Flickers of movement caught in the corner of the eye, phrases from overheard conversations that rang out louder than others, hidden thoughts of the hundreds of passers-by as they went about their private lives. All was so close yet impossibly distant.

She looked up at the crimson domes of the palace atop the hill and wondered if Anathasius was watching. Her curious look transformed into a glare.

She imagined Anathasius contentedly strolling along the gardens of the terrace while she had to pretend to be a common peasant girl. Melea had no idea how to be a peasant and the thought of portraying commonness was laughable.

Normally, she was able to step into her training, just like pulling on her well worn boots. Repetition of practiced maneuvers calmed her mind, stopping it from racing, allowing her body to take over, to intuitively understand what she was supposed to do. Where was the training for this mission?

Lamps were being lit to fend off the night. Every house had a lamp near the door and most shops had several. Many of the streets in Azra blazed throughout the night to support the faith of the Shining Empire. Great towers were situated throughout the city, the wide bowl at the peak fed all night with fuel to burn bright and triumphant. Azra embodied the vision of Anathasius and shone proudly as a symbol of his divinity.

Melea was no stranger to these streets but she was unfamiliar with the section near the wharf where the meeting was to take place. She took a side street leading toward the Gulf, leaving the brightness of the more traveled routes behind.

The buildings became increasingly ramshackle, having the feel of clustered tenements. The architecture abruptly changed, reverting to the style favored in the time of Cambor. Once grand houses of brick now had the appearance of cracked and broken smiles.

A stink of trash and waste hung in the air as it emptied into the street to drain away to the water. Melea wrinkled her nose. The location was beginning to make more sense. This was far from the most desirable area of the city. Tall masts with rigging loomed over the declining buildings.

Others braved the stench and darkness; grizzled men with dark tans, who Melea took to be sailors. A small hanging lamp illuminated a worn placard bearing the name Hog's Ear Tavern in red lettering. Beneath the sign was a door of the same red with a dried hog's ear nailed to the doorframe. Melea rolled her eyes. She pushed through the door and was assaulted by pungent smoke. A swirling cloud pervaded the entire interior, bringing tears to her eyes. The place reeked of stale beer and unwashed bodies.

Much of the smoke billowed out of a stone fireplace set against the far wall, but a shocking amount also escaped from the lips of the patrons. Several tables of men puffed on pipes and hand rolled cigarettes, between swigs of beer. None of them so much as turned a head at her entrance and the bartender only gave a passing glance before continuing to fill tankards. Melea headed to the rear section of the tavern, looking for a booth with a man sitting alone.

She waded through the smoke until a loud cough from a nearby table caught her attention. Melea was surprised by the informant's appearance; he was cleanly shaved and actually quite handsome. He regarded her with cool eyes as she slipped into the booth. The informant signaled the bartender for two drinks without asking what she wanted.

"Always best to order a drink at a bar, looks suspicious for folk to be siting here with no drinks between them. The beer at this particular establishment is palatable if you don't care about the taste."

Melea only responded with a head nod, causing the informant to give a puzzled look.

"A quiet one hey? Rare trait in an informant. I'm Trinn, no last name, never needed one." He extended a hand in greeting and Melea squeezed hard. Trinn tried to return the grip but flinched ever so slightly.

"My name is Shamara, I was told you had some information for me?"

Trinn chuckled. "Straight to the point hey, I was told you're new at this, so let's go over some basics first."

The bartender arrived with the beer and actually looked at Melea for the first time. "A little young to be in here, aren't you?"

Trinn produced some coins for the beer and added what Melea considered to be a generous tip, as well as a slimy smile that gave her the creeps. The bartender swiped up the coins.

"No funny business in the tavern. A room will cost extra."

Trinn extended the oily grin. "No need, friend. We'll soon be on our way."

The bartender grunted and cast an appraising look at Melea before leaving. The look only lasted a second but it made her feel like a piece of meat being inspected for quality.

Trinn shot her a sly look. "Now that you're a whore there will be no follow up questions. The only question whores are ever asked is, how much?"

"I'm not a whore."

He flashed a smile so winsome that it was hard to believe he was capable of the repulsive look just given to the bartender. "You're not a common peasant girl either, but that is the identity you must assume to complete your mission. With one look and a few well placed coins I gave you a new identity, one that makes you forgettable, an afterthought." Trinn raised an eyebrow as he came to a realization. "Well, I suppose a whore only elicits one thought, which is also good." He placed his hands on the table and looked at her seriously. "A persona is useful but money is infinitely more valuable. Money almost always quiets tongues and is even better for loosening them."

Melea's patience was nearing its end. "Anything else?"

"Bribery is the most basic trick of the trade, hardly a man that doesn't have his price, and if he don't have one, well I bet you can guess what comes next." He scrutinized Melea's appearance. "But I doubt if strong arm tactics would work for you, women usually use other physical means."

"You'd be surprised what I'm capable of."

Her hand instinctively went to the knife on her hip, she had been unable to leave it behind. She had also pocketed the matches since they were always useful to have on hand. Trinn took a drink of beer and gave her a smile and a wink.

"We all have our methods," he said. He pressed his fingers together while looking seriously at her. "The less I know about you the better. The less anyone knows, actually. Stay below people's awareness until you find the mark. Once you find your mark, then you say and do anything you need to in order to get the information. That is your job, information is your currency, your only reason for existing. Don't forget that."

Melea nodded. Perhaps this would not be so different than her previous missions. "Speaking of marks?"

"Right," said Trinn as he raised his mug again. "You will need to find a man named Gerboa. He runs a group of pickpockets and smugglers in the old section near Stone Park. Rumor has it that he and his gang live in the ruins. They're a slippery bunch who seem to be mostly young folk about your age. I've arranged a room for you at a nearby inn called the Black Lotus—it's paid up for two weeks. The proprietor owes me a favor so I got him to give you a room with its own entrance" A dark look passed over Trinn's face. "Blackmail is extremely successful in this business. If you own a man's secrets, then you own him." Trinn slid a key across the table, finished his drink, and moved to leave. "Those were my directions, do not try to contact me, I will contact you if I am told to. I must go. Rumors to uncover and others to disperse."

He snatched up her mug and downed the contents in one long drink. He belched, then stood and indicated for Melea to join him. "Try to give a giggle or something, play the part. It only needs to last until we're outside."

They moved through the smoke, the acrid fog curling around them. The bartender gave Melea a more lingering look and her pulse jumped as Trinn placed a hand on her hip. Her hand shot to Trinn's wrist and his whispered words were all that prevented her from wrenching his arm off his body.

"Now would be the time to giggle. Take my hand and lead me outside."

Melea hooked her fingers around Trinn's and attempted a lighthearted giggle but it came out flat and cold. She stepped into the cool night air and released Trinn from her grasp.

"You need to relax, Shamara. It doesn't matter who you were before. You're not that person now. Become whatever is needed."

He gave her a peculiar look and a brief nod before leaving. Melea stood on the corner, dizzy from the smoke. At least she thought it was from the smoke.

"Keep moving ya skinny brat—unless you want to lose a fistful of hair."

A woman walked towards Melea, her movements stiff and aggressive. Garish makeup could not conceal the bruise on the woman's cheekbone.

"Think you can take this spot from me?" Melea challenged. She was tired of being told what to do.

The whore stopped, her long coat swinging open to display large breasts partially concealed by a low cut shirt. Melea looked into the woman's eyes. Something was wrong with them. They were halfway dead, lacking the spark of imagining a world outside of the present circumstances. *Is that how she looked when she died?*

"This is my territory and you're trespassing. Move along bitch."

The glazed eyes offered no indication of where the aggression came from. The whore was drunk or drugged, and she was having trouble keeping her balance. Melea was repulsed by the lack of control.

"Is this worth a few coins? Choosing to put yourself through beatings and worse?" asked Melea.

"I need to eat and it looks like I'm doing better at that than you." The woman spit at Melea but missed. "And I have nicer clothes."

The woman wobbled from foot to foot. Her anger fading then returned when she remembered why she'd walked over there.

"You a chet or something? Who do you think you are? Judge me?"

She reached for Melea. The attack came in slow and awkward. Melea grabbed onto the woman's wrists. The woman squawked in distress. A jolt of energy passed from her and into the whore. A spark of life flashed in the woman's eyes. For an instant, Melea saw the person the streetwalker might have been under more fortunate circumstances.

Melea released her grip, turning in the opposite direction, and moving steadily away from the stench of the waterfront.

Many of the streets she approached blazed with flickering light. Melea tried to avoid them as much as possible; she did not want to draw any undue attention as a young woman alone in the city after dark. She was used to navigating shadowy pathways and the act of subterfuge brought about a sense of familiarity that put her at ease.

Melea knew she was getting close to Stone Park when more of the buildings were built of huge slabs of rock. The structures in this area were of a completely different scale.

She chose a dark alley to avoid traveling down a particularly bright street. The alley was in disrepair, obvious even in the dark, and it soon came to a dead end. Melea silently cursed her wrong turn, then froze at the sound of concealed movement behind her.

The scuffling noise sounded too large to be a rat and a ragged wheeze left few assumptions as to its owner. The reek of stale alcohol and soiled clothing was accompanied by a dark form moving down the alley to block her exit.

"Don't think you can slip by me in the dark missy," came a rough voice. "I can see yer every move."

Melea doubted the drunkard's claim and angled away from his advancing figure. She moved stealthily along the wall, slipping beside his probing arms that swayed slowly in front. With the drunk behind her, Melea turned to sprint into the open. Before she could run her feet were suddenly lifted off the ground as two strong arms slipped around her chest. One arm crushed her ribcage and the other was moved to clasp around her neck.

Her captor chuckled. "Got her, Jeb."

He smelled worse than his companion, body odor rank as a dead dog. Her dangling feet kicked helplessly. Jeb returned, whistling softly in delight.

"I apologize for lying t' ya, sweetness, I couldn't see ya but Karn here could with his shine glass."

*How did these two drunks get a shine glass?*

"Take her to the hole," said Jeb.

Melea seethed. So that was how she had been caught. Karn had waited by an opening in the wall while she had been herded over in his direction like a stupid animal. She did not plan on becoming another victim.

Melea raised her right leg as high as it could go and smashed her heel into Karn's shin. He grunted in pain but kept his grip. She gave two more quick kicks before the third attempt was interrupted by a punch to stomach from Jeb.

"Stop squirming, sweetness—I don't like squirmies."

She was winded but could feel energy burning inside. She kicked out with both legs, pushing hard off Jeb's chest to slam Karn into the wall. His grip around her chest loosened slightly and she opened more space with a sharp elbow. An arm became free and instantly went for the knife on her hip.

Karn's hold around her neck intensified. She swung backward wildly with the blade and felt it glance off bone as it sunk deep into her captor's hip. Karn howled in pain and released his stranglehold. Melea sprang toward him as he stumbled backward, plunging the knife into his chest. He made chortling noises as he fell to the ground.

Melea heard Jeb scramble away into their hideout. She snatched the shine glass off Karn's face and placed them over her own eyes. The alleyway did not burst into light as she expected. Objects adopted a subtle hazy outline and only one of them was moving. Melea could clearly make out a man sized shape bobbing further into the structure. The would-be captor could run, but he couldn't hide.

She exited the dank alley, stepping into the open street to breathe in the lamplight like fresh air.

"Daughter of shadow, you are alone," rasped a brittle voice.

The knife was immediately back in Melea's hand, ready to face another assailant, but she only saw an elderly beggar. He sat propped up against the wall of a fabric shop beside the dark alley. His smile showed more gum than teeth. He motioned for her to come nearer.

"We have not spoken in a very long time, little one."

Melea returned the knife to its sheath, the naked iron feeling out of place in the lamplight of the deserted street. "What nonsense do you speak of? We have never met."

The old man had a pleasant expression, examining Melea like she was a long lost relative. His eyes glittered, conveying more life than his malnourished body. Many necklaces of different colors and designs drooped around his neck, sliding across his chest toward the ground.

"Once, but not here, oh no, not in this place. You are more beautiful than I remember." He locked eyes with Melea. "But also much colder, I can feel the chill from here."

"You must have me confused with someone else, or maybe with a figment of your imagination." She nodded toward the alleyway. "A poor victim of those scum in the alley there, but they won't be hurting anyone else."

"Terrible men, consumed by foulness that spreads through them like a disease. They cannot bear the light so they hide in the shadows." He looked up at the lamp, watching fat-bodied moths flutter around the glass. "Do you feel safer here in the light? Why avoid it and travel down paths of darkness?"

"It is your safety you should be concerned with," said Melea, fingering the hilt of her knife.

The man cackled. "I see you, daughter of shadow, oh yes, I see. The eye does not stop seeing when it is closed, it is always searching."

The man began to sing a slow song Melea had never heard before. The sombre melody was one of loss. "Left alone far from home, they wander on, their purpose gone, run and hide from the shame, never can escape the blame."

The singing concluded as the old man looked beyond the lamp, up into the night sky. Melea followed his gaze but the glow of the lamplights only allowed for the hint of the moon to be glimpsed.

"There is much to be seen in darkness as well as in light, but I think you already know this, young one, or else why would you walk as you do?" He pointed a gnarled finger at the moon. "See how lonely she is, lighting the darkness by herself? The moon does this great task but her gift is obscured by our creations. But we know better, don't we?" He grinned a gummy smile at Melea.

"The moon cannot illuminate the streets enough to make them safe. Walking in the dark places is dangerous. I was attacked in the alley."

The old man clucked his tongue. "That was not real darkness, that is the danger, it is only a shadow cast by light. You know of what I speak, a darkness so complete that it is the absence of light."

A sensation of vertigo overwhelmed Melea's mind, like she was staring into the memory of a place she had never been. "I think you are a crazy, old man."

The beggar laughed as though this was the funniest comment he'd ever heard. "This is a dream we are living in, can you not feel the sunlight on your sleeping eyes? It is hardest to see with your own eyes—you cannot know the world if you do not know yourself, and the self is a mystery if you ignore the world."

"What do you mean?"

"You're not asking the right kind of questions."

"Who are you?"

"A better question, a question with direction, but not helpful in my case. The trick to having no name is to have many, you have just gotten another one, haven't you? There is no hiding behind names, oh no, there is always somebody for the naming and for the knowing."

The beggar cackled, a grating sound of bone on bone. A feeling of pressure built within Melea's head, pushing against the inside of her skull. The pressure intensified into needle sharp pricks and she struggled to turn her focus away from it. Vision blurred as involuntary tears stung her eyes. She could no longer ignore the pain. Her instincts screamed at her to run, so she ran.

"Run and hide, wash your hands of those who died, run and hide, run and hide." The singing followed her down the empty street.

The pain threatened to overwhelm her as she ran with no thought of direction. After several blocks of reckless sprinting, the pressure started to decrease, and she stopped to wipe her eyes. She felt ashamed and angry and not sure why. As she continued to walk, the pressure eventually dulled to a tolerable throbbing.

Melea saw a sign declaring 'Black Lotus'. Somehow, in her mad dash, she had arrived at the intended destination. She avoided the front entrance and circled the building. Facing another person was unendurable at the moment; her mind was whirling. After trying two other doors she eventually found a side entry that opened to her key.

The click of the lock echoed in the ramshackle stairwell. At the top of the staircase was a small bedroom that had more the feel of a closet than an actual room. Melea sat on the tiny bed and lit the candle on a nearby dresser, the only other piece of furniture in the room. She took off her boots and placed the knife under the pillow. She lay staring into the flickering shadows until sleep finally claimed her just before dawn.

*Slanted yellow arrows of sunlight shot through the dark recesses of the forest. Songbirds offered their melodious chatter from the forest canopy. In a grassy clearing a stag tensed, all senses alert. A discomforting scent drifted by on the breeze, a momentary scent of smoky, tanned animal hide partially obscured by dirt and sweat.*

*Two figures sprang into the stag's vision, quickly advancing on his position from the east and west. The stag bolted into the adjacent woods, heading north into the shadow filled forest.*

*Tangled underbrush did not slow the stag as it leaped over and around obstacles in its headlong escape. A large, half-seen figure rushed in from the right side, causing the startled animal to immediately alter its direction. The stag now raced down a worn forest path, the sound of rushing water rumbling in the distance.*

*The sun had ascended higher in the sky and streams of light came pouring through the trees ahead, signifying an upcoming clearing. The stag angled left, attempting to retreat within the dense wood, but at that moment another large figure appeared to cut off the desired route and force the stag into the sunshine.*

*The clearing continued for a short distance, narrowing as it went, before abruptly ending at a cliff. A turbulent river thrashed between rocks far below. The stag skidded to halt and turned back to see multiple figures emerge from the forest, blocking the way it had come.*

*Men. The group approached the cornered stag in a tight semi-circle formation. No fear was reflected in their eyes. Only the cold certainty of inevitability, animated by adrenaline-fueled excitement.*

*Each man held a long, wooden spear with a pointed stone attached to the top, which they held out sideways to form a crude fence. Each hunter also had an axe strapped onto their backs, a large triangular stone visible over the shoulder. One of the men passed his spear to the man on his right, removed his axe from its bindings and advanced towards the stag.*

*The man had broad shoulders, arms of corded muscled, and long dark hair that flowed around his neck like a mane. He hefted the axe lightly in hand as he approached, crouched, ready to strike, eyes never leaving his prey.*

*The young stag almost always relied on its speed to escape predators but now there was nowhere else to run. Survival instinct dictated that he lower his bony crown to swing and lunge violently whenever the man got too close.*

*The man was lithe and amazingly light on his feet as he danced around the stag's antlers, all the while looking for an opening to use his axe. A series of rapid attacks by the man threw the stag off balance and one sweeping slash nearly connected with its jugular. Out of desperation, the stag reared up on its hind legs to smash the smaller man from above.*

*In one fluid motion, the man slid under the upraised hooves and slashed at the unprotected underbelly of the beast, emerging on the other side with a bloody axe in hand. The stag let out a throaty bellow of pain and collapsed to the ground as its innards spilled out of the gaping wound. Before the dust could settle from the impact, the man had sliced its throat and the hunt was over. He turned to his companions with a triumphant smile. His shout of victory never got the chance to leave his throat.*

*A flash of blinding white light erupted above the treetops, emanating from all directions at once. An intense heat followed in the wake of the flash, rolling in a wave pattern. A moment after the blast, the calm morning air turned incredibly dense, making it impossible to pull breath. In the next instant the air seemed like it was trying to rip itself apart as a screeching tempest arose out of the silence.*

*The wind tore in every direction. A shudder ran through the core of the earth. The rumbling vibration lasted for an impossibly long moment and then collapsed. With the silence came darkness.*

## Streets of Azra

Melea took another bite of the biscuit while she watched her target move through the jostling crowd on the street. The tough biscuit was all that remained of her breakfast of spiced sausages and fried potatoes. The greasy sausages were savory and the bland potatoes filled her stomach.

Several days of nearly continuous prowling around Stone Park had not revealed much information. She was tired. Dreams of hunters chasing a stag and a violent storm disturbed her sleep nightly. But there was no time to rest; she needed to be out on the street.

By Melea's assessment, the streets seemed to operate on two different levels. On the surface there was the unending day-to-day routine of merchants hawking their wares and commoners haggling for a fair price, each side usually satisfied that they had gotten the better of the other. Included in this were the solitary priests of the Sanctuary who performed countless tiny miracles, seemingly removed from the swarms of people; immovable, yet still part of the flow like stones in a stream.

There were also the patrols of the city guard, always in pairs, who displayed varying forms of protection, extortion, and indifference. At night, there were the teams of street cleaners who filled cart after cart of animal excrement and human waste in the dim lamplight. The monotonous clip-clop of hooves continued all night, as mules carried the waste outside of city limits.

Azra continued as a city because of these different support structures but their usefulness was ineffectual to Melea's cause. She needed to find the second level of street life, where those who lived between the supports operated, those who eroded the outermost layer of society just enough to scrape out a living.

Thief guilds had been in Azra since the time of Cambor, and the Binding Doctrine had not removed them, only forcing them to be more discreet. The way to track a thief seemed obvious to her—follow the flow of money. Find the main arteries where it was easiest to siphon off excess currency, and she would find her target.

A week of hunting down and questioning pickpockets, burglars, and other criminals provided little of tangible value, besides shaking down a few of the suspects for coins to replenish her purse, of course. Only one common thread kept emerging—a reference to the Sanctuary.

The Sanctuary, her entry point into the Shining Empire. Where Anathasius had come to get her. The black walls of the temple loomed in her memory, immovable.

One astoundingly drunk city guard corroborated this rumor, after accepting the shine glass as a bribe. The guard claimed to have met a man who was asking questions about the Sanctuary and if he knew of any soldiers who could be bought off as muscle for a short mission. Melea pressed the guard for more information, but he passed out shortly after making this claim.

Lacking any real leads, she had decided to stakeout the entrance to Stone Park day and night, to see if anyone went in or out and then shake them until they told her what she wanted to know. The second floor of a derelict house on the edge of the park provided a decent vantage point for this task. The crumbling walls concealed her presence and the many small openings allowed for good sight lines. She sat in her hideout for two days and nights but nothing of interest appeared. Finally, in the early morning fog of the third day, she spotted movement.

A boy who looked to be around twelve years old crawled out of a crevice in the shattered stones. He was unremarkable in every way, but his ruddy complexion and dull brown hair etched themselves into Melea's memory. She followed at a distance, memorizing every street and every stop of his route throughout the city. Afterward, she returned to the Black Lotus for much needed sleep.

Two days later she had found him again. She casually watched the boy as he moved in front her, oblivious to her pursuit. As she watched him work, she could not help but be impressed by the skill of his young hands. He was just a boy but he was an expert pickpocket. His hands were incredibly nimble and his sense of timing was nearly preternatural. He always placed his body at exactly the right angle to make a quick pilfer, in and out before the unobservant passerby was even aware.

He wore a loose fitting tunic that must have had some sort of inner rigging to hide his purloined goods and quiet their jingle as he moved. At least Melea assumed this was the case because he should have had a fair amount of coin stashed on his person by now.

The boy appeared to reach a similar conclusion as he looked to exit the crowded marketplace. Melea tossed the biscuit crust into the sandy gutter and hurried to follow. The thief walked swiftly, floating throughout the crowd as if he were alone on the street, never having to stop or move around an obstruction. Melea found herself struggling to match his progress. He was much better adapted to Azra's streets than she was and it showed. A sharp turn around a corner took the thief out of eyesight so she sprinted to catch up.

Melea rounded the corner and froze. A pair of horses snorted as the driver cracked a whip to urge forward the cart barreling directly toward her. She jumped out of the way. The driver shouted an insult without slowing down.

In the process of evading the cart, Melea had smashed into a man on her left. He grumbled at the unexpected collision but she ignored him, keeping her eyes on the crowd. She raised herself up on tip-toe, trying to catch a glimpse of the boy. A familiar brown head bobbed its way further down the street. Melea spotted an opening in the traffic and moved to take it but was held in place by a firm grip on her shoulder.

"Not so fast," said the man she had bumped into. "You nearly plowed me over and I demand an apology."

She whirled to face the man. His dark eyes glinted with malice. A big man accustomed to using his size to get what he wanted. She let his hand remain where it was as hers shot forward to grab his belt to pull him closer. The man grunted in surprise as he was forced to shuffle forward a step. The corners of his mouth flicked upward as he looked down at Melea.

"It's to be that type of apology, is it?"

Melea matched his smile but there was no mirth in her emerald eyes. "The blade should be hot, but alas there is no time."

Confusion swam on his wide face, followed by a flash of fear as he cast a look downward. Melea's knife was pressed firmly against his sack. He went to grab her with his other hand.

"Uh-uh, I wouldn't do that." She pressed the point of the knife through the cloth and his movement stopped.

"I am going to beat you for this," he growled. His eyes made a quick scan of those nearby to see if anyone was watching.

"Doubtful. Now be a good boy and don't follow me."

Melea switched her grip on the knife and hammered the hilt into the man's groin. He doubled over as she reentered the crowd, jogging to catch up to the thief.

She cursed under her breath as she jostled with other pedestrians. The boy was nowhere in sight. She recalled his route from the previous day to guess where he would be going. Perhaps he had not fared as well in the other market as Melea thought. He could be heading towards richer pastures.

Activity on the street was dense as the majority were headed to the main bazaar. Melea didn't know Azra's routines well enough to formulate why this bazaar would be seeing a sudden onrush but she went with the crowd anyway. If there were this many pockets in the bazaar then there was a good chance that the little thief would be plying his trade here.

The smells of spices, fish, sweat and countless other substances flooded her nostrils. In the distance, she noticed the olive waves of the Gulf. Merchants shouted relentlessly from beneath brightly colored canopies. The bazaar was overcrowded, forcing Melea to slow, so she methodically made her way along the market while looking for the boy.

"Several Nefaran ships arrived this morning," said a man nearby. Melea paused. "I hear it's the most anyone has ever seen here at one time. Everyone wants to see what they have."

"Nefara? I could get something for the wife before swindlers like you gouge the rest of us."

"Imagine the women I could get with a rare gift from the deep, dark jungles. But then again, think of the profits! Let's hurry up."

Melea watching the two men, spotted the boy hurrying down the street ahead of them. She pushed through the crowded marketplace in pursuit.

The brine of the Gateway Gulf slowly replaced the aroma of spices. The road made a sharp decline as it angled toward the harbor. Tall ships rose up like a floating forest.

Eight ships were grouped together, slightly apart from the rest, and distinctly different than the others. They sat lower and squatter, their hulls so black that they looked to feed on sunlight. The sails were tethered but a myriad of swirling colors could still be seen.

A semi-circle of shouting, gesticulating men had formed in front of the Nefaran fleet, as the traders had apparently barely made it off their ships before being confronted. The image of a hive of bees descending on a particularly sweet discovery came to Melea. She stalked the perimeter, searching for a thief.

From her vantage point the wares attracting the men of Azra might as well have still been in Nefara. Melea's nose crinkled. Merchants were odd creatures, buying and selling without creating the product or using it for its intended purpose. They moved items from a place of plenty to one of scarcity to reap a profit. She didn't know if she found them disgusting, pitiable, or clever.

She completed her sweep of the perimeter, having to stop where the extensive dockworks began. She'd lost him.

Melea walked away from the harbor, leaving the jostling crowd behind. An excited flurry of bartering gave her pause. The assembly seemed to be taking on the form of an auction. Melea turned to see a disagreement escalate into a shoving match.

"Thief!"

Melea moved closer the group.

"Thief!"

A thin man slipped through the front line, into the open space between the merchants and Nefarans. He looked to flee but did not have anywhere to go—ships and water on one side and an angry horde on the other.

With a lack of viable options, the thief did what most trapped men in a desperate situation would do, and took the faint glimmer of escape over certain doom. Melea knew this internal calculation of the odds, the cry for survival that sparks movement, because to stand in place is to die. She saw all of this coalesce inside the thief in the moment it took to blink. Melea forced herself through the same gap made by the thief and watched as he made a mad dash towards the wide eyed merchants from Nefara.

A heavily-muscled, bearded man wearing a yellow turban moved to intercept the thief. He must have been a guard for the envoy as he removed a stone cudgel from the cloth belt at his waist with practiced ease. He crouched, ready to pounce. The thief attempted to dodge past the man. The cudgel connected with the thief's arm and a wince-inducing crack splintered through the crowd as the arm was now undoubtedly broken.

Melea barely even noticed the sound of breaking bone. Something much more interesting occurred when the blow connected. The thief appeared to wobble. Not his body but the outline around his body. The discrepancy was similar to the wavy lines around an object viewed at a distance on an especially hot day. She would have missed it if she had blinked.

The thief collapsed to the ground and as he made contact, the trembling around the contours of his body appeared again. Melea's pulse raced. She was sure she had seen it. The thin man's blonde hair became an unmistakable brown for an instant before returning to its normal lighter hue.

Melea recognized the look in the bearded guard's eyes—a predator waiting for the final jerky movement from its prey that would call for the killing blow. She quickly considered her options, moving before the thought could reach a conclusion. Melea barreled into the guard, latching onto his chest and shoulders. He stumbled backward, trying to regain his balance to deliver another bone-shattering smash with the cudgel. She slammed her forehead into the bridge of the guard's nose. He made a guttural noise as blood streamed from his nose.

She hefted the thief up by his good arm, pulling him past the dazed guard, toward the ships. None of the other Nefarans made any attempt to stop them and the Azran merchants seemed too confused by Melea's sudden involvement to intercede. She half carried the thief as they ran to the ships.

The black planks of the hull loomed overhead. Up close to the wood Melea saw intricate swirls and whorls hidden within the blackness. The guard had recovered enough from the surprise attack and charged in their direction with his weapon held high.

"Let go and you die," said Melea.

She looped the thief's good arm around her neck then pressed her palms against the hull. A rush of energy steamed through veins to converge in her hands. She felt her fingers sink into the wood of the ship as she scrambled vertically hand-over-hand up the hull and onto the main deck. Melea glanced down at the bewildered guard.

"Come on," she said, pulling the thief across the deck.

She went for an open doorway to what looked to be a main hatch leading below decks. A tug on her arm slowed Melea at the doorway.

"We'll be trapped," complained the thief.

"I've gotten out of worse and if you don't follow me they will kill you and it likely won't be done quickly."

The thief's throat bobbed as he gulped. He obediently followed as she disappeared into the hatch.

Darkness was thick below decks, the dimness hindering their movement more than Melea would have liked. They bumped into cargo and other supplies as she tried to find a stairway to the lowest level. The thief stumbled into a support beam at one point and screamed in pain. After feeling around with her arms out in front, Melea finally found another staircase and they descended further into the ship.

She led them to the rear of the ship which was stocked with a row of barrels. Melea climbed atop the barrels; the sound of water lapping against the hull told her this spot should be just about right. She placed her palms on the wood once more, feeling the exhilarating energy return.

Melea could feel the wood grain in her fingertips, sense the formidable weight of the ship in her chest. The sensation seeped through her fingers and into her hands, placing more pressure on her chest—a stone slab slowly being lowered onto her wincing ribcage. The pressure became too intense and Melea ripped her hands free with a ragged inhale. Daylight and seawater poured into the ship.

Melea looked through the opening she had created as another wave splashed against the hull, some of the water dribbling through the gap. The thief eyed her with undisguised distrust.

She shrugged and gestured to the hole. "Not like you have any other options."

The look of suspicion remained, but the thief raised a hand for Melea to help him up.

"I'm going to lower you through. We'll swim around the other ship and come up on the dock. If we're quiet we can slip away while everyone is searching the ship."

The small hole was just wide enough for their thin bodies to squirm through.

"Can you swim?" she asked.

"More or less."

"What is it? More or less? If you're splashing around like a wounded seal they will catch us."

"I can swim," he said, pushing past her her and climbing into the opening.

He got stuck halfway and Melea carefully lowered the thief by his feet into the water. Pounding footsteps above signaled the arrival of the Nefarans. It was time to go. She hoisted herself into the opening and dropped soundlessly into the water.

Melea woke with a gasp, disoriented by the unfamiliar surroundings. A smell of earth permeated the enclosed space to give it the feel of a burrow. Roots and vegetation burst through cracks in the fallen stone but the straight lines and smooth surfaces of the huge stone slabs suggested human design.

The debris lay at odd angles all around to create a crude dome. Melea remembered where she was. A tomb for the past. A warning.

Melea looked at the sleeping thief, his chest rising and falling steadily. She had been taught how to treat basic wounds and had used this training to set his arm in a splint so that it might heal somewhat correctly. The sooner a wound can be treated the better the chance of it healing. *Wash it, set it, sew it, or amputate but do not leave it to fester.* Gruff wisdom given to her by an army medic. The thief had passed out immediately after the treatment and sleep claimed her soon after.

They had managed to make it off the docks before the city guard came marching into the harbor. The rest of the journey to Stone Park was fairly easy since the thief seemed to know every street in Azra. He led them back without error, despite his obvious exhaustion. Melea was confident that she could have done the same but would have been at a loss once they arrived in Stone Park.

The thief led her to a different tunnel than the opening the boy had emerged from, which immediately branched off in several directions. The buried core of the park was a maze of uneven passageways. Mapping the interior would have taken weeks in itself. Melea had no doubt that she would have gotten hopelessly lost on her own.

They were in a chamber approximately the size of Melea's room in the palace, which was the largest open space she had seen within the ruins. She used the matches to light a ring of small candles situated around the perimeter. Melea walked beside the candles, taking the chamber in fully, but nothing stood out except for an opening opposite of the one they had entered. She returned to the center and noticed that the thief's breathing had changed, he was now only pretending to sleep.

"Your name?" she asked. No response. Melea picked up a pebble and flicked it off the thief's forehead.

"Ow! Didn't your mother ever tell you to not throw stones?" He sat up, rubbing the red spot on his forehead. "I'm Gerboa, but I have a feeling you already know that. Who are you? I mean besides a rude bitch and my unlikely savior."

This was her man. Melea had captured her target, yet the realization came without a sense of satisfaction. The thief was taller than Melea and incredibly thin. He had a mop of brown hair that drooped over his eyebrows, a small button nose, and expressive brown eyes. Melea was having difficulty placing his age but he couldn't have been more than thirty years old.

"I heard rumors on the street, whispers about a man, a thief of all people, asking about the Sanctuary. I couldn't explain it but I knew he must be someone like me so I've been searching for him."

"Like you, huh," said Gerboa.

"Except," said Melea as she withdrew the knife. "I am not a traitor scheming to overthrow the Emperor."

Gerboa blanched. "Neither am I!"

Melea slowly walked closer, the knife loose in her grip. "So you say. How many of you are there?"

"Just me, I swear it!"

Gerboa moved to get up but Melea kicked out his legs. He grimaced at the impact to his arm.

"Stay," Melea commanded. "You will explain everything or you will die." She crouched, angling the knife closer.

"All right!" Gerboa eyes never left the knife. "I'll talk, I'll tell you everything. I was taken as a child, I was an orphan so nobody came looking for me. They brought me to the Sanctuary and tossed me in with the others to see if I had any ability. I didn't know that I was a vessel but the priests, they break you down, force you to become an animal. One night I conjured an illusion and escaped. Swam until I was picked up by a fishing boat. Been hiding in Stone Park since."

Melea sheathed the knife. "What do you intend to do?"

"I have unfinished business."

"And the Emperor?"

"He can do what he pleases, he's a God after all. I just need to return to the Sanctuary this one time."

Melea watched the thief, contemplating his disclosure. The image of the Sanctuary dominated her mind. Streams of thought that had been circulating since first hearing of the rumor regarding the Sanctuary coalesced. The memory of her time there was opening like a scab being torn off.

How to proceed? Her mission was to uncover threats to the Emperor's status as leader of the Shining Empire. Whatever Gerboa planned to do at the Sanctuary could be damaging to the Empire's aims but she doubted that it could oust Anathasius.

An unsettling pull squeezed her chest. Melea knew this sensation—she was going to die again. *Not here, not now*! Melea's nails dug into her palms as she fought to stay in control.

A woman's face appeared in front of her. Startling blue eyes framed by blonde curls. Lips red as blood. The pain in those bluest of eyes called out to her. The pull in Melea's chest sucked the air out of her lungs in one forceful jolt and then faded, along with the woman. Death lost its grip.

Gerboa watched her intently. She heard her words as if someone else was speaking.

"I, too, have unfinished business at the Sanctuary, I will join you."

Gerboa nodded enthusiastically. "Deal."

"How soon?"

"Things are in motion, a little time and coin are needed to make the rest happen."

"How much coin?"

Gerboa looked to his splinted arm. "More than I can steal until this is healed."

Melea doubted her current supply would be enough to finance the excursion. "I can get the rest. Now get up, you're coming with me."

"In the streets? I'll be recognized, my arm is a dead giveaway. Then it's the gallows for me."

"You are a master of illusion, give yourself a new appearance. I tracked you when you appeared to be a boy."

"I can't. Used too much energy this morning."

Melea lifted Gerboa to his feet. "Then you'll just have to take your chances."

The vision of the blonde woman troubled her mind as she led Gerboa toward the Black Lotus. *What was that*? Melea fumed—this made no sense. She did not make mistakes; weakness was unacceptable.

"What is your name, anyway?"

"Shamara."

A dread realization crept over Melea, the sense of crumbling, a slow erosion of the unseen aspects of herself. The first premonitory stones skipping down the mountain before the inevitable landslide.

Melea's intuition hinted that bringing Gerboa to the palace and washing her hands of the situation would not help. Her mind was rebelling against her will, each day holding it together became more difficult. She needed answers.

## Double Vision

The smell of fear was rank in the grand bedroom of Karaccus castle. Dozens of candles spread the scent to every corner of the room with their flickering light. The windows were shuttered and barred even though the night was quiet and the wind calm. An iron latch bolted the thick wooden door shut from the inside. Duke Elgarth Karaccus was nowhere to be seen.

Decorative carpets of deep reds, drapery of rich greens and vibrant gold smothered the room, conveying a sense of established wealth. A massive four-poster bed with a peaked canopy dominated the center of the bedroom. Large portraits of deceased dignitaries boxed in by ornate frames adorned the walls. Each dignitary stared into a random corner of the room; a taste for affluence apparent in their proud features. Wealth and authority grown comfortable over generations as nothing incubates frivolity like inherited wealth.

A coat of arms decorated the wall directly across from the bed: a roaring lion above crossed swords set in front of an imposing forest. Real swords were attached to the wall and one was absent from the fixture. The doors to the tall mahogany wardrobe in the corner silently opened and the sharp point of the missing blade reached out warily.

Duke Elgarth Karaccus of Asyrith emerged from the wardrobe, brandishing the weapon taken from his family crest, his frightened eyes sweeping the room. Several tense moments of scanning every corner confirmed he was alone. He lowered the blade with an irritated huff.

"I'm becoming a superstitious fool."

He strode to the door and leaned his head near the frame. "Lion?" A shout from the other side responded, "Roars!" This was the signal to inform the Duke that his guards remained vigilant at their post. Elgarth rapped on the door twice in quick succession to notify message received.

The Duke breathed a sigh of relief and sat on the edge of the bed, staring at the emblem of Asyrith. The sword remained loose in his grip with the blade across his lap. He looked to the painted forest behind the lion's fangs—his family was the strength that kept the danger of the forest at bay. It was they who controlled the trade flow through the Chuku Bartha Pass.

The Duke considered his relatively small contribution to the Karaccus legacy. A sneer rose unconsciously at the thought of his father's bold partnerships as he attempted to network Asyrith into the upper echelon of the Calanthian states, trying to attain the former glory Asyrith had once known.

He fidgeted with his wispy mustache as he considered the wisdom of the recent tariff increases he had placed on transport and protection. Talks of war between Calanthia and the Shining Empire had allowed him to raise the tariffs to an exorbitant amount. The Duke had also made thinly veiled threats to close the trade route altogether when complaints had been voiced.

Most men lacked the fortitude to make such audacious decrees but Elgarth was cleverer than most, he had foresight. Duke Karaccus had reached a secret agreement with Emperor Anathasius months ago. He knew they would not go to war with him over his tariff increases. Not while they remained allies.

He was to let the army of the Shining Empire through the Chuku Bartha Pass and into central Calanthia, with the understanding that he would be allowed to remain in control of Asyrith. His forces were too small to impede the Shining Lord's ambitions for long and Elgarth did not fancy turning the green hills of his homeland into a ruin of mud and blood as the front line of Calanthia's defense. His soldiers would appear to put up a resistance and then be quickly overwhelmed. He had been well paid for this future charade. Still, those rumors circulating about a certain nefarious individual in his domain were disconcerting.

He returned the sword to its place on the wall, a wry look replacing his worried expression. Elgarth went to the door and tapped it in a short, fast sequence. The proper response was given and the Duke set about extinguishing candles. He let the large candle nearest to the head of his bed burn, its glow illuminating the bell sitting on his bedside table. The Duke placed a thin dagger beside the bell as he disrobed. He knew that some of the minor nobles called him a coward behind his back but he saw himself as well prepared. Those disloyal subjects would be dealt with once he was afforded the authority attained by his carefully laid plans.

Elgarth caught his nude reflection in the shimmering sword blades. Still fit, still strong.

When word of an unknown agent conducting business with important individuals in Asyrith had reached him, a sinking feeling of dread had filled his stomach like a toxin and fueled Elgarth's paranoia. The Duke ordered a doubling of the sentries on the castle walls and for his personal guard to attend to him for the rest of the day.

His fear had grown until verging on overwhelming, so the Duke had retired to his bedchamber shortly after dinner, complaining of a headache. The anxiety only abated upon entering the small, dark space of the wardrobe. His normal sense of security was restored as logic overcame his unfounded worry. No suspicious activity had been discovered and he felt proud of his prudence. Elgarth smiled at his former distress, the mirror image of his face warped by the blade.

A shadow descended from the canopy of the bed behind the Duke, disturbing the reflection.

He felt the darkness enlarge behind him. Goosebumps pricked his naked flesh. He closed his eyes, trying to swallow the incapacitating fear. *Let this be a tired man's delusion*, he silently begged. Elgarth tensed his right fist to turn and strike.

A slight tickle against the throat forced Elgarth to crack open his eyes. He watched a crimson droplet of blood dribble onto a curved blade pressed to his neck. The cold iron of the sickle enhanced the color of his blood and the sight of it made dizziness swam behind his eyes.

"Don't faint on me, Duke," whispered a hoarse voice. "We wouldn't want any accidents to happen."

Elgarth's eyes snapped open, an involuntary shudder ran up his spine. The slight pressure applied by the blade froze his words.

"Ssh there is no need for you to speak."

The voice grated like sandpaper, invoking an instinctual urge to flee. Perspiration dotted the Duke's forehead and armpits, his feet stuck fast to the floor.

"Relax, you are not dead yet." The rough voice was terrifyingly calm. "You are a greedy man, Duke of Asyrith. It was unwise to betray the faith of the Emperor." Elgarth's mind spun as he fitted the pieces together—he was dead—or might as well be.

His captor tossed something on the mattress. Out of the corner of his eye, Elgarth spotted a letter with his seal of approval. The message was coded but that hardly mattered now. Elgarth closed his eyes and exhaled deeply in defeat, he had been caught.

"You know this letter, yes?" teased the voice.

Elgarth knew the letter, it was written in his hand and sent to the King of Calanthia who ruled out of Marikal. The message detailed how Elgarth had been strong-armed by the Shining Empire into standing down at the border. It also proposed that King Monchiet send reinforcements to hide along the edge of the Eternal Forest and trap the invading army between Calanthian forces after being allowed through the Pass. The letter had never reached the intended recipient.

"You were well paid were you not? Promised to remain in control of Asyrith?" The tone of the questions intimated no answer was necessary. "These gifts were not good enough for you."

Beads of sweat streamed down Elgarth's face. The speaker leaned in closer, his words crawling over Elgarth's skin like spiders. "The deal was made dear Duke, there is no going back."

A sharp crack on the back of the head sent Elgarth stumbling to his knees. The sickle was gone, replaced by a gag that was shoved into his mouth. His hands were forcefully tied behind his back. A kick between the shoulders slammed Elgarth to the floor and his feet were presently bound together. Elgarth squirmed onto his side, casting a fearful look at his assailant.

The slim man was dressed all in black, his eyes darker than the shadows. His mouth was filled with serrated fangs. The Duke was in the least fortuitous situation in all of Rua—at the mercy of Morokko Kachina.

The assassin crouched beside the whimpering man. "You will not disobey your orders again, I will make sure of it." The words were fangs that cut into Elgarth. "Don't worry, this will be fun."

Elgarth cowered before the Teeth in the Darkness.

"The problem is that you are looking in two directions, trying to play both sides to your advantage." The assassin withdrew a small packet. "Your choice has been made, you must be reminded of this fact."

From the packet, the assassin removed a needle, casually holding it aloft to inspect it in the light. Elgarth trembled at the sight of this small object. His eyes followed his captor's every movement; anything to look away from that face.

"You seek to be doubly rewarded, gaining at each turn, scheming to avoid loss. But loss is where much learning takes place." The assassin flicked the needle into the air and caught it between his thumb and forefinger. "You cannot help but look in opposite directions, it is in your nature. I have discovered a solution to your problem."

Without warning, he was grabbed under the armpits and heaved onto the mattress, pinned down by the assassin. The Duke's breath was heavy against the gag and he tried to look away from the assassin's predatory gaze. His captor waited patiently and Elgarth's eyes slowly returned to stare into their dark counterparts. The assassin's eyes held a fierce glow that at once terrified and entranced the Duke.

"You have too many eyes, dear Duke. There is only one path for you to follow, this is not in your nature but I will help you see it. You will assure King Monchiet that your troops will be able to stop any attack by the Shining Empire. You will stop all news of the Shining Empire's progress from reaching your former King's ears."

The needle reappeared in the assassin's hand, slowly descending toward Elgarth's left eyeball. Elgarth watched the needle descend, his mind already screaming. Searing pain lanced through Elgarth at the instant of contact, filling his skull with a fear beyond anything he'd ever felt before. He squirmed but several powerful blows to the gut forced him to cease. His eyelid was forced open and the needle descended again. The process was repeated twice more until pain was all the Elgarth truly knew existed in the world. His last sight was the demonic grin of his torturer.

## Thieving

The stag and hunters again. The sky exploding. Floating in an infinite blackness. Luck of the dead.

Melea rubbed her nose, trying to remove a burnt, acidic smell clogging her nostrils. Nothing new ever happened in this dream, vision, or whatever it was, but the outcome was always the same.

At first she had been able to brush the imagery off as an anomaly, but the nightly repetition of the identical scene was making her wonder if death was attempting a coup through her dreams. A cunning attack; coming at her sideways, sneaking under and around her defenses.

Melea scanned the interior of her room at the Black Lotus. Empty. She jumped out of bed. Gerboa was gone. The rope she'd used to tie him to the bed-frame was cut.

"Stupid! Stupid! Stupid!"

Her anger pushed aside the lingering after effects that accompanied the vivid dream. The strange images and empty nothingness were irritating but ultimately they were false. This failure was real.

Melea roughly scrubbed her face with both hands. The door swung open and she leapt up, knife in hand.

Gerboa raised his good hand. "Don't kill me. I brought breakfast."

Melea sat on the edge of the bed. Gerboa reached into a satchel slung across his shoulder then tossed her a sweet-roll.

Gerboa smirked. "Thought I'd run off, didn't you?"

"Something like that."

Gerboa bit into his own sweet-roll. "You can trust me. I don't have any other options. None good for my health anyway."

Melea knew he was right: she knew his identity, the location of his hideout, and he was injured. But she still didn't want to trust him.

"I have somewhere to be," she said. "You wait here."

"Gladly."

"Give me what you used to cut the rope and pick the lock."

Gerboa handed over a small, thin metal rod equipped with a sharp edge on one side and and a curved tip. Melea left the thief in her room, locking him in.

She entered the tavern of the Black Lotus and took a seat at an empty table. A few elderly men were seated on stools near the taps. Men who worked hard and didn't ask for much but complained about everything. One codger was regaling his cronies, ranting about his newest perceived slight.

"My grandson hasn't invited me over for dinner in a year, not since he got that uppity wife." A series of grumbles and mutterings were given in agreement. "I practically raised the boy, taught him everything I know, showed him how to use his hands, and this is the thanks I get?" More grumbling.

"Children these days have no respect," offered another man.

Melea sidled over to the far end of the counter, motioning to the bartender as the serving girl was nowhere to be seen. She ignored the complaints of the old men. Family issues were a foreign subject, only known of in theory, like arithmetic or sailing.

A serving girl appeared out of the back, carrying two steaming plates. The scent of bacon and eggs was intoxicating. She set them down in front of Melea and left without explanation.

Trinn emerged out of a back room and joined her. He immediately began eating.

So," he said between mouthfuls of scrambled egg. "You're still alive, that's a good start. Find your man?"

"The mission is progressing."

"In what way? Get the goods and get out."

Melea shook her head. "Not yet."

Trinn thought this over as he chewed a hunk of fatty bacon. "I'll report your findings to my superiors, but most spies don't decide when their mission is over."

Melea wanted to tell Trinn that her superior outranked his and that she was able to do as she damn well pleased but reluctantly decided to remain neutral. "I'm not most spies."

"I think we're done here." Trinn pushed his plate away even though Melea hadn't yet touched her meal. "I'll contact you."

He left without giving her a second look. *So long and good riddance*, she thought, waving a piece of bacon at the back of her supposed mentor. Melea suddenly felt a little closer to the disgruntled old men as she picked up the fork to eat the cooling meal alone.

She returned to her room to find Gerboa dozing on the floor.

"Show me how to steal," said Melea.

Melea found that she took to pickpocketing quite well. She couldn't match Gerboa's deftness, at least not yet, but thieving was easy enough once she knew what to look for. Her dexterous hands probed with precision, ruffling through unwary pockets in the crowd. Soon she had coins stashed all over her person and needed to return to Stone Park. Melea considered getting a basket and making a false bottom to stash her stolen copper, silver, and gold pieces while walking the streets, but decided the item would be too bulky to carry. Her methods were never finished until they were perfected—if she was going to be a thief, then she was going to be the best thief there was.

To her surprise, Melea discovered she was actually enjoying this. Each theft was a short mission and the targets came in many forms. There was the ubiquitous mercantile crowd in the busiest streets, sailors on shore leave, lone pedestrians, pompous officials, and countless other uncategorized citizens going about their daily lives. Why these people did not guard their money better was perplexing. The cold metal meant so much to them but most seemed unable to hang on to it for long. Melea took out a coin to inspect it, she had never considered money in depth before.

The edge of the coin was dinted on one side but the silver still shone. The sigil of the Shining Empire was imprinted on one side and Anathasius' face on the other. This little object made so much happen in the world. Such a small and unassuming item; a tool to be used for various designs. Not so different than her knife, really—hardness applied with the right force to influence people in the desired direction. An exchange based on choice and want. Coins just had a duller edge.

Perhaps that was why she was suddenly interested in money. She had a design in mind and enough coin would make it possible. Her knife might also get the job done, but things would be a lot messier that way.

Every day she felt greater urgency to return to the Sanctuary. Something about the place seemed solid in her mind. The feeling was strangely reassuring when so much of her current situation was unstable. She entered the passageway to the meeting place in Stone Park, only taking one wrong turn this time. Gerboa was waiting, his broken arm wrapped in plaster to hold the bones in place, an expensive procedure that most could not afford.

"Is this where my coins are going?" asked Melea.

"No, and so what if it was? I need both my arms. It's your fault this one is broken, anyway."

She dropped the money in front of Gerboa, the coins clinking in the soft dirt.

"That's all?"

His disappointed tone stung. She had thought this to be a good haul.

"How much more?" asked Melea.

"Two days at most," said Gerboa, confidently.

She returned to her room at the Black Lotus. A small slip of paper lay on the floor just inside the door. The note read: *Continue—Reports daily.*

Melea ripped the note into pieces. Time was running out. She needed to get to the Sanctuary before being ordered to return to the palace. She left the room, walking swiftly down an arbitrary street, her mind focused on how to get the necessary coin that night.

A little girl skipped across Melea's path, forcing an abrupt stop. The girl hummed a tune to herself, blonde locks bobbing with every small skip of her tiny feet. A man scooped the girl up by the waist, lifting her into the air as she squealed in delight.

"Father!"

The man smiled and kissed the girl's forehead before placing her back on the ground. The child looked past Melea to a woman selling herbs.

"Mother. I'm going with father to get a treat."

"Bye honey." The mother smiled. The girl started off with her father, hand in hand. She suddenly released her grip and raced back to her mother as fast as her little legs could take her.

"Natalya, where are you going?" called the father.

"One more hug." The mother embraced her daughter, pulling her in close. "And a kiss."

Natalya giggled and then skipped back to her father, delicate hand curling around two of his big fingers.

The familial scene annoyed Melea. Her mouth went dry, yet tasted gritty and bitter. She stalked off in the opposite direction of the happy father and daughter, feeling a dark cloud following closer than her shadow. She needed to come up with a plan, and fast.

The walk eventually eased some of the tension out of her body but an unpleasant taste remained. Melea found herself in front of a tavern called the Lightning Bolt. At least a drink would remove the sour taste in her mouth.

An idea struck: she could find a wealthy patron inside the tavern, wait for him to get drunk, then ambush him on the street. An easy target.

The Lightning Bolt proved to be a popular place and Melea was forced to take a small table in a dingy corner. The interior of this tavern was better lit than the Hog's Ear and was relatively smokeless, compared to the wharf tavern. Servers showed a great deal of cleavage, whether they had some to show or not, as they bustled around the many tables. The server nearest to Melea had perfected the easy laugh that makes drunk customers feel special without wasting any undue amount of time on them.

The nearest serving girl ignored Melea's attempt to request a drink in order to make a strategic lean-in to show her ample bust to a table of men while refilling their mugs. Loud cat calls and drunken boasts filtered through the room. As Melea scanned the interior for potential targets, a server swooped in to deliver a glass of sparkling wine the color of sunlight passing through amber.

"I didn't order this."

"It's from the two gentlemen at the bar. They ordered drinks for every unattended woman in the tavern."

The server gave Melea a wink and left. Melea scanned the crowd to find her would-be wooers. Her search ended quickly as it was immediately obvious which men were casting drinks out into tavern like fishing lures.

They were both tall and dark and lean with crow black hair. One had his hair tied in a ponytail and wore a short sword on each hip. The other wore a wide, flat brimmed hat and a longsword across his back. They were young and appeared almost identical to Melea. The men were laughing and carrying on with those around them, each with a woman under one arm and drinks in both hands. They were unknown to her, but the wine tasted sweet with a hint of nut, so at least the two men had decent taste. Melea sipped the drink and watched the crowd.

The glass was empty before she knew it, so Melea looked to see if there was an opening at the bar to order another. No vacancy appeared but she did spot a bulging coin purse practically spilling out of the pocket of a paunchy man. The animated drunk was rambling on, his companion only half listening, appearing more intent on avoiding being sprayed by the drunkard's saliva. The hefty lout was an easy target and she could likely pluck the coin purse right now. Melea made her way toward the fat man, trying to be as casual as possible.

Slowly, carefully, she angled closer. After a few moments of waiting, the man turned his head in the opposite direction and Melea darted in.

Nearby, the young man in the hat was telling a story to the women in front of him, exaggerating the exploits with hand gestures. The man with the pony tail was gone. The women laughed at the reenactment, but the energetic portrayal caused the man with the hat to spill an entire drink directly on Melea's head at the exact moment she made her move for the purse. Beer sloshed into Melea's face and onto the fat man's hairy hand.

"Bloody thing," he said, adjusting his coin purse to fit snugly in his pocket.

Melea ripped a mug from the hand of a man beside her and hurled it at the young man in the hat. He was already turning to follow the direction of the missing beer from his empty mug so he managed to catch a glimpse of the object hurtling toward him. He ducked and the mug sailed past the brim of his hat, directly into the forehead of another tavern patron. The mug splintered into an explosion of foam and shards.

A startled man cried out in pain and anger as he tried to wipe the blood and beer from his eyes. "Who did this?!" He pointed an accusing finger at the man in the hat. "You!"

The man in the hat gestured at Melea. "Whoa! It wasn't me, it was her."

"Been buying drinks for every woman in the bar all night, then blame a girl. I'm going to tear you apart, ya gosser."

"Hey, not for every woman in the bar, that's just a stupid waste of money. I only bought drinks for the *unattended* women, see the difference?"

Several others congregated behind the man hit by the mug. He spat and advanced. "You're a dead man."

The man in the hat still appeared calm despite being outnumbered. "Well now, you seem overly confident. Besides, that nick on your nose adds character, and you could use some by the looks of it."

The man with the pony tail arrived in hurry. "Taisto, I think it's time for us to go."

"What did you do now, Dacre?"

Dacre had a guilty but proud look that is seen far too often on young men. "May have arranged a meeting with someone I'm not supposed to. Anyways, I've been spotted so we have to go." For the first time since arriving he noticed the escalating distress. "What's going on here?"

Taisto jabbed a thumb at Melea. "Ask her."

Dacre looked at Melea. "You're not a dangerous man's daughter are you?"

Melea's attempted explanation was crushed into silence as the group of men rushed Taisto and Dacre. Fists flew around her head like an angry swarm. Taisto landed a straight jab and followed the momentum forward. Dacre shoved his way into the narrow gap between the press of men and leapt onto a table, sending drinks splattering in a spray. Swords appeared in his hands. Melea grabbed a mug and smashed it over the head of the closest thug. Taisto was now grappling with two men. Panic started to rise in the tavern as the patrons struggled to avoid catching a stray blow.

Taisto ducked a chair being swung at him, but one of his adversaries was not as quick. The chair shattered against the man's back, dropping him to the floor.

Melea crossed her arms and watched— they started it, he shouldn't have dumped a drink on her head. Two drunk womanizers were none of her concern.

More men moved towards Taisto, and it was clear he would soon be overwhelmed. "Brother!" he shouted.

Dacre was off the table and scrambling around the room but it was obvious that he would not be able to reach his brother in time. Melea sighed, and picked two broken chair legs off the floor. She hefted one before hurling it into the head of the man wrestling with Taisto. The man thumped to the floor, as did his companion a moment later. Taisto gave Melea a quick salute and whooped with joy as he sprinted toward the staircase. Dacre was on his brother's heels as they bolted up the stairs. From the second floor came a shattering of glass and a gust of fresh air.

The two men Melea had struck with the chair legs were back on their feet and moving toward her. The main entryway was blocked by a crowd shoving one another to get outside. Melea evaluated her opponents—one was limping and the other's eye was swelling shut—it wouldn't take much to drop them for good. She glanced back at the crowded doorway, and the thought of cutting her way out crossed her mind.

The men were nearly on top of her. They would not know what hit them if she attacked. Except that they might, because of the scene she'd made at the dock, and word would definitely spread about her actions. Melea squirmed. She was not supposed to be a merchant of death on this mission. Shamara the thief would flee so Melea smothered her instincts and ran.

She hopped over the bar countertop and pushed through a swinging door, heading for the back of the building. She sped past an older man, who must have been the owner, as a torrent of obscenities ripped out of his beet red face. She found the back door and kicked it open.

A breeze pushed humid air into her face as she rounded the corner of the building, sprinting into a back alley to avoid the crowd near the entrance. The street was empty and the tavern muffled the sound of shouting so that it barely reached her. She soon found why the alley was deserted; it ended in a high brick wall.

Men came rushing out of the back entry like a pack of wild dogs. They tore towards Melea, malice in their eyes. *Good*, thought Melea, she was never one for fleeing anyway. She reached for the knife, but a concussive thud in her chest halted the motion. *Not now!*

Her vision narrowed, obscured by a smoky mist, limbs going rigid and unwieldy. Melea collapsed to the ground. She clenched her jaw, teeth shut tight as a lowered drawbridge, but the last of her air escaped anyway. Pounding footsteps vibrated through the ground, barely registering in her numbing mind. *Could a body be killed if it was already dead?*

In her fading vision, Melea saw something sail overhead to hit the ground in front of the approaching men, followed by a whiff of thick smoke. The lights went out. Melea tumbled into darkness.

No voice. No footsteps. Only a brief fluttering of invisible wings.

"Hey, syla."

An object materialized in Melea's vision, slowly coming into focus, limitless possibilities of shape shifting into distinct lines. A face framed in starlight. A smile. Melea blinked.

"Thought we lost you for a moment there," said Taisto.

They were on top of the brick wall at the end of the alley, and a thin black rope was bundled at Taisto's feet. Dacre looked over the shoulder of his crouching brother. Melea felt uncomfortably exposed laying on her back. She shoved the ruffian and jumped to her feet.

*An enemy is someone who is not useful to you. The role may be reversed depending on the situation,* These were the words of her tutor Mandrikos. These two might not necessarily be enemies, the verdict was dependent on what they wanted from her.

Taisto raised his hands, palms up. "Plucked you off the ground so those mongrels couldn't get at you. Didn't think someone your size would be so heavy."

Dacre cuffed Taisto. "Never mention a woman's weight."

The men below had retreated to the rear entryway of the Lightning Bolt where they were currently being berated by the owner. Someone would have to pay for the damage and it was not going to be Melea or the brothers.

"Send your women to the Outskirts if they want some real men!" Dacre bellowed while grabbing his crotch. He disappeared over the other side of the wall.

Taisto grabbed Melea by the hip without warning, dipped her back, and forcefully kissed her lips. Melea was too stunned to stop him. The kiss tasted of beer and sweat and was over before she knew what was happening. Taisto removed his hat in a bow.

"Until next time." He too disappeared into the darkness.

Melea stood on the wall in shock for a moment. The bastard had kissed her and gotten away with it. Anger simmered across Melea's skin—a cold blue flame that made her hair stand on end. Taisto had taken something from her and she couldn't get it back. Control had been stripped away for an instant and the feeling was numbing. But the warmth of his hands and touch of his lips endured.

The kiss was unwanted and he had forced it on her, caught her off guard, and the unpreparedness made her feel weak. Shame at her weakness fueled the cold flames. But there was something else within the anger, crackling along the surface of it. Something nourishing, invigorating in way she had never felt before. Part of her found the kiss thrilling. It was unexpected and passionate and stirred her more than she wanted to admit.

Melea shook her head at the boldness of the young men. Imperial law stated that members of the wandering Bands who inhabited the Outskirts were to be killed on sight if captured within the borders of the Shining Empire. They raided caravans, ambushed fringe army barracks, and were a general nuisance to the civilized world. They even had an insult named after them, one used by people when given a raw deal, or when conducting business with a particularly dubious individual: oustid. The men paying reparations to the owner of the tavern could legitimately claim to have been oustid in this instance.

The two rogues had probably robbed a carriage on route to Strakos and were blowing the Azran merchant's loot on women and drinks in the city. Fingers were now being pointed at Melea's position on the wall, so she took her leave, clambering across rooftops until she was a safe distance away to climb down to the street.

Melea's musings about the brothers from the Outskirts were interrupted as a familiar, paunchy figure lumbered into view. The owner of a poorly guarded coin purse waddled alone down the street in front of Melea and appeared to be even drunker than before. He sang something unintelligible as he staggered along.

She quickened her pace to close the gap. Sure enough, the purse was clearly visible as it bobbed half-out of the man's pocket. The street was mostly empty; she would not be denied this time.

The man pulled a ring of keys from another pocket and went to a house with a large oak door. He fumbled with the keys, struggling to find the right one for the lock. Melea decided to abandon stealth and reach for the purse on the run. She sprinted the remaining distance, lightly plucking the coin purse from the man's pocket. Her arm jarred as the purse would not move any further, it was connected to a chain attached to the man's creaking belt. He looked down in confusion.

"Huh?"

Melea yanked on the purse but it would not budge. The man finally figured out what was going on.

"Oh."

Out flashed Melea's knife to slice the edge of the purse connected to the chain while the man's alcohol-sedated brain prevented him from reacting. The soft leather sliced easily under the well honed edge. Melea caught the purse, the weight of the coins inside felt like victory.

As she turned to escape, a small wooden sword flashed out of nowhere and smacked against Melea's wrist with a solid thwack. She dropped the purse. A young boy brandished a play sword at her.

"To steal is no fair deal." The boy scooped up the coin purse and bolted into the night.

"Ha," barked the drunk. "There it is," he said as he produced the correct key to unlock the door.

Melea raced after the fleeing boy. He was quick and scurried through alleyways like a feral cat.

"Hand it over, kid," called Melea.

"Heroes don't shake hands with villainous demands," huffed the boy.

He slipped through a hole in a crumbling section of a wall that was too small for Melea. She picked up a chunk of the stone wall, focusing her mind on the feel of it in her hand. The stone shifted on her palm, dissolving downward as if being eroded. Her hand became considerably heavier and her fingers could not close fully to make a fist.

She delivered a wide arcing punch to the wall adjacent to the hole. The stones crumbled, widening the hole enough for her to fit. Red scratches marked her knuckles, and the sleeve of her blouse ripped as she squeezed through the opening.

Melea spat out a phlegmy ball of mud. Her nose crinkled. She hated the sensation of the stone in her blood. Feeling came back to her hand in the form of intermittent tingles as she ran. A patter of small footsteps told Melea which direction the boy had gone.

The sound of footfalls led her through winding streets that were steadily becoming more labyrinthine. This area was a confusing jumble of engineering, as new and old construction intersected at seemingly random points. Melea stopped. She could no longer hear footsteps.

"Forever a boy, forever able to annoy with joy." The boy's voice echoed in the street.

Melea charged in the direction of the voice, seeing a shadow flit around a corner. "Taking what you don't need is greed," called out the boy in sing-song.

She was done with this chase and his irritating antics. She followed him into a circular courtyard occupied by a broken fountain in the center. He was trapped. Only a few lamps lit the entire courtyard. Most of the space was covered in shadows. Melea slowed, listening for the boy's movement.

"Close is closer than most but is no reason to toast." The mocking words moved around the circle.

"Enough games."

"Playing is fun, the best thing to do under the sun, but all you do is run, run, run."

Melea angled around the fountain, the voice originating from somewhere behind it. She saw an object shift in the shadows and pounced. The boy scrambled out of reach, a hairsbreadth from her grasping fingers, darting around the fountain. He looked over the stagnant water at her.

"Heroes don't fake, they don't rob or take, they give and help and make."

"I get it, you like rhyming. Now give me the coins."

The fountain was too large for Melea to jump so she considered which way to direct the boy. His dark eyes glittered across the water. They made Melea notice the winking starlight above. The night was quiet between the two as they continued their stare-down.

"Choice is the voice of the young, comes from the tongue, a weapon to be swung."

"You stole from me. Not very heroic behavior," she scolded.

The boy took off towards one of the larger buildings. He bounded up a small stairway with Melea right on his tail. He stopped at the top of the landing before a set of double doors, dropping into a crouch with his sword out in front.

"This is no toy, prepare to be stung by the blade of the Forever Boy!" He hacked at Melea with dramatic flourishes that she easily dodged. Melea grabbed an overemphasized lunge and held on tight.

"This is a toy, and this game is over."

The boy pulled on the handle with both hands, unable tear it from Melea's grip. His little face squirmed in frustration. Melea yanked the sword away and sent it clattering down the steps.

"Well, that was fun," she said dryly.

The boy waved his hands in front of his face and tossed out a few strikes in an attempt to intimidate Melea with his prowess.

"Kids can do more, adults are such a bore." He set his jaw, ready to do battle if Melea so much as moved.

She sighed. "I don't want to hurt you, but I need those coins."

"Need, need, need. Greed, greed, greed." He kicked out at Melea.

"Alright, Mr. Hero, why did you take the coin purse?"

He glanced at the doors. "Need, need, need. Feed, feed, feed."

Melea saw faded letters carved into wood above the doors of the rundown building. A single word: Orphanage. A piece of Melea's chest fell away and settled heavily in her stomach.

"You need it this badly?"

The boy shook his head. "The forgotten ones that nobody misses, never known their mother's kisses."

She experienced a sensation of floating, not in water but in a thicker, more buoyant substance. Her vision blurred and dizziness made her temple throb. She was going to collapse for the second time in under an hour. The sensation disappeared as quickly as it occurred, instantly replaced by blazing sunlight.

Melea raised a hand to her face, the long nails were cracked at the ends and thick with dirt. Intense sunlight blasted her tanned body. She held a jagged shard of mirrored glass in one hand that glinted fiercely in the midday light. Melea felt trapped within her own body as she watched herself tilt the mirror into the sunlight and reflect it on the hot stones at her bare feet. Melea noticed that she was naked but oddly enough, she didn't seem to mind.

The heat from the sunlight was focused by the mirror and she used it to incinerate the red ants swarming across the stones. One by one she roasted the ants with detached awareness. There was a sound of water crashing over rocks nearby but her focus was intently directed at destroying the ants. Melea killed a good number of them before noticing the design carved into the stone beneath their twitching deaths.

A tree stump appeared to be growing out of the stone. Melea blinked and the stump looked as though it had sunk into the stone. Whatever the case, the smooth surface of the stump was deep inside the rock, its shape a series of dark grooves. Inside the carved circumference of the stump was a gnarled tree with bare branches and twisting roots. The trunk, branches, and roots of the tree were hollow—connected to the circuitous tree rings within the rougher bark perimeter. Melea traced the lines of the design, her mind drifting in the maze of connected channels.

The symbol flashed dull red, startling Melea. It flashed again, brighter. Again. In the same rhythm as her heartbeat. She became aware of someone watching her.

An elderly man casually gazed at Melea, quietly observing her. His eyes were almost colorless, just a touch of indigo. He stroked a long white beard and waited until he had her full attention. Melea knew this man but could not recall from when or where. He walked over, his gait steady and sure for a man of such a pronounced age. Melea looked up expectantly at the aged face; skin smooth and taut, too old for wrinkles.

"Are you finished?" His voice was like an ancient elm creaking in gale winds. He spoke with a strange accent that emphasized syllables in a jarring manner. Melea felt herself nod, tangled hair waving in her face.

"Tell me: what have you done." The words were a command.

"I killed some ants." Her voice was high pitched, that of a child.

Stern eyes drilled into her, she could feel them searching, scouring her entirety.

"Why?"

The question challenged Melea's childish mind, she did not have an answer and was about to panic because of it. "Because."

*Melea held up the shard of mirror as if it was an explanation in itself. The silence and the man's austere, unblinking eyes threatened to overwhelm her. She felt like she was in trouble but had no idea why.*

*"Did you know what would happen?"*

*She nodded again. The old man stroked his beard, his eyes thankfully leaving hers as he looked to things unknown.*

*"Why their sacrifice?" The question was heavy, it slammed into Melea as though it could force out an answer.*

*"Because I could."*

*"Hmm and why is that?"*

*"Because I'm stronger than them." This seemed like a good answer to Melea, something the man would be unable to refute.*

*"Yes. I am stronger still, can I do the same to you?"*

*Melea's heart jumped, she suddenly felt vulnerable and weak. Salty tears dribbled down her chubby cheeks. The man crouched down before her, he extended a gnarled hand to pick the twigs out of her hair but then pulled back before doing so.*

*"Become stronger, Melea."*

*Melea wiped away her tears. "I will, Grandfather."*

The out of body experience dissipated in an instant and Melea was once again standing in front of the orphan thief. He gave her a quizzical look. Melea raised a hand experimentally to see if it would respond. A rush of relief washed through her as she realized full control was restored.

The boy watched her closely, his eyes squinting in the starlight. Melea watched him as well but thoughts of obtaining the stolen coins were not on her mind, she was just trying to keep from falling down. The boy unexpectedly lobbed the coin purse over.

"Remember," he said as he opened the door and slipped inside the orphanage.

The door slammed, leaving Melea alone on the stoop. The sliding and latching of metal sounded as several locks clicked into place. Melea blankly looked at the coin purse and walked out of the courtyard in a daze.

## Tomb of Kings

Ritika gazed upon the Tomb of Kings and prayed. Beside her stood Draggar Vol, Remori General, and advisor. Her tall, lean frame and black skin contrasted with his paleness, broad shoulders and blonde beard.

"Thank you for accompanying me," said Ritika.

"My Queen, he was your father, but he was also my dearest friend."

"What would he say if he were here?"

Draggar shook his head. "I don't dare speak for a king."

Ritika observed the resting place of her father's bones. A grassy mound curved out of the earth like the shell of an enormous turtle, a shaded tunnel where the head should have been. Chalk white stones the size of carriage wheels ringed the base of the mound, a circle of protection, a sign of veneration. Smoothed blocks of stone the height of a man stood upright in a perfectly straight line from the top of the opening across the curvature of the hill to create a carefully ordered row of sentinels.

Ritika's attention was drawn to the the High Priestess, who placed a string of laurel leaves across the stone lintel which was supported on either side by two upright pillars. A squat white candle was placed on the ground between the stones, the single light too weak to illuminate the details of the earthly confines further down the passageway.

The High Priestess raised her bare arms to the blaring sun, which was directly in line with the row of white stones atop the mound. The many colored beads in her hair jangled as she angled her face to catch the sun. With closed eyes she squeezed blood red berries in her palms, the juice running down her forearms. She smeared the berries on the pillars around the opening, signifying the sacred burial mound was ready to be entered by the living.

Ritika attentively watched the performance of the Rite of Entry. She was envious of the information known only to the High Priestess, of the mysteries of death and rebirth passed down in an unbroken chain of matrilineal lineage.

Hekäli Mu'godis, High Priestess of Rhezaria, was an intermediary between worlds, an arbiter on religious matters and keeper of inviolate knowledge. She was short and old. Sagging skin hung from sharp cheekbones and fuzzy whiskers sprouted from her chin, but her eyes retained a powerful vivacity. Ritika felt comforted by Hekäli's presence—the High Priestess was a woman to be respected, fearless as she moved with the assured grace of one with a foot in the afterlife.

The High Priestess wore a loose fitting black gown cinched around the waist and chest by a spiral pattern belt of animal bones. Ritika had seen this outfit of death once before, at her father's funeral.

Ritika wore a gown of mourning as a sign of respect for her father. The color purple was lightest around her ankles, transitioning through shades until a band of black circled her throat.

Hekäli motioned Ritika forward, the jaws of a small skull clacking together as the aged woman shook her arm, the tiny predatory fangs snapping in time with Ritika's steps.

"Do you speak on behalf of the people?" Hekäli's brown eyes were fiercely unblinking.

"I do."

"Do you honor your God and forefathers?"

"I do."

Hekäli opened a gnarled hand to blow a fine dust into Ritika's face. The dust sparkled in the sunlight and carried a musty aroma. Ritika's eyes widened immediately, the light becoming invasive, burrowing into her skull.

"Go then. Enter the cycle without interruption." The High Priestess stepped aside to allow Rhezaria's Queen to enter the tomb of her ancestors.

Ritika's vision instantly adapted to the gloom of the passageway, narrowing in the softer light of the candle, which she took with her. Specially crafted stones lined the walls, floor, and ceiling of the passageway but the clever engineering could not deny the sense of crushing earth all around. The tunnel narrowed, forcing Ritika to crouch as she shuffled deeper into the mound.

The passageway abruptly ended, opening into a curved chamber large enough that the candlelight could only brighten a circle around Ritika. A heavy stillness coated the air, the scent of time contained.

Ritika walked to the center of the chamber, stopping at a black stone altar. The bones of her father lay across the stone. She was unable to recognize what remained as the man she had known. They could have belonged to anyone. The regal clothing was the only feature to distinguish the assemblage of bones as belonging to someone significant.

"Father," her voice sounded out of place in the tomb, that of an intruder. She bowed her head. "I ask for guidance. Rhezaria has finally been stabilized following your death. Do I bring us on a new course or stand firm?"

Ritika stared at the bones poking out of the rich fabric; they seemed false. This could not be the man who had held her as a child. Where was the look of love in his bright eyes? The strength that kept enemies at bay?

Had Ritika completed her training as a disciple of Tehlo maybe she could have saved her father from an early demise. If only she was more capable—stronger, wiser, better—than she was.

Ritika stared up into the impenetrable blackness, unable to look at the remains of her father any longer without coming to tears. A rustling stirred in her mind, a roughness of stones grating or claws scratching against the outside of a door. *War*. The sound intensified, clear as a violent gust of wind in the empty chamber. *Blood and death*.

The noise stopped as swiftly as it appeared and Ritika looked down once more at her father's skeletal grin.

Ritika exited the chamber, moving quickly through the passageway to emerge into the light. Hekäli stared at her with a penetrating gaze. Draggar stood a little ways back, watching Ritika with a questioning expression.

Hekäli began chanting, a high keening wail, as her servants rolled a circular stone to barricade the entryway.

"He is not as I remember him," said Ritika.

Dragger sniffed, his beard wagging back and forth. "Aye, none are to mortal eyes once they've gone to Mar'Edo Kon's Hall."

"The dead only speak of death."

"Something the living do their best to ignore," said a raspy voice from behind.

Ritika hadn't noticed that the wailing had stopped. She turned to see the High Priestess standing at her elbow.

"No man knows when their time is up, they must do what they can while they may," said Draggar.

Hekäli fixed him with a mischievous look. "Yes, no man."

Draggar cocked his head, opened his mouth to respond and then thought better of it. He looked to Ritika. "What now, my Queen?"

*His Queen*, thought Ritika, *the King's daughter*. Decision maker and mouthpiece of Mar'Edo Kon, who sat on the Hezraaka throne. She had the answers that would direct the fate of her people. Ritika wished she knew what those answers were.

## The Sanctuary

Melea raced along the side streets. Everyone around trucked with mud sucking slowness while she floated past, her movement effortless, like the agile steps of a long-legged waterstrider. Everyone except Gerboa. He kept pace with her step for step on the opposite side of the street. The plaster cast had been removed that morning and the thief had insisted on joining Melea during her circuit.

His arm was still too weak to be of much use, but Gerboa managed well enough. They pinched much more as a duo than Melea ever did alone; the extra profit almost worth having a partner. Gerboa caught her eye and motioned to stop. Melea sunk back into a staircase and temporarily lost sight of Gerboa as he slipped into his own hiding spot. She listened intently for what must be coming. Soon enough came ragged breathing and mumbled curses.

"Damnbloedeththieves." The swear came out in one long wheeze.

Melea peeked out to see a heavyset man charging down the street. He looked like he might pass out at any moment: arms swinging, back drenched in sweat, darkening his shirt into a distinctly different color. The same man Melea had nabbed a plump coin purse from the night she met the Forever Boy. The man was once again under the numbing influence of alcohol, but the sun was still up, so he was not yet blind drunk.

"Wring...their little...necks."

He let out a belch that became a dry heave of disgusting intensity. He stopped momentarily until the episode was over, hacked out something vile, then raised his plodding feet again, his drunken determination not yet spent. Those nearby wanted nothing to do with the sweaty mess of a man, ignoring his rambling questions about two thieves—questions that sounded more like accusations. Melea melded back into the crowd, walking in the opposite direction the man had gone. Gerboa's thin frame sidled up beside her and they walked a few blocks before speaking.

"What a lard ass," Gerboa commented.

Melea was surprised at how comfortable they had become around one another. They had met daily for a week now and their interactions expanded from terse statements about Melea's progress to casual conversations about more personal topics. Gerboa in particular had opened up, often talking about his sister who lived on the streets with him. For all that he talked about her, Melea had never seen this sister.

"If he was a pig we could probably sell him for more than what we took off him today," said Gerboa.

"A keg with legs, Azra's finest fermented pork."

Gerboa laughed and Melea snatched a quick look as he looked away. He was slightly taller than her so she had to peer up out of the corner of her eye.

Laughter made her uncomfortable; she had difficulty deciphering if it was directed at her or what she said. Making jokes was a rare occurrence in her life, as was interacting with others for an extended period. Melea had no friends. The thought struck her like a bolt of lighting. *Was Gerboa her friend?*

Melea liked him well enough, he was kind and had a sharp sense of humor, and she had actually enjoyed most of their time together. *There is a reason why you are with him*, Melea reminded herself. They were not neighbors or family—she was sent to find him, to uncover his secrets. Melea could not lose sight of her objective. Gerboa was planning something treasonous, something that threatened to undermine the Shining Empire, thereby becoming a direct assault on Emperor Anathasius. The thief was also the one who would take her to the Sanctuary.

She had serious doubts that one thief, no matter how nefarious his schemes, could injure the Empire.

"How much more do we need?" Her most asked question this past week.

Gerboa scrutinized her appearance and shook his head. "Why am I clean and your clothes are filthy? We went to all of the same places." He dropped his voice to a whisper even, though the busy crowd never paid attention to anyone's business but their own.

"We leave tonight."

*Tonight*! She was supposed to meet Trinn for a report tonight in the tavern of the Black Lotus but Gerboa would want to leave before that could happen. She would need an excuse to slink away and notify Anathasius. Certain measures had to be set in motion while she still had control of the situation. Melea reasoned she could handle Gerboa herself, but the full scope of his plan was still a mystery and she was not one to leave things to chance. Too much within the world of the living was orchestrated by the callous hand of luck. Only the dead were excused and Melea's cursed existence caused her to be caught in between. She wanted access to the Sanctuary but the thief's plan, whatever it was, could not be allowed to succeed.

"What about supplies?"

"All taken care of," said Gerboa. "We go to Stone Park after lunch, wait for nightfall, and then we're off."

Melea quickly analyzed potential options for relaying a message to the Emperor. Now, it had to be now.

"I just need to stop at my room and pick up a few things. I'll meet you there."

"I'll join you," said Gerboa, who appeared to be in a particularly chipper mood. "Everything is taken care of. We could stay at your room instead, doesn't really matter."

"No"

"Why not? It's much closer."

"I don't have any food," Melea cautioned.

"No problem. We'll pick something up along the way."

Unable to draw up any other excuses, Melea started in the general direction of the Black Lotus. Her blood boiled at not being able to hammer a fist into Gerboa's gut and demand that he wait for her at Stone Park. Using words to politely dance around what she wanted was infuriating. One more night and she would be within the walls of the Sanctuary, then maybe the strangeness in her life would end.

Just a little more pretending to be a thief and then she could go back to what she knew, back to the palace and back to carrying out missions without needing to rely on anyone but herself. She could leave the cluttered streets where all these people inexplicably chose to live out their lives.

Gerboa darted to the left and flipped a few coins to a vendor. He returned with two pitas, twin tornados of steam escaping from the small openings at the top.

"Here you go. I got you the sweet sauce because I know you don't like it too spicy."

Melea took a bite of the warm bread, the crunch of fried vegetables and tender chicken blending beautifully with the spices and sweet onion sauce. Pitas were her favorite discovery. They were relatively inexpensive, quick to make, filling, delicious, and easy to eat on the go. All in all an exceedingly efficient meal.

Gerboa was the only person in the Empire who knew of her preference of sweet over spicy, the only one who knew she liked pitas for that matter. The realization troubled her, making Melea feel more alone than she had in a long time. Which was strange since the thief was walking right beside her eating his own pita, spicy whiffs wafting her way with every bite he took. The smell bothered her for reasons she could not understand. She crunched another bite but barely noticed the flavors.

"So you've organized everything and yet I don't have the faintest idea what the plan is. About time you fill me in, don't you think?"

Gerboa took a large bite. "Shamara," he gulped the food down. "Have you killed before?"

"Yes." The answer came to her lips automatically.

Gerboa nodded, expecting this response. "You'll have to kill again if we are going to pull this off. The priests at the Sanctuary are evil and they must not be allowed to continue. You know what they do to the children there, and tonight we're going to change all of that."

"How? Kill all of the priests? We'll never get out alive."

Gerboa stopped eating and stared straight ahead. "We'll get out and we won't be alone. We're going to release everyone held within the Sanctuary and kill whoever gets in our way."

Melea dissected this new information. The thief did indeed have big plans, but now she knew for certain that Anathasius was not part of them. She should take Gerboa down and end this mission. Melea knew this is what her training demanded; what Anathasius would want. But she wanted something else.

The dreams that left her feeling exhausted upon waking, the memory of Grandfather, the woman in the vision—it all had to stop. She needed to put an end to the sensation of inner instability and the implication of weakness. The Sanctuary was central to her dilemma, Melea felt this to be true even though she could not yet prove it.

They turned a corner, the Sanctuary rose up, swallowing them in its shadow. Melea blinked, and the Black Lotus came into view.

She put her head down until they were in her room. The small space felt cramped with two bodies, the angles disjointed, like too many items cluttering the inside of a pocket.

"We'll need a ship," she said.

"Have one."

"We'll need swords."

"I hired some mercenaries, they'll be joining us at the docks."

"So you take everyone and put them on your ship and then what? You won't get far. The Empire will send a fleet after you."

"Thought of that," said Gerboa. "Where would you go if you had a ship full of escapees?"

Melea considered the options, recalling a map of Rua in her mind. She made herself memorize such a map prior to her first attempted escape from the palace years ago. The Sanctuary sat on an island to the south of the Shining Empire west of Calanthia and north of Rhezaria. Calanthia would soon be swarming with troops from the Empire, Rhezaria was likely to behead them, Strakos might return the escapees to the Empire or turn them into slaves to row on their galleys, Nefara and Fyn were too distant, and the isolated Six Isle Republic was practically out of reach. That left the North, which had just been annexed by the Shining Empire and Melea doubted that Gerboa was oblivious to the turmoil there. Only one inhabited area remained.

"The Outskirts," she said.

Gerboa nodded, looking quite proud of himself. "Yep, we make the short trip to Kannark then sneak north past Azra into the Outskirts."

The plan was dangerous and foolhardy, but Melea could not criticize Gerboa's choice of destination. The Outskirts hated the Shining Empire and would surely accept any who chose to leave their longstanding enemy. Gerboa might even be seen as a hero by the marauders within the Outskirts. If successful, the damage to the Empire's reputation would be severe as word of the escape leaked. Melea thought back to the brothers from the Outskirts she had encountered. Such brash individuals would shout the tale to all corners of Rua.

"What about supplies? You know—food, water—that sort of thing."

"Being loaded onto the ship right now, should be enough to reach the Outskirts."

"The harbormaster at Kannark will turn you in," Melea warned.

"I've heard from a reliable source that the man has a hefty gambling debt so I'm guessing a large donation will see us on our way." Gerboa smiled, pushing hair out of his face. "A bribe is much better than loyalty—fits in the pocket quite nicely."

Even after hearing this insane plan, the urge to return to the Sanctuary remained, increasing into an acute longing. Melea would never get another chance to enter the priest's island fortress if she turned Gerboa in now. She was told where to go, unable to request her missions or take time off.

The black stone walls were calling, a steady pulse in Melea's bones, troubling her at every moment of inattentiveness. Phantom whispers taunted her embattled mind. A longtime enemy she had yet to vanquish. She felt the strain almost constantly now, attacked by the ghosts of her cursed existence.

"A solid plan," said Melea.

This seemed like the thing to say. There were too many aspects of Gerboa's plan that could go wrong for Melea's liking. She had no intention of actually letting him succeed so she kept the revisions to herself.

"Returning will be strange."

"Just this one time and then we'll never have to think about the Sanctuary ever again," said Gerboa.

"I hope so." Gerboa would never know the honesty layered within that statement. "So, what now?"

Gerboa yawned. "Probably should get some rest. The next few days are going to be hectic."

"Good idea." Melea meant it this time. Gerboa stretched out on the floor and was soon snoring away.

Melea lay on the thin mattress, watching dust motes float by on shafts sunlight. Sleep was now an enemy, one that she was hesitant to engage, not when she was unable to control what dreams might visit. Death always lurked on the periphery. Best to face it with eyes open.

Eventually, the motes were rendered invisible as the light leaked away. Melea gave Gerboa a tap with her boot, he rubbed the sleep from his eyes, and they walked out of the room in silence. Gerboa went first, completely unaware of the message Melea had carved into the top of the dresser while he slept.

Gerboa buzzed with excitement. He constantly scanned the crowd as they walked toward the harbor, head bobbing nearly as fast as his twitching fingers. He licked his lips as if his mouth was unreasonably dry. Melea barely recognized the nervous wreck as the smooth and skillful thief she had been working with.

"Gerboa, you need to calm down."

He started at her voice and stopped, wobbling for a moment, shifting even though he wasn't moving. Melea found the action disorienting, akin to crossing one's eyes while staring at the tip of one's nose. A priest in white robes brushed past, distracting her from Gerboa. The priest strode confidently into the large factory across the street. Smoke and dust billowed from the chimneys above and settled on the priest's shoulders, marring the clean white fabric. Melea looked back to Gerboa and he seemed to have somewhat calmed. She peered at his thin frame but could not detect any of the inconsistency that she thought had been there a moment before.

"Right, thanks."

He walked more smoothly now but his fingers continued to move on their own accord. Pigeons cooed from rooftops but bats had emerged for the evening to control the airway above the streets. They swooped silently, feasting on insects drawn by human refuse.

"You have everything covered, remember?" Melea felt the need to reassure Gerboa, the action so peculiar it brought goosebumps to her skin. She would not like to see how he handled the stress of the situations she was often placed in.

"Right, right," Gerboa mumbled.

They continued toward the harbor, causing Melea to recall her first meeting with Trinn. She was supposed to be meeting with Trinn several hours from now at the Black Lotus. She hoped he would check her room after growing impatient. She had no doubt that the informant could get access to her room and, by her estimation, the delay would provide enough time to reach the Sanctuary before Trinn could notify the authorities and seal off transport to the island. The navy would be mobilized, and Melea could feel satisfied that she had done her duty by relaying the message. She could then simply return to the palace, once Gerboa and his mercenaries were captured.

Rows of ships lined the wharf as far as Melea could see in each direction so she followed Gerboa's lead. They passed boats of all shapes and sizes. Fishing vessels that could be manned by only a few fishermen sat next to their hulking cousins who required an entire crew. The dark hulls of massive traders loomed ominously in the calm water, their tall masts jutting outward like the quills of a beast best left alone. She had no idea how much these ships weighed and found it amazing that they were able to float.

Melea had never been on a real ship. She had traveled on a barge once as it meandered down the Choisis river. They had encountered some strong winds but no river was a match for the Shallow Sea. The Sanctuary was not overly far away and they should arrive by midnight. Melea only hoped the sea was calm.

Gerboa approached a ship that looked to be decades older than the others. It appeared to be held together by its most recent repairs. Melea didn't want to wager as to when those repairs occurred. It might have just been her imagination but she swore the ship looked lumpy. Three stern men stood before the boat, trying to appear casual but achieving the complete opposite, as it was obvious they were anxiously waiting for someone.

The shortest, a stocky man with a grizzled face, stepped toward Gerboa. He wore a black wool cap and his face was a network of half-healed scars, some partially hidden by patchy facial hair. The other men were younger: one wore an eye patch and was of average height and build, and the other was tall and lean. They were content to stay back while their leader conducted business. He did not offer his hand or give a greeting.

"I'll take our payment now."

Melea felt her ire rise at the man's gruff approach but Gerboa seemed unperturbed. He reached into his jacket to retrieve the payment. Melea reached out to stop the motion. Gerboa pulled away quickly.

"What's the big idea?" grunted the mercenary.

Melea ignored him and stared straight at the thief. "Not out here in the open. Payment on the ship."

Gerboa gulped and nodded, removing an empty hand from inside the cloak. The mercenary scowled at her then motioned for his comrades to head up the short walkway connecting the dock to the ship's deck. Melea shot Gerboa a demanding look, causing him to look away in embarrassment.

They followed the hired killers onto the boat to find the deck deserted. No crew or captain appeared to greet them so the five stood quietly, the two groups apart from each other, unsure of what to do next. Melea studied the mercenaries while she waited for something to happen.

Their leader, who she had dubbed Scar, scanned the deck aggressively, looking for someone to bark an order at. The man with the eye patch she named One Eye. He looked unbothered by their current situation, seemingly content with picking food out of his teeth with a thumb nail. The taller man was different, he stared right at Melea with an intensity that made it difficult to decide if he looked out of anger or fear. Melea guessed the reaction to be fear, sensing a flighty vibe from the man as he looked away from direct eye contact. She called him Skittish. Thankfully, someone emerged from inside one of the small cabins to break the silence.

"A quiet crew, eh? Good. Do what I tell you and everything will work out just dandy."

The speaker was a short bald man with an enormous gut. His stomach was barely contained by a sleeveless shirt, hanging over the creaking waistband of his pants like a ball of dough. Nobody responded so he raised his voice.

"I'm Captain Luger and this lovely lass is the Bethuna. Take your thumbs out of your arses, drop the gangway and lower the sails, let's get this girl moving. Hop to it, ya cretins!"

The three mercenaries jumped at this last command, even Scar, who spit a wad of chewing tobacco over the side as he went down the gangway to release the ropes securing the ship to the dock. With the way these men immediately responded to authority there was no doubt in Melea's mind that they were former Chosen. Probably deserters, which meant their lives were forfeit if discovered. No wonder they were willing to accept Gerboa's suicidal mission. Captain Luger ambled toward Gerboa and Melea, a well chewed cigar drooping over his bottom lip.

"Everything is loaded up tight below decks, Mr. Gerboa, it's all there and accounted for. Nows, for the matter of my fee?"

Gerboa tossed a bag to Luger that made a soft jingle against the ship captain's heaving belly before Luger tucked it into his pants. He winked at Melea and then marched past them to direct the mercenaries. Scar appeared at Gerboa's shoulder like a wraith. Those who risk their lives for coin acquire an uncanny sense of knowing when it is presented.

"We're on the boat now," said the mercenary.

Gerboa tossed a bag that the mercenary plucked out of the air. "The rest when we put in at Kannark."

Scar spat, marking a dark stain on the deck, and stalked away to finish with the departure. Gerboa walked to the bow of the ship and stared out across the waves. Moonlight cast silver ripples on the water when it peeked out from behind inky clouds. Melea moved beside Gerboa, watching his carefully laid plans unfold before him.

"How long?" she asked.

Gerboa continued to look out into the night. "Too long," he said. "Give or take."

Melea stared into the distance. The wiry thief could have spent his coin in Azra's finest brothels or he could have opened a legitimate business, he could even have bought a modest house. But instead he had been living in rubble, where no one else wanted to go, so that he might be able to stand where he was now. Sailing into the darkness to his almost certain demise. Melea considered why someone would choose to do this. The Bethuna kicked off the dock and carved through moonlight reflections until the harbor disappeared behind them.

Luger could handle most of the duties himself once the ship got going. The ship was unburdened by weight, the seas were fairly calm, and when he did need assistance, One Eye was willing to lend a hand. Scar sat with his back to the mast, meticulously honing the edge of his sword. Skittish lived up to his moniker as he paced back and forth across the ship. Melea noted that he made sure to avoid whichever side she happened to be on.

She had been in too many fights to ignore the premonitory tingle on the back of her neck that always preluded them. The man made her uneasy and she was not going to let a cowardly deserter interfere with her entering the Sanctuary.

"Would someone be kind enough to get me a refill? I'm drier than a camel's twat up here," Captain Luger bellowed from the helm.

"Get your own damn drink," Scar shouted.

"I would but Bethuna has a fat ass and none of you know how to treat a big boned gal."

"I'll carve a piece out of your fat ass if you don't shut up." Scar's voice had the unmistakeable rage of a man who was unwilling to accept his poor lot in life. One who had to fight for everything, but was much more accustomed to losing.

Luger laughed, only incensing Scar. "I just want a teensy drink. A little drink served by a little man. Seems like you fit the bill."

Scar leapt to his feet, newly sharpened sword in hand. Melea stepped in front of him before things could escalate further.

"Enough," she said. "I'll get it. Both of you stay where you are."

Neither man commented. The command in Melea's voice was enough to make Scar stomp away and sheath his sword. Melea walked up the short stairway to the small semi-enclosure housing the ship's wheel. Between the wheel and Luger's girth there was little remaining room in the enclosure. He handed Melea a battered canteen.

"Rum is in a cask belowdecks. Thanks, girly."

Rotted stairs led into to the bowels of the ship, the smell of decay cloying in the still air. Melea measured her weight carefully on each step, feeling a sickly crunch beneath her boot, and waiting for the crack of splintering wood that would send her tumbling down. But the stairs held. Melea doubted they would be able to support Luger's weight, which was probably why he made such a fuss about someone getting his drink.

Weak light from an oil lamp made the Bethuna seem decrepit rather than just in poor repair. She noticed a few crates stacked in the corner; Gerboa's supplies. Melea took a quick inventory: five loaves of bread, two jugs of water, a couple shanks of dried meat, and a bag of bruised apples. Meager rations for the amount of people he expected to be leading. The thief must have run out of money paying for Luger's and Scar's services. He still had a harbormaster to bribe as well. Melea now sensed how desperate Gerboa really was.

A cask of rum sat beside the supplies, purchased with Gerboa's coin no doubt. She twisted the tap to release the bittersweet liquid, the tinkling of its flow against the metal of the flask temporarily overshadowing the steady sound of water slapping against the hull. The moment of calm came to an abrupt end, as the door at the top of the stairs slammed shut. Muffled shouting came from the deck.

Melea dropped the flask, and leapt up the rotted stairs two at a time. She heaved her shoulder into the door. It held fast. She could hear Luger cursing at the mercenaries. The captain suddenly went silent. There was a heavy splash, followed by a crackling. Tendrils of black smoke curled under the gap at the bottom of the door.

"Bloedeth cowards."

Smoke streamed through the gap. She could hear the blaze intensifying just beyond the door. Rage filled her up. Energy coursed through her veins, volatile and insistent. Melea inhaled deeply, balled a fist, and cocked her arm back. She released the breath as her knuckles made contact with door. Energy exploded out of her fist like lightning, destroying half of the door in a storm of splinters.

Melea stepped through the sagging door and into an inferno.

Luger lay on the deck, his gut rising up, his legs and head were already consumed by the fire.

Smoke stung her eyes and the heat pressed aggressively against her skin. Melea spotted a missing rowboat. She put her head down and angled toward the edge of the ship, hopping from space to space to avoid the flames. An endless expanse of black water appeared. A lone boat rowed away, still near enough that she could make out individual faces. Melea dove off the Bethuna.

The cold water shocked her senses for a moment, but Melea came up to the surface with purpose. She swam after the traitors, gaining on them with uncanny speed. A shout of alarm came from the boat. Scar and One Eye manned the oars, while Skittish sat next to Gerboa. Melea caught the glint of iron in Skittish's hand.

The boat was within reach. Melea gripped the gunwale with one hand and pulled herself in. Skittish stood, brandishing the knife. His fearful eyes bright as the moon above.

Melea rolled out of the way of the initial swipe. She closed the short distance between them, scurrying on her hands and feet like an animal. Skittish swung again but Melea caught him by the elbow and wrist, twisting the knife out of his hand and into her own. His eyes froze in disbelief as the knife came away, the blood as black as ink.

His hand clamped over the gash in his throat. Melea grabbed the mercenary by the belt and leather jerkin and shoved him overboard.

Scar held a sword to Gerboa's throat. One Eye had his sword out as well, but looked more likely to dive out of the boat than fight.

"Demon," Scar hissed.

Melea grinned. One Eye trembled.

"Jordo saw you fight the bear-man," said Scar. His eyes darted to the waves where Melea had tossed Skittish. "You're cursed."

"Then you know what I can do to you," said Melea.

Scar slid the edge of the blade closer to Gerboa's jugular.

"You reek of cowardice," she said, as she lowered the knife. "Kill him. He means nothing to me."

Scar and One Eye exchanged a panicked look.

"Don't," Gerboa whispered. "Shamara, please. She's in there."

The wind whistled over the boat and the waves lapped against the hull.

"Your sister," she said.

"Yes," said Gerboa.

Melea feel sick, not like the temporary nausea caused by a large wave, but something more disturbing. This was an old hurt, one Melea had not felt in some time, a pain she didn't want to be feeling again. Returning to the Sanctuary would dispel this pain, it had to.

"I can see your cowardly hearts beat faster and faster," she said to Scar and One Eye. "Take us to the Sanctuary or be devoured; those are your options."

"Don't listen to her, she's trying to trick us," said One Eye, shifting nervously.

"Shut up," Scar hissed. "I'm thinking."

"You're deserters," said Melea. "That makes your lives forfeit. Row us to the Sanctuary and take your chances."

"Shut up," said One Eye, his voice rising.

"Close your mouth, you whoreson, or I'll gut you myself," Scar snapped.

"Or I kill you both now," said Melea.

Scar released his grip on Gerboa and slowly sheathed his sword. One Eye whimpered quietly. Melea sat. Her rage was now down to a simmer. The mercenaries picked up the oars and started rowing.

Gerboa exhaled, rubbing his neck. The thief's words kept spinning in Melea's mind. *She's in there.* The guilt at leaving his sister was palpable.

The island became visible on the horizon—a dark smudge between the black surface of the water and the night sky. She needed to return to the Sanctuary. She felt it in her bones.

The mercenaries angled the boat to the backside of the small island, skirting rough coastline that led to cultivated farmland. Stony waterfront was replaced by rocky crags and cliffs as the incline of the terrain steadily increased along the curvature of the island. The outline of the Sanctuary came into sight, a hulking black mass blotting out the stars.

The Sanctuary squatted atop the island's highest point and was the only structure Melea could recall ever seeing on the island. Beauty was absent from the Sanctuary's design—windowless stone walls of straight edges without walkways, gardens, or parapets. Emperor Anathasius might commission structures of grace and beauty, like the Palace of Light, but the Sanctuary was an antithesis to form. This was the first time Melea had seen the Sanctuary at night and it reminded her of a smaller version of Mt. Skarskaard.

A tenet of the Binding Doctrine seemed to pour forth from the Sanctuary: *Carry the candle of Light within as you step into Darkness and be not afraid.*

The Sanctuary sat high above, a crusted shell growing outward from the rock. Melea saw no trails leading upward and even if the cliff was climbable there would be no way of escaping in any hurry.

"That's where I escaped from," said Gerboa. "There's a hidden passageway cut into the cliff that leads into the Sanctuary."

The water calmed as they passed by the larger rocks acting as a breaker for the waves to smash into. Chains of smaller rocks in the cove played tricks on Melea's eyes. The rocks appeared to be moving.

"What the?" said Scar, noticing the same effect.

Melea looked closer at the strange rocks, they were littered with bones bleached by the sun. The boat passed nearby and she saw that the bones were small, that of children. The movement of thousands of tiny bodies made the rocks appear to shift. Black shelled crabs scuttled across the rocks in their multitudes.

"Most who leave the Sanctuary don't do it wearing a white robe," said Gerboa.

"Bastards," Scar cursed. His face compressed into a fierce glower. Melea wondered if the mercenary had children of his own.

Gerboa directed them to a small rocky shore, the crash of the boat's hull sending crabs hurrying for the safety of the water. Melea looked up at the moon. It was already descending, somewhere between midnight and dawn.

"We enter through there," said Gerboa, pointing to a hole the height of a man carved into the rock.

"What about guards?" asked Scar.

"There are no guards, but there will be priests. Probably not a lot patrolling at this time of night. Kill any you encounter because they will do the same to you. Remember, we're not supposed to be here, nothing like this has ever been attempted, so they will be unprepared."

Melea knew the mission was destined to fail, she had arranged for it to be so. If Trinn had received her message there would already be warships en route to the island.

"This mission is bloedeth to the balls," she said.

Scar actually smirked.

"Find his sister and get them out of here," she said, staring pointedly at the mercenaries. "Do this and I'll let you continue to eek out your shitty existence."

Scar's smirk dropped.

"Right," said Gerboa. "Let's go." He stepped into opening in the rock and the small procession followed in single file.

The smooth walls and floor of the passageway led upward in a spiraling route. The journey didn't take as long as Melea expected as she bumped into Scar's back to find the others huddled together.

"There is a door up ahead," Gerboa whispered. "The problem is that the door is locked and cannot be opened from this side, and any noise will alert the priests."

"I understand," said Melea, continuing ahead.

The powerful energy that emerged earlier was absent. A cold hearth would not ignite without fuel. She would be unable to open the door without tapping into the power. Melea approached the door and placed her hands on the cold iron.

The door was seamlessly merged into the rock, with no markings or protrusions. Melea closed her eyes, unnecessary in the total darkness, but the action helped her focus. She became conscious of her breathing and followed its pathway into and out of her lungs, acquiring a sensitivity to the feel of it, noting every aspect of her body—the connectedness. As she focused, the feeling became noticeable yet unimportant.

All distraction was pushed aside as she followed her breathing until eventually even that faded away. A calmness settled over her, an extended moment where the chattering of her anxiety went silent. This focusing technique had been with her for as long as she could remember, often becoming her place of refuge as a child when the world became overwhelming. Countless hours of her life were spent inside this empty space within her own mind.

She felt a spark flicker in her chest, a tiny flame that leaned away when observed, as if shy of contact. Melea whispered to the flame, trying to coax it forth. *Come*, she asked, but the flame did not move. She reached, trying to pull the flame closer but it eluded capture. Frustration flared, causing the flame to dim until nearly vanishing altogether. *Remain still and do not allow the frustration to build.* Melea knew this was the action required—passively acknowledging the unhelpful prickles of irritation was the only way to remove them. The taunting jabs of doubt would increase if she gave them attention. She needed to be distant to herself, yet completely attuned. To be aware without being involved.

Distraction was the enemy, an aspect of herself that would erode her resolve if she succumbed to its nagging insistence. Instead, she coiled her focus like a well toned muscle. When she was ready, Melea mentally directed her concentration on the task at hand. The flame returned to awareness.

She watched the flame, but not as closely as before—aware of the flicker but not concentrating on the image. The sight behind her eyelids moved outward, extending like branches from the trunk of her core. She could sense her hands on the door even though they seemed to be stretched far out in front.

The solidity of the door began to lessen, she felt gaps within the makeup of the structure's firmness. Minuscule sparks dancing across her palms. Melea felt her way through these gaps, peering further into the door. The flame flickered at this movement but she ignored it, leaving its illumination on the periphery of awareness. *Please*, she asked. She did not know who she was asking or why, but it felt like the proper thing to say.

The flame brightened. Melea thought of why she had come to the Sanctuary, the unspoken need rising within. The flame burst into light and with it came an accustomed rush of energy. This energy extended throughout her body. Her hands moved to an edge where the door met the wall. Her fingers pushed through the iron like warm butter, disappearing up to her wrists. Melea pulled back and the door swung open soundlessly on greased hinges. She removed her hands from the door. A long bolt lay across her palms, part of the locking mechanism from the other side.

The bolt felt warm and malleable in her hands, so Melea flattened an edge, pressing one end into a thin point. A priest in white robes stood a few meters in front of her, unaware of her presence. A crystal set into the wall cast soft red light on the priest. The hallway was absolutely silent, daring Melea to move and break it. She raised the piece of iron she had fashioned into a knife and snapped it forward with a well practiced flick of the wrist. The priest let out a soft groan as the crude weapon sunk into the back of his neck. Melea caught him before he hit the ground and dragged the body back to where the others waited.

"Demon," whispered Scar.

"Even demons get homesick," she said. "If you have any honor left, this is the time to show it."

As she walked through the doorway Melea realized that she could have left Gerboa to the mercenaries and continued on her own. She was making things complicated by getting involved; many levels beyond deviating from the plan. This was her plan though, she could alter it as she saw fit. Gerboa, against all odds, had made it this far, and Melea was not about to allow a couple of second-rate mercenaries stop him from seeing his sister.

Melea jolted to a dead stop. The blonde woman with the piercing blue eyes materialized out of the wall in the hallway. A half-formed face emerged out of the stone to stare directly at her, vanishing as quickly as it appeared, and leaving Melea blinking in the red light of the wall crystal.

"Shamara?"

She motioned for Gerboa to continue.

Melea could sense something above them, calling out to her but the call was weak. This is why she needed to come here, there was an odd energy in the air, one that Melea recognized. For a moment she forgot about her mission, the mutinous mercenaries, and the betrayal that she knew was coming.

Crystals were set into the wall every few meters which made navigating the halls quite easy once their eyes adjusted. They traveled at a jog, the silence and the bare stone walls giving the impression of moving through a tomb. Dust stirred in the confined space, temporarily disturbing the stale mustiness.

Melea checked every intersection before they crossed but they didn't encounter any other priests. So far so good. She slowed their pace as they approached a familiar crossroads.

The hall branched off in four directions, each leading to living areas where potential vessels were separated by level of ability and the amount of time they had spent in the Sanctuary. "Let's try this one," said Gerboa, pointing down the third.

Melea nodded. This is where she would leave them. She would head for the upper levels, where the call was urging her to go.

Gerboa looked Melea in the eye—grateful, fearful, and excited all at the same time. "Thanks," he said before starting down the third hall, with the mercenaries trailing.

An itch started in Melea's chest as she watched him go. When Gerboa was almost out of sight he suddenly collapsed to the floor and lay completely still. The itch in Melea's chest escalated to a pang of alarm as she ran to his fallen form.

The thief flailed his limbs weakly and tried to rise but lacked the strength. An outline around his body began to fluctuate, wobbling and distorting the air, making Melea dizzy as she watched. His form shrunk, becoming smaller and more youthful. Melea's jaw dropped as he transformed from a thin man into the young boy with brown hair she had seen scramble out of Stone Park.

Dark rings hung under his eyes and his arms were a mess of scars. Some of the marks were long healed but the majority looked fresh. He was exhausted, his body could not hold the illusion together anymore. Gerboa had reached the limit of energy he could sustain.

Melea wanted to be impressed with the boy for orchestrating this masterful deception but instead felt embarrassed and betrayed. He smiled weakly. "Surprise."

"You little sneak."

"I had to. Nobody would have listened to me otherwise." Gerboa broke into a coughing fit.

"So that would make her..."

"My older sister," finished Gerboa.

Melea clenched her jaw, calculating the remaining time available. "Come on, let's go."

She hefted his light frame up, draping an arm across her shoulders, silently cursing herself for this act of foolishness. Scar rubbed his stubbly chin and One Eye paced, but they followed.

She did not know this section, only staying in the first two before Anathasius arrived. Her time in the Sanctuary involved group living quarters filled with a daily routine of various forms of mental, physical, and emotional abuse. The priests broke the children down to their most basic human states in those initial sections, in order to rebuild them as vessels capable of using blood rituals. The reconstructed individuals who left the Sanctuary became righteous bearers of the Emperor's Gift, their power manifested in a unique ability that was to be used for the betterment of the Shining Empire.

Melea had arrived wilder and more chaotic than the rest of her counterparts, already presenting ability far beyond what she should have known. The priests were baffled, unsure of what to do with her, as none of their methods seemed to work. She injured more than a few priests, and the beatings they delivered did nothing to break her spirit, forcing them to place her in solitary until Anathasius had arrived.

This section appeared to be for the more advanced as each person had their own individual quarters. The doors to the apartments were without locks and all had a small round window cut into it. Most of the doors were closed for the night but a few remained open. Melea carried Gerboa to each door they came to so he could peer inside. Finally, as they crept past an open door, Gerboa tugged on Melea's sleeve to get her to stop.

Asleep in the bed lay a girl who could have been Melea's sister. The resemblance was so similar that Melea brought a hand to her cheek in shock. Gerboa's sister had the same dark hair and smooth complexion and looked to be around the same age as Melea. Gerboa stood under his own power, making sure of the sturdiness in his legs before entering the room. He knelt beside the bed, reaching out to shake his sister awake, but drew back his hand as he reconsidered.

"Leanna," he whispered. "Leanna wake up."

She opened her eyes, brown like her brother's. Leanna needed a few blinks to push away her sleepy confusion. Gerboa smiled and for an instant all the exhaustion on his young face disappeared.

"It's me Leenie, I came to rescue you."

Leanna blinked again in confusion. "Who are you?"

Gerboa's smile fell and Melea's heart dropped with it.

"Gerboa, your brother. Come, we don't have much time."

Leanna sat up, her face serious. "I have many brothers, all within the priesthood are brothers and sisters. Leave me, you aren't supposed to be in here."

Gerboa reached for her hand but Leanna pulled away. "You have to remember me," he pleaded. "You have to come with me now, we're going to be free to do what we want, we'll be happy like we used to be."

Leanna's eyebrows furrowed. "I'm happiest when serving the Emperor."

"You're not! You only think that, you have to believe me." Tears of frustration bubbled from Gerboa's eyes. He looked to Melea in desperation. "Tell her Shamara, tell her it's the truth."

"Go now," Leanna said forcefully.

"Gerboa, she is beyond help." Melea's words sounded dull to her own ears.

"I can't leave her again!" Tears streamed down Gerboa's cheeks.

Leanna stood on the bed and began to shout, Gerboa grabbed her ankle and tried to pull her off the bed. Doors were opening as others were alerted by Leanna's shouts. Gerboa looked to Melea again—the pain in his eyes caused an internal rupture inside of her. It was all too much. She tried to apologize but the words got stuck. Melea turned her back on the estranged siblings. The mercenaries had already fled. She sprinted down the hall past the curious onlookers.

At the crossroads where the hall split, she headed for the staircase she had used to leave the Sanctuary years ago.

*How could one escape what was inside of them?* Melea would have given anything for an answer.

She sped by an oncoming priest. He started at the disruption of his nighttime routine. One thump on the top of the head with the pommel of her knife sent his body slumping awkwardly to the stairs.

Melea reached the landing for the main level. The upper levels were sure to be swarming with priests. The call was growing stronger, a primitive drum beat registering in the marrow of her bones. A primal rhythm oftentimes called intuition told her to continue upwards—outside. She scanned the arched hall for an exit that might lead outside. The large hallway was silent for now but Melea knew this solitude would not last much longer.

Up ahead, on the left, Melea detected the first hints of the sun's rays leaking in through a large opening framed by two massive pillars standing like obelisks on either side of a set of stairs. As Melea rounded a pillar she ran smack into a priest carrying two buckets of water slung across his shoulders on a wooden staff. The water sloshed from the contact but to the priest's credit he did not drop either bucket.

She lashed out by reflex, delivering a lightning fast right-left-right strike combination to the priest's jaw and temple. He dropped to the floor, this time spilling the contents of the buckets.

Melea was already stepping around the priest, running into a courtyard dominated by a large fountain in the center. The statue in the fountain was made in the Emperor's likeness, one stone hand outstretched and reaching toward the rising sun. The beckoning call carried Melea beyond the fountain, the sense of urgency screaming that she was nearly at the destination.

She crossed the courtyard and ran down a grassy incline to find a peculiar building, a small temple of some kind. The structure was triangular in shape and several times her height with a flat rooftop. The dark stone of the structure was different than the rest of the Sanctuary, muted, as though brighter colors soaked into the rock to leave more somber pigments behind. She saw no doorway but the call attracting her to this spot had stopped at her approach. She traced her fingers along the weathered surface, stone pebbled and worn from seasons of wind and rain. Inside resided an answer, Melea was sure of it.

Melea pressed both palms to the stone. She could sense the spaces within its structure just as when she had pushed through the iron door. Heat spread across her palms until they felt on fire. She focused on her breathing, centering herself, feeling calmness spread out from within. She pushed into the stone and her arms disappeared. Melea stepped forward and passed through the stone.

The stale air within the temple made it immediately clear that none had entered this room in an age. Shafts of sunlight streamed through tiny holes in the ceiling. The walls looked like they had once been adorned with complex motifs and calligraphic writing but all that remained were shallow imprints. A shrine of some sort stood in the center but the crumbling facade no longer contained its treasure. Melea walked slowly toward the shrine. In the silence each step transformed into a heavy stomp.

She stopped, and stood perfectly still, feeling out the ancient room. A subtle scent of death lingered. Melea knew this scent anywhere. She was born in death, bathing in it time and again in service of the Emperor.

Inside of the shrine, there were enormous roots, each offshoot thicker than her waist. The tops bore jagged splinters as if the tree was ripped, rather than chopped down. Splotchy markings on one of the roots were darker than the surrounding wood. Melea leaned in to inspect the marking. She had been in enough fights and seen enough wounds to be able to recognize a blood stain. The hairs on the back of her neck stood on end.

She was not alone in the room. She sprang back from the shrine, knife in hand as she crouched, prepared to attack or defend.

A portly man looked at Melea. He sat in the shrine, beside the roots. A few wisps of hair clung to his temples, flowing over the tops of his ears even though there was no wind in the structure. He watched Melea with a contented smile on his cherubic face.

"Please put the knife away. I have seen enough of knives in this place," he said.

"Where did you come from?"

The man smiled broader. "I have been here longer than you have. I should be asking that of you. Come, sit."

The man sat and crossed his legs, golden robe billowing around him. Melea did not sense any intentions of harm or detect any foul play so she sheathed her blade. But she was not yet ready to sit like an adoring child in front of her kindly grandfather.

"My name is Wasi," he said. "Nice to meet you Melea. I have heard much about you."

Melea's muscles coiled. "How do you know my name? You're not the first weird old man to claim he knows me."

Wasi looked amused. "I cannot account for the claims of other weird old men, only for this one. Your mother has told me all about you. She told me to give you a message if you wish to hear it. Do you?"

*Her mother?* Melea had never met her mother. She was an orphan. Alone until the soldiers brought her to the Sanctuary.

"You may relay the message."

Wasi clapped his hands together. "Splendid. She says, be wary of Grandfather, trust in your intuition. She apologizes for the burden of carrying death's mark."

Wasi's words hit Melea like a hammer. There were so many questions she wanted to ask but she could not utter the words. She had spent a long time forcing the words down, burying them where they would not be found, directing herself in other pursuits so they were unable to surface. Despite her best efforts the questions remained; they could not be eradicated by neglect and were impervious to rejection. Now was the opportunity to ask them and she found herself totally unprepared.

"How?" was all she managed to choke out.

Wasi's eyes drooped. "I am sorry Melea but I cannot tell you more. You will have to discover the answer on your own. We do not have much time and there is more I would say. Come, please."

He motioned her forward. Melea's wariness had evaporated with the mention of her mother, and she moved closer to the old man without a second thought. Wasi reached gently into the soil beneath his feet with both hands, retrieving something, cupping it before him.

"For you. Put out your hand."

Melea obliged, feeling the dribble of dry soil spill into her palm. In the center lay a lime-green seed the size of the tip of her smallest finger. Thin pink lines covered the surface of the seed in intricate whorls and spirals. The beauty of the seed astounded her.

"This is a gift. You may give it to whomever you choose."

"When do I need to plant it?"

Wasi laughed. "Always the pragmatic one. Do not worry about the planting. The seed is stronger than it looks. It will persevere as long as you keep it safe."

"Why me? Why give me the seed?"

"You have seen the rune of rebirth." Wasi looked past Melea. "They are coming."

Melea turned in time to see the entire wall come crashing down.

Rocks tumbled and skidded across the floor, dust gusted in like the exhale of a mighty sandworm of Fyn. Priests swarmed in through the opening. They did not utter battle cries, but the barely contained fury in their eyes screamed of hostility. Melea recognized bloodlust, the desire for vengeance.

She burst past the priests, too fast for their grasping hands. The seed gripped tight in her fist, she raced toward the shore. The huffing breath of the priests followed as they gave pursuit.

A sudden jolting pain in Melea's legs caused her to trip. The constricting pain traveled up her calves, into her thighs and lower back. Her legs went numb, no longer responsive. Melea could feel the invasive energy creeping into her back. A ritual—she tasted the energy attaching to her body.

*The seed.* Melea knew the priests would take it from her. With great effort, Melea raised her fist, prying her fingers open with her other hand. She couldn't leave the seed here and hope to find it again. The priests were almost on top of her. Melea forced her mouth open and slammed the seed inside.

The priests circled her, attacking simultaneously and from all sides. A dozen hands shoved Melea to the ground and a knee between the shoulder blades pinned her in place. Slowly, the hands were removed but Melea found that she was still pinned. It actually felt like more priests had piled their weight on top of her, even though she knew this to be false, as she could see their feet a short distance away.

Two droplets of blood displaced the dust next to her head. Melea tried in vain to see who approached but her eyes could only tilt high enough to glimpse a red robe. The weight felt like a boulder had been rolled on her neck.

"Sneak into my temple."

The statement was followed by a kick to the ribs. Melea was incapable of flinching, the intense weight held her in place as the kick shuddered through her.

"Kill my priests."

Another kick. Even her throat was subjugated to the pressure suppressing her body, her cry of pain stifled before it could begin.

"You may be the Emperor's little bitch but you're in my domain now."

A kick hammered into Melea's temple and everything went black. She felt the unnatural bonds restraining her fall away as she drifted downward, weightlessly, without worry, like a leaf on the wind released from all connections.

## Sickness

Daymon was distraught. The crops would not grow and he knew Master Pompae would be displeased. The priest blamed himself for this failure—every failure was his. A priest must uphold his duty to give himself as an offering on behalf of his Master, which made the failure of the crops the greatest disrespect. Surely the problem was only a simple error that could be corrected, a mistake in the calculations or in his preparation,.

Daymon mentally retraced his steps once more, even though he knew there was nothing new to find. A solution could not miraculously spring forth from training he did not have. The only training he had ever received was for this particular ritual and it should have worked just as had in the past. Daymon had performed this ritual many times, having perfected it long ago at the Sanctuary.

The taste of the morning oatmeal, the names of his fellow disciples, and the feel of his cot were all grey and indistinct. The possible inaccuracy of his memory did not trouble Daymon because there was a powerful truth that superseded all else and tied him forever to the Sanctuary. Years of exertion finally culminated in a moment of soul-quenching triumph. The dry, dusty road of his existence was instantly transformed by a celestial downpour that saturated his life with incomparable meaning. One singular moment continued to direct his future, and upon reflection, had directed his entire life.

The thought of that moment brought forth tears of frustration. *Why wouldn't it work?* If only he could feel the familiar rush of power needed to complete his duty, the task he was destined to provide for the people of the Shining Empire. But there was nothing. Daymon was tapping a dry cask and expecting a foaming mug of ale.

He stared into the dirt, trying to summon a sprout to burst through by sheer force of will. The effort made Daymon's head swoon and he used what balance remained to keep from collapsing into a heap on the dusty ground.

Daymon sat cross-legged, back hunched, head hung low. He rolled up the sleeves of his robe to stare at his bony arms—usually capable instruments that had betrayed him without warning. His arms were criss-crossed with scars, the many lines looking like an attempt at crude artwork or lazy torture. Each cut was self inflicted and a mark of honor for Daymon. Every scar was a lasting reminder of his purpose, a fulfillment of the inner becoming the outer. Stitches holding together a vessel intended to transfer divine power. Daymon mindlessly counted his scars. The shock that he would never add another turned his mind into a blank instrument, impervious to grief or pity. The realization of his useless condition was impossible to process.

The sweltering air made Daymon feel heavy, pushing down on his chest and shoulders. Sweat dribbled down his forehead, the beads trickling off his nose to land in his lap. His armpits were soaked, his body odor rank. In his distracted state, Daymon didn't notice the crunch of footsteps approaching.

"Daymon, what's the problem, friend?"

The priest looked up at Jerome Bogan, the estate overseer, the man who managed the day to day operations. Everyone called the portly overseer Big Bo, or just Bo in more formal situations. He wore a wide brimmed hat to cover his rapidly thinning hair, which he tried to counter with massive sideburns. He always wore a long-sleeved shirt under an unbuttoned leather vest despite the season, which did nothing to hide the two dark splotches of sweat soaking through.

"It's cursed hot out, as scalding as my wife's tongue." The overseer gave a bark of laughter at his own joke.

Daymon continued to look at his arms. Big Bo adjusted his hat, blue eyes squinting at the priest as if they could squeeze a response out of him. "Now ain't no reason to be disrespectful, friend."

"I'm sorry Bo, it's just that..." He wanted to say that he was broken but that word was not quite right, the problem felt bigger. More discordant than broken—broken things could be put back together. Daymon was now forever out of sync.

"Just what, friend?"

Another drip of sweat dropped into Daymon's lap. He spoke in a whisper. "There's nothing left. It's gone and I can't even feel it anymore."

Big Bo crouched down beside the priest, his protruding gut filling Daymon's vision. "What's gone? Are you referring to the Emperor's Gift?"

Daymon gave a nearly imperceptible nod. Big Bo pushed off his thighs with two meaty hands to stand, his face shaded by the hat as he looked down at the priest.

"I'm sorry to hear that, I truly am. There comes a time in every man's life when he can't do the things he once could, but most never receive the Emperor's Gift." Big Bo spat into the dirt and looked out across the field. "A damn shame, but there's nothing that can be done to bring the Gift back." He paused, extending a hand to help Daymon to his feet. "No use sitting here. Let me help you back to the villa and I'll get everything sorted."

Daymon's weight was partially supported by the fleshy bulk of the overseer as they walked back to the living quarters. The best he could muster were stumbling steps. Big Bo took the priest's weight in stride, talking like they were on a leisurely stroll.

"Used to be that you couldn't grow wheat in this area. They tried a couple of times but it would never take. Think about that, all this prime territory being wasted. The Sanctuary changed all of that, brought the impossible within reach and then made something useful out of it. But you know of this, son, you've taken care of this estate for how many seasons now?" Big Bo continued without waiting for an answer. "You've done your best, Daymon, you done a lot of good work, fed a lot of mouths in the Empire. You aren't the first to have this happen to them; there's a procedure for priests in your situation. Don't worry, Daymon, you can still aid the Empire."

The hot, sticky air suddenly seemed less clingy. Daymon had not considered that other priests could have encountered the same dilemma. The thought invigorated his sapped limps with newfound determination. His legs felt sturdier beneath him and he was able to stand upright under his own power.

Priests were solitary by nature, rarely associating after their training was completed, but his spirits were buoyed by learning that others had been where he now was. Daymon was not relieved, far from it, but the thought of his future was no longer a solid wall of despair. Master Pompae's grand villa appeared on the hill overlooking the estate. It spread luxuriously over the expanse. The architecture was designed to work with the environment rather than dominate it, and Daymon found the effect calming.

This had been his home for years, the only home he ever had outside of the Sanctuary. He looked longingly at his small suite located on the westernmost section of the villa, imagining the comfort of resting his exhausted body. Fatigue seeped throughout Daymon. Big Bo was still chatting away but the words could not penetrate Daymon's foggy mind. They were nearly at the stables before Daymon noticed the overseer was leading him away from his room. The sickly sweet smell of hay and manure disturbed Daymon's cloudy awareness.

"Where?"

"The procedure, remember? We've got to get you sorted."

"What procedure?" asked the befuddled priest.

Big Bo set his mouth in a hard line, leading Daymon into the rear of the stables. The clang of a blacksmith's hammer sounded.

Big Bo propped Daymon on a stack of hay and went to talk to the shirtless blacksmith. Daymon had never been in the smithy before and the heat of the furnace made his lungs retract on themselves with every breath. *Why were they here? Was he going to become the blacksmith's apprentice?* Daymon shook his head, that was a stupid, it was difficult to think, and his throat was parched. He shambled over to a bucket of mostly clean water and scooped handfuls into his mouth. The tepid water soothed his throat some so he turned to ask Bo why he was needed here.

Daymon wanted so badly to sleep, he would only ask to take a nap, surely that would be alright. They could discuss his future at the estate later. The overseer had approached while Daymon drank and clamped his big hands over the priest's wrists.

"Easy now, don't struggle."

Fear lanced through Daymon, but he was too weak to have any hope of escaping Bo's grip. The overseer grunted with effort as he roughly forced Daymon to the ground, pinning him with a knee to the chest. Daymon was in full panic, feeling helpless beneath the larger man's bulk. Another hand, stronger even than Bo's, forced Daymon's mouth open. He struggled futilely to free himself from the blacksmith's painful clasp.

A red hot blade descended into Daymon's view like some sort of exotic bird, wisps of steam trailing its passage. The blacksmith brought the blade down with one smooth motion. Daymon smelled the stink of burning iron as it passed his nose. He instantly lost consciousness as the blade sank into the soft flesh of his tongue.

## Secrets

Time laughed at her pain. Bursts of agony made her body scream for life and her mind plead for death. Time held her close, blocking all exits of escape.

Melea didn't know where she was, or how long she'd been there. She wanted time to end, to take her beyond life, outside of death.

She lay curled on a stone floor in a small room, pitch black from an absence of windows. The cold stone sent violent shivers through her naked body but she barely noticed them anymore. Her mind was fatigued beyond exhaustion, yet sleep remained out of reach. Something about the smoke of the herb they had placed under her nose. The same herb they used on her as a child to force an inhuman level of exhaustion in an attempt to break her will.

She desperately needed to go somewhere beyond thought, beyond her body, beyond the present. But she did not know how to stop what was happening to her so Melea, who had been called Shamara, lay shivering in the cold, her body numbing until she could no longer distinguish her skin from the floor. Despair trickled in, a toxic liquid that she could drink herself to death with.

Her mind moved in fragmentary jumps, never settling on anything for long. The anguish in Gerboa's desperate eyes, the words hiding behind the searching gaze of the blonde woman, the smear of Skittish's blood on her blade—but mostly she recalled the sound of her tormentor's breathing. The punctuated grunts and exhales as he vigorously went about his business, systematically inflicting as much suffering as possible.

During the ordeal, Melea had retreated into the refuge of her mind, shifting her awareness into an empty, weightless space forged of a material stronger than iron. She floated near the ceiling while her tormentor conducted his grisly work. He had started with her feet and finished with her fingernails. Once he finished, there was a moment of lucid sunshine before she faded out of consciousness.

She woke to a room drained of warmth, her anger filling the confines like a living being. The snarling beast inside of her lashed out against the encroaching despair that lapped against her like the current, each wave slowly dragging her farther from herself. The will to live does not go quietly, even when everything has been taken and this was why she always killed quickly. Time was not as merciful as she had been to her victims.

Melea curled her fingers into her palms but could not press them into fists because of the damage done by the needles pressed under the fingernails, one by one. She wanted someone to enter so that she could make them feel as bad as she did. Soon, before her strength left.

The door creaked open, grating on rusty hinges, allowing a sliver of light into the room. Someone tossed clothes at her and left, leaving the door open.

Was this a new torture? Were they daring her to make an escape so they could inflict more punishment?

Her tormentor had been uninterested in questions. There was no interrogation, just methodical punishment. She still had her secret. They did not know about the seed.

The realization imparted strength, providing energy Melea thought was extinguished. The beast of anger bared its teeth and advanced into the waves, pushing them aside with each step. She was not finished living, not yet.

Melea had never owned a secret. Not a real one anyway. With the secret of the seed came a sense of purpose. Something that was hers and hers alone; none knew of the seed and none could take it away. The realization allowed Melea to envision more than her damaged body.

She felt the seed inside, sensed it come to life, hot as an ember. Melea turned her focus on the sensation, awareness piercing through her fogged mind. Slowly, carefully, she reached for the seed.

Her will had been beaten low, tortured into something feeble and ineffectual. The indomitableness assumed to reside within her was treated to the harsh reality of human wickedness and it had slowly crumbled under systematic cruelty.

Some of the former iron inside began to harden.

Wasi had said she could give the seed to whomever she chose. Melea decided right there on the freezing stone that she would keep going until this task was completed. She would not die with this secret, she would give the seed away as a gift, as was intended. A decision to be made when she was ready.

She opened her eyes and saw the seed resting in her palm—delicate, resilient, beautiful. She squeezed the seed tight.

No more cowering naked in the corner. She would leave this horrid place. Melea refused to die here, to give in to the unknowing, and succumb to the emptiness in her life. Better to live and battle back against the hollowness intent on consuming her.

Melea winced, forcing herself into a sitting position. The soles of her feet were burned from hot pokers so she crawled forward on hands and knees to retrieve her clothing. The effort of dressing was exhausting. She tucked the seed into a hidden pocket inside of her shirt that she had fashioned for stashing stolen coins.

The pad of footsteps announced someone's arrival. Melea panted on the floor and looked up, hoping it was her torturer so he could see that she was unbroken. Her pride swelled and then abruptly deflated as she looked into stern faces.

Three Chosen glared at her. She tried to rise but could not lift herself. Two soldiers knelt down and scooped her up, carrying her between them and out of the room. The light dazzled her eyes. She felt as if she were floating in a strange dream. None of it seemed real even though she knew it was happening.

Soon they passed through two huge black pillars and into the sunlight. She lapsed in and out of consciousness as the Chosen carried her away from the building. They seemed to be moving toward the small harbor but the clouds spun, making her dizzy, so she shut them out.

The sharp cry of gulls floated above. She watched how easily the birds soared below the voluminous clouds, so effortless in their movements that she hated them. Exhaustion claimed her as they stepped onto the ship.

She knew this place. Her room in the Palace of Light. The sensation of the mattress was pure luxury. To move and break the supreme comfort seemed like the greatest sin. Right now, all she felt was the softness of the mattress beneath her and the comforting blankets above. Her bed had not been this comfortable before, she was sure of it.

It seemed like ages ago when she had last slept in this room. She scanned the space, noticing a dozing guard sitting on a chair near the door. Melea lay quietly, savoring the moment of peacefulness. Her body felt good, surprisingly good, but she was not ready to disturb the feeling by getting up and allowing cold reality to turn its gaze on her damaged skin. The outside world was unaware of Melea and she was content to remain in a state of blissful ignorance, but her own body mutinied against the tranquility. She needed to use the bathroom. Now. She squirmed out of bed, her limbs feeling more of stiffness than pain.

The guard jolted to attention. "You're awake! Where are you going? You must remain here."

"There's no bathroom in here so get out of my way or else your boots are going to get wet."

Melea hustled past the guard, out the bedroom door, and into the adjoining bathroom. She heard the guard race down the hall, no doubt informing his superiors about her stirring.

She returned to an empty room, surprised at the ease with which she walked. Her body had felt infinitely worse the last time she was in it. The reflection in the mirror showed a thin, pale girl with dark, matted hair. Dark circles ringed her eyes but the eyes themselves sparked fiercely. Melea's stomach grumbled loudly. How long had she been out? Her blank expression offered no answers.

Fresh wounds should be underneath her fingernails but they seemed to be mostly healed. The nails were a mottled blue-black and there was only a dull throbbing. Melea raised her shirt to see where the hot metal poker had scorched her ribs. The scar from that branding should have been red and raw but Melea saw no mark at all. Her skin was one smooth, unmarred surface.

Melea sat on the edge of the bed. She checked as much of her body as possible but there were no wounds to be found anywhere. *Was it possible to have a nightmare feel that real?* Confusion and doubt swirled in her mind. Maybe she had imagined everything.

An idea occurred to her. A way to discover the truth—find the seed and she would know for sure. Melea's hand went to her chest, where the concealed pocket held the secret cache. The spot was empty. Melea's hopes sank, there was no seed. The emptiness of her palm mirrored the feeling in her heart when she realized how badly she wanted the seed to be there. Her secret would have been worth the pain of betraying Gerboa, as well as the pain inflicted by the torturous devices.

Melea looked down to her shirt, it was longer than it ought to be, far longer actually as it hung to her knees. She was wearing a bedgown. Someone had changed her clothes!

She hunted through the room until finding a small pile of clothes in the bottom of a large dresser. Leggings and a belt flew over her shoulder as Melea tossed items across the room while looking for the shirt. At the bottom of the pile lay the crumpled shirt, which she nearly ripped apart in her search. Melea shoved her fingers into the pocket and did not come up empty handed.

The delicate beauty of the seed was as marvelous as an untainted pearl, a flawless gem, or a mysterious crystal storing unknown life.

She returned to the bed and lay down with her right hand closed over the seed, contemplating the significance of its existence.

The Emperor entered the room. "You look well," he said.

Melea sat up, the seed concealed in her hand. She placed her hands in her lap. "I feel good, better than I should. I can't really remember what happened."

"My priests at the Sanctuary can be quite passionate at times."

Her mind flashed back to the sense of crushing weight on her back and the crack of multiple kicks to the ribs. The one who delivered that beating remained out of eyesight but he must have been high ranking. She kept quiet, unsure how much to reveal.

"But that is to be expected. They did not know you and you were found in a most forbidden location. All signs pointed to you infiltrating the Sanctuary and killing several priests, so my disciples were simply fulfilling their duty."

"Yes," Melea mumbled.

Anathasius continued casually. "How do you feel? The extent of your injuries was quite severe, the priests were...thorough."

Melea stretched her neck from side to side and arched her back. She was sore but no more so than from a hard day of training. "I feel," she said, searching for the correct term, "rested."

"You truly are amazing Melea, unlike any other I have seen. Almost completely healed in only seven days time."

Seven days. She could not believe it. Melea nodded absently, absorbing the significance of the information.

"I am curious as to why you entered the Sanctuary." The Emperor's tone was sunlight on a silver blade, beautiful but unmistakably dangerous.

She wanted to sound confident and assured but what came out was a babbling stream of cryptic responses. Few could think straight when this close to the Emperor.

"There was this dream with a stag and an old man and a vision of a woman's face and then Gerboa mentioned the Sanctuary and I didn't know how many men he had working for him and I didn't even mean to enter the temple but just stepped through the wall. I didn't kill anyone, well, one priest, and Gerboa's operation wasn't about removing you as Emperor and then I was tortured and then you arrived."

Melea let it all out and the Emperor waited patiently until she was finished.

"Sometimes I forget how inexperienced you are," he said quietly.

For some reason this comment made Melea's chest tighten and she could feel tears welling.

"You wouldn't lie to me would you?"

A single tear dribbled down her cheek. Every heartbeat screamed danger. The sliding tear burned her pride. Melea felt ashamed for showing weakness in front of Anathasius.

"I owe everything to you."

The Emperor watched her impassively, letting the silence drag out, regarding her with his luminous eyes. The presence of the seed made her palm sweaty, she felt it throb guiltily but could not bring herself to show it to Anathasius.

"This Gerboa, what were his intentions for infiltrating the Sanctuary?

"To rescue his sister, a priest in training. He acted alone."

"Besides your help," said Anathasius. "I am disappointed that you found it necessary to enter the Sanctuary. You deviated from the mission to serve your own purposes."

"My actions were unacceptable."

"What did you see in the ancient sanctum?"

Melea sniffed back further tears. "Nothing really, an old shrine and a stump. The priests barged in and imprisoned me soon after I entered." The lie was not a conscious decision but the words were already spoken and she knew there was no going back.

"You mentioned a dream and a vision?"

Melea nodded. "The dream doesn't make any sense. There are some hunters and a stag in an unknown forest, and a violent storm. I don't recognize the woman in the vision but she appeared to me several times, most vividly at the Sanctuary."

"How do these relate to your mission?"

Melea shrugged and looked away. "They don't, really, but they wouldn't leave me be. I thought that maybe I could find answers at the Sanctuary because that's where my life truly began. Where you found me."

Anathasius sighed. "Why did you hide this from me? Why not ask my permission?"

Melea dictated a tenet from the Binding Doctrine. "Beware the influence of dreams as they are spawned in Darkness. Be wary of their unstated intent as it is their desire to lead one astray, to separate one from the flock." She looked into his eyes. "I'm sorry, Martinus. I let myself be led astray."

The Emperor stared back at Melea, his authority absolute. "Yes, you did. You should have known better."

Tears welled in her eyes again as she fought to control her emotions. *What was wrong with her?* The lack of self-control was irritating.

"I apologize for this failure," Melea whispered. The apology floated as delicately as butterfly wings across the distance between them.

"You are stronger than most but are still susceptible to the subversive nature of Darkness. What else is there? You have not told me all yet."

Melea's head sagged, the seed burning in her palm. There was so much more that she should tell Anathasius, but how to begin? How would he respond? She said nothing.

Melea felt the pressure in the room thicken as though the movement of the light slowed. The Emperor's face was calm but his eyes flashed bright with power.

"You will answer me," Anathasius commanded.

Melea's head snapped up, eyes defiant, and then her head drooped. She could feel the energy pulsing out of the Emperor, twisting and turning all around her.

"I feel like I am crumbling," Melea whispered. "From the inside-out."

The pressure in the room intensified, slamming Melea flat against the bed, then dissipating as quickly as it had come on.

"How many chances must I give you?" asked Anathasius. "Your strength will soon be needed. I offer a final chance to regain your strength; a covert journey to Strakos to deliver a message to their king. The concern is if you can be trusted at this moment."

Melea sat up straight. "I will prove my worthiness with this mission. Take my head if I fail to meet your expectations."

Anathasius smiled, a look so winsome that it wrapped her in its embrace and Melea never wanted it to let go. "I will take more than that. You have this mission to return yourself to the flock, to show that you will follow my orders without deviance. Become the Melea I have always envisioned, a being of truth through action."

"I will."

"Your return will signal the horns of war."

"I won't fail you."

The Emperor left Melea alone in her room. She was too nervous and excited to unclench her hand. She was not ready to share her secret, the thrill of concealing it was enough for now—revitalizing in the possibilities offered.

Some time later, she dressed, making sure to put on her dirty shirt and stashing the seed in the inner pocket. She placed a shirt of finer material over top, one baggy enough to fully conceal the rags beneath. Her stomach groaned in displeasure, so she headed for the kitchens. She would enter through the double doors as Melea. The time for playing pretend was over.

## Queen of Clans

Ritika gave the signal to commence the festivities. A booming note rumbled out of a horn the length of two men and tens of thousands of Rhezarian spectators roared and smacked the stadium seats in response. Ritika sat straight in the tall oak throne and scanned the assemblage of her people.

Her black hair had been dyed bright red on the left side and hung over her shoulder in a long braid tied together by silver bands. The red in her hair matched that of her blouse and was accented by a wide silver belt, all of the features complementing each other to enhance her light brown eyes. She wore black leggings and knee-high leather boots. Ritika crossed her long legs and looked out at the great stadium.

Warrior delegations of the united Clans were in attendance as were many common folk who had come from all corners of the nation. The massive stadium was oval in shape and sectioned into six divisions; one for each Clan, with the sixth reserved for the ruling families of each respective Clan. Each division was marked by a mountain native to traditional Clan territory. Towering replicas extended from the external walls to cast shade down on the seats below.

Each mountain had been carved with great detail, impressively conveying the strength and magnitude of the real mounts. Ritika always thought that Union stadium looked like it had been carved downward from one enormous rock. Stonework and engineering conducted by her ancestors greatly overmatched the skills of her clansmen. The secrets behind their many works had been lost to the passage of time but great stone edifices remained, as solid as the day they were completed.

Ritika looked to the section in the shadow of the smallest carved mountain. The Nataga cheered and smacked their seats with fervor. The gleam from their shiny hair reflected brightly, even from this distance. Nataga men shaved the sides of their heads and greased the middle row into spikes. Ritika thought all Nataga men looked the same. They were all on the shorter side, stocky, brown skinned, and had brown spiky hair. Only the older men did not adopt this style, instead keeping their hair extremely short.

She hoped for their competitors to have some success during the Union Games to quell their notoriously hot tempers—she did not want to deal with another insurgency. Mercy would be withheld if the Nataga claim to the throne was reignited.

Ritika turned her gaze to the section across from the Nataga, to her own people, the Rhezi. They were the last Clan to be formed in Rhezaria, having been established by a collection of various survivors after the War of the Gods. The Rhezi were taller and leaner than the Nataga and much darker skinned, but there were a few blondes and redheads interspersed within the sea of black hair.

Ritika had always assumed the coloring had come from the seafaring Remori, who were predominantly of this nature. She did not share any resemblance to the Remori, her high cheekbones and ebony skin were the spitting image of all of those within the Dracarion line.

The Remori were a Clan of pale skinned giants. They were seated in the section next to the Rhezi. Typically, they sported long beards, which her people rarely did. Next to the Remori, was the Clan of the Kon mountains, the enigmatic Sando. These reserved people always traveled in a group of four when out of their mountainous homeland, and were in the habit of wearing leather caps with the earflaps hanging loose. The Sando did not make differences for men and women in these groups and the makeup was often a mix of both. Lastly, Ritika looked at the only section still cheering.

The Uzanaki continued to holler and pound on their chests. Uzanaki men and women tended to be enormous and did not wear clothing on their upper bodies, so the sound reverberating off their chests made quite a din. This southernmost people were bedecked with an abundance of obsidian jewelry, since their highest peak was in actuality not merely a mountain, but an active volcano.

Many of the men's bodies were covered with tiny black markings made from their warrior rituals. It was obvious to see which men had been in the most battles as their bodies were a whole shade darker than the others. Ritika smiled, the Uzanaki would be loud no matter the outcome of their representatives. They might get into a few fights once the drinks started flowing but she would not have to worry about them unduly.

The inaugural event to commence the Games was to be hand to hand physical combat. Ritika leaned forward to hear the announcement of the combatants but listening was a lost cause as her retinue immediately began bickering about the skills of each warrior.

Draggar Vol, her General of Remori descent, was the loudest. "Well sure, that Nataga boy is strong, but he's no match for the Uzanaki prince. Have you seen the size of his hands? Could slap an ox unconscious with those meathooks."

This statement caused the Uzanaki chief to swell with pride. "My son could do it, and then he'd eat the whole ox."

Draggar roared with laughter. "I don't doubt it, my southern friend. I hope Luka is as fearsome as his appetite."

Ritika saw the doubt on the Chief's face, which was the only section of his upper body not covered in tattoos. "I wish it were so but my boy is too gentle. He does not have the kholar. His true warrior spirit is lacking."

Draggar smiled and elbowed the Sando to his left. "Did you hear that? Koacachoa says his boy is too gentle; a gentle Uzanaki, now that's a contradiction. That means he'll just break your bones but he won't kill you."

Obsidian earrings jangled as Koacachoa O'kanhana'etim shook his massive head. "Luka has never killed anyone. I worry for my son. My father would be ashamed."

Draggar erupted into laughter. "The Skull Crusher! Thank benevolent Tehlo that he isn't around to compete anymore. He won how many times? Three? I hope Luka finds the kholar but only after this competition." Draggar paused. "Speaking of sons..."

Ritika rolled her eyes, she knew what was coming next. Draggar continued, stroking his well-trimmed blonde beard, and raising his voice a little so that the conversation was no longer only between him and the Uzanaki chief. "Reyner has a good chance of winning this competition. There's no Remori even close to his prowess."

A snort came from the leader of the Nataga. *Here we go.* The peace lasted longer than Ritika thought it would.

Chief Soren Daro sauntered over to Draggar. The Nataga kept his hair shaved to signify his status as an elder. He wore black leather gloves, a black long-sleeved shirt and dark blue slacks with a braided belt of the same two colors at his waist. He looked up at the taller Remori, his brown eyes did not reflect the smile on his lips.

"Your son might be good but he is not on a boat. He does not know how to stand without the waves pushing him around. My warrior is too fast for a lumbering Remori."

Draggar stared back at Daro, the strength in his broad chest displayed by the trim black uniform. An ivory pin fashioned into eagles wings attached to Draggar's chest was at Daro's eye level. "Being fast and being small are not the same thing, Daro. Your man can run but there is no room to hide in Verangor's Ring."

Daro stepped closer, his misleading smile growing wider. Draggar closed the gap. Ritika rested her chin on her hand and watched the two men size each other up. General Vol and Chief Daro were of a similar age and both were still in excellent fighting shape.

"Man enough to make a wager?" asked Draggar. "If your warrior wins, then I'll lop off these fingers to bring myself down to your level." Draggar waved the ring finger and small finger on his right hand. "If Reyner wins then you lose the rest of yours, except for one to scratch your head with when wondering why you ever dared to go against me."

Daro's eyes glinted menacingly and Ritika cut him off before he could speak again.

"That's enough boys. If I want to see your balls, I'll have the pruney things removed and brought to me. Put them away and enjoy the fight."

Both men turned away bearing stony expressions, moving to either side of the Uzanaki, using the man's impressive girth as a human wall.

No banners were allowed within the stadium except for the official flag of Rhezaria: sky blue behind five peaks linked by forged chain rising from a war hammer. This measure was instituted at the original Union Games because the competitions were meant to symbolize the coming together of the Clans. All could display their worth and receive honor without coming to bloodshed. The competitors soon devised a way around this rule though, as it was now customary for competitor and spectator to wear the colors of their particular Clan.

Reyner Vol strode confidently into the arena sporting the gold and white of the Remori. The Nataga warrior followed wearing an outfit identical to that of Soren Daro. Nataga and Remori supporters cheered for their warriors, heckling one another as the two men made their way across the sandy ground to the circle of stones. The stones were said to come from a boulder smashed by the war hammer of Verangor Dracarion, first king of Rhezaria, as it was hurled at him by Mar'Edo Kon himself.

The two young warriors were accompanied by an official who tossed ceremonial crushed oak leaves around the perimeter of the ring. The fighters could enter, now that this offering was made.

The rules were simple—a fighter could be thrown or knocked out of the ring up to three times and could continue if they were able to make their way back into the ring. However, they could not step out of the ring under their own power, to do so was instant disqualification. A victor could also be determined if a fighter was knocked unconscious in the ring or voluntarily submitted.

Reyner removed his shirt and stepped into the ring. The Nataga entered opposite of the Remori. The crowd roared when each man gave a small bow of respect as the final custom before the fight commenced.

The Nataga dropped into a crouch and began circling Reyner. He was lightning-quick as he darted in for an opening, trying to get the larger Remori on the ground. Reyner managed to evade this attack and launched a counter strike but the Nataga stayed outside of his long reach.

"He won't even stand and face him, this is a fight not a race. If he wanted to run he should have waited for the Pursuit," Draggar muttered.

Ritika was not sure but thought she could hear Chief Daro's teeth grinding on the other side of the big Uzanaki. Daro's mood quickly changed as his warrior dashed in and landed several quick blows to Reyner's chest and abdomen. The Nataga chief cheered and Draggar immediately quieted.

Reyner stumbled backward trying to gather himself but the Nataga rushed forward. The Nataga landed a few ineffectual blows and then overreached himself going for a more substantial connection. Reyner grabbed one of the Nataga's arms with both hands and showed excellent footwork as he spun in a tight circle to gather momentum and launch his opponent out of the ring. The Remori section went wild, as did Draggar Vol. Now it was Daro's turn to mutter under his breath.

The Nataga re-entered the ring but with a slight limp. Reyner crouched, slapped his face with both hands, and advanced quickly. The Nataga moved around as well as he could while lashing out with fast punches but Reyner turned them all aside. It was plain to see that the Remori was energized by the crowd and wanted to end this fight quickly. He landed a few jabs of his own trying to set up a knockout blow. The Nataga sensed what was coming, ducking under a wide swinging punch, exploding up into Reyner's midsection, and knocking the Remori to the ground. Reyner covered his face as the Nataga scrambled on top to unleash a bombardment of furious punches.

A communal outcry escaped from the Remori section, which was countered by the cheering and seat smacking of the Nataga. In a moment of pure luck or perfect timing, Reyner broke his cover and threw out one big fist that caught the Nataga on the chin. The Remori shoved his disoriented attacker away and leapt to his feet. Reyner closed the distance in two large steps, charging straight through the Nataga's punches before hefting him up onto his shoulders and into the air. With a roar, the Remori youth hurled the Nataga into the dirt, the force of the impact bouncing the Nataga out of the ring. The Nataga rolled onto his stomach, tried to rise, but was unable to lift himself from the ground.

Reyner turned to the ecstatic Remori section and opened his arms wide. Draggar whooped and slapped Koacachoa on the shoulder. Soren Daro briskly turned to leave, his dark features contorted into a scowl. Ritika clapped and gave her general a smile to show her support. She ignored Daro's angry exit since any intervention would only make things worse.

Koacachoa laughed along with Draggar Vol. "Your son has much kholar, a fine fight indeed."

Draggar beamed as if the victory were his own. "I was a little worried when he was sent to the ground but I never doubted him. What did you think of the fight, Queen Dracarion?"

Ritika turned to look at her general, aware that everyone nearby in the section was straining to hear her response. "I agree with Chief O'kanhana'etim, it was a fine fight and all Remori should be proud of Reyner this day. The Nataga warrior fought valiantly and the fight could have gone his way, but it was not in desires of Mar'Edo Kon for him to win this competition."

Draggar smiled. "Yes, Mar'Edo Kon showed favor on the Remori today. Speaking of which, have you, Queen Dracarion, considered showing royal favor upon potential suitors?"

*Not now, you jackass, not in front of the nobles.* Ritika forced herself to remain composed. Draggar was feeling much too loose from the elation of his son's victory. She took a deep breath before responding.

"My *appointed* General, this is not the time for such questions. I do not wish to discuss royal favors, as you so put it, during the Games. What I would like to do is watch the representative of the Rhezi compete."

Perhaps Draggar Vol sensed the anger beneath her words, because he did not press further. "Of course my Queen, let's enjoy the fight."

Ritika looked straight ahead toward the center ring, ignoring the sidelong looks and partially muted conversations.

The third fight was between Rhezi and Sando. Luka, the Uzanaki prince, had already won the opening match against the reigning champion, a fellow Uzanaki. Not much hope to be a repeat champion when the heir to the Clan is making his first entry into the Games.

The Rhezi champion was a big man, although not as big as Reyner, but he still loomed large over the wiry Sando. Life in the high mountains required specialization and each Sando trained a specific sense to extreme sensitivity. A pack of four Sando could survive indefinitely in any environment, so good were their hunting and tracking abilities.

The Sando's head was shaved even shorter than Soren Daro's. Ritika did not personally know the Rhezi fighter but she had heard the name of Ulaar Tremana bandied about. He was a veteran soldier who was well-loved by his comrades. The two opponents entered the ring, bowed, and began.

Tremana wasted no time in attacking as he opened with a combination of jabs and kicks. The Sando did well in blocking and evading these strikes but he withheld from counter striking. Tremana danced around on the balls of his feet trying to find an opening in the Sando's defenses, whereas the Sando mirrored the Rhezi's movements but did not seem intent on attacking. The Rhezi brought the fight to the Sando but was again rebuffed at every angle. Frustration was starting to show in the tenseness of Tremana's movements.

The Rhezi attacked again and this time with wilder and more powerful kicks and punches. The Sando stepped in sideways as Tremana swung, grabbing the Rhezi's wrist to transfer the momentum in one smooth motion so that Tremana was flipped onto his back. Tremana immediately sprang back on his feet.

He circled the Sando more cautiously now. The Rhezi warrior offered some jabs, testing the Sando's reaction, but the Sando only blocked them and moved out of their path. Tremana surged forward with a flying knee strike. The Sando sidestepped then dropped into a low crouch, sweeping his leg to trip up Tremana where he landed. Tremana hit the ground then got back to his feet, but not as swiftly as before. The Sando crowd cheered but were not nearly as loud as the Remori or Nataga had been. The Rhezi fans embodied the frustration of their fighter and urged him on.

Tremana shook his head and came at the Sando again, trying to break through and hit his elusive target. A series of jabs allowed Tremana to get in close where he grabbed the Sando on each arm and delivered a powerful head strike. The Sando's body went limp as he dropped.

Ritika saw the Sando subtly shift the position of his wrists as he fell. The Sando landed smoothly on his back, rolling Tremana over top, kicking upward with both feet to send the Rhezi rolling in the other direction. Both men got to their feet at the same time, rushing toward each other to exchange a spurt of blows that ended with the Sando delivering an open palm strike to Tremana's sternum. Tremana stepped back gasping and this time the Sando initiated the attack.

The Sando warrior attacked with speed and force as he pushed Tremana toward the circle's edge. The Rhezi saw what was happening and tried to sidestep around his adversary but as he did so the Sando spun on his heel and landed a kick to Tremana's chin. Tremana staggered but remained standing. The Sando was on him in an instant and an elbow to the temple sent Tremana to the dirt where he stayed. The Sando spectators called out in a strange high-pitched call that echoed off the stone walls. Apparently, the Sando warrior had impressed the Uzanaki because they cheered loudly and many in the stands mockingly reenacted the final knockout blow.

Draggar whistled in amazement. "Well, that was unexpected. Tremana is as skilled as they come, but you never know what to expect from the Sando."

Ritika looked for the Sando chief who was some distance from her position. The Chief stood and bowed in the direction of his victorious warrior then sat looking quite pleased. He felt her eyes on him and turned to look in the Queen's direction. Ritika stood and gave a small bow, impressed as always with their uncanny awareness. The Sando stood and returned a salute.

Ritika sighed. The Sando were always the easiest to deal with. Her own Clan would be in an uproar tonight. The Rhezi representative had fought well but the Sando simply had a better strategy and executed it to perfection. Tremana should have taken the fault by getting knocked out of the ring to re-group—patience won more battles than stubbornness. There were now only three fighters left in the competition and everyone eagerly awaited the announcement of the next fight.

The great horn blew once more as Reyner joined the Sando warrior in the center ring. They were attended by an official who placed five wooden cups on the surface of the largest stone in the circle. Only one cup had a token inside of it and whoever picked that cup would face Luka O'kanhana'etim tomorrow. The other would await the victor and then fight for the championship.

Reyner pointed to the cup in the middle and the Sando chose the one on the farthest right. The middle cup was turned over but proved to be empty. A cheer went up from the Remori and groans of disappointment could be heard from the Nataga side. The official turned over the Sando's choice and a small blue egg fell to the ground. At once a great cheer went up from the Uzanaki, Sando, and Remori. The Uzanaki and Sando were excited at the chance for glory and the Remori relieved that they would not have to face the Uzanaki behemoth.

"That proves it," said Ritika. "Mar'Edo Kon is truly on your side today, Draggar. I hope Reyner is wise enough to be thankful for avoiding Luka in the next round."

She was tactful enough to suppress the urge of blurting out that Reyner getting his face smashed in might force a little humility on the swaggering Remori. Draggar humphed and started talking with Koacachoa about the upcoming fight.

The fighters exited the arena, as caretakers hustled to disassemble the ring so that tonight's festivities could begin in full. Dancing and music and drinking would take place, only ceasing when the first rays of sunlight crested the hill. Ritika stood to leave.

The Union Games were a time for celebration and relaxation for most of Rhezaria as the Clans gathered to reaffirm their cohesive identity, but this was not the case for Ritika. There was the stress of having so many nobles in one city, as well as the headache of preparing the city of Draccar for the oncoming horde. Feeding so many mouths was a monumental organizational task in itself, yet no less important was the duty to keep order when the inevitable emotionally charged outbursts occurred. Lastly, and most unpleasant, was dealing with ambitious nobles and warriors trying to climb the social ranks. Ritika hated this last aspect most of all. She could delegate the other tasks to capable officials, but she alone had the burden of listening to the often outrageous and contradictory demands of her royal subjects.

Ritika Dracarion appeared calm as she steadily made her way through the royal section of the stands. Her stomach becoming more knotted with each piece of small talk as she slowly made her way to the exit. None had the gall of General Vol to blatantly offer up their sons but that time would come. The Games had only just begun.

Trangdon Wulfstom, captain of the Wavebreaker, and cousin to Draggar Vol approached. Wulfstom was an influential Remori trader who had once commanded their fleets in battle. He was shorter than the General, his blonde beard unkempt and looking like it had never seen a razor.

"Queen Dracarion, how good it is to see you again. I have been spending far too much time out on the great blue and not enough at home. Even worse, I have not spared a moment in almost two years to make the trip inland to your lovely city. Please forgive my absence and accept my condolences for the outcome of your Rhezi fighter."

Ritika smiled as she looked down at the shorter trader. "It is your wife you should be apologizing to. Leaving such a spirited woman alone for so long must surely be a crime. My guess is that you made a tidy profit on your extended excursions, and as for my warrior, I suspect he could use some time aboard one of your ships to escape the scathing ridicule he will be subjected to by his comrades."

Trangdon returned the smile, or so it appeared by the movement of his thick beard. "I believe he would enjoy the reprieve but you Rhezi are not seafaring folk, too tied to the trees and hills. Your assessment is correct my Queen: the winds of trade have been gusting in my direction almost as forcibly as the demands of my err...feisty wife." The Remori trader chuckled and Ritika smiled politely, feeling her stomach crunch tighter as she waited for the proposition.

"Furthering trade routes is why I approach you now," said Wulfstom. "The Shining Empire, as I'm sure you know, is preparing for war with Calanthia. It is only a matter of time. The Shining Lord has deep pockets and he will pay handsomely for Rhezarian armor and weaponry."

Ritika dropped her smile. "Captain Wulfstom, I acknowledge your desire to increase the Rhezarian treasury, but we will not be fortifying the advancement of the Shining Empire."

Ritika knew that the Remori trader did not care about the Rhezarian treasury, it was his own vaults that he wanted to fill, and to silence his demanding shrew of a wife in the process.

Unperturbed, the trader continued. "My Queen, this is a golden opportunity—golden being the operative word. The Shining Empire will attack Calanthia so it might as well be our weapons doing it."

Ritika furrowed her brows slightly, looking straight into the sailor's grey-blue eyes. "The answer is no. I understand there is no love lost between Rhezaria and Calanthia but we will not support this upstart empire so that Rhezarian weapons may one day be used to kill those who made them."

Wulfstom struggled to mask his frustration. "Queen Dracarion, it would be foolish to sit idly by and watch this boon dissolve before our eyes."

Ritika silenced the Captain before he could continue. "This is the last time I will tell you; any sale of weaponry or armor to the Shining Empire will be considered an act of treason and any dealings will be met with the penalty of death. To disobey my command would be truly foolish. I would appreciate it if you made this knowledge known to those in your circles. Now, if you will excuse me, I must take my leave."

Ritika brushed passed the sailor, his pale eyes cloudy as rising storm clouds. *Foolish*! The trader had the audacity to call her foolish. She was tired of constantly having to deal with older men who assumed they were speaking to an inexperienced girl. Ritika was never supposed to lead Rhezaria, but then again, her father and brother were supposed to still be alive. No one had wanted this arrangement, but there was no changing matters now.

Two guards approached, holding a doughy man between them who was clearly unimpressed with his predicament. Ritika waited, as she knew they were looking for her. More duties; they never ended.

She recognized the man being held as a Rhezi merchant who had been charged with supplying the majority of the food for the Games. His name was Zlakos and he was a middleman, he operated between the farmers and the restaurants, butchers, bakeries, and market. Zlakos had become exceedingly wealthy by distributing the goods of others.

The guards stopped before Ritika, forcing their captive down to his knees. When he did look up there was fear in his eyes but he seemed to be more embarrassed than afraid. The guard on the right, a Lieutenant, wore a silver pin fashioned as an eagle talon on his cloak.

"What is the meaning of this, Lieutenant?"

"My apologies, Queen Dracarion, I did not wish to interrupt but he insisted."

The Lieutenant trailed off and what went unsaid spoke volumes. Ritika then understood why the merchant had been brought to her. Zlakos was a well connected and powerful man in Draccar, and the Lieutenant was worried about the repercussions of sentencing him on his own authority.

"Go ahead, Lieutenant," she said.

"It was discovered that the merchant Zlakos has been stealing from the farmers instead of paying them. Word has it that some were killed when they spoke out against him, and one risked death by alerting the guard. The farmer gave estimates of how much was taken and said that no receipts were given. I've asked around and those who were willing to talk corroborated the claims. The city guard stormed Zlakos' warehouse and found goods numbered nearly identical to that of the accusation."

Ritika looked to the merchant, who was nonplussed by the Lieutenant's words. "What do you have to say about this?"

Zlakos raised his palms in defense, although he could not raise them very high because of the guard's firm grips on his arms. "Your highness, you know me and all the good I have done for Draccar. This is obviously an attempt by a competitor to frame me. I assure you that the farmers were paid. I am a man of status and conduct my business in a fair and honorable manner. Those goods were already in my warehouse in preparation for the Games."

Ritika was unconvinced. It was law to produce a receipt written on a small clay tablet for all merchant transactions. "If you were framed, then how do you explain the lack of receipts?"

The merchant shrugged and looked away. "Farmers are not known to be the most intelligent of people, most cannot even read what the receipts say. They likely threw them away or lost them."

The arrogant tone provoked Ritika's ire. This man believed himself above the law; he was used to throwing money around so that he could do as he pleased. Ritika ignored the merchant for the moment. "Lieutenant, how many farmers did you speak to?"

"Twenty two, my Queen."

"How many are reported to be killed?"

"Three and they all happened last night."

Ritika stared down Zlakos. His double chin quivered under her scrutiny. "You're telling me that twenty-two hardworking men, whose back breaking labor creates your wealth, simply tossed away the only piece of evidence for their work?"

Zlakos didn't flinch. "Twenty-two is not a very large number. Because of my work, many more than that are able to feed their families. I can't be held accountable for the actions of a slovenly few."

"I think you underestimate the severity of this accusation. If found guilty, you are facing ten years imprisonment."

"Queen Dracarion, I would never do such a disservice to Rhezaria, much of Draccar has been built with the help of my donations. Your father and I completed several agreeable deals which have only benefited the people of this city. I see no reason why we cannot continue to build on this foundation. The profit made from the Games will be more than enough to commission a new garrison."

Ritika stopped the merchant with a raised hand. "You will find that I am not my father. Your greed disgusts me. At the moment, I think the best way to improve Draccar is to remove you from its streets."

The smug look dropped from the merchant's chubby face. "But my Queen, who will feed the thousands of mouths for the Games? I was commissioned to do so."

Ritika smiled at Zlakos. She saw panic sprout in the merchant's eyes. "I am the Queen. Have no worries. I will make sure that my people are fed and that they are paid for their work." Ritika nodded to the Lieutenant who, together with his comrade, dragged Zlakos towards the exit.

The merchant's piggish eyes bulged and spittle flew from his mouth as he struggled to plead his case. "Queen Dracarion, do not act so rashly. Surely we can reach an agreement!"

Ritika ignored him, standing still as an oak as the guards carried him away. She started towards the exit after his shouts and curses could no longer be heard. Her brown eyes were fuming and those around the Queen gave a wide berth as she passed. She was almost at the exit when a large figure filled the opening.

Reyner Vol beamed at Ritika as he stood in the doorway. He bowed deeply.

"It was my honor to compete in the Games while you were in attendance, Queen Dracarion."

Reyner was one of the few people that Ritika had to look up to, as his physical stature truly was impressive. Draggar Vol had long been trying to encourage Ritika to court his son but she always declined. Reyner was five years her junior and never struck Ritika as the most intelligent of individuals. She had to admit that he was every young maid's dream, though. The Remori warrior had an athletic grace to go with bulging muscles, a strong jaw, blue eyes, and thick blonde hair.

"You fought well, Reyner. Perhaps a little impetuous, but determined all the same." She kept her tone polite but clipped. She wanted to leave, to be alone for the rest of the evening.

"Eternal thanks my Queen. In a few days time I will be Champion of Verangor's Ring and have the honored status that comes with it."

"You do not lack for confidence. May Mar'Edo Kon be in your prayers so that victory may be granted to you." Ritika waved the back of her hand at Reyner.

He moved enough of his large frame for a small opening to appear.

"A little more perhaps?"

Reyner took a step to the side so that Ritika could pass. As she moved to the exit he subtly leaned in and said, "Perhaps my status as Champion will allow me to become suitable in your eyes."

Ritika's mind went blank and her body reacted as if Reyner had spoken a witch's spell instead of a clumsy act of seduction. Her leg flashed out to swipe Reyner's out from underneath. His eyes went wide with shock as he fell. Ritika caught him by the collar just before impact.

"Another disrespectful word and I'll tear out your tongue. One more lustful look and I'll pluck your eyes out. Solicit me again and I will kill you. I am the Queen—you already belong to me. Do not tempt me to take your body before you're finished with it."

All of his bulk was meaningless as Reyner hung there looking like a scolded boy. He nodded and kept his mouth shut. Ritika let go of the fabric and stepped over the Remori warrior as he slumped to the ground.

Ritika was once again obligated to sit upon the ancient oak throne of her people. The Hezrakaa throne, meaning seat of God. She could feel the weight of ages soaked into the dark wood. Each time Ritika sat beneath the expressionless visage of Mar'Edo Kon carved into the top of the throne, the words of Hekäli Mu'godis, High Priestess, came to her. That conversation five years past still inspired Ritika.

"You must take the path that is before you," said the wizened High Priestess.

"But I am learned in the teachings of Tehlo, I am to be a healer," said Ritika. "No queen has ever ruled outright."

"Then your fool of a brother shouldn't have gotten himself killed hunting for the Odon'kul."

"He aimed to make a mark on history by wielding the legendary weapon."

"Vain," Hekäli snapped. "Your father's untimely passing was unfortunate but now he resides in Mar'Edo Kon's Hall."

"My mother—"

"Queen Kianna's mind is unraveling, it is best for everyone that she remain in the Singing mountains."

Ritika had looked at the High Priestess, at the headdress she had wanted to wear since she was a girl. "I'm supposed to be your successor."

Hekäli batted the thought aside with a wrinkled hand. "No one is *supposed* for anything. Do you know why you were chosen as my successor?"

"Because of my last name?"

"No. Because you are a leader."

Ritika still felt the strength of Hekäli's conviction. She had used that passion to claim the Hezrakaa throne and put down the Nataga rebellion. She had claimed the disputed land between Nataga and Rhezi, an area home to the sacred Singing mountains. Chief Daro's small and ring fingers were also claimed by the new queen. He would have to live with the shame of being unable to wield a weapon.

Ritika looked over to the far right of her hard won throne to where Daro sat with his small retinue. The Nataga chief had been surprisingly composed during the Games after his incident with Draggar Vol on the first day. Nataga victory in the spear toss and melee had tempered his earlier anger. From her left, Ritika heard Draggar laughing and carrying on. The aging general had been in a near constant state of euphoria after his son had been named Champion of the Ring.

Luka, the Uzanaki prince, had used his tremendous strength to overpower the cagey Sando in their matchup, moving on to face Reyner. The fight was one for the ages as the two huge warriors battered each other with devastating blows that would have killed other men. Reyner managed to land an uppercut that sent Luka stumbling over a stone to fall flat on his back. Too dazed to continue, the Uzanaki prince had to withdraw, and Reyner Vol was named the victor. Chief Koacachoa had looked down on his wide belly, slowly shaking his head while Draggar sang the victory song of his ancestors.

Today marked the final day of the Games and a scorching summer sun hung over a strangely quiet stadium, a stillness that is only possible when thousands of people are actively trying to be silent. Ritika's favorite competition was nearing its finish—the Standing Prayer. Five long poles stood in a straight line across the center of the arena facing Ritika's section. Competitors stood atop the flat surface of these poles, which were barely wide enough for their feet.

Each man had his arms extended outward to the side and from each hand hung a weight on a length of chain. The men were tied to the pole by a rope around their waists and had to remain standing without dropping the weights or falling from their precarious perch. Only the Rhezi and Sando contestants remained as the Uzanaki had fallen and the Nataga and Remori had each dropped one of their weights. This competition required finely controlled concentration to remain balanced as well as the strength to uphold the dangling weights.

Ritika knew this Rhezi competitor personally—they had been lovers on and off for years. Her relationship with Garret Tumino was not necessarily a secret, but it could never be a public courtship because of his low birth status and standing as a common soldier.

Garret appeared untroubled on his pillar whereas the Sando was beginning to show tell-tale signs of fatigue. Veins bulged in the Sando's neck, taut from the exertion of holding the weights, and soon his body was shaking with tremors of fatigue. The Sando section urged their warrior to continue but the effort became too strenuous as one of the weights dipped and he lost his balance. He fell, careening forward in a pendulous swing before coming to a stop at the end of the rope. Garret opened his eyes and dropped the weights to the ground.

A thunderous cheer went up from the Rhezi section and Ritika found herself cheering with them. The Sando chief stood and gave Ritika a small bow which she politely returned. Ritika's heart was beating fast.

"Redemption for the Rhezi against the Sando!" Draggar bellowed. "Wouldn't you say so, Queen Dracarion?"

Ritika smiled, amused by the boyish look on her general's face. "Indeed my wise General, hereby ending the rivalry that began all of six days ago."

Draggar cast a sidelong glance in Soren Daro's direction. "Aye, some feuds are shorter than others."

Ritika shot Draggar a fierce look and he got the message to bite back any further comments. The great horn sounded again to signal the end of the Games, eliciting a long roar of approval from the fans. Ritika allowed herself to let out a small sigh of relief. These had been the best Games of her tenure. There had only been a few drunken fights, no deaths, and all of the Clans had garnered enough honor to be satisfied until the next Games.

The old warriors were finally beginning to believe that Ritika was a strong and capable leader. Ritika felt pride stirring in her chest as she watched the parade of Champions enter the arena for one last appearance before the adoring crowd. The Champions completed their lap and the crowd began to disperse.

Draggar clapped his hands together in excitement. "Now we feast!"

Anselmbao castle snaked its way up the two hills rising from the center of Draccar. A substantial area of land was sectioned off by three rings of high walls separating areas within the castle complex, creating an entirely closed off community from the city below. A squat rectangular structure dominated the lowest section, a garrison housing thousands of soldiers. The middle area was split between training grounds for the soldiers, stables, and royal gardens. The highest section was reserved for the castle itself.

The castle stood dignified on the hill, evening blue stone glimmering in the moonlight. Many turrets were set to face attack from any direction, protecting the massive rectangular complexes within. Legend said the stone heart of Rhezaria was held together by a mortar made of the indomitable will of its fearsome people.

In the castle proper, the nobles feasted with the Champions, dining in a hall larger than most houses. Oil lamps lit a spacious room lined with dozens of tables and benches. A stone ceiling arched overhead, supported by wooden beams bent like the ribcage of a whale. The elite of Rhezaria dined on an extravagant meal to commemorate another successful Union Games.

There was roast boar so succulent that it fell off the bone, pomegranate glazed pheasant, spicy squash soup, smoked lake trout, fresh goat cheese with herbs, honey oat bread, and a whole assortment of varied custards and pastries. Ritika sat at the head table and looked out over the congenial scene.

The Queen wore a white silk blouse with voluminous sleeves and a silver necklace to match the silver bands in her hair. Her pants were loose-fitting black silk trousers and her shoes were simple black flats. Ritika heard that queens of other nations only wore extravagant dresses but things were done differently in Rhezaria.

She took a sip of blood-red wine, toying with the idea of going for a hunting trip in the Sawtooth mountains. The rams would be bashing their heads together in attempt to gain status, oblivious to the world around them. Easy targets for a hunter. Ritika scanned the room, noting a few heads she'd like to put on the wall.

She spotted Draggar, who appeared to be celebrating harder than usual, which was fine as long as he did not dip too deep into his cups tonight. He had difficulty restraining his mouth at the best of times and would undoubtedly insult someone. Even if he did, Ritika could excuse his behavior on this occasion. It was not everyday that one's eldest became a Champion of the Games. Ritika noticed another Remori making his way from table to table.

Captain Wulfstom appeared to be in good spirits but he had not approached Ritika further on the topic of trading with the Shining Empire. She watched him and wondered how many of his conversations this night were centered on that subject. Laughter from a group of Champions caught Ritika's attention and she looked to see Garret leading the conversation amongst them. An unconscious smile came to her face as she watched the Rhezi Champion entertain his comrades.

Garret held a large mug of beer in one hand as he gestured with the other. The Champions spilled the contents of their own mugs with the unworried air of the intoxicated. Ritika noticed that not a drop fell from Garret's mug. She knew this would likely be his only drink of the night, that he would not become as inebriated as his companions. She respected this inner control—there was a reason why many warriors could not win the Standing Prayer. Garret always appeared so composed and at ease. He did not panic or become overly excited.

"I knew you had an eye for Champions, my Queen."

The statement startled Ritika. The combination of drink, a satisfying meal, and daydreaming had caused her to miss Draggar's return to his seat at her left. Draggar Vol's eyes were beginning to swim and his enlarged pupils had lost some of their focus but his voice remained calm and relaxed. No one else would have the gall to make such a comment but Draggar was like an uncle, an uncle she liked, and he had always supported her when her father could not.

"Some perhaps. They are the best of Rhezarian men after all; paragons of youth and vitality."

Draggar grunted. "Aye, seems like a lifetime ago that I was a Champion. My back pains me in the morning now, and my eyesight is not as sharp as it once was." The General looked at his son, who was laughing and drinking with his former opponent, Luka of the Uzanaki. The two made quite the duo and had many female admirers fawning for their attention.

"There was a time when I was that strong, when I had my pick of women."

Ritika laughed. "Were you also that daft? Those two are overgrown boys—look how they drink and eat and talk of nothing but their own strength."

Draggar bristled. "They are only boys because they have not been tempered by the flame of battle, they have never known war."

"Are you saying that I should start a war to toughen up the young men of Rhezaria?"

The tight lines in Draggar's face relaxed. "No, my Queen, I am not saying that. You have done well to keep the peace and quell the ambitions of that laughable Nataga. And yes, I was that stupid or nearly so. I was lucky enough to be leaning on the shoulder of your father instead of an Uzanaki prince though."

Ritika made a pouty face. "Sadly, there is no heir of Dracarion lineage for bold Remori Champions to befriend. There is just a Queen whose intimidating beauty is only surpassed by her strength." She leaned over conspiratorially. "I fear that many men find it emasculating, Remori in particular for some reason."

Draggar guffawed and smacked the table, spilling half of his drink in the process. "More like a spinster who doesn't listen to advice given to her by her wise General." Draggar looked away, lost in thought. "Your uncle has a son about Reyner's age but the weakling could never hope to be a Champion."

Ritika took a drink before responding. "General Vol, you are an excellent military man, but a terrible matchmaker. It's unfortunate that Reyner was duped into employing your services. The poor lad never gave himself a chance."

"I wouldn't have to play matchmaker if you would come to your senses and realize what a catch Reyner is." Draggar put his mug down, punctuating his comments wildly with his hands. "Look at it this way. Along the Remori coast there is a type of fish that grows so large and powerful that even the sharks do not bother it, a sailor is lucky to see one of these fish in a lifetime, let alone catch one, and it is a sign of good luck and long life. Reyner is such a fish."

Ritika wrinkled her nose. "I don't care for the taste of fish. We Rhezi are hunters, not fishermen." Ritika paused to judge Draggar's reaction. "Besides, why would I want something that not even the sharks would take?"

Draggar finished the rest of his drink while watching Ritika over the lip of the mug, his blue eyes searching hers. He finished and wiped the foam from his beard with the back of his hand. "I see now why your father's heart was in such battered shape. Thank Mar'Edo Kon I was only given sons."

Ritika giggled, glad that she had gotten under Draggar's skin, while effectively avoiding a conversation about courting Reyner Vol.

A sentry entered the hall through the massive double doors and closed them. The chain mail he wore over his green and yellow uniform jingled as he walked swiftly toward the head table. He wore a gold pin shaped like a war hammer, signifying his status as captain of the castle guard. He stopped in front of Ritika, standing at attention until she gave her approval to speak. Ritika saw the uneasiness on the soldier's face. Whatever his message was he did not seem glad to bring it.

"What is it, Helgernon? The message appears to be urgent."

Helgernon squirmed slightly, aware of the many eyes pretending not to watch him in the dining hall. "Perhaps I could deliver the message somewhere more private?"

Ritika considered leaving with the Captain but that would only turn the hall into a storm of speculation about the news. Only Draggar and herself were close enough to hear Helgernon's words.

"Best to speak of it here and not cause a scene."

"Yes, my Queen." He required a moment to choose his words. "An envoy from the the Six Isle Republic just arrived and claims to have gifts for you and the nobility. They are asking for admittance into the hall."

"Six Isles?"

"What are those readers and scribblers doing here?" Draggar hissed. "We have no alliance or war with them."

"What was their reason for coming to Rhezaria?"

"They said they intended to come for the Games but travel was slowed by rough seas. Their leader is with them and he said," Helgernon looked up into the rafters as he tried to recall the exact words, "that he brings a great and unexpected gift for Rhezaria."

"Unexpected is right," Draggar grumbled.

Ritika was intrigued. She had heard of this faction that had broken away from Strakos to create their own kingdom, but had never met anyone from these distant lands. They were said to be great intellectuals with more written documents than any other kingdom in Rua.

"Have you searched them for weapons?" asked Ritika.

"Yes, the few soldiers they have do bear weapons but they seem to have only been needed to defend the ships during the voyage. We searched the gifts they brought and found no sign of treachery."

Draggar's curiosity was also piqued. "What did they bring?"

The guard gave a fleeting smile. "Well, they brought one hundred bottles of their finest wine, in honor of Rhezaria's Champions."

Ritika watched her general's eyes open wide. "My mind is made up. I say send them in."

Helgernon waited for Ritika's response. Everyone would undoubtably find the guests fascinating and enjoy the gifts, but why would the leader of the Six Isles travel across Rua without first sending word? Ritika sensed this arrival had more meaning than she could presently discern.

"You can send them in, Helgernon. Stand ready in case anything else unexpected occurs."

Draggar's face lit up. "A bold decision but I, for one, am curious to see how it plays out."

Ritika took a sip of wine. Perhaps it was also her curiosity that had powered her judgement. She took a knife from dinner and clanged it against the cup to gain the attention of the hall. After several moments, the various conversations and chatter quieted as all eyes focused on their Queen.

Ritika stood to address the crowd. "I would like to congratulate the Champions on their performance in the Games, as well as the exemplary conduct of all the peoples of Rhezaria during this time of celebration." A cheer went up along with the swish of liquid. "It has recently come to my attention that some unexpected guests also wish to pay tribute to Rhezaria and the Champions. Our esteemed guests have traversed dangerous waters to journey here, and only just arrived, so I would not do them the dishonor of missing this great feast." Helgernon's head poked through the doorway and he gave Ritika a nod. "This royal envoy hails from the Six Isle Republic and today marks the first official meeting of our two kingdoms. I am uncertain as to how long our guests will be staying in Rhezaria, but let us show them every hospitality while they remain in our care."

The hall exploded into a low rumble of whispered conjecture. Perhaps it was the wine, but Ritika allowed herself a smile, a rare pleasure, and one she found to be fiendishly enjoyable—to reverse the tables by catching the nobles unprepared.

The heavy doors of the hall opened wide causing Reyner and Luka's entourage to scramble out of the way of the procession. A clamp of boots preluded the envoy's entrance. Stiffly marching guards of the Republic entered the hall in rows of four. A long sword hung from the hip of each guard and a crossbow was held in the crook of the right arm. No bolts were knocked within the crossbows and the guards did not carry any. Ritika, like most of the crowd, peered intently at the metal bows. The Six Isle Republic was the only nation that knew the secret to their construction and kept it carefully guarded.

Following the several rows of armed guards were others who carried chests containing what must be the aforementioned gifts. Next entered what Ritika considered to be the nobles. These men and women were dressed in rich colors indicating their high standing.

Most of the men were short of stature and portly and some wore spectacles. Ritika noticed that many of them had discolorations on their fingers from ink. Draggar made the same observations as he muttered with some distaste, "scholars." The women were about the same age as Ritika's mother and carried themselves with quiet confidence. The procession lined up in front of the head table and a man in crimson and black smoothly made his way to the center. The entourage placed their right hands over their hearts and bowed to Ritika.

"Guests, your arrival is unexpected but not unwelcome. We have heard of your Republic but only by second-hand accounts, as it lies such a great distance away from our kingdom. Why have you made such a long and dangerous journey to Draccar?"

The man in crimson and black gave Ritika a wide, sincere smile. His hair was jet black and he kept a goatee like some of the soldiers. Ritika noticed that he was younger and taller than the other nobles. She was curious to see if he knew that to address her in any tongue other than Hokrail was a monumental insult, a mistake that would force his immediate eviction from Anselmbao.

"Gracious Queen Dracarion," he said in a warm voice, his command of Hokrail impeccable. "I am Jai Alvarros, Chancellor of the Six Isle Republic, and I humbly thank you for your hospitality." He spoke in a voice loud enough for everyone to hear, his tone comfortable and relaxed as if he was amongst old friends. "I will explain our reason for travel in due time, but first I would like to present our honored hosts with their gifts. Do not presume us to be rude or misleading but we have carried these gifts a great way and fought off marauders along the Sunken Coast, then nearly lost the chests when our ship almost capsized during a storm. In the Six Isles it is customary to first exchange gifts as a token of goodwill before conversing on business, but to be honest I would be happy to get them out of my care before any other misfortune falls upon them."

Ritika wondered how much of the story was true. "Chancellor Alvarros, it is customary in Rhezaria to agree on what business is being discussed before gifts are accepted. I do not want my hospitality to allow you to assume that any agreements will be made."

The Chancellor was unfazed. "A most understandable position Queen Dracarion. I make no such presumptions, but these gifts are to remain in the possession of your noble chiefs." His tone was jovial but firm. "Business or no business, these gifts are yours. Allow me this one infraction and then there will be no more pomp or ceremony. All questions will be answered in full."

Ritika surveyed her chiefs. All this talk about the gifts likely increased their desire to see their particular prize. She looked back at Chancellor Alvarros and waved a hand. "So be it."

The chests were carried to the five chiefs and set in front of them. The Chancellor calmly strode to the nearest, the Remori, and began to describe the contents. "Chief Akklad, I offer you these knives fashioned from the fangs of a beast washed up on the easternmost island of Strakos, in the hope that they bring you luck on the ever mercurial sea."

The creamy white fangs were quite long and wickedly serrated. They were set into intricately carved metal handles. The three braids in Chief Akklad's red beard swished as he scratched the edge of the blade against a thumb.

Draggar whistled when he saw the gift. "That was one big monster."

"What was it?" asked Ritika.

"Blasted if I know, but I'm glad it's dead!"

"And you're the supposed fish expert, hmm?"

Draggar only glared as a response.

Chancellor Alvarros continued onto the Nataga. "Chief Daro, please accept this exquisite artwork from Nefara that is as beautiful as it is mystifying."

Soren Daro held the frame of the portrait at arms length to view his gift. He looked shocked, then interested, and then strangely calm. The canvas swirled with colors that slowly moved by their own accord without stopping, creating vibrant images that transformed just before comprehension of the design could occur.

Next were the Sando. "Lord Xoatal, your Kon Mountains are the coldest region in all of central Rua. From the finest seamstresses of the Frozen Tribes in the far north I bring clothing of unparalleled warmth and natural beauty."

The quiet Sando chief held coats of supple grey hide trimmed with pure white luxurious fur. He fingered the bone decals embroidered on the sleeves, clearly impressed. By this time Koacachoa had scoured the contents of his chest but had yet to remove them while he listened to the descriptions of the other gifts.

"Chief O'kanhana'etim, for you I present stone birthed from a volcano on the island of Fyn. This turquoise jewelry has none like it as this was the final work of a master craftsman who is now deceased." Koacachoa's grin threatened to burst its seams as he reached into the chest with both hands, lifting out handsome necklaces, rings, armbands, and earrings.

Chief Abi'Ragaz sat with his arms crossed, thin face expectant as no chest was given to him.

"For you Chief Dracarion, I present hounds from the finest bloodline Calanthia has ever produced to assist during hunts." The Chancellor made a sharp whistle that resounded throughout the hall and two large dogs raced in from the corridor to stop at his side. The beasts were enormous, sleek but muscled, with short coarse hair. One was black as night and the other a tan the color of driftwood.

"I don't hunt anymore," said Abi Ragaz, arms still crossed as he scrutinized the dogs. "Was thrown from my horse last summer and shattered my leg."

The Chancellor of the Six Isle Republic stuttered, obviously unaware of this recent injury. "My apologies. The only other gift in my possession is the wine and that is intended for the Champions."

Abi'Ragaz's face was sour, his bald head gleamed. "Such is to be expected for the second born, my line is destined to receive inferior gifts. Give the dogs to my niece, she is a leader and a Rhezi."

The Chancellor abruptly turned on his heel and returned to face Ritika, the dogs following at his side. Ritika looked at the hounds, immediately noting the intelligence in their inquisitive eyes. She transferred her inspection to the Chancellor, his face was relaxed even after the failure with her uncle.

"What say you my Chiefs? Do you approve of these gifts?" Hurrahs went up from other tables. "The gifts were well chosen Chancellor Alvarros, splendors from all the corners of Rua, except for the Shining Empire and your own Republic."

"Queen Dracarion, your intelligence is as astute as reputed. I promised answers and you shall receive them." He paused, portraying a pained expression. "Please accept my apology for not sending word of our arrival. There are many who would be displeased to discover that I am meeting with you. One such individual is Emperor Martinus Anathasius. The Shining Empire aims to bring war to Calanthia and the Emperor will not be satisfied until he has conquered the entire world.

"I believe that he would have attempted to stop our meeting by any means necessary, so you can see why we bear no gifts from the Shining Empire. The founders of the Republic could not tolerate the oppression of Strakos so they left to establish their own council and this sentiment remains strong in my people."

Alvarros paused again and for a brief instance looked slightly flustered. Ritika blinked and the composed Chancellor was once again in front of her. "I have brought gifts from all of Rua for the Clans of Rhezaria but for the Queen of Rhezaria I offer the greatest gift in my possession." Jai knelt on one knee. "Ritika Dracarion, I offer my hand in marriage and with it the rule of the Six Isle Republic."

Ritika was too shocked to immediately respond. Absolute silence filled the hall until manifesting into a smothering presence. A hand slammed loudly on a table, breaking the spell, and the hall burst into shouting.

"Silence!" The hall quieted as Ritika fixed Alvarros with an intense look. "A speech about an imaginary threat and a few trinkets are supposed to persuade me? What would I want with a handful of islands on the other side of Rua? There will be no agreement, Chancellor."

Alvarros rose and did not blush or become angry at these remarks. "You are right, the gifts and islands are a paltry offer to the leader of such an impressive kingdom. They are mere baubles, inconsequential tokens; the true value of my offer resides in the knowledge contained within the libraries of the Republic. The warriors of Rhezaria are strong but the Shining Empire is advancing and we cannot afford to doubt the power of Martinus Anathasius. You need the resources of the Six Isles."

Ritika's fingernails dug into her palms. "So you intend to use blackmail and fear to coerce me into extending the protection of Rhezaria. You are either very brave or very stupid but I'm inclined to go with the latter. Rhezarian leaders have killed envoys for far less disrespect than this, perhaps I will feed you to my new hounds. You will wish that the oceans took you to their depths rather than to Rhezaria's shores."

The Chancellor didn't flinch, instead taking a step closer to the head table. Ritika noticed they were nearly of the same height, the Chancellor's eyes only a hair lower than her own.

"Rhezaria's army is large and the Republic's is not, but if Calanthia falls there may be no stopping the Shining Empire. This worry does drive me to seek Rhezaria's aid but it is not my true reason for approaching you in this bold manner. Do you believe in love, Queen Dracarion?"

Ritika's eyes bulged. What was this madman playing at? The Chancellor did not wait for Ritika to respond. He looked into her eyes and matched her fierce gaze with one of tenderness.

"I saw you in a dream and instantly fell in love. I heard tales that your strength was overmatched by your intelligence and beauty, but now I see now these tales are only pale shadows of the truth. Allow me to prove my love so that you may see its sincerity. I would give all that I have to simply stand at your side."

Ritika did not know how to respond, no man had ever told her that he loved her. Not her austere warrior king father, her older brother, or Draggar Vol her gruff general. Not even Garret Tumino. Ritika felt the silence in the hall thinning rapidly so she found the words.

"Love and leadership are like oil and water. You would sacrifice the lives of your nation for love?"

"No, my Queen, it is only love that may save my people. I know there are proper procedures for courtship but there is no time to waste on etiquette."

Ritika peered into the Chancellor's unwavering brown eyes, searching for the weakness that must reside within them. She spoke slowly, as if they were alone in the room and not surrounded by hundreds of onlookers watching in rapt attention.

"You are mad to travel here and proclaim your love but you are the most well-spoken madman I have met." She stared out at the shocked faces of nobility. Reyner Vol looked like he wanted nothing more than to wring the life out of Alvarros. "I am curious to see which of your words, if any, have truth to them. Truth is found in action. You may stay, but your actions will be tested and I alone will be the judge. Know that if you choose to remain here that I will decide the fate of your life as well as the fate of your Republic."

Jai stood straight and proud. "I will remain."

Grumbles of protest diffused but no one interrupted Ritika to voice their complaints directly.

"As you wish, Chancellor, your life is now in my hands. Seeing as you missed the Games, I will allow you to witness them firsthand. You will face three Champions of my choosing and if you are still alive afterward we may speak again. Until then you will receive instructions from General Vol."

"My thanks, Queen Dracarion. We will retire to our camp outside of the city."

The Chancellor bowed and turned to leave, the retinue following in his wake. An older man in a maroon doublet looked around nervously and did not seem to realize that his leader was leaving.

Draggar called out to him. "You there, word scribbler, what about the wine I was told you brought?" The Republic noble came to his senses at this call and grabbed a nearby guard. A few moments later several guards retrieved five cases filled with twenty bottles each.

"Pass me a bottle would you? I could use a drink after all that." Draggar took two bottles from the guard. "Might as well pass them all out, nobody will be able to sleep after that performance."

Ritika left her seat, using her private exit to enter the royal hallway. A cacophony of shouting voices echoed from the dining hall.

She walked briskly to her chambers, only noticing the hounds when arriving at her personal chambers, where she commanded them to stay. They sat on the floor on either side of the door and appeared to be content.

"My most successful Games yet; not one issue with the Clans." Ritika leaned against the door and began to chuckle, her laughter escalating until verging on hysterical.

## The Serpent

Early morning light was just peeking above the eastern gate as Melea rode through, leaving the walled city behind her. The dun mare kicked up small clouds of dust as Melea urged it into a gallop. Conflicting emotions prompted Melea to push the mare as fast as it could go. The speed and power of the horse was exhilarating.

 A thin cloud of dust trailed their passage before sinking back down between the stones of the road to become dormant once more. The rush of the wind against her face and the warming rays of the sun did their part to distract and delight. Melea leaned forward in the saddle, the strength of the horse making anything seem possible.

 The sun grew larger and hotter as Melea raced toward it, losing herself in the steady pace of the horse's hooves and snorting breath. The mare was in peak physical condition and had been well trained, hardly needing Melea's commands at all. That was fine with her, she was content to point it south-easterly and let it thunder down the ancient road known as the Serpent.

 Before leaving, Melea had consulted with Goldwin, her geography tutor. She'd found him in his office, a neatly organized space filled with detailed maps. Goldwin was a large man, big hands and forearms, and a small head that seemed out of proportion for his size.

 "I'm going on an important mission and can't tell you anything about it," was her introduction.

 "So, the usual," Goldwin rumbled in his deep drawl. "Which direction?"

 "South, deep south."

 "By land? Seas are ideal for travel during this time of season. Viktair Garrengar set out into the ocean that came to bear his name around this time and—"

 "Land."

 Goldwin had a habit of giving more information than necessary.

 "Not a good time for that, talk of war in the air, you know." Goldwin mused. "If you must travel by land then speed is essential. Take the Serpent. Goes south through the Pass, straight through Marikal, and into Cheton."

 "Through Marikal?"

 "Yes, a busy place. Looks suspicious if you go around. They question all who do and bypassing the checkpoints would add another week. Higher chance of bandits on the smaller roads, besides you wouldn't want to deal with the mud after a downpour. Serpent is the only continuous stone roadway."

 "What's longer—the road or your description?"

 Goldwin was unfazed. "Longest road in the world, composed of irregular shapes and sizes that fit perfectly together; no gaps or breaks anywhere. Thousands and thousands of individual scales custom fit to match every curve of the Serpent's length. The world changes around the Serpent, while it remains as solid and true as when the final stone was laid."

"What of Cheton?"

"Hmm? Oh, the floating city. They say it only floats atop the water because the law decrees that it must."

"What does that mean?"

"You'll see," Goldwin said with a chuckle. "The first settlers in Strakos—"

Melea left before being subjected to more ponderous details.

She traveled light, her pack loaded only with food and camping gear. A scroll stamped with the Emperor's seal was stashed in her cloak, the parchment pressed tight against the tiny protrusion of the seed hidden in her undershirt. The shirt containing the seed was stained and torn but Melea had been unable to leave it behind, instead choosing to wear a finer garment overtop.

Her freshly oiled leather boots were given a liquid sheen by the glaring sun. Huge white clouds moved slowly across the blue sky, only temporarily blocking the sun before continuing on their way.

The Serpent shot out east to the edge of the Eternal Forest, then south through the Chuku Bartha Pass before crossing the boundary into Calanthia. Melea found it peculiar having to cross the entirety of a nation she would soon be at war with. *If one is to be victorious one must have contingencies for every conceivable possibility as well as be able to compel the enemy into choosing the option you desire*, as General Cathair, the Emperor's top strategist, had explained to Melea years ago. There was more to war than the clash on the battlefield.

Morokko Kachina was supposed to have made arrangements for her to pass safely through Marikal. Melea could guess how the assassin had made these arrangements and hoped she would not have to speak with the vile man. Kachina always seemed to be watching her with a hungry look, a concealed desire more disconcerting than the normally dead stare in his eyes.

After Marikal, the Serpent meandered across Strakos, traversing the many bogs and marshlands that stretched from the Sunken Coast to Cheton. Melea calculated that the journey would take a month round trip to complete. One young girl traveling alone was not going to raise any suspicions. Few, if any, within Calanthia and Strakos, knew her identity.

She slowed the mare's pace to a comfortable trot once Azra was no longer visible behind her. Melea felt her shoulders loosen up, unaware of the tension constricting them until this point. The road stretched out through farmland as far as the eye could see. Golden fields of wheat waved in the wind between tall patches of corn and mounds of potatoes set in organized rows. Stones passed beneath the mare's smooth stride, swallowing up the distance as if horse and rider were floating. For a moment Melea felt between events in her life, a brief interlude where time and action had no effect. She was on her own, able to move freely without the constraint of sending reports. Better yet, Melea did not have to pretend to be somebody else, because this was a companionless mission.

Inside, Melea knew it was not independence, that the notion was only a fantasy. Her journey had a directed purpose and was not merely a joy ride to the floating city. The distance covered by the horse's hooves could never exonerate her past, but the moment of respite was needed. She relished the solitary responsibility, taking it as an indication that the order of her world was reset, that she could go back to how things had been in the past.

She stopped her mind from wandering into unwanted territory; any thoughts concerning Gerboa's fate. The circumstances regarding Gerboa and the Sanctuary were confusing but she could leave them behind, remnants of her past like so much else in her life, debris that would eventually be forgotten completely.

Melea rode until dusk before making camp in the lee of a rocky outcropping on the side of a hill. A small stream provided water for the horse and Melea gave the mare a few pats of respect for a good day's work. She tethered the horse nearby, removing the saddle and gear to give it a rub down with a coarse brush while it munched on tall green grass.

The night was warm so she decided to forego making a fire, choosing to eat a cold supper of bread and cheese. She rolled out the bedroll and stretched out under the stars. Sleep soon claimed her and she slept soundly for what felt like the first time in years. She was up before dawn and decided to skip breakfast; the road was calling.

Patches of long yellow beans and plump red tomatoes interspersed fields of wheat, corn, and potato; stretching out on either side of the road, and arranged into rectangular sections. The fields looked healthy and the crops were nearly ready to be harvested. As Melea helped herself to the vegetables, she wondered how much food would be coming with the army when it marched down this road in a month's time.

The people of the Shining Empire would not starve due to the army's voracious appetite. The actions of the priests working on these farms guaranteed multiple harvests to feed the Empire's ever growing number of stomachs.

She passed several farming villages, communities where the tallest building had two levels and the people went without shoes. The words of the curmudgeonly group from the tavern of the Black Lotus sprang to mind: *Everyone clings to their patch of dirt hoping to pull something out of it, or build something on top of it, before being laid to rest underneath it.*

By nightfall she was into an area of rolling hills and the sea of crops was replaced by herds of grazing livestock. Melea's eyes closed to the sounds of bleating sheep and mooing cattle in the distance. There was a peacefulness in the noises of the animals, a sense of distance conveyed by the travel of their calls. Crickets chirped out their love songs in the tall grass, unconcerned by the prospect of war.

As the air chilled, the hum of mosquitos displaced the comforting sounds. The bloodsuckers tormented her all night, forcing her to pull the blanket over her face to create a protective cocoon. The pests were relentless in their pursuit, finding tiny openings to gain access to her skin. At one point it seemed as if though there were enough thrumming mosquitos on top of the blanket to lift it up and carry her away.

By mid-afternoon of the third day she reached the Chuku Bartha Pass. The area was the only open stretch of land between the Eternal Forest and the western coast. Few chose to live in the area as they were afraid of the beasts that lived in the forest. Those who did live here were so poor that they had nowhere else to go.

The Pass was named after the ape men who dwelled inside the forest. Their name, Chuku Bartha, derived from the rough barking sound they commonly made. Melea could not recall ever seeing one of the ape men, but that was to be expected as they only lived in areas people tended avoid. The Eternal Forest was such a place. Over the centuries different groups of settlers had tried to encroach into the forest but each met with disaster. Those who avoided a grisly end ran for their lives, spreading tales of man-eating monsters and a living forest bent on consuming all who entered.

The Serpent curved in close to the forest, a barren strip of land separating the two as if a pact had been agreed upon. Melea peered across the expanse at the dense wall of green, wondering if anything was looking back. The Chuku Bartha Pass was a favorite spot of ambush for raiders from the Outskirts. The heavily laden carriages traveling between the Shining Empire and Calanthia were too tempting to pass up.

She glanced up at the sky, dark clouds were building and the wind had been rising all afternoon. There was not much for cover in the Pass, not much of anything really, and in this section there was an absence of farmhouses as well. She decided to push onward as far as she could before the storm hit, hoping to find a decent spot to weather the rain and wind.

A brilliant flash and booming thunderclap came sooner than expected, spooking the mare. Melea stroked the mare's neck as it whinnied. The sky had gone black and Melea felt uncomfortably exposed on the stone roadway. Lightning flashed again, instantly followed by the boom of thunder. The clouds opened, releasing sheets of rain like a volley of arrows.

She placed her hood over her head and sat still in the saddle, deciding what to do as a veil of water streamed in front of her face. A lack of shelter behind her and none in the vicinity so she continued forward at walk. The mare's hooves skittered on the wet stones every time the lightning was too close but Melea kept her under control. The wind howled as the last of the light seeped away. Violent gusts pushed and pulled at her as if they were unhappy with her remaining vertical. The mare stamped a hoof and snorted in dissatisfaction with the situation but continued forward when Melea kicked her heels into its sides. The pounding rain finally forced her to dismount. She led the mare along the road while the swirling wind tossed rain and debris in her face.

Ishtanvor and the Gate of Asyrith were further south, likely a half-day's travel. No sense in wandering aimlessly off to the west in the hope of finding a farmhouse. She knew the forest was directly east, she could enter the fringe and hunker down for the night. The soaked foliage would not offer any warmth but at least she would be out of the wind. Melea stepped off the road and started toward the forest, slipping with every step on slick grass that was quickly turning into mud. The mare followed obediently until they reached the tree line.

A fortress of black, darker even than the night, barricaded the way. The trunks of mighty oaks stood as still as sentries, protecting the outer wall against intruders. Twigs and pine needles crunched underfoot as outstretched branches scratched at Melea's face. She walked with one hand out in front with the mare snapping off branches behind.

Finally, they entered far enough into the forest to be out of the gusting wind. Branches whipped back and forth violently overheard but the melee was less severe at ground level. Melea squatted beneath the sweeping boughs of a massive fir. Most of the rain was blocked by the branches and the droplets that made it through dripped softly into the soil. She was tired—this was far enough. She tied the mare to a thick branch and sat down near the base of the trunk, rubbing her icy hands together and wishing she had something dry to burn.

The storm continued all night, content to have a party, or a tantrum, without regard for Melea's desire for sleep. Flashes of light emerged from deeper in the forest, seemingly excited to join the fray, matching the intensity of the occasional bursts of lightning. Glowing balls of orange and red moved about in the forest canopy, quickly leaping from place to place.

The action looked as though fireballs were being tossed about in a reckless game of catch. A thin trail of light trailed the fireballs each time they moved to a new location. Melea watched the flames in fascination until they were gone completely, leaving her alone in rain.

Several hours before dawn the storm ended, allowing the forest to attain a sense of profound stillness. The trees seemed to relax with a collective inhale and bask in the undisturbed freshness brought by the rainfall. Melea nodded off during this moment of quietude but true sleep was elusive, leaving her feeling even more exhausted when the sun finally appeared.

She groaned and stretched her aching body, trying to limber up cold joints for the day ahead. The movement helped her muscles but not her mood. She knew she was alive, but her body felt dead. Her strange double lives were merging. *Great*, thought Melea.

She untied the mare and started for the tree line. No monsters lunged out and neither did the forest attempt to swallow her up. Apparently, even monsters were respectful enough to avoid disturbing the stillness of the morning. Melea rubbed her eyes as she pushed past the final branch and into the sunlight. The mare stepped anxiously and huffed.

Ten meters away from Melea stood a naked man holding a spear. His dusky skin bordering on blue. The man's body was covered in tufts of grey hair which grew longest from thick patches on his elbows. He had a wide face and flat nose with deep set black eyes. Purple markings were painted across his cheeks and forehead. He studied Melea carefully, and she noted the appraising look in his eyes. She knew the look; he was deciding if Melea was worth the trouble.

He tilted his head back to let out a loud warbling howl. Several more howls within the forest echoed a few moments later. A decision had been reached.

The pitch of the howl stirred something inside of Melea, something primal and forgotten. She instinctively knew the call was meant to bring reinforcements and that the man had no intention of letting her escape. The sound also brought a realization that should have occurred immediately—this was no man. Melea stared at the Chuku Bartha as he stared back, apparently content to wait for his comrades. She knew little about the ape men except for the legends of them stealing unsupervised children and raising them as their own in the forest. This particular Chuku Bartha might have such a plan in mind, but from the way he gripped the spear it seemed unlikely.

Her throwing knives were on her hip, her sword attached to the saddlebag. Her gauntlet with the poison darts was stored away with the rest of the gear. Melea wanted to leap onto the horse and ride away, but doing so would give the ape man a free shot at her with his spear. She could fight him but would have to let go of the mare and the frightened horse would bolt. But she definitely could not wait around for the others, who were no doubt getting closer with each passing moment.

"Get out of my way hairy," she said. "Shoo, move along."

He stared back impassively.

"Go!"

The Chuku Bartha raised an arm slowly, palm cupped and facing the sky. He made a clucking, growling sound that could have been, "chuku bartha." The words, if they were words, meant nothing to Melea but the ape man stared at her as if they should.

Melea repeated the gesture but jarringly and in a mocking fashion. "Chuku Bartha," she said in her best impersonation.

The ape man smiled, showing wide teeth framed by two sharp fangs.

"Now that we've said hello, it's time for me to get out of here," she said.

Melea moved to climb into the saddle. He howled and bared his teeth as he sprinted across the separating distance. She reached for the two knives on her hip while keeping the reins secure in her right hand.

The mare spooked and reared up on her hind-feet. Melea found the throwing knives and snapped them at Chuku Bartha. He sidestepped the projectiles and was nearly on top of her before she could swing herself properly into the saddle. The mare took off with an outraged snort.

Melea hung on to the terrified animal's neck, struggling to wriggle her way into the saddle. The horse leapt over the road, its back hooves knocking against the stone with a loud crack. The mare kept going, trying to place as much distance as it could between itself and the wild beast that had attacked it.

Melea clung to the mare until it slowed enough for her to regain control. For the next few hours she stayed parallel to the road on the western side, nearer to the coast, feeling safer with the Serpent between her and the Eternal Forest. Logic dictated that the road could not stop any attacks, but the sense of having a barrier eased Melea's nerves, which in turn soothed the skittish mare.

The Chuku Bartha did not pursue her so she rode in solitude for the rest of the morning. Around noon she passed a wiry farmer and his young son, digging at a patch of dirt with a hoe, but neither party exchanged words of greeting. A mangy dog barked its displeasure at Melea's arrival from the boy's side. The farmer eyed her suspiciously. She glanced over her shoulder and saw the farmer still watching her even though the dog's barking ceased. His form grew smaller in the distance until it disappeared completely.

Melea continued into the afternoon without any further encounters. The Serpent should have been far busier. The border between the Shining Empire and Calanthia was not officially closed, but few merchants dared to take the risk of being trapped on the wrong side should hostilities suddenly erupt. The quiet was fine with Melea except that every snap of a twig or rustle near the forest caused her to swivel her attention to the Eternal Forest. She was becoming paranoid of being followed.

Melea's paranoia grew as the adrenaline from the Chuku Bartha encounter was replaced by the exhaustion of a freezing night with no sleep. The swaying movement of the mare rocked Melea into inattentive lulls where she would burst back into awareness at the flutter of a bird's wings or the scurrying of squirrels as they stashed nuts in locations that only squirrels remember.

She tried chewing on a chunk of beef jerky to keep herself awake. The activity kept her going for a short time but the bit of food created a rumble of hunger in her stomach. Weariness seeped into her bones, slowly forcing her eyelids closed for longer and longer periods of time.

A persistent shiver that had clung to her since the storm only compounded the effects of sleeplessness and a growling hunger, eventually forcing her to dismount. She sparked a small fire from tufts of grass and a jumble of twigs, her body hungrily soaking up the heat. Lunch consisted of a couple of roasted potatoes. The warmth and the food did wonders for her body, and Melea felt that she was back where she wanted to be. The only problem was getting back on the horse.

Heavy limbs and drooping eyelids argued against Melea's logic that the distance from the ground to the saddle was much too high. Her logic dictated a truce that was eagerly agreed to—a short nap and then her body could continue. Melea grabbed her short sword from the saddlebag and lay down with it in the crook of her left arm. She was asleep the moment her eyes closed.

Frightened snorts from the mare woke Melea from a dead sleep. Her eyes shot open, hand reaching for the hilt of the sword.

"Easy, syla, I wouldn't do that." The voice was confident and oddly familiar.

Four Chuku Bartha stood in front of Melea, still as ominous statues in their grey-blue skin. All held spears with flint stone blades and each gazed down at her with impassive eyes. The ape men kept their stony expressions when she sat up, but leveled their spears at her head, ready to attack if she moved again. Melea glared at the Chuku Bartha directly in front of her, the same one she had encountered that morning. He barked some animalistic sounds at her. Melea craned her neck around and saw a man atop her horse.

The man wore a flat brimmed hat, shadows obscuring his face. His shirt was black and rumpled and his boots were of a style that was new to Melea. They looked soft and as though they conformed around the contours of his feet. A distinctive cloth belt was the only article with color: thick threads of red, blue, yellow, green, indigo, orange, and violet were placed beside each other in a tight weave.

"My friend here likes you, he wants to know if he can keep the knives you threw at him," said the man seated on her horse.

"What do you want?"

The man shrugged. "A good time, some excitement, a little glory, a little fame, more wealth than I had this morning."

The flippant attitude stoked Melea's ire. "You won't be getting any of that from me. Get off my horse before I hurt you and tell the ape man to give my knives back."

The man chuckled. "You're a feisty one, that's for sure." A figure stepped beside the horse—another man. This one with long hair in a pony tail. He wore baggy brown pants and a brown vest over a white shirt. His boots appeared to be of the same odd style and the end of a colorful belt drooped down to his thigh. The second man smacked his leg as he looked at Melea.

"The Lightning Bolt! I remember where she's from, did you, brother? She started quite the ruckus, if I recall."

"Seems to be in her nature. How could I forget one as beautiful as her?"

She suddenly recognized the two bandits. These were the two men from the Outskirts that had started the brawl in the Lightning Bolt tavern. The one with the hat had spilled his drink on Melea's head. His name eluded her but she remembered the arrogant look on his face. He had kissed her and then escaped into the night. Her anger flamed white-hot. She leapt to her feet and swept the sword out of its sheath to block the incoming spear points.

The Chuku Bartha came at her from all sides. They were cautious and appeared to only want to contain, not to kill. The two men from the Outskirts watched the scene unfold. She lunged at the Chuku Bartha between her and the bandits, knocking a spear aside and following it up with a punch to the ape man's jaw. The Chuku Bartha went staggering backward as Melea sprang through the opening toward the men.

Two of the ape men rushed her from each side while another followed closely behind. Melea grabbed the wooden shaft of the spear on the right and spun swiftly into the Chuku Bartha, delivering a smash to his temple with the hilt of her sword. The ape man slumped to the ground. The other two advanced together, once more between her and the bandits.

Melea attacked with fervor, her sword a blur of movement as she put the ape men on their heels. They knew how to fight, but their footwork was no match for Melea's, the one benefit of putting up with Derclerq's pompousness.

She stepped between them, ducking as one ape man jabbed his spear at her, only to impale the shoulder of his comrade. The wounded Chuku Bartha yelped and Melea kicked out his leg, sending him to the ground. She spun around to deliver a fist to the other ape man's stomach followed with a smash to the back of his neck with the pommel of her sword. Melea stepped past them, striding toward the men from the Outskirts, who were still casually watching.

The man on the horse twitched his wrist and kicked his heels into the side of the horse to make it back up. Only then did she notice the length of rope in his hand go taught. The rope that was now looped around her ankle.

Melea's feet flew up from under her as she slammed onto her back. She retained her grip on the sword and moved to chop the rope securing her but a second loop drifted over her head, tightening around her neck. The man on the ground pulled hard on the rope and quickly ran around behind her as the man on the horse continued to retreat, stretching Melea out from both ends. Melea's eyes rolled as her head was snapped back. She tried to swing her sword at the rope around her neck but a crack on the wrist from a Chuku Bartha spear knocked the sword loose.

The Chuku Bartha expertly looped ropes around her wrists and other foot and pulled them taught. Melea was completely suspended by the tension of the ropes. She seethed at her capture. Energy churned within her chest, begging to be released.

"Easy now! Don't hurt her!" shouted the man on Melea's mare.

The comment temporarily stalled the burgeoning destructive energy within Melea. They had won. Why would they stop now?

"We only want to talk to you, syla. You won't be harmed if you can stop yourself from attacking for a moment."

The others waited for a response but Melea was unable to speak because of the snug rope around her neck. The man on the horse realized what was going on.

"Dacre, slacken your line so she can talk, no need to strangle her."

The rope around her neck loosened enough for Melea to move her jaw and neck.

"Do you yield so that we may talk?" asked the man on the horse.

Melea grunted. "Give my horse back and I won't kill you."

"That's not exactly the answer I was looking for," said the man as he rubbed his chin.

Melea felt energy building, the air in her lungs was hot, like it was turning into steam before it could be released. The ropes around her wrists began to sizzle, a slight crackling sound like butter frying in a hot pan. The Chuku Bartha holding the ropes made excited noises, apparently reaching an agreement as they dropped the ropes in unison and bolted. They picked up their unconscious comrade and carried him away, moving swiftly toward the refuge of the forest. Melea jumped at the opportunity for freedom. She snapped the ropes attached to her wrists forward like whips.

One rope made contact with the man on the horse, knocking his hat off as he shouted in alarm. The rope around Melea's neck cinched up, constricting her windpipe. Melea was dragged backward along the ground, the back of her head bumping hard on the tip of rock protruding from the soil.

"Stop! You can have your horse back." The now hatless man dismounted and dropped the rope that was secured around Melea's ankle. "Let her go, Dacre."

"Not sure if that's a good idea, brother," said the owner of the voice reefing on Melea's neck.

"She won't kill us, this isn't how I die."

"That's fine for you, but what about me?"

Silence followed, and then the pressure around Melea's neck lessened as Dacre let go of the rope. Melea pulled the noose away and sat up, glaring at the man in front of her. He raised his hands slightly in supplication before returning to a relaxed posture. The steadiness of his gaze and the certainty of his statement piqued Melea's interest but she still wanted to pulverize his face. She pulled the loops of rope off her wrists and ankles before getting up.

"I could kill you right now in any number of ways," she said evenly.

"No, you can't." Again with an assuredness that belied the situation.

"I'll have to show you a few ways I've thought of."

"Taisto, I don't think she's joking," said Dacre behind her.

Melea snapped her head around to face him, trying to intimidate with her glare, but Dacre simply watched her like a threat he was trying to avoid but would engage if needed. These two would not go down without a fight. Despite their youth, they appeared to be experienced in combat. Melea faced Taisto.

They stood there for a moment, just staring at each other. Without his hat Melea could see how young the bandit was, in fact he was probably not that much older than she was. Likely was not able to even grow a full beard yet.

"You won't kill me if you're a woman of your word—here's your horse."

Taisto smacked the mare on the rump to make it trot over to Melea. The horse nickered as Melea grabbed the bridle, seemingly tired of this debacle. Her eyes narrowed into two green slits. She was out of daggers but her eyes shot them at Taisto nonetheless.

"Since when do Outskirts bandits return what they've stolen?"

"When they've made a mistake by taking from those who need it more than they do. We could use another horse but you obviously need it more. It would take you much longer to run away without this fine mare."

"Why do you say I'm running away?"

Taisto smirked and Melea wanted to smack the look off his face. "I come from a people who survive by fleeing, who have run to the only corner of Rua that will hide them. I know a runaway when I see one."

Anger boiled in her gut but the intensity of it was rapidly fading away. Taisto leaned down to pick up his hat, dusting it off before placing it on his head. Melea considered her options. These two deserved a beating for the trouble they caused her and she could give it to them, but she was tired, and hungry, and had lost enough time already. She shot Taisto a nasty look, and Dacre as well, before hoisting herself into the saddle. No sense in wasting more time. Melea gave the mare a kick and turned to the road.

"It's not out there," Taisto shouted.

"What would you know?"

"Whatever you're looking for. Believe me. My brother and I have traveled much of this world and have seen wild things, wilder even than you, and we haven't found it yet."

Melea flipped him the middle finger without looking back. She heard Dacre laugh, smacking his thigh as he hooted. The mare's hooves clacked against the stone of the Serpent. Melea kicked it into a canter, speeding away from the bandit brothers, focused on reaching Cheton and delivering the Emperor's message.

## A Shepherd and His Flock

Belenus crumpled the paper between his palms. He felt like spitting, like shouting in rage, or pounding his fists and breaking something beneath their force, but he did none of these things. Instead, he unfolded the crinkled paper and read the last line again.

*Keep the bitch on a leash.*
*Kronus Pompae, High Priest of the Sanctuary*

The arrogant prick. Pompae had the audacity to sign the letter with his full name and title because he believed himself superior to Belenus. The cretin was a little more than half of Belenus' age, yet he had risen to the pinnacle position within the Sanctuary. Belenus loathed the egotistic leader of the Sanctuary and as a result had not set foot in the temple where he had been trained so many years ago—not since Pompae had attained the seat of power.

Unfortunately, the courtesy had not been returned and Belenus had been forced to feel Pompae's roiling contempt on several occasions when the High Priest of the Sanctuary met with Emperor Anathasius at the palace. Belenus was not included in these meetings. He probably should have used his status as Beacon to be involved in all priestly matters, but he wanted nothing to do with Kronus Pompae. All men were equal in the faith of the Shining Empire but that did not mean Belenus had to like them equally.

Belenus crumpled the letter again, then opened it up to tear the message into tiny pieces. Shreds of paper drifted to the floor to settle in a small pile. Belenus kicked the pile, sending bits of paper scattering across the room. He felt a little better.

How was he supposed to control that assassin girl? She answered only to the Emperor, which normally was fine, but now she had interfered with the priests of the Sanctuary. The priests were used to their secluded lifestyle and regarded all members of the Palace of Light as one entity. Melea was lumped in with Belenus even though they had hardly exchanged words. He was a shepherd, yet he shared the same halls with a wolf.

What was she doing over there anyway? Pompae's letter stated that they found her in the abandoned shrine, a structure that was sealed ages before Belenus' time at the Sanctuary.

That blasted girl, muddying up the order of things. The Emperor was lax on her faith studies, allowing her to prowl around like a domesticated cat, by all appearances harmless, until natural predatory instincts took over.

Belenus clenched his fists together, raised them to his chest, and did an angry little dance. He lowered his hands to smooth out the bunched wrinkles in the robe, slicked back his scraggly hair, which immediately sprang back up to stick out at all angles. He should talk to this girl, find out what she was doing there.

She was an odd case, arriving at the palace one day without explanation—wild and unmanageable. The child was a terror who constantly needed to be restrained by guards, oftentimes taking the combined effort of several strong men to calm her. Belenus was never asked to instruct her on any matter, as Emperor Anathasius did so himself. The Emperor showed Melea more attention than any other individual Belenus could recall.

A rumor claimed she was his daughter and the mother was dead, but Belenus did not believe such things. The girl looked nothing like the Emperor and taking her on as a pupil was different than displaying love to a daughter. Emperor Martinus Anathasius was eternal, a paragon of Light sent to vanquish Darkness, he had no need for an heir.

Belenus never questioned the Emperor about Melea's arrival or lack of tutoring from the priesthood but he had brought up the peculiar ability apparent in the girl. Melea could enact the Emperor's Gift without drawing blood. An act that Belenus found to be profoundly disturbing because it placed the mysterious girl somewhere between the priests and the Emperor himself. When asked, Emperor Anathasius had said, "She is a manifestation of my vision brought to aid in the struggle against our enemies." The response was beyond reproach.

The Emperor may be infallible but irksome Melea was not. Belenus left his chambers to find the palace attendant, the man knew all of the happenings within the Palace of Light and would know the location of the assassin girl. The Beacon of Azra was not going to wander around like a lost puppy.

As there was no public address or ceremony scheduled for the day, Belenus decided to wear an old robe from before his time as Beacon. The color was starting to fade, turning more grey than white, but the material was soft and less constrictive than his official attire. His slippers scraped the floor as he went in search of the attendant.

The attendant was a thin, well groomed man who gave the perception that he had never had an idea of his own. He was polite and his skills were polished but his own thoughts were never voiced. The man was well seasoned, having been in the palace for many years now, but Belenus was having difficulty remembering his name. Belenus wondered if it was because he was getting old or that the attendant was completely forgettable.

He found the attendant in the main entry hall in his normal state of attentiveness.

"Beacon Wicket, how may I be of service?"

"Just Belenus will do. I need you to tell me the whereabouts of Melea, I would like to speak to her."

The attendant's face squirmed as he looked uncomfortable about giving unwanted news. "I regret to inform you that she has left the palace and I do not know when she will return. She left on horseback."

*Riding off to disrupt someone else's day no doubt.* "Thank you my good man, that will be all."

The attendant shuffled off and the priest started in the other direction. Belenus wondered if he should pursue the girl's destination when a name burst into his head. The attendant was already at the end of the hall but Belenus called out to him anyway.

"Goodbye, Hector!"

Hector smiled, or at least Belenus thought so, as he squinted and waved before disappearing around a corner. Belenus continued walking, his joints were feeling good today and he was enjoying the reprieve from his ailments. He looked over both shoulders to make sure no one was watching before running a few strides as fast as his skinny legs could take him. The robe swished around knobby knees as he returned to a walking pace, his heart beating vigorously as a few drips of sweat beaded down his armpits to trickle across ribs. Belenus smiled to himself, the previous anger forgotten.

The smile slowly faded as Belenus realized that he had nothing to do today. No task required his attention, no group needed his sermon, no assassin girl was to be found in the palace. He should be busier. This realization was coming to Belenus more and more.

Daily life had been much more hectic several years ago when Belenus oversaw the requirements of the priests in Azra as well as the surrounding area, but that was while he was still putting the structural system in place. The system he designed and implemented could run without him having to constantly check up on his subordinates. Every priest was extremely competent and handpicked. Nowadays, Belenus was only contacted in cases of emergency. He still met with the heads of each division on a monthly basis, to check in and give his input about how things should proceed. The next meeting was still a couple weeks away.

Belenus paused—he could go and check the files of recent activity to see how the priests were carrying out their duties, but that was boring. Adrenaline from the sprint left Belenus feeling energized, antsy, seeking more stimulation. Belenus made his way to the long stairway leading down to the dungeon.

Kerak sat cross-legged on the floor of the cell with his eyes closed as Belenus approached. The shaman opened his eyes and smiled when he saw who was visiting. The smile rattled Belenus, shattering his expectations. He thought the shaman would greet him with a scowl or a rude comment, not with a friendly expression. Maybe Kerak was just desperate for company. Rats and prisoners did not make for the best companions.

"Beacon, it is good to see you," said the shaman.

Belenus was completely thrown off guard. Was the shaman playing at something? He had come down to the dungeon for a fight. He just expected Kerak to be the instigator.

"Your frozen bones finally thaw and let some Light in?"

Kerak smiled again but not as big as before. "My bones and the glacial ice are one and the same. They will not melt for any amount of heat."

"Figured it was too good to be true. Why are you so happy then you old crow? It can't be to see my wrinkled face."

"You and I are not so different," said Kerak.

"Yes, we are."

"We are both men of ability, the voices of our people, and yet we are both caged. We both choose to be imprisoned, we have offered ourselves up in the belief that our sacrifice will be of benefit to the people."

Belenus wondered what the shaman was getting at. How could his situation be helping the Frozen Tribes? The fool's actions on the Skar had hurt his people's reputation, and sitting in a dungeon helped no one. Belenus dedicated his life to serving the Shining Empire in the priesthood, which could perhaps be construed as a form of sacrifice. He could not take a wife or have a family; the price of accepting the Emperor's Gift.

Kerak was mistaken though, Belenus was not the one behind bars, in fact he had too much free time on his hands. Time was a very different reality for Kerak. For him it was a pit that he could not escape, a chasm that was slowly swallowing his hopes and dreams. Belenus almost pitied the man's captive state but Kerak only had himself to blame.

"Some sacrifices are more beneficial than others," said Belenus.

Kerak nodded in agreement. "This is true, but knowing which one will have the greatest effect is never decided in the present. Those who will come after us will look back and know."

"What will the histories say of you, Kerak? Will you be an ally and honored disciple or a rebellious unbeliever and nuisance?"

The shaman shrugged before getting up to stand level with the priest. "That is not for me to decide. I will act as I must and it will be written. I am more concerned with what manner my story will be told, in how it will be shared around the fire from elder to child. I would prefer my name added to the song of my people rather than shouted from the podium to the masses as a warning."

"I'm inclined to never mention your name in public again. The world will be better off for it, and a Beacon does not shout to the people, he speaks with them," said Belenus.

"I wonder if you understand the difference," Kerak said as he looked past the priest.

"I understand that the Frozen Tribes are now part of the Shining Empire, that they are without their voice, that their old crow has the power to aid them in this time of transition but he is too arrogant to put their lives before his pride. The Frozen Tribes will now be granted the safety from nature that comes with cities and the light that they bring."

"Is that so?" Kerak said glibly. "Separating oneself from nature is impossible, so I fail to see how this can be achieved for an entire community."

Belenus felt his ears growing hot. "Your pride and blind faith will be the death of you. This self sacrifice is meaningless. You'd help more people if you weren't so pigheaded."

Kerak smiled wide, then burst out laughing, his head tilting back as he roared. Belenus paused, stunned for a moment, all worked up with anger, but the shaman's laughter was infectious. A chuckle escaped and soon he was laughing along with Kerak.

"You crazy bugger," Belenus muttered between laughs.

Kerak wiped tears from his eyes as he finally stopped laughing. Belenus thought he could see a weight dissipate from the shaman's shoulders. He stood straighter than before, more comfortable and relaxed, even though his predicament remained the same. Kerak looked at Belenus with something close to friendship, a moment of silent kindness that only lasted the length of time it took to cross the distance between the two men.

Belenus had a sudden realization that made him erupt into a laughing fit. Kerak watched Belenus curiously, waiting for the joke to be explained.

"It's funny," he said. "I'd rather limp all the way down here to visit with an imprisoned pagan than speak with a certain fellow priest."

Belenus shook his head, pondering the unknowables between people that bring them together or drive them apart. The shaman waited patiently with a knowing look on his stoic face. Belenus had come to the dungeon to argue, but instead he found himself feeling quite comfortable. He wanted to talk about things that had been brewing inside for some time, things he could not share with his brethren.

"I'm bored, Kerak. I'm too old to be out on the frontier anymore, the Empire is stronger than ever, the priesthood is becoming more adept every day, and not even a dissenting shaman shouting from the mountaintops can shake the people's resolve."

A shadow fell over Kerak's eyes as his voice grew serious. "That is an undesirable luxury to have. Are you not the Beacon? Can you not do more?"

Belenus struggled to think of anything. Kerak answered for him. "Help the Frozen Tribes adapt to the Empire's ways."

A light flared to life in the depths of the priest's mind. His experience and skills made him the perfect man to help ease the Frozen Tribes into the Shining Empire. He could stop further bloodshed. It would be exciting. Why was this the first time he'd considered the idea?

He was slipping, not as sharp as he'd once been. The thought skittered through his mind but Belenus refused to acknowledge it. Better to focus on what was needed to reach the Frozen Tribes. He would need to ask Emperor Anathasius to sanction the excursion. Belenus doubted that Kerak would be allowed to return with him.

"What will become of you?"

"That is unimportant. My people must survive and you may be able to help them. They need to be strong; strong enough to withstand the sickness. It spreads more everyday, I used to catch its scent on the southern wind."

Belenus was yet to witness the rumored sickness.

"This foulness consumes all that it touches and, as of right now, it is unstoppable," said Kerak, outraged.

"The Emperor has everything under control."

Shadows covered Kerak's eyes but Belenus could feel the flinty greys staring into him. "The situation is worse than can be explained and the sickness is growing. It's coming for all of us, Beacon."

"You seem pretty certain about that, shaman but there is only one aspect of the sickness which concerns me." Belenus pointed a finger up at the ceiling. "The greatest healer in Rua, a living God who brings life to the dead and dying, is up there. I think we'll be fine."

"Perhaps," said Kerak, looking up at the ceiling. "But the Emperor is an individual, he is only one and the people are many. An individual cannot live forever but a family can last for generations. He should bow before eternity to truly influence the great wheel of life."

Belenus found the Emperor as he exited the stairwell. The exertion of the long climb had overpowered the priest's adrenaline, allowing former aches to resurface.

"Belenus, I'm told you are looking for Melea. Perhaps I may be able to answer for her," greeted Emperor Anathasius. The Emperor wore a simple white tunic with gold trimming and white trousers with light gold sandals.

Belenus limped over, trying to force his leg to find its regular stride. "My Lord," he bowed in respect. "That's not important anymore but I do have something I need to speak with you about."

The Emperor smiled and motioned for Belenus to continue.

"I've been thinking and it makes a lot of sense for me to go north and assist with the integration of the Frozen Tribes. It's been a while since I've been on the frontier but this body still has some punch in it."

"Belenus my friend, you can barely even walk over here, traveling to the northernmost point of the Empire would be quite the challenge. Summer will soon be over, I fear your joints may seize up completely with the first freeze," said the Emperor in a soothing voice.

"Nonsense," Belenus grumbled. "The day you stop rising to life's challenges is the day you become old."

He was about to add that he was an infant compared to Anathasius, but remembered his station. One did not talk to a God in such a manner. He bit back his words and limped alongside the Emperor's smooth gait.

"I know you wish to help, your service to the Shining Empire has been invaluable, particularly to the people of Azra. You cannot go to the newest disciples because the city needs your abilities once again."

Belenus was intrigued, but unable to shake the disgruntled feeling of being denied what he wanted. The emotion was childish and he knew it, he should be overjoyed to help in whichever capacity available. He had let the shaman's words stoke the flames of his bored imagination into an unrealistic dream. All of his life, Belenus had needed to rein in his imagination, which often threatened to undermine reality, to take him away into the unknown, distancing himself from his faith.

"What's this?" he asked.

"War with Calanthia is unavoidable as you know. Their history and ours runs deep, the scars of the past will never be fully healed, scars that mar the reputation of the Shining Empire and sully the name of our faith even though they do not belong to us. Remind the people that the Shining Empire is something new, an ideal that is unconnected to Cambor and all that has come before. Calanthia is unwilling to acknowledge this difference, they cling to the old ways and will attack to halt our growth—it is only a matter of time until they reach this conclusion. Speak to the people as only you can, you are their Beacon, the impetus of faith in their hearts to drive out this unparalleled Darkness."

The Emperor's words made Belenus feel acutely foolish about his earlier request. Yes, helping the newest members of the Empire was important but he could not neglect the core of his flock.

"It would be my honor, your highness," said Belenus. He felt energized again, an inner burn that was more sustainable than the temporary rush felt earlier. "Let me be so bold as to ask that I choose the method of relaying this message to the people."

"Of course," agreed a congenial Anathasius.

"The priests will not fight this war, but they will contribute to its victory. I will recruit every priest within Azra and the surrounding area to march through the streets. The people will see that we are behind them, that they have our support, that after the war they will return to a land in better condition than which they left."

"A wonderful idea, my friend." The Emperor smiled and Belenus reveled in the beatific aura.

The embarrassment in Belenus' chest was replaced with the warmth of veneration. Emperor Anathasius, divine leader of the Shining Empire, a living embodiment of their faith, was willing to place trust in him. To listen to his words and call him friend. Belenus suddenly felt like the awestruck boy he was when his uncle first told him the wondrous story of how Emperor Anathasius liberated the city of Azra.

The inspiration of that moment had never left Belenus, shaping him into a man capable of performing minor miracles of his own. His recent lethargy combined with the letter from Pompae had caused him to forget this source of inspiration, but that very source, Emperor Anathasius, was there to remind him of it, to allow Belenus to share his passion with all of Azra. Belenus looked to the Emperor but the words to describe the sentiment eluded him. The Emperor found the words for his Beacon.

"Remind them, Belenus. Give them the strength to endure this strife so that they may achieve immortality."

Belenus marched confidently at the front of the line. His knee ached painfully from overuse, but he did not care. This was now the fifth time that Belenus had led his fellow priests through Azra's streets to offer support by proclaiming their faith. The people responded so well to the first gathering that Belenus decided to continue until the Chosen left the city. The sounds of inspiration would carry them forward as if their armor was weightless.

The importance of this duty gave Belenus a focus he had been lacking for years. His mind and heart spoke as one and the effect was astonishing. His voiced boomed out during the marches, more forceful than it had ever been. Blood dripped down his hand from the latest incision in his forearm, seeming to follow the contours of his tattoo all the way to his fingertips before dropping to stone below to be trampled by the many feet following behind. More people joined in with the priests on each occasion, adding their voices and passion to the rally.

The Beacon called out to his flock. "When Light has eradicated Darkness, you shall live forever!"

The crowd responded with a unified, "Light fill me up!"

Belenus felt the strings of energy trailing behind, tying themselves into a braid that pushed him onward.

"Sacrifice is necessary but Emperor Anathasius has made it so that sacrifice has meaning, so that it will lead to something greater. The sacrifices of old were transient; pointless bloodshed that only begat further bloodshed. The Shining Empire is different, unique, an example to the world of the change that must occur. Priests combine their blood with the Emperor's Gift to advance the Shining Empire, and our progress cannot be denied!"

The crowd shouted their support at this proclamation. More citizens joined the throng, Belenus could feel them by the new connections humming through his body. This was the peak use of the Emperor's Gift he had enacted and the sensation was thrilling. Belenus felt as if he could accomplish anything, that he could fly if he was so inclined, that he could bring his followers with him into the ether. He spoke of the past so they would be able to understand the future that could be made possible. A glorious existence free of death.

"You have seen the progress made in your own lifetimes, how each generation has improved in every aspect since Emperor Anathasius arrived as our savior. We cannot be content to horde our accomplishments to ourselves, to ignore the rest of the world and bask in our own glory. These actions breed arrogance and slothfulness. We must bring passion, the burning Light within each and every one of you, to the rest of Rua. Share this faith and it will grow, horde it and Darkness will consume you. Do not fool yourselves. Darkness will storm our borders if we allow idleness to reign. We live in a carnivorous world, one that requires consumption, where every creature strives to devour in order to survive, and nothing is hungrier than Darkness."

Each step sent a jolt of pain racing through his leg but it barely registered in the Beacon's mind. The world was a golden ocean of languid waves that he strode across. Each word was a footstep on the surface of the liquid, creating ripples which radiated into his flock. His voice was the wind that stirred the ocean with invisible motions, making waves to prevent stagnation.

"Immortality is within our reach, but the task is ours to attain it. You may not get to see this wondrous existence with your waking eyes, but your children or children's children certainly will if we hold true. Do not fear death as the Light you take with you from this life will allow you to walk the Illuminated Path."

The buildings fell away as the Gateway Gulf opened up before Belenus, the expanse sparkling like countless tiny diamonds. The rush of the glittering visual stopped him in his tracks. He turned to face the congregation, tightening the strings connecting them so intimately. His heart felt full enough to burst. He drew from this boundless reservoir and emptied it on his people. Each string an individual stream providing nourishment meant only for them.

"Courage is needed to reach our ultimate goal, as the ultimate sacrifice may be asked of you. Calanthia is not the end, it is but a step in the right direction, a statement to the world of our cause, a statement to ourselves, an affirmation of our conviction to banish Darkness, to conquer death, to live forever in harmony. So I ask you—do you have the courage?"

The crowd let out a deafening roar. It seemed as if Azra itself cried out in response. Belenus felt weak from the exertion and thought his knees might buckle beneath him. The cheering of the crowd helped to keep him aloft. The brilliant domes of the Palace of Light arched gracefully in the distance, high above the city. Belenus looked to the palace and knew the Emperor was watching.

"Go now my friends and share these words with all that you encounter. Hold them in your hearts as dearly as you hold your loved ones."

Belenus felt the loss as each string was cut away. The ties binding him to his flock straining as they stretched, before finally snapping and severing the connection. His heart wept at the amputation. The loss was desolation. Belenus felt an intense loneliness, the crowded street transforming into a barren wilderness.

Fingers twitched spasmodically in distress, an unconscious effort to create warmth. Belenus clenched his hands to stop his trembling fingers but the vibration moved into his hands, shaking them in place like the beat of hummingbird wings. The exaltation of leading the people, their hands on his heart, was gone. Golden light drained from the environment, leaving a landscape far bleaker than any remembered by the old priest.

Belenus stood still, trying to appear calm as the people of Azra dispersed. His mind traced every sensation inside of his body, trying to analyze each particularity so that he could gain understanding. Control would follow understanding. Belenus knew this sequence to be true, his sensitivity to the functions of his body and the Emperor's Gift had allowed him to gain mastery over both. This time was no different; he would attain control. Belenus fought for focus but the shifting movement of people was too distracting.

He turned away to remove the stimulus from sight. The water of the Gulf spread out like a dull blanket, the reflections of sunlight sparking like flares. The color drained from Belenus' face as he stared out at the water. His heart felt exceptionally empty, a dried husk, staying true to form as a scarecrow resembles a man.

Thirst consumed him. Belenus needed a drink, his survival depended on it. On rickety legs the priest staggered down the hill and into the water. He waded in up to his knees, until walking met resistance. A strong hand on his shoulder held Belenus in place.

"Beacon?" asked Gern, his personal guard.

The heightened concern in Gern's voice snapped Belenus into awareness. "Nothing to worry about, just taking a dip in the wash bucket of the world. Worked up a mighty heat during the congregation."

The soldier's worried look softened but his eyes remained skeptical. Ryndell, stood ankle deep in water, looking equally concerned. Belenus splashed a few handfuls of water on his face.

"Are you alright?" asked Gern.

"Much better."

Belenus walked towards Ryndell, sloshing water with each step, as Gern followed.

A solitary priest in a white robe stood a few meters back from the water. The man looked young enough to have recently left the Sanctuary.

"Who might you be?" asked Belenus.

"Arnul Aderat."

"Pleasure to meet you, Arnul. How may I be of service?"

The younger man eyed Belenus with caution, unsure of how to respond. What was wrong with the youth of today? As far as Belenus knew they still spoke the same language so there was no reason to get tongue tied.

"Come," said Belenus, placing an arm around Arnul's shoulders. "Walk with me."

"Beacon, we should return to the palace," said Gern.

"In due time," Belenus responded. "Arnul, what is your speciality, your unique task to the Shining Empire?" asked Belenus.

Arnul remained silent.

Belenus rephrased the question into more specific terms for the bashful priest. "In what capacity do you enact the Emperor's Gift?"

"I've just left the Sanctuary and am being stationed at a large farming estate. I specialize in yielding more harvests."

Belenus clapped him on the back. "Good on you, there are always more mouths to feed. From the time we're born with little hair to the time we go out with even less, it's what goes in the stomach that drives a person. Speaking of which, let's find us a hot plate." Belenus laughed and he could feel the priest's shoulders relax under his arm.

Ryndell quickened his pace, going ahead to choose a dining location. They found him several minutes later, standing next to a tavern door. Gern directed the priests inside. The server's jaw dropped at the sight of the Beacon.

"I thought he was jesting..." the server muttered.

"Two plates of your finest, if you please," said Belenus.

The server hustled off without responding so Belenus ushered the young priest into a seat by a large window overlooking the water. The tavern was furnished with wooden tables stained dark and smelled of frying fish. Ryndell remained outside the tavern and Gern stationed himself near the door.

"Tell me about yourself and your time at the Sanctuary, it's been some time since I've visited," Belenus said cheerily.

The young priest squirmed slightly under the request, an action Belenus attributed to shyness. "I started at the Sanctuary at a very young age. The greatest honor is to serve."

Belenus nodded absently, he was having difficulty following the dialogue. He clenched his thighs to keep his fingers from shaking. The server returned, setting down two heaping plates of fried salmon, grilled sausage, and pickled cabbage with sliced red beets.

"On the house," he said awkwardly and left.

Belenus nodded at the steaming food. "Ah delicious, shall we?"

The Beacon tore into the food, thankful for the warmth it granted his depleted body. Arnul hardly touched his plate. Belenus made short work of his meal, leaving his plate free of scraps. He stopped short of licking his fingers, remembering his guest across the table.

"Nice meeting you Arnul Aderat. Now, if you don't mind, please grant an old man some privacy. It's been an eventful day and I'd like to collect my thoughts."

Arnul nodded politely and left. Belenus glanced at Gern, who was staring out of the window, and slid Arnul's plate across the table. He ate and ate but the emptiness inside could not be filled.

## Choices and Chance

Melea was a fool.

Worse, she was incompetent. She checked and rechecked for the tenth time even though she knew it was gone. The scroll carrying the Emperor's message was missing. Anathasius would take her head and he had every right to; her death was deserved for being bested by hairy forest dwellers and half-wit bandits.

"Idiot," she said.

How could she have lost the only item necessary for the mission? It must have fallen out of her cloak during her encounter with the bandits. That was a day's ride behind her and who knew what condition the scroll would be in when she found it. If she found it.

A feeling of vertigo assaulted Melea's mind. The earth beneath her feet stretched out far below. The dirt beckoned her with magnetic force. Her vision clouded over, limbs stiffening with the finality of rigor mortis. Melea stood like a rotted tree not yet willing to return to the soil.

The wind pushed her over.

Melea was unsure how long she was out; time flowed differently for the dead. Light crackled around the contours of her body. The enveloping blackness was more than a lack of color, broader than a lack of light—it had depth. So thick was this space that Melea thought it to be a substance that she could move within. She tried to swim through the void but her luminous feet just kicked uselessly.

Her vision returned to see two floating faces. Taisto smiled.

"I was hoping we'd catch up to you before you made it too far," he said happily.

"I figured you'd stick to the road," said Dacre, nodding to himself.

Melea felt her hackles rise. She was too aggravated to deal with these gossers right now. "You have something of mine," said Melea, her voice cold. "I want it back."

Taisto raised his eyebrows questioningly. "Can you identify the item? Why are you on the ground?"

Melea lurched upright and the bandits jumped back. She reached for her sword but it wasn't there. Taisto held it at his side like a walking stick.

"Do you have it or not?" Melea snapped.

Dacre folded his arms. "Have what?"

Melea's hand twitched, desiring to feel the weight of her knives, but she'd lost them as well. "A scroll," Melea growled.

Taisto snickered, stopping when Melea shot him a withering glare. Taisto walked to the nearby horse and reached into the saddlebag. He held the scroll before him, waving it slowly back and forth. A purple wax seal, the Emperor's personal identifier, was clearly visible. "Ah yes, we have one scroll in stock. Lucky for you there isn't much trade on the Serpent these days."

"Give it to me...please." Melea remembered that being polite meant using words like please.

"Certainly," Taisto said cheerily. "Why do you think we made haste after you?"

Melea felt some of the stress melt from her shoulders. The widening chasm of her disappearing future began to narrow and form into a solid path again. She had made a mistake, a thoughtless error, but luck appeared to shine on her so that she could still move forward.

"There's just one thing," said Dacre.

"This is an important piece of parchment, sealed with the Emperor's own personal sigil, which makes it extremely valuable," said Taisto.

"Potentially valuable," added Dacre.

"Yes, potentially," agreed Taisto.

"How could you possibly know that sigil?" asked Melea.

"We tend to operate outside of the law, trading the obscure and rare to earn a living. It's a requirement of our occupation to know such things," said Taisto.

"And as you can see we are neither dead nor imprisoned, so I think it's fair to say that we're good at it." Dacre inclined his head as if he were stating an obvious fact.

Melea scowled and Taisto raised a hand to stop her. "Now don't be alarmed. We haven't opened the scroll and do not intend to blackmail you for an exorbitant fee to get it back. We have just one request and if you agree to it then the scroll will be handed over free and clear."

Melea waited for the request but it never came. Eventually, she had to ask. "Well?"

Taisto looked quickly to Dacre as if finalizing their decision. "We would like to join you on the delivery of this scroll. Not all the way to the actual moment of delivery but simply to accompany you on the journey."

What were these two playing at? There was no way she could allow them to join her. The success of her mission was dependent on secrecy and these two loudmouths would be like traveling with a carnival.

"That is not an option," she said.

"Told you she'd say that," Dacre remarked.

Taisto also seemed to expect this response. "How about this? We will only accompany you as far as Marikal, and after that you will never have to see us again. Unless of course, you want to. That's a pretty fair deal."

The Calanthian capital was four days away. Melea was loathe to lend her trust to anyone and she was not about to team up with two bandits from the Outskirts on a whim. But Marikal was still a week from Cheton. They would never discover the true intention of her mission. Melea considered these cartographical details while the brothers watched her expectantly. She could fight them, but they'd likely come prepared after last time, or else they were complete fools and Melea was giving them too much credit. She listened for any signs of the Chuku Bartha but only heard the sounds of nature going about its business on a calm summer day.

"Why?" she left the question hang open ended between them. Dacre seized the moment.

"The truth is," he paused. "The truth is we can't go to Marikal. Not without you anyway. Turns out that you are the only one who can help us, me in particular. It was a gift from the universe that we bumped into you. The Eye spins on our location."

Melea furrowed her brow. "You did more than bump into me." Her chafed neck still itched from the strange fiber of the rope.

"Sorry about that," said Dacre. "A misunderstanding."

"Why would you possibly need me to go to Marikal? I'm dying to hear the explanation." Dacre answered straight faced, features honest as a child still young enough to only believe the good in the world. "For love, for a boy and a girl. The love of my life is being held prisoner in Marikal and you are the answer to my prayers. With your help—"

"Minor help," Taisto interjected.

"Yes, minor help, I will be able to rescue her from her overbearing and all-around asshole of a father."

"Step-father," said Taisto.

"Right, no blood relation," Dacre agreed.

Melea was unimpressed. "You're joking, right?"

"Afraid not," said Taisto. "Everything he said is true. I was doubtful at first but came around to the idea when I saw that he loves her, or something that resembles love, at any rate."

Dacre scowled at Taisto before looking back at Melea questioningly.

"You two are insane," she said. Melea had had just about enough of this farce. She needed that scroll. There was no time to be involved in fairy tale rescues. "I'm not doing it."

The brothers were undeterred. "What does your gut say?" asked Dacre.

"It says stab you both and take the scroll."

"Very funny," said Taisto. "You helped us before, back in Azra when you didn't have to, and that says a lot about what kind of person you are. You went with your instincts and look where they've led you. There are no accidents. Go with your gut until your heart takes over, your gut knows what's right, your heart knows what's true."

Taisto's words reminded her of Gerboa. The little thief had followed his heart further than he should have, further than she would have believed possible. He had trusted her to help him, believing she would help him save his sister, and she had betrayed him. Melea did not like where her thoughts were leading. She was considering deviating from the plan, which would compromise her promise to Anathasius.

Perhaps this was an opportunity to balance her actions. There was no making things right, no going back, but maybe she could even out the scales. The thought tasted of blasphemy on her tongue—bitter and forbidden yet powerfully compelling. But it was not enough. Melea trained too hard and was too loyal to throw that all away by taking a chance on these brothers. Outcasts from the Outskirts no less. To lose her head over them would be an ultimate oustid.

Dacre spotted the doubt in her eyes. "There's more. The Chuku Bartha talked about you, they said they know who you are."

Melea's pulse jumped. That must have been why the ape men ran away. They recognized the energy flowing out of her. *How could they know?*

"They were spooked pretty bad, were saying all kinds of things that didn't make sense to me and Taisto."

"Like what?" asked Melea.

In that moment they knew they had her and Melea knew it as well. Her past was pushing through again, an iceberg set adrift by her actions at the Sanctuary. She needed to know; the questions were slowly consuming her. The more Melea tried to ignore them the more persistent they became.

"Kept repeating the word, *stonemen*," said Dacre.

"You can speak with them? You understand their language?"

Dacre shrugged. "Yeah, no one can really speak with a Chuku Bartha unless they are Chuku Bartha but Taisto and I can talk to them better than most. They like us, even work with us on occasion, as you found out."

Was Melea crazy that she thought the seed against her chest pulsed at the thought of speaking with the ape men? The importance of the mission dictated that she could not go back. But there might be time after she completed the mission. "What would I have to do?"

Dacre was all excitement. "We have everything figured out, mostly. You'll make the whole operation go so much easier. Basically, all you have to do is turn us over to Fitzroy Jenks."

"Who is he, exactly?"

"We'll explain as we go," said Taisto, hoisting himself into the saddle.

"Do we have an agreement?" asked Dacre.

Melea nodded. She felt numb. Dacre walked over, spit into his hand then scooped up a handful of dirt, rubbing it between his palms.

"You do the same," he said to Melea.

"Makes the deal official," Taisto added.

Melea watched the brothers warily. She dripped a tiny bit of spit into her palm and reached for a handful of earth. Dacre stepped forward and clasped her hand in a firm grip.

"The fluid of our bodies binds us and the earth notifies the world of our deal. If there is any betrayal, the spirit will be held accountable."

Melea rolled her eyes. "I suppose spit is the least disgusting of fluids you could have picked."

"The least fun too, but this is about business." His face serious.

Dacre nodded and released the handshake. Taisto tossed over the scroll which she quickly stuffed inside her cloak.

Taisto gave a warm smile, his teeth straight and white. "Now that we're joined in a business venture, it's time for proper introductions. I'm Taisto Salero of the Xahyr, son of Zelimir and Chizoba, and this is my younger brother Dacre of the same lineage. Obviously. What, perchance, is the name of the lovely lady?"

Melea paused. Using her real name was out of the question and the idea of returning to Shamara the thief was abhorrent. "Natalya," she said, quietly.

Taisto looked up at the sky as if he were searching for something. "Well, we should get going, there's still plenty of daylight left."

The brothers fell in beside Melea as they rode in silence down the road. The silence built until it began to make Melea feel claustrophobic. Finally, exasperated, she had to say something. "What—"

"Ssh," scolded Taisto. "We're trying to get to know one another."

For some reason Melea accepted this response, and they continued without speaking. Over the next hour, they passed several farmers in homemade wagons being pulled by mules, and one four horse carriage that raced past them in the other direction. They rode until dusk before turning off the road to make camp.

The brothers buzzed about while setting up camp, acting as if they were all old friends, the rule of silence apparently only mattered while on the road. Dacre got a fire going and Taisto cared for the horses. They went about their tasks like the three of them had done this same routine many times. Melea felt dazed by the surreality of the situation.

She brought her horse to get a drink in some murky water accumulated in a low reedy area, needing the space to help make sense of everything jostling around in her head. Frogs croaked and a long legged heron hunted for them. The world seemed oblivious to the deal she had made with the Saleros despite Dacre's solemn handshake.

When she returned, Dacre was roasting meat over the fire on a stick, slowly turning it so that it cooked evenly. Fat dripped down, sizzling in the glowing embers. The stars were starting to come out, blinking like fireflies between gaps in a dark mass of clouds.

"So what's your horse's name?" asked Dacre.

Melea looked into the mare's big eye but the horse offered no response. "I don't know."

Dacre laughed and shook his head. "All those demands and threats over the horse and it doesn't even have a name? You're hilarious."

Melea was offended by the remark. *Why should she bother naming arbitrary things?* The mare was just a tool to be used for the mission and then never seen again. Her boots were without names and they were the longest tenured items in Melea's possession. She was used to moving on, to never becoming attached to anyone or anything—life was easier that way. She could name the mare but the animal was unable to understand anyway. No point in wasting her time.

Taisto returned and sat by the fire, rubbing his hands together in anticipation as he looked at the sizzling meat. Melea stood by the mare, not feeling like becoming part of the group but not sure where else to go.

"Horse with no name," said Dacre, jabbing a thumb in Melea's direction.

Taisto gave her wistful look. "That doesn't surprise me, but it does leave only one course of action. Let's find a title befitting that wonderful beast."

"How about Beihr the mare," said Dacre.

Melea was clueless, unfamiliar with the word. Dacre shot Melea a sidelong look. "Beihr means feminine strength in Ouskert, the language of the Outskirts. There are dozens of languages used by the many different peoples within the Outskirts but Ouskert is the common tongue. Every person knows at least some of it. Most everyone around here thinks the Outskirts is a clump of dung that needs to be cut out of the fur but it's actually quite a complex place."

"Still, that name doesn't quite fit," said Taisto. He stared at Melea and the mare as if he could find a name hidden in them if he looked hard enough. "Rannakitch," he said finally, looking satisfied.

Dacre nodded his approval.

"It means *gift of the journey*," Taisto explained.

Melea mulled the meaning of the name, rolling the word around on her tongue like a smooth lake stone. It still did not sound quite right.

"Call her Ranna for short," offered Dacre. The name stuck in Melea's mind. She looked at the mare and it seemed to fit.

"Ranna," she said, barely above a whisper. The mare's ear flicked and she nuzzled Melea's shoulder.

"Looks like it's official," said Taisto.

Melea ignored him and led the mare over to the other horses to get it prepared for the evening. *What was she doing?* The question bothered Melea as she finished with the mare—with Ranna.

This situation was nothing new. Melea had done this before; she could be someone else to get what she wanted. She had spent two weeks with Gerboa. What were four days with the Salero brothers? Melea strode confidently toward the fire, resolved that she could complete this task. But first she wanted every detail or else she would discard the arrangement and carry on to Marikal alone.

"Who is Fitzroy Jenks and how would turning you over to him get you his daughter?"

"I thought you'd never ask," said Dacre.

Taisto patted the ground beside him for Melea to sit down. She chose to sit on the opposite side of the fire.

"All men rule with power," Dacre began. "Some are given this authority by the people because of natural leadership qualities, some take it ruthlessly by force, others scheme and plot and sneak their way in. Some do all three. All men eventually walk one of these paths if they want to remain in power. Fitzroy Jenks is all of this and more. His power in Marikal is secondary only to that of King Monchiet. He fancies himself a king in his own right, sovereign of all criminal activity."

"You two want to get on this man's bad side?" asked Melea.

"We're already there," Taisto laughed.

"That's why he'll let us walk right into his home if you turn us in," said Dacre, a wicked flash flickering across his eyes in the firelight.

## Blood Ties

Belenus pushed the plate away, unable to finish breakfast. A pounding in his head had yet to relent since the moment he opened his eyes. The sound of his grinding jaws caused a pulsing in his temples. He needed to limit the incoming noise as much as possible.

His eyes felt tight, stretched taut like animal hide drying on a rack. The soft whites of his eyes itched, burnt from staring into the sun. Trapped in the grasp of a powerful dream, Belenus had stood in waist high water beneath a starlit sky filled with foreign constellations. A bright glow beneath the waves drew his attention. He dove under the glasslike surface, fascinated by the illumination. Belenus swam and swam, somehow able to breath like a fish.

The deeper he dove the brighter the light became, but he could not seem to reach it. His body went cold and his head pounded from the depth of the dive. He dove deeper than the reach of the stars yet the submerged light still eluded capture. Without warning, the ability allowing Belenus to breath underwater abandoned him. He gulped water in a panic. Belenus swallowed more water than was humanly possible, causing him to sink at a faster rate than he previously swam. The orb of light appeared, blindingly bright, surrounding Belenus and suffusing the water filling his lungs. He had awoke woken up at that moment of powerlessness, bolting upright in bed with a ghastly headache.

Belenus leaned forward, elbows on the table, eyes closed, rubbing his temple to relieve some of the pain. To return to bed and lounge until the pressure in his skull departed was a luxury he did not have. He needed to get dressed, an important meeting with Emperor Anathasius awaited.

The Chosen would soon be leaving Azra.

He put on a white robe with an image of a sun radiating energy across the chest. He left his chambers, the door slamming with a wince inducing bang.

"Feels like a malevolent goat is prancing around in my head," he complained. A nearby guard raised an eyebrow at this remark. "Carry on, son, your strength and diligence are of no aid to me in this matter."

"Yes, Beacon," said the guard as his eyes returned to an arbitrary spot on the wall.

The meeting was set in the grand conclave—a circular room whose walls were decorated with artistic depictions of the Shining Empire's accomplishments and filled with plush furniture intended for visiting dignitaries. The room was on the second floor of the palace, two below Belenus' chambers, and these days he appreciated every chance to go down stairs rather than up them. At least he would not enter the meeting hobbling and winded from the walk.

Two soldiers flanked the doors to the conclave. One was kind enough to open the door for Belenus. The movement from the walk and the guard's gesture helped to alleviate some of his headache. This momentary relief was squashed as a familiar robed individual stood with Emperor Anathasius to greet Belenus.

Kronus Pompae stood with his hands clasped, a thin smile on his narrow face. Pompae wore a white robe to match the Beacon's but it was embellished with the symbol of the priesthood: three circles in a triangular formation inside a larger circle.

"Belenus, come join us," said the Emperor, motioning for Belenus to sit on a padded chair beside him.

Anathasius sat beside the Beacon, with Pompae directly across, alone inside the massive room. Belenus guessed that Pompae had requested to meet here. Nothing was ever good enough for that snob. Basking in opulence was second nature to the leader of the Sanctuary.

Belenus came from a wealthy family but compared to Pompae he was a peasant. The Pompaes were the largest landowners in the Shining Empire, akin to the dukes of Calanthia. The head priest of the Sanctuary was used to having others beneath him, born into a station of status, and his service to the Empire had only increased this authority.

"So good to see you again," said Pompae. "You never visit."

Crooked teeth, a hooked nose, and pointed eyebrows gave Pompae an appearance of constant accusation. Belenus was surprised to see his colleague without the customary sneer: he had thought the look to be a permanent fixture. No doubt that Pompae was hiding the sneer due to being in the Emperor's presence. With the absence of blatant arrogance, the man could almost pass for human.

Belenus would visit the Sanctuary upon the removal of Rua's biggest ass. A shame that such a pivotal location in the priest's life had become tainted by one individual. "Didn't expect you to be here."

Pompae's light brown eyes sparkled, the challenge unmistakable in their countenance. "Delivered with the cheery elocution befitting the Shining Empire's finest speaker."

*You hook nosed goon.* Insults flooded Belenus' mind but he choked them all back. Thankfully, the Emperor spoke. "Today marks a momentous occasion. The beginning of the Shining Empire's campaign into the southern expanse of the continent. Such an undertaking requires leadership, which is why I will be joining the Chosen."

There was no fault in the logic of the Emperor's decision, but Belenus was still shocked to hear the words spoken out loud. He should have foreseen this development. The Emperor was not going to stay in Azra while the army marched to Marikal and beyond. Pompae's presence in the meeting was starting to make sense. More priests would be needed to aid the people as the army would draw on the supply of resources.

"You two men are the most capable and dependable of any I know, each with a long history of providing valuable service to the Shining Empire. I have asked you here to perform another act, one of greater responsibility than any other." Anathasius looked to each priest, Belenus licked his lips and nodded slightly. "Azra needs to be led while I am away and together you two will accomplish this task."

Belenus was at once excited and appalled. He was honored that the Emperor would entrust the safety of the city to him, but this honor was tarnished by having to work alongside Pompae. He would have daily interactions with this loathsome man, even having to compromise and agree with Pompae's opinion. Under different circumstances Belenus would have refused, but the importance of the duty meant he would have to put aside his personal feelings for the good of the city.

The Emperor's luminous eyes melted the Beacon's anger. "Belenus, you will remain my voice for the people of Azra. Keep them along the path, fill their hearts with passion for the upcoming victory, and temper their spirits as they patiently await my return."

Belenus was confused—he was to remain the Beacon? That could only mean one thing. Anathasius looked to Pompae, the leader of the Sanctuary sat calmly, awaiting the news of his promotion.

"Kronus, your efforts at the Sanctuary leave no doubt in my mind that you have the experience to manage the affairs of Azra. I have set everything in order for you to oversee that the city and the people continue to flourish. My attendants and various administrators have been informed of the temporary replacement and will meet with you later in the day."

Belenus was beside himself with disbelief. He was now subservient to Kronus Pompae, a person who, along with the boy who beat Belenus up when he was eight years old, was categorized in his short list of enemies. This had to be part of the dream, Belenus must still be trapped in the nightmare. Belenus jabbed a fingernail into his thumb and felt a sharp pain that proved he was not sleeping.

Anathasius looked to each priest in turn, his voice as soothing as it was inspiring. "Together you will maintain what has been carefully built, adding a new layer to the foundation of this great city. Belenus, I ask that you continue as you have always done, remain a pillar of strength for the people. Do you accept this task I ask of you?"

"Of course."

As if he had a choice. He would excel at this obligation, despite the bitterness of resentment he was feeling inside.

Anathasius closed his eyes, nodding once in approval, the gesture at once humble and profound. "Thank you, my friend. Kronus and I still have matters to discuss. Please allow us to continue."

"Yes." It was all that Belenus could manage.

The palace was made toxic merely by the presence of Kronus Pompae. Belenus needed out. *But where else to go?* The quandary caused him to realize that he was quite alone despite his conception of unity with the people of Azra. His father and mother had both passed on, he was wifeless, and had sired no children. Only his brother Barroc remained in the city. When was the last time he had ventured to the family shop for visit?

The memories were blurring together, but Belenus was fairly certain that he had a beard at that time. He had shaved the thing a decade ago because the tangle of grey sorely aged his appearance. That settled it. He would pay his brother a visit.

Belenus exited the carriage he'd ordered, a few blocks from the shop, walking the remaining distance with a limp. He took a moment to observe the exterior of the family business before entering. The shop looked much the same as he remembered. The only difference was a fresh coat of red paint given to the placard above the door —Wicket Family: Expert Craftsmanship In All Things Metal.

The shop hardly passed as a family business anymore. Barroc ran the place by himself and had no children to transfer it to when he passed. Belenus struggled to fight the creeping guilt of leaving Barroc alone with their father. His mother had been there but in body only, her presence like that of a quiet mouse hoping to remain unseen lest she be attacked by the larger predators. Hentavio always had a temper. Belenus witnessed it firsthand on too many occasions to count. He sighed, pulling open the main door. How many times was Barroc subjected to Hentavio's wrath because of Belenus' decision to leave?

The interior of the shop was gloomy. Weak light illuminated what should have been gleaming shelves of bracelets, rings, pots, pans, utensils, farm equipment, and a myriad of other carefully crafted products. Belenus wiped a finger through the layer of dust on a nearby shelf. Cobwebs drooped from the corners. This was no longer a place of business.

He strolled through the shop, a place that seemed far more distant than the one in his memories. Apart from not being boarded up, the only clue that the shop was not completely abandoned was a flicker of candlelight coming from the back room.

Belenus found a pretty woman going through sheafs of work orders. Her blonde hair was cut to shoulder length and she appeared to be copying the transactions into a ledger. She jumped when he rapped a knuckle against the half open door.

"We're closed. I recommend the trinket shop down the street," said the woman without looking up.

"I'm not here to purchase anything. I'm looking for Barroc Wicket."

The woman carefully closed the ledger, standing to face Belenus. "He's extremely busy, I'm sorry, he won't be back here anytime soon."

The state of the shop made that evident. "Pardon me, I haven't introduced myself, I'm his brother Belenus. And who might you be?"

"I'm his wife, Mariam. Barroc never mentioned he had a brother."

Belenus' tongue stuck to the roof of his mouth. He could understand why his brother would want to cut him out of his life, but how could Barroc never even mention that he had a wife? One that was half his age, no less.

Recognition flared in Mariam's eyes as she observed the symbol on the robe of her uninvited guest. "You're the Beacon!"

Belenus nodded, still coming to grips with how out of touch he was with his family. But when was the last time he and Barroc spoke? Five years ago? Ten?

"That I am," said Belenus. "Barroc took up the business when I entered the priesthood. It seems that we are not as close as we once were."

"To think that I've been related to Azra's Beacon this whole time," Mariam stammered.

"How long have you been married?"

"Eight years this fall."

The number smashed Belenus in the chest like a hammer blow. That many years since he had even seen his brother, his only living relative, a man who lived in the same city he called home.

"Do you and Barroc have any children?"

"We do," said Mariam. "Elowen is seven, Janna is five, and little Hentavio just turned four."

Belenus nodded glumly. "Just one more thing. Where might I find Barroc? It appears that a conversation is long overdue."

"Barroc would berate me for telling someone this but you are his brother after all, and besides, how could I refuse the esteemed Beacon? He's where he always is these days, at the factory near the harbor."

"Thank you, Mariam."

Belenus quietly left the shop. The Wicket family business would not die with Barroc. There would even be another Hentavio in charge some day. What exactly constituted that business was a mystery though.

Belenus flagged down a rickshaw to take him to the factory. He wondered what his nieces and nephews looked like. He hoped they got their looks from their mother.

The street in front of the factory was lined with horse-drawn carts. Soldiers in crisp blue uniforms loaded the carts to capacity with heavy packages wrapped in burlap, tied with string. Belenus moved closer to inspect the products of his brother's factory. Sword hilts peaked out from the opening in the parcels. The rounded shape of lumpy packages in another cart led Belenus to believe it was carrying armor. Several soldiers watched Belenus but none interceded as he entered the factory.

The heat of the interior was immediate, gusting into the priest's face as if he had walked into a giant furnace. After a cursory look around, Belenus gathered that the building did, in fact, house an enormous furnace as well as many smaller forges. The air stank from the incessant smelting process of usable metal being extracted from raw ore. He found it hard to breathe between the heat and the smell.

A constant chime of hammers on anvils rang out as smiths went about their work. Men carried armfuls of wood to add to various furnaces. Every once in a while there was the indignant hiss of hot iron being dipped into water. The scene was one of focused activity but Belenus was still able to locate his brother. Belenus did his best to dodge around others as he followed the sound of Barroc's yelling.

"More heat! I could piss this fire out. Bellows now!"

Sweaty men raced to enact Barroc's commands. He stood beside the largest furnace in the factory, glaring at everyone around him. The heat was intense but apparently below the desired level. More shovels of coal were tossed to feed the flames. Two men feverishly strained to work the massive bellows needed to pump air into the fire.

Belenus watched as Barroc directed the men, diligently monitoring every detail of the process and shouting adjustments. Barroc's bald head gleamed with sweat that poured down to drip from a bulbous nose. He was two years younger than Belenus and his arms and shoulders displayed great strength, seemingly flexed at all times from decades of hard labor. Barroc stomped from station to station, his hunched back pulling him forward as he walked. It was only when he was completely satisfied with the status of the furnace that he approached Belenus.

"This is no place for softness, you'll get your nice gown dirty."

"Good to see you as well brother," greeted Belenus.

The priestly robe was slick from the blazing heat and had somehow acquired a few sooty smears. Barroc's hunch forced him to look up at Belenus, his dark eyes peering from beneath thick black eyebrows.

"I stopped by the shop," Belenus said casually, "and met your wife."

Barroc only grunted as a response.

"You've been busy," said Belenus as he appraised the factory. "All of this in addition to raising three children."

"What are you doing here, Belenus?"

"Recent changes at the palace got me thinking about the past and it dawned on me that I haven't been a very good brother. I've allowed my responsibilities to turn me into an absentee in your life."

Barroc scowled, his fire baked face forming into creases. "You deserted the family, left us for your glorious dream."

He was right, Belenus could not argue with the assessment. Except, that he did not leave to follow a dream; he left to follow his faith. Belenus only found the strength to stand up to his father through his belief in the future promised by Emperor Anathasius. Clarifying such details would be meaningless now.

Belenus was the one who made the choice to ram a wedge between himself and his family.

"I don't blame you for it though," said Barroc, his face softening. "It wasn't your path to stay with us. You were always useless around the shop anyways."

Belenus laughed, it felt good to let it out. He smacked Barroc on the shoulder, who grinned as well. For a moment it seemed as though the laughter might dissolve the years of separation but the fleeting sentiment could not erode the thick crust of accumulated neglect. The work of the furnaces proved that intense force was needed to remove the valuable qualities hidden within hardness. One congenial moment was insufficient effort to wear away the past of the Wicket brothers.

"So what do you want, Belenus?" Barroc growled.

Belenus had wanted to visit his brother so that he could return to his childhood, to once again be filled with limitless optimism, but that was impossible. They were old men now, men who were in places that their past selves likely could not have predicted. Belenus gestured at the activity around them. "Why this? Why abandon the shop?"

"You saw Mariam. A woman like that wouldn't look twice at me if I didn't have wealth."

Belenus agreed, Barroc had been an awkward boy who grew into an ugly man. During their teen years Barroc buried himself in learning the craft as an excuse to be alone, which Belenus always considered to be an excuse used to avoid talking to the neighbor girls.

"Besides, I'm good at it, better than good actually. The finest iron in the world is produced in this factory," Barroc said with pride.

"Used to make instruments of death. The Wickets left that behind long ago."

"Aye, they did but the fighting didn't stop did it? People still kill each other don't they? Humans kill one another in countless ways for all sorts of reasons and will invent new reasons if they don't have one. Our ancestors embraced this truth and benefited from it. I have no issues with profiting from human nature."

Belenus recalled the carts being loaded until they were heaped with weapons and armor. "Aren't there enough weapons in the world? Why choose to make so many more?"

"There can never be enough weapons," Barroc spat as he chopped downward with his hand to emphasize the point. "The rise and fall of warriors is as constant as the tide."

An ocean of corpses floated in the priest's imagination, the freshest bodies on top embedded with Wicket iron. Would Barroc have chosen this path if Belenus stayed to run the shop as his partner?

"You are right, I took one path and you another. It is serendipitous that they have merged to aid the same cause," said Belenus.

Barroc wiped his nose with the back of his hand, then rubbed it on his tunic. "You kiss babies and warm hearts with your pretty words, you keep the people happy and content while the army is away fighting. I provide the iron claws and iron skin that makes it possible for fathers and sons to return from the battlefield. My weapons will give them a chance to win this war."

"I am not happy and content."

"You better be. You're the bloody Beacon."

"That's not all I am. Today I learned that I'm an uncle."

Barroc grunted.

"Invite me over for dinner sometime. I want to see if your children were unlucky enough to inherit your nose."

Barroc gave the slightest of nods and then returned to the furnace, barking orders at the nearest man. Belenus started for the exit. The heat was becoming too much for him. On his way he noticed two men pull handkerchiefs over their mouths and noses before entering a side door. No one wore masks in the main room. What was on the other side of that wall? His curiosity piqued, Belenus turned to follow the men.

A peculiar smell floated around the door, one Belenus was unable to recognize. He reached for the handle but thick fingers attached to a hairy arm reached past him to push it closed.

"I don't pry into your line of work brother, so don't pry into mine." Barroc's face was serious, but Belenus could not resist agitating him further. Speaking with his brother had stirred old associations.

"Have an even prettier wife hidden back there?" Belenus teased.

Barroc stared up at Belenus, his eyes like the heat pouring from the furnaces. "I'll wager there are parts of each our crafts that are best left unseen to those who wouldn't understand."

Belenus deliberated whether he should press the issue, Barroc seemed dead set against him entering. As the Beacon, he could probably order that he be granted access but it could be considered rude to ignore your brother for a decade then show up unannounced and go traipsing around his factory.

"Alright, but you owe me a dinner."

Barroc kept his hand pressed against the door. "Fine."

"I suppose I should be going. Plenty of important business to be carried out. Should I contact you about the dinner or..."

"I'll let you know a day that works," said Barroc. "I know where you live."

"Excellent. I'll see myself out."

Barroc remained by the door as Belenus left, guarding it like a dog over a buried bone. The fresh air was a balm against Belenus' skin as he stepped outside. Soldiers continued to load cart after cart.

## The Golden City

As they neared Marikal, the signs of civilization became unmistakeable. The impenetrable mass of the Eternal Forest was at their backs, and the land they rode was thoroughly domesticated. Farms were set beside each other in organized strips of land, small communities popping up after every hill like their own form of crop, and the Serpent was becoming increasingly busy with traffic.

The people here looked similar to those of the Shining Empire. The only differences Melea noticed were in clothing. Most obvious was the assortment of headgear: the men wore small, flat topped hats and women kept their hair beneath shawls. Dacre explained that the different colors signified social class.

Melea noticed that the women decorated their scarves in unique patterns rather than copying the solid colors of the men.

"Choice cannot be completely silenced," was Dacre's explanation when Melea brought this up.

Taisto had removed his broad hat and replaced it with a smaller silvery cap to designate him as a merchant. Dacre wore an identical one, tying up his long hair into a compact pony tail. They gave Melea an orange shawl covered in black dots which she wrapped loosely around her neck and head. The brothers also exchanged their colorful belts for plain leather ones. It seemed that people from the Outskirts were held in the same esteem in Calanthia as in the Shining Empire.

Shirtless workers toiled in the field on either side of the road, stretching out in rows as far as Melea could see. Sweat dripped down the bare heads of these men, women, and children.

"What of them?" she asked.

Dacre sighed as he watched a nearby group work. "I misspoke earlier. There are certain conditions when choice can be silenced."

"And that is?"

Dacre nodded toward a portly man with a thick mustache, walking amongst the group of field workers. The man wore an open white tunic, stained a dull grey from his constant sweating. His head was covered by a tall black cap and he cracked a whip as he walked. Each worker he passed pretended to go about their task as if the overseer was invisible but Melea saw them tense up until he moved on.

Taisto watched the scene as well, shaking his head slightly. He licked his lips as he looked away before unexpectedly turning to Melea, his eyes hardening but a softness underneath tried to float to the surface. They smoothed over, becoming an opaque black as he pushed the unspoken emotion back down.

"Choice is denied to them and all who live as part of that particular class," said Taisto. "They are slaves, the lifeblood of Marikal's prosperity. Not all were born slaves, but once one becomes a slave, he will certainly die a slave's silent death whenever his master wishes it."

"They should rise up, the lot of them, and overthrow their masters," said Dacre, careful to keep his voice low. "Escape to the Outskirts to be free."

Taisto gave a weak nod. "Most men will not fight unless they know they can win and for that, hope is needed."

Melea mouthed the word, breathing it out like smoke. *Hope.*

Taisto stared down the Serpent, eyes roving to distances only he could see. "There is much gold in Marikal but little hope. Often that is the way the scales are weighted."

"Why do you admonish their methods? Look at what Marikal and Calanthia have been able to achieve through the use of their slave workers," she said.

Taisto and Dacre both jumped in the saddle, looking as if they were stung by a hornet. They looked at Melea as if she had just dropped from the sky.

"That seals it," said Dacre. "She's definitely a Shiner. No other people are so clueless about the ways of the world yet are ready to pick up its nasty bits."

"What do you mean?" Melea huffed.

Dacre gave a lopsided grin, a hint of sadness twitching at the corners of his mouth before the grin fell. "Few things are worse than slavery. I'm going out on a limb here but I'm guessing you haven't heard about the origins of the Outskirts?"

Melea shrugged and looked away. Everyone knew that the people of the Outskirts were raiders, wild folk who were a nuisance to the Shining Empire and Calanthia.

"Extermination is what follows when even slavery is deemed too good for a people," said Taisto, voice was stiff with controlled anger.

"She doesn't understand the basics so let's start at the beginning," said Dacre. "Which as it often does, gives glimpses of the end. How does one act toward the weakest and most vulnerable?"

Melea was silent. They were not her tutors. They were not even experienced veterans. Dacre continued anyway.

"I'm asking you, Natalya, how would you treat those who are unable to care for themselves, who are at the mercy of those around them?"

"Are you talking about the slaves? Because they look strong enough to me." Her voice was more stern than she intended, but maybe it would be enough to end this lecture.

Taisto chimed in. "What happens when one, and I am not only referring to the slaves, is injured so that they are no longer able to work? This is an extremely common occurrence. A rarer occurrence is when one beats the odds and grows old enough that work becomes impossible, what then?"

Melea shrugged, glaring at Taisto to intimidate him. She opened her mouth to answer but was interrupted.

"You might say that you are strong now so what does it matter? That you are a warrior who is untroubled by the thought of old age because you won't live to reach it anyways. If you are indeed from the Empire then you might also be inclined to state that what happens in this world is of little meaning because you await immortality. All are fair responses but they deal with the present and the future. Let's look back to the beginning, to the event of your birth."

"What about it?" she snarled. "It doesn't matter."

A softness returned to Taisto's eyes. "A human child is the most vulnerable thing in the world, incapable of feeding itself, of defending against harm, of even cleaning its own mess. We all come from this state of absolute dependence, which means that someone cared for us and tended to our needs so that we might become strong enough to take care of ourselves."

Melea clamped down on uncomfortable thoughts. *Grandfather*. The man's pale indigo eyes flashed in her memory. A slick sheen of sweat covered her forehead and her hands felt clammy. A shiver rattled through Melea despite the warmth of the sunlight. She was an orphan but had she always been alone before entering the Sanctuary? How else could she have survived to reach that age? She shook her head against these thoughts. She would not go there, couldn't, not now, not ever.

"But there is something else," Taisto said in a soft voice. "With humans there is always more than meets the eye even though we try to deny it."

Melea's heart jumped. She needed to look away. She stared out across the fields, careful to avoid looking at the slaves, but unable to ignore the violent crack of whips.

"Our strength is shared," said Dacre. "One man or woman can accomplish a great deal in their lifetime if they are disciplined and work hard, but all are limited by their lifespan. So much of our lives are spent as defenseless children or feeble elders. The assistance of others is needed and when it is given it seems that there is no limit to what humans may create. So I ask, does it matter if creation is attained with the lash of the whip or with the aid of an open hand?"

Melea spoke slowly, still looking out over the fields. "It doesn't matter as long as the goal is completed."

Taisto sighed. "You speak as if you come from a place of power, where people are only possessions to be moved about but—"

"But what?" Melea spun back to Taisto. "You don't know anything about me."

He remained calm, thoughtful even as he regarded her. "From the way you're running I'd wager you aren't royalty, that you're from the dregs like the rest of us, where the common person is one unlucky incident away from being one of those poor bastards." Taisto motioned towards the slaves but Melea ignored him, staring down the road ahead.

They rode in silence for a time through the fields, listening to the somber singing of the slaves bent to their task. The Green river now ran parallel to the

the Serpent, flowing toward the sea from the distant Kon mountains marking the border with Rhezaria. Melea thought the water looked more of a murky brown than green but the vegetation along the banks of the river was indeed a lush green, so maybe that was how it had gotten its name. River barges traveled lazily in both directions, easily navigating their way on the wide waterway.

Pleasant weather had allowed them to make good time and they now neared their destination. At one point Dacre took it upon himself to act as a guide, pointing out locations of note to Melea as if they were on a leisurely tour of Calanthia. Melea soon became versed in Calanthia's history.

"There," Dacre said, pointing to a small hill covered by a crumbling fortress. "That's the southernmost edge of the former kingdom of Asyrith. It was sacked long ago with most of the other outposts. Asyrith was annexed by Calanthe, and most of its former land was taken, making Asyrith the smallest dukedom in Calanthia."

The day before, Melea and the brothers had passed through the Gate of Asyrith on the dukedom's northern border. A toll was required to gain passage through the heavily guarded gate. According to the brothers, the price of the toll was twice as high as last summer. They called the gate the "siphon of the Serpent".

"Duke Karracus might as well shake us by our boots," Taisto griped. "He makes a fortune by allowing travelers to cross an arbitrary line." They chose to bypass the nearby city of Ishtanvor out of spite.

She knew Asyrith occupied the area closest to the Shining Empire and Marikal was the Calanthian capital but that was the extent of her knowledge. Dacre's mention of Asyrith once being a kingdom was baffling.

"How many dukedoms are there?"

Dacre perked up, ready to resume the history lesson. "Six. They were all independent at some time or another, but have all sworn fealty to Calanthe. Each still keeps their customs and beliefs, but I doubt the King cares as long as their swords are pointed away from his back."

"I thought we were in Calanthia, what is Calanthe?"

Dacre gave her condescending look. He pointed to the road in front of them, to a tree in the distance, to rooftops of a village poking over a hill, to a slave working the fields. He swung his right hand in a circular motion. "This is all Calanthe. Kings live to own things and everything here falls under King Monchiet's possession. Calanthe was the first king's original domain, before Calanthia, named after his wife from way back when. Named the whole nation after her once it was unified. What kinds of things do you fill your head with?"

*The finest tutors will help you to become my champion.* The Emperor's promise to Melea when she submitted to his mentorship. Various tutors had entered Melea's life to dictate their lessons, which she was expected to reverently absorb. They tended to respond negatively to her questions.

"Why would the others submit if they still want to keep their own ways?"

Dacre glanced over at Taisto with a knowing smile. "Is she serious? Calanthe has the biggest army, of course, and the most powerful drainers."

"Drainers?"

Taisto chuckled as Dacre made a slicing motion across his wrist. "Priests, shamans, ritual users—those who trade their blood power. It's what we call those outside of the Outskirts."

That made sense to Melea. It was said the Outskirts denied the power made available through the offering of blood. A troubling thought occurred to her—*if the priests of the Empire got their power from the Emperor's Gift, how could the Calanthians use it as well?* The source must be a bastardized imitation, a cheap replica lacking the fullness of the original. *Impure.* The word drifted into her mind, pulled up from a lesson she'd half listened to in the palace.

Impure. The word perfectly described the priests and their conduct within the Sanctuary. Melea had not cared for the robed clergy before the incident at the Sanctuary but now she detested even the thought of them. Her wounds had healed but she would not forgive the inhumane treatment she had been subjected to in the torturer's chamber. The head priest who captured Melea must have known who she was, but chose to exact punishment anyway. His time would come. All choices had their consequences.

"Don't speak too harshly of them," said Taisto. "Aren't we traveling to Marikal for a drainer?"

"Yeah, yeah," Dacre muttered. "I never saw that coming." His expression softened, fading into a particularly sweet memory. "Want to know how Iribi and I met?" he asked Melea.

"Not really."

"Don't bother, he's going to tell it anyway," said Taisto as Melea tried to protest.

"Let me tell you a tale," said Dacre. "It was during the harvest festival," Dacre intoned theatrically. "A swollen harvest moon reflected the golden domes of Marikal like a coyote's eye, the streets were packed to bursting, and you could feel an energy in the air. We had just completed our first and what would turn out to be our only job for ol' Jenks. We'd done well, our pockets were filled with coin. The girls skipped through the streets with their festival dresses trailing behind them, so what choice did we have but to stay?"

Taisto motioned for Dacre to get on with it but Dacre ignored him, continuing at his own pace. "We probably walked all of Marikal that night, trying to see everything we could, and ended up by the river in a small square. My feet were killing me but there was music and drink in the square so it was as good of a place as any. It was there that I saw her. She entered my sight like a glowing vision, wearing a flowing white dress. You could see every curve of her body." Melea rolled her eyes and Taisto chuckled.

"She danced by herself, ignoring every man that asked for her hand. I was speechless, mindless, forgot my own name, couldn't even remember how to stand while I watched her dance."

"Still managed to finish three more pints," Taisto interjected.

Dacre paid him no mind. "I needed to speak to her, to hear her voice, to know if she was real or just a beautiful vision. So I summoned the courage and got up to dance. I listened to the notes of the lute, to the singer's voice, moving along with the music. I danced my dance and she danced hers. We moved our way around the square carefully so that we never faced one another, but always certain of where the other was."

Taisto burst into laughter. "Funniest thing I've ever seen. He lumbered around using steps I haven't seen before or since."

"The music told me how to move," said Dacre, puffing up his chest a little. "When the song ended we were standing back to back. I wanted to turn around and grab her, to kiss her and hold her in my arms, but I couldn't. Instead, I said..."

A fly buzzed around Dacre's face, he stopped his story to swat at the pest. Taisto and Melea snickered at the interruption. Dacre glanced around to make sure his winged adversary was gone for good before continuing.

"I said, my name is Dacre Salero and I have never known truth until I saw you. She giggled and took a step backwards so that her shoulders touched my back. She told me that I still hadn't found truth and that her name was Iribi. I said that knowing her name was close enough."

The fly returned, buzzing around Dacre's head.

"Get away!"

He swatted at the fly and tried to compose himself so that he could finish the story. "Where was I?"

"She had just told you her name and you melted into a puddle at her feet," said Taisto.

"Ah yes, she laughed lightly and took my hand, we turned to face each other. We danced hand in hand all night and watched the sun come up over the river."

Taisto groaned. "Gets more dramatic with every telling."

Melea was silent. She was unfamiliar with such stories, but found that she liked the telling of it well enough. A buzz tingled across her skin. The sensation was rubbed off by the warm breeze, leaving Melea with a lump in her throat. The passion in Dacre's voice was unsettling, delivered in a certain tone, with a force that Melea was having trouble deciphering.

How could someone speak with such intensity about a single experience? About one night? He placed such great emphasis on the individual aspects, as if each were momentous and full of meaning.

"We spent the rest of the festival together and met several times afterward," said Dacre. "I had no idea who her father was and I didn't care."

"Good thing she was paying attention," added Taisto. "Jenks gave us another job, but the swine double crossed us, planning on taking us out so he wouldn't have to pay. Iribi warned Dacre and we barely escaped with our necks."

"Bless her heart," said Dacre. "We met in secret for a while until he caught her sneaking out one night and found out who she was going to see. He's been after us ever since."

A group of soldiers in green bearing the insignia of a diving falcon passed them on the road, their peaked helmets reflecting the sunlight. The leader cast a suspicious look over as he rode past, noting the headwear of the Saleros.

The terrain was becoming increasingly hilly, as many steep inclines paced either side of the river. The road angled upward, and after cresting a tall hill, Marikal finally burst into view. Melea inhaled sharply at the sheer size of the city sprawling out before her.

The end of the city could not be seen, stretching out with the river and the hills for what seemed like infinity. Enough gold sparkled from rooftops, towers, and statues to make one think Marikal had a limitless supply of the lustrous metal. Melea had thought Azra to be large but Marikal dwarfed the Emperor's city. An uncountable number of structures dotted the view, many appeared to be dug into the hills, their rounded windows poking out like eyes. Other buildings towered high above the twisting streets as they reached toward the sky. She wondered if those that led underground reached as far down.

Three separate walls protected the city, cutting directly through the different districts as they wound their way around. The final wall was a barrier specifically designed for the palace and king's court. Melea marveled at the palace; it sat atop the highest hill overlooking a cliff with a precipitous drop to the river. The palace loomed like a colossal termite mound, starting wide at the base, then slightly narrowing as it rose straight up to end in a series of rounded points. The material was rough, a deep brown color like sandy clay or stained wood, conveying strength and immense weight.

"She's something, ain't she?" said Dacre. "They say Calanthia can never be defeated while the Pillar stands. If you think that's something, wait until you meet Iribi."

Melea could see why the people of Marikal would put their faith in the strength of the Pillar. The structure was the largest manmade creation she had ever seen. It towered over the city, imposing its will across the landscape. Glittering rooftops of red and gold reached right to the edge of the wide brown river, where tall ships glided beneath large curved bridges. Green flags flapped listlessly along the walls, too many to count. The shocking intricacy of the city took Melea's breath away.

"You ready?" asked Taisto.

Doubt clawed at her throat, attempting to silence her words, to strangle them in a dampening grasp. Things were becoming complicated, picking up momentum as she interacted with more people. The security of the Palace of Light was behind her, and Melea was hesitant to accept that it might never come back. She wanted out of that stifling atmosphere so that she could be on her own, but this?

"Natalya?"

"I'm ready," said Melea.

The walls of the golden city loomed high above them. A string of figures were carved into the top of the wall depicting a war party hunting lions. An immense statue of Ziya'Sybel, God of Calanthia, made of stone the darkest shade of blue straddled the gate. In the God's left hand was a massive broadsword which crossed over the top of the opening. Melea understood the implication—all who entered would be judged by this God's laws. The statue's right hand held a staff sprouting a plume of wheat. He was both the ruler of life and final judgement; a deity to be respected on both fronts.

Ziya'Sybel glowered down at her as she passed through the gate. Anathasius claimed that Ziya'Sybel had abandoned his people, that his presence was long removed from Rua, that Calanthia lived in denial of this fact. She wanted the Emperor's words to be true.

The cold, serious eyes of the statue did not feel like those of a dead god. The eyes burned into her, making her feel naked, transparent to her core. The uncomfortable sensation passed as they entered Marikal and her confidence returned. Alive or dead, Ziya'Sybel no longer ruled this city, that privilege belonged to another. Jenks was only a man and Melea feared no man.

Melea stood at the edge of a marble dais, looking up at Fitzroy Jenks, who sat on a gilded throne. He glared down at her with beady eyes. From the size of the manor it appeared that Jenks truly did imagine himself to be a king. The opulence of the room shouted his wealth from every corner—sculptures arranged along each side of a red carpet leading to the throne, paintings of nudes teasing the line between expressive and crude, tapestries depicting regal authority, and a magnificent chandelier hanging above it all at the center of the room. Fifteen slaves in yellow togas stood quietly in various locations around the hall, ready to attend to the whims of their master.

Jenks even wore a marble headpiece, inlaid with gold, similar to that of King Monchiet's crown. Melea noted that his clothing was expensive but improperly fitted, hanging off his skeletal frame to make the crime-lord look like an impossibly old child playing dress up in his father's finest outfit. Two enormous bodyguards stood on either side of the throne, staring straight ahead.

"My reward?" Melea's question was more of an expectation than a request.

"Tell me again how you captured them?" Jenks hunched forward, his glower intensifying. The two guards behind Melea held tight to the hooded captives as they struggled, their voices muffled by gags.

"I found them passed out drunk at the south end of the Chuku Bartha Pass—looked like they had recently robbed a carriage stocked with wine—there were bottles everywhere."

"What were you doing there?"

Melea held Taisto's hat in her hand which she used to smack the hooded Dacre over the head. "I was supposed to marry him, but he said he was in love with someone else, and then ran off. I followed them and waited for a chance to get my revenge."

Jenks' eyes widened and his nostrils flared, making the protruding nose hair visible even from this distance. The bodyguards at his sides tensed, preparing to silence her.

"You have done a good thing," said Jenks. The guards relaxed but still looked ready to spring into action.

"He said this girl was your daughter," she said. "He said that he was coming to rescue her."

Jenks slowly pulled apart his pursed lips into something closer to a snarl than a smile. "They thought they could steal my daughter away from me? They actually thought that they could walk into this house and leave with my daughter? Too damn funny. Humor is a sickness, one that needs to be eradicated."

"He was a little simple minded now that you mention it. Probably for the best that things didn't work out between us," said Melea.

Jenks produced another toothy snarl. "A reward bestowed upon yourself, a lesson learned and a life that will no longer be wasted on Dacre Salero."

Melea feigned indignation. "Surely they are worth more to you than that?"

Jenks gripped the armrests of his throne, eyes fixed squarely on Melea. "This is a most gracious reward I offer, or would you prefer to be fed to the hyenas? The beasts were a gift and they have a sense of humor that I do not. They appreciate a good laugh."

Melea looked away in silence and Jenks leaned back, comfortable in his authority. She stared at a colorful tapestry, chewing her bottom lip while tapping her right foot, counting the seconds as she tried to look upset.

"The hyenas will get a great laugh out of these two," Jenks mused. "I'll feed them the older Salero first and put Dacre in the cell below so that he can be covered in the excrement that was his brother."

"At least let me see the woman Dacre left me for. I need to see the face that stole his heart," said Melea.

The plan had been for Melea to cry at this point but tears could not be forced. She sniffed loudly and hoped that would be good enough.

Jenks rapped his fingers on the armrest, considering her request. He waved a hand at one of the bodyguards to retrieve Iribi. The bodyguard soon returned and Iribi stepped out from behind his large form, clearly upset with her father.

"What is the meaning of this? I told you I don't want to be involved with what you do." Her harsh tone cut like a razor but Jenks seemed immune.

Iribi wore a soft blue satin dress. It was light and ended above her ankles. After seeing the decor of the room Melea had expected a complicated dress with an exquisite train stretching out behind. This dress was much simpler, and almost garishly tight, displaying Iribi's curvaceous figure.

Iribi's eyes matched the color of the dress, shining vibrantly against the contrast of her smooth, pale skin. Her thick hair was the color of flame, reaching to the middle of her back, bouncing with every step. She turned to Melea, her eyes focusing on Taisto's hat, then to the two figures whose heads were covered. Dacre winked at her as she tossed his hood to the floor. Iribi slapped him hard across the face.

"You said you wouldn't get caught!"

Melea glanced at Jenks. Iribi kissed Dacre on the cheek where she had slapped him, whispering, "I'm sorry."

She stepped in front of the bandit to glare at the man who had become her father until he grew bored with her mother.

"If you kill him, then you'll have to kill me as well," she said, body stiff in defiance.

"I can do what I want. You are mine, and now they are mine," Jenks stated.

Iribi turned her rage to Melea, looking as if she might slap her as well. Melea shot her a quick wink just as Dacre had, which stalled Iribi, while she considered what it might mean. Melea looked to Jenks, who was still savoring every moment of this encounter.

"I understand now," said Melea.

Jenks looked pleased with this response.

"I understand why you covet your daughter and lock her away behind these doors, why you fear the Saleros and the choice they offer her. She has made her decision, yet you do not honor it because your pride exceeds even your vanity."

Jenks' eyes bulged, making him look even more like a vulture as he slapped the armrest with his palm. "You are as foolish as the imbecile who left you. Guards!"

The two bodyguards sprang into action, moving swiftly toward Melea. Iribi gasped, hand rising to her mouth. Melea remained still until the bodyguards were directly in front. She pulled back the sleeve of the cloak and leveled her forearm at them, knocking the release on the gauntlet. The darts shot out and the burly men collapsed to the floor, clutching their throats. Now it was Jenks' turn to gasp.

Melea spun back, launching into the air to smash an elbow into the face of the guard holding Dacre. Iribi plucked the sword off his belt as the guard stumbled backward and promptly knocked him on the head with it, sending the guard crashing to the floor. Dacre hopped over to Iribi and she sliced the binds on his wrist. He pointed at Melea then at the other guard before brushing past her to advance on Jenks, taking the sword from Iribi as he went by.

The second guard let go of Taisto, fumbling for his sword with panicked fingers. Taisto smashed his heel down on the guard's toes. The guard never saw Melea's attack as she dropped him to the floor with one strike to the windpipe. Melea cut Taisto's ties and he removed the gag from his mouth.

"We make a good team," he said.

"Team? I did everything," Melea said wryly.

Taisto's attention was pulled to the throne before he could respond. Dacre stood in front of Jenks, who remained seated, his eyes spiteful as a cornered badger.

"Too damn funny, hey?" said Dacre.

Dacre casually hefted the sword in his palm. His body itched with energy. Melea could see that he so badly wanted to release his pent up frustration. Dacre extended the sword toward Jenks, plucking the expensive headgear off with the tip of the blade.

"This hat is funny," he said as he smashed the stone crown to the floor.

Jenks never moved a muscle, his eyes radiating pure hatred at Dacre.

Dacre spread his arms wide and glanced side to side. "This is funny." He pointed the sword at Jenks' chest. "You are funny. A thug who fancies himself royalty."

Jenks lunged forward, a knife clenched in his fist that must have been concealed in his clothes. The younger man smoothly stepped aside and lopped off the crime-lord's hand at the wrist. Iribi screamed and Jenks dropped to a knee as blood gushed from his stump of an arm. "Funny," said Dacre, his voice as dark as his eyes.

The slaves moved for the first time since Melea had entered the room. They quickly and quietly raced out of the hall without looking back. No one was going to rush to the aid of their master.

"Well, I wish we could stay, but it's about time we hit the dusty trail," said Taisto. "So nice of you to have us over, Jenksy boy. I'd say let's do this again sometime but we both know that we won't be able to top this party." Taisto hopped up the stairs and grabbed Jenks by his good arm. "Right this way sir, let me help you to your seat."

Taisto tied Jenks to the throne, giving him one of the guard's shirts to slow the bleeding. "One more thing," said Dacre, sprinting out of the room.

Melea ground her teeth. They should be leaving. Immediately. Her frustration grew to the point where she was about to leave the others and go her own way just as Dacre rushed back into the room. He was winded and grinning from ear to ear.

"What are you waiting for? Let's go!"

"This way!" Iribi shouted.

They ran up the stairs, from where Iribi had entered. At the top of the stairs she shoved through the doors to her room, striding to the balcony, which had been crudely boarded up. The brothers began prying the boards off, and soon enough were removed for the group to squeeze through one at a time.

They slid down the rooftop, feeling the heat of the sun reflect back from the red clay tiles. Iribi kicked off her shoes, and barefoot on the slippery tiles, led them around to the side of the building, where she scrambled down a mass of climbing vines. She dropped to a narrow ledge, took a couple quick steps and leapt across to a lower rooftop.

Dacre grinned. "She's something, ain't she?"

The others followed her to race across the tiled gold and red rooftops of Marikal. Melea's heart pounded as they ran, a scent of spice wafted up, reminding her of Gerboa. The little thief would have enjoyed this.

Iribi still looked the part of a debutant in her expensive dress, but played the role of an alley cat as she set the pace. She led them expertly along the rooftops as they gradually made their way to ground level. They did not speak or celebrate the escape, instead walking swiftly toward the river, only slowing down when the sluggish water came into sight.

"It's killing me," said Taisto. "What did you run off to do back there?"

Dacre gave a sheepish smile and shrugged. "I let the hyenas out. Figured he'd see the humor in it."

Iribi's face blanched, but she said nothing. She wiped away a few small tears and pulled Dacre forward by the hand, leading the way across the street to the banks of the Green river. The reunited lovers stepped onto a small river barge as Taisto turned to face Melea.

"Thanks for your help. We won't forget our part of the bargain." His expression was solemn, like they were saying a final goodbye. He leapt onto the barge and shoved off, starting upriver.

Melea jogged a little further down the street before finding the bridge where the brothers had said it would be. It was a massive stone arch, wider than most streets in Azra. She hurried toward it, anonymous amongst the bustling crowd, and wondering if Natalya's actions made up for Shamara's. She pushed the thought aside. More pressing matters contended for her attention.

She needed to find Kachina's contact and leave the city. Revenge would be swift and savage whether Jenks lived or not. Someone in his network would be after the Saleros as soon as the details of what occurred were known. The exits out of the city would soon be monitored; Jenks was sure to have his hand in the pockets of the city guard.

A group of people swarmed the entryway to the bridge, their togas dirty and disheveled. They shouted into the crowd, some actively trying to stop individuals, forcing them to listen to the oration. The leader had a wild beard and tangled hair, his eyes held the unblinking stare of a fanatic, his voice filled with the ferocity of a true believer.

"The end draws near! Ziya'Sybel has forsaken us, know the truth and lament!"

Melea paused at the similarity of the man's decree to the claims of Anathasius.

"We are not worthy. Our hubris seals our demise! The temples ask naught but for the offerings of silver and gold!" The man laughed, high and eccentric. "Purchase your salvation. Curry favor with a departed God and feel content!"

A pedestrian shoved the speaker to the ground. "Silence your blasphemy."

The fanatic retained the wild look, leaping to his feet only to be shoved to the ground once more. "A new God will rise! The name is yet to be revealed but all shall know!"

He caught Melea watching and scrambled over quicker than she expected. She looked into his eyes, at the madness glazing his expression. Yet his voice was lucid. He lowered his tone, speaking only to her as the rest of his congregation shouted in the background. "The new God rises."

Melea pushed past him, placing one foot onto the bridge. Her progress was halted by a hand gripping her shoulder. The man released his hold as she turned, he looked off into the sky, gaze lost in the distance. "Daughter of shadow."

"Get away from me," Melea snapped.

"He will come for you."

The man turned away, returning to the head of the group, arms raised as he resumed pontificating. Melea started across the bridge, her mind buzzing with the man's deranged words. Her thoughts were displaced by the sound of a sweet melody, sifting through the open spaces along the crowded bridge.

A trio of musicians wearing canary yellow caps had secured a space near the end of the bridge. Their playing was carefree as they smiled to every passerby who dropped a coin into the basket on the ground in front of them. Each man played a different type of stringed instrument which made its own distinct sound, the distinguishable notes blending together perfectly. The only instrument Melea recognized was a lute which the musician plucked with deft fingers.

The singer's voice was strong and pure, easily carrying his words across the distance to Melea.

"She is love, bright and shining, warm and caring, tender and fierce
giving without thought
all that is good yet she cannot sustain herself
love cannot live alone, it does not dwell in solitude
love is shared or it is not at all
it is not stored or hoarded, but is passed on, given and received,
never owned but possessed by all
she is love made visible to my heart
so that my eyes may not be blinded

> love cannot live alone
> love is truth"

Melea continued pushing her way through the crowded bridge.

She noticed that the citizens of Marikal wearing hats were vastly outnumbered by those who went without. Slaves pulled rickshaws, carried goods, worked in labor crews, manned the boats on the river below, and carried out dozens of other tasks that Melea was unable to identify.

A line of stooped men shuffled past Melea, their wrists and ankles shackled. The lead man had a hollowed out look. The next man's eyes darted in every direction, catching on hers. His desperation was palpable through the brief connection before being cut short by a shove from behind. A man with a tall black hat knocked the slave on the shoulder to keep him moving. The slaves went on and so did Melea. Each was not in a situation they wanted to be but unlike them she was able to alter her path.

Originally, she was supposed to meet the contact near the main gate so that he could usher Melea through Marikal while resupplying her for the next leg of the journey. This meeting had not happened, of course. But she was only a couple hours behind schedule so she thought the missed rendezvous could be excused. The Saleros had informed her of how to get in touch with her contact when she mentioned the name of the man.

Melea approached the side door, as recommended by the brothers, knocking in the pattern they said was needed for entry—two fast, pause, one high, two low. A small slit opened in the door which Melea dropped a ten piece coin into. The slit closed and the door opened a moment later. A large bald man filled the doorway, barring entry. He seemed unimpressed to see her.

"What do you want?" Annoyance clear in his rumbling voice. He spoke in Gren, the tongue favored in Calanthia even though many spoke Simanu as well.

Melea knew Gren. She had been trained by a tutor when first arriving at the Palace of Light. "To see Vand. I missed my appointment earlier today."

The doorman was already closing the door. "Too bad. No rescheduling."

"Morokko Kachina arranged the meeting," said Melea in a hushed tone.

The name stopped the doorman dead, he tilted his head down and to the side, as if he could shake the name out of his ear. Melea had not dared to mention that name to the Saleros.

"This way," he said, ushering Melea inside.

The hall darkened when the door closed. The doorman led the way without a light. Wooden planks were peeling off the walls and holes spotted the floor. At the end of the hall was an iron door which the doorman opened with a key hanging from a string on his neck.

On the other side was a large warehouse of sorts where five carriages were being unloaded. The workers kept to their task, uninterested in who entered. She was surprised at the size of the warehouse, the building was larger than it appeared from the outside. How the carriages entered the warehouse was unclear, which made her wonder how much further the building extended. The doorman turned, leaving the carriages and workers behind so she followed. He stopped in front of a dilapidated stone fireplace, motioning her forward with a sweep of his hand.

"Get inside."

She raised an eyebrow at the request.

"Stand there," said the doorman, pointing to a spot that was less dusty than the rest of the area.

Melea obeyed the command this time, standing on the indicated spot. She looked up the chimney to see that access to the open air was blocked off. The doorman reached into the chimney to pull a hidden lever. There was a creaking of ropes and pulleys as the floor descended smoothly. Her last sight of the warehouse was the doorman's retreating footsteps. Smooth stone was her only view for what seemed to be a considerable amount of time before the descending floor stopped. Melea stared blankly into a stone wall before realizing to turn around.

Tables of men played cards, threw dice, and stacked gaming tiles between stretches of silence and bursts of expletives. Red curtains hung from the ceiling on the right side of the room, concealing the activities over there. The grunts and moans left little to Melea's imagination. Topless women strolled amongst the tables, providing drinks and food, as well as mingling with men lounging on couches. The room was well lit and a sweet fragrance pervaded the air.

A woman approached her. She wore a thin silk outfit of orange and pink that was open on the sides, displaying the curves of her hips. Her hair was elaborately supported by ivory pins and her arms jangled with dozens of gold bracelets.

"Mr. Vand is waiting for you," she said.

The woman spun on her heel, starting off in the opposite direction of the red curtains, bypassing the tables. Melea was quick to follow, noticing that every man in the room glanced over at her, even those who pretended to not be paying attention. The woman brushed through a green curtain at the back of the room to knock on a nondescript door. A dimly lit hall extended in either direction far enough that she could not see the ends. The hostess left Melea, who stared at the door for a moment as she gathered herself. She entered to find a man seated in a high backed leather chair. He motioned for her to take a seat on the other chair in the room. Melea closed the door behind her and sat down.

"I am Lucius Vand. Welcome to my establishment."

Vand was short, his chubby legs barely reaching past the edge of the chair. He was middle-aged and his hair was mostly gone, but black tufts still clung to sides of his head. Many rings of different shapes and sizes glinted in the light as he moved his right hand, which held a glass of amber liquor. His clothing was fine cut silk and tailored much better than that worn by Jenks.

The room was a ramshackle collection of miscellaneous items: a full suit of armor stood upright in the far corner, the eyeless skull of a gigantic horned beast stared down from the wall, stacks of leather bound books lined shelves above the fireplace, an intricately welded birdcage hung from a stand but without the bird, and a statue of a nude female dancer struck a graceful pose near Vand's chair.

The proprietor of the Dirty Penny took a sip of liquor before addressing Melea. "Thought we missed you. Didn't anticipate that you'd to make your way here, but what else to expect from one of Kachina's associates? I say associate because you cannot be a friend. That man has no friends, and if he does then I shudder to consider the state of the world. Anything I can get for you?"

"Supplies and a way out of the city."

"Ah but that is a trivial request. I was hoping for something more obscure."

Melea watched Vand intently. This was a man who liked to hear his own voice, who was soothed by the sound of his confidence. The room was filled with objects as in Jenks' hall, but these were not blatantly ostentatious. They were the hoarded treasures of a packrat.

"Since you're here, it means you've changed the plan, which means something has gone wrong, which means that you cannot leave as easily as before. You need me to smuggle you out of Marikal. Am I right? Of course I'm right. I am right, aren't I?"

"Yes," said Melea in Gren.

Vand nodded, smiling at Melea's accent. He switched from Gren to Simanu, clearly trying to impress her. "It can be arranged. You will be out of the city before night falls." He took another sip. "You can trust me you know. I'm not so bold as to wrong that man, not when I so enjoy living." Vand waggled his eyebrows at Melea. "Daring of you to be involved with Kachina. I can only imagine what you two are up to."

She continued with Gren, noting the spark of challenge flare in Vand's eyes. "We aren't involved." An edge crept into Melea's voice. "Why am I meeting with you instead of one of your lackeys?"

"Kachina requested that it be so," Vand said airily, reverting back to Gren. "Made it quite clear that I must personally make sure you were outfitted. It was quite rude of you to stand me up at the gate. Once you are no longer my responsibility I shall also be free of him."

The choice of words grabbed Melea's attention. "Morokko Kachina only considers a debt repaid with death."

Vand chuckled softly. "I don't owe him anything. I'm not nearly daft enough to be in that lamentable position." He pointed a stubby finger at Melea. "You are an add-on to a prior business deal, the final undertaking that will make me exceedingly wealthy. On that note, let's get you where you need to be, wherever that is. It doesn't much matter to me."

Melea considered Vand's words. Something about them was not quite right. He was willing to go to great lengths to get her out of Marikal, to take a dangerous risk simply by being alone with her, and to associate with a murderous assassin to accumulate a little more wealth. He was being quite open with her but she could not be sure if it all was just a show. Vand rested his glass on a crystal saucer and moved to rise.

"More coin will not buy your freedom. You will always be indebted to him," said Melea.

Vand relaxed in his seat and pulled a gold coin from his pocket. He held it between his thumb and forefinger, spinning it as he spoke. "Fate spins, my dear and this right here *is* freedom."

"I don't think so. It's only a small piece of shiny metal." Melea's voice sounded solid, as if the thought had not just jumped into her mind.

Vand smiled and tucked the coin away. "The shine makes all the difference. Soon I'll have enough of that shine to do whatever I please, and that my dear, is good enough for me."

For the second time that day she listened to an affluent criminal claim they could do whatever they wanted because of the power lent to them by ill-gotten coin. The first speaker was likely being devoured by his own pets. Melea wondered if anything better was in store for Vand, but could not bring herself to care about his fate.

"It binds you as tight as any other chain. The only difference is that you strive to place these shackles on yourself," she said.

Vand's eyes narrowed, and for a moment Melea saw the predatory instinct that drove him. "We're all bound in our own ways, but not all of us are fortunate enough to have deranged killers backing us. I have to pay for mine."

Melea gave a wicked smile, switching to Simanu—the language of the Shining Empire was much more effective for conveying malice. "I don't mind getting my own hands dirty."

Taut silence bridged the space between them on invisible strings, as each weighed the other's words—each using their own scale to decide worth, sifting through the potential options. Vand stared hard at Melea but she was content to wait him out. He abruptly leaned back in the chair, resting a hand on his belly, chuckling softly.

"This is why I love this line of work; you never know what to expect. Time to get you out of here, girl. Your carriage is already loaded. There's a guard on the south gate who is coming on shift just about now and the poor sap hasn't fared so well at the tables lately."

Melea stood but Vand remained seated.

"Charmonix will see you out."

Melea felt as though she had passed some sort of examination. Vand ignored her presence, apparently he was finished with her. She opened the door to find the hostess waiting.

"This way please," said Charmonix.

She started down the hall, her garment sashaying with each swaying movement. Charmonix brought Melea to a narrow staircase. She stood at the entrance, waiting for Melea to lead the way. Melea climbed a few steps before looking back to see if Charmonix was following but the hostess was gone. The woman had a quiet grace about her which allowed her to move as silently as a feather on a breeze. Melea continued to the top of the stairs to find a thin line of light separating the wall in front of the landing. She pushed against the wall and it swung open easily.

She stepped into a small warehouse almost entirely occupied by long iron boxes. The open space was filled by a carriage attached to two horses. The room reeked of sulfur and ash, the smell could only have been coming from the contents of the boxes.

"You must be my passenger," said an elderly man on top of the carriage. "Come now, I'll take care of everything. You just sit tight."

Soon they were clattering down the streets of Marikal. The whole situation was moving much faster than she was used to and the action of being bustled throughout the city made her feel queasy. This mission was acquiring different moving parts at an alarming rate. She was getting herself involved again.

Involvement with others caused trouble. Others were difficult to control, requiring continuous alterations of her plans. But how else was she going to find someone who could speak to the Chuku Bartha? Could the brothers even do as they say, and would they honor the deal? They might have used Melea, made her into a pawn for their own plans.

How could she even be sure if the carriage was actually taking her out of Marikal? The thought forced a sickly sweat onto Melea's forehead. She rubbed her clammy hands together while considering the possibilities. Her mind spun like the wheels of the carriage, turning darker as thoughts of her mistakes gathered momentum.

Silence stirred Melea out of her spiral. The sounds of the streets were gone. All that remained was the crunching wheels of the carriage and the occasional chirp of a bird. She was out of the city.

A human noise floated over the extraneous racket of the clattering wheels. The carriage driver hummed a slow, sad melody that rose and fell in contrast to the swift, direct travel of the carriage. She felt the difference in the road beneath her as the driver steered them from the stones, wheels bumping against the ruts of a dirt road.

Melea jumped out as soon as the carriage stopped, quickly scanning her surroundings. They were in a wooded area. Fresh marks in the grass showed where the carriage had deviated from the path. A horse's nicker caught Melea's attention. Her eyes followed the noise to find Ranna's ears twitch above the branches of a small raspberry bush surrounded by a stand of poplar. At least the Saleros were true to their word on this part.

"It's all about who you know," Dacre had remarked.

Melea was beginning to realize how true that was. Vand had also delivered on his promise. She turned to the carriage driver who was staring straight at her. He chewed his bottom lip, making a soft smacking sound. A thought occurred to Melea—*how had the driver known exactly where to take her?* He could not have known where her horse would be waiting.

He spoke before she could ask. "So you think you can outrun darkness, now do ya?" The driver produced a smile that was more gums than teeth. "Can't escape something that's inside of you."

Melea suddenly recognized the tune the driver had been humming. The same one sung by the crazy beggar on the streets of Azra. The old man's many necklaces jangled as he leaned forward.

The coincidence seemed absurd, but her driver, one of Vand's employees, was the same man who had confronted Melea on her way to the Black Lotus. His face looked differently than she remembered but she was certain this was the man. She doubted it was coincidence for them to meet again.

"Why are you following me?"

He gave a gummy smile. "Who says I am? You've come to me both times while I was just sitting around minding my own business. So what does that mean? The boy is right, you know."

Melea disliked this man. He rambled as if he knew all about her life. He never answered her questions either. "Leave. I am finished speaking with you."

Melea went to Ranna and stroked the mare's neck. Her saddle and replenished gear sat in a pile to the side. Melea began preparing Ranna for travel, ignoring the looks from the old man. The smacking of his lips grated on her nerves. *Ignore him and he will leave, he is just a strange old man.* The creak of the departing carriage indicated her assumption to be correct.

"You can't outrun it." His tone was a cheerful warning, like that of a grandfather advising a child not to touch the fire. *Careful, it'll burn your fingers—what did you learn?*

His quavering voice carried as he sang.

"Left alone far from home, they wander on, their purpose gone, run and hide from the shame, never can escape the blame.

"Wounds have healed but have not been sealed, shed a tear for the abandoned four, their legacy lives on forever more."

The song faded out as the carriage rolled away. Melea concentrated on saddling Ranna. After a quick check of her bags to make sure all of the gear was where it supposed to be, Melea was riding south again. Ranna was full of energy so Melea kicked her into a gallop. The big mare was enjoying the outburst, but Melea slowed the pace, her mind distracted from the task at hand. The last thing she wanted was a broken neck because of a senile old man's nonsensical, twisting words.

Words did not have meaning, they were just a less tangible variety of coin—meaningless bits of refuse used to placate others and acquire possessions. Melea gasped when she found herself humming the carriage driver's tune. His laughter echoed in her mind.

Melea slowed Ranna, bringing her to a full stop. She fumed at the man's influence. She had already wasted enough time thinking about him. Complete the mission and return to Azra to cement Anathasius' trust; that should be her only concern. Her actions at the Sanctuary gave the Emperor reason to doubt her reliability, and she would rectify this shortcoming.

She started down the Serpent at a good pace, pushing aside all thought, and focusing only on the road in front of her.

That night she dreamt again of a stag and a group of hunters, waking with a gasp as the sky exploded.

## The Floating City

Melea followed the Serpent as it slithered between Cheton and Marikal. She had always considered Azra to be the head, the location directing movement, failing to recognize that it was the rear which propels a creature forward. The Saleros had called Cheton the godless home of coin counters and policy makers.

Huge ships became visible through gaps in the foliage, gliding along like a dream. From the road, Melea could not see how these ships navigated the swamplands but she'd heard that magnificent canals cut through the constricting vegetation to connect Cheton with harbors on either coast. The Serpent took a sharp bend, leaving the ships behind.

She had reached her destination. The Serpent unceremoniously ended at the edge of a murky expanse of water. She approached the ferry needed to bring her across the half-submerged landscape and into Cheton. There were no signs or markers to designate the area, but other, smaller boats navigated the waterways as well, each choosing their own route through the wide spaces between clusters of trees rising out of the water. Thick vines drooped from overhead, draping curtains of green moss that hung still in the stagnant swamp air. The place had a motionless, closed-off feeling, an environment that adhered to its own set of rules.

The ferryman sneered when Melea approached leading Ranna. "Citizenry card."

Melea shook her head.

The ferryman scoffed, as providing explanation was apparently beneath him. "You'll have to pay the outsider tax then."

"I'm a special envoy from the Shining Empire," Melea explained.

The ferryman shrugged. "So you admit you're an outsider. Tax is five croniqs on top of the ten to ride the ferry."

"I don't have any croniqs," she said, producing a gold coin bearing the insignia of the Shining Empire.

"Exchange fee is another two croniqs." The bored disregard in his voice was as effective as if he'd demanded payment. She handed over three gold coins to see if that was enough payment and received four small octagonal coins in return. He stepped aside to let her board.

Mosquitos and flies buzzed in massive swarms above the boats, as large reptiles floated within striking distance in case anything fell into the water. The ferry cut smoothly and silently through calm water covered in broad almond shaped leaves. Melea looked over the side to see twisting roots strangling submerged trunks, pushing deep into the dark mud below. The only sign of civilization was the amount of traffic on the water as smaller, swifter boats passed the more cumbersome ferry. No one talked to Melea but a few gave her critical looks as their eyes flicked to Ranna, who took up most of the space near the rear of the boat.

As they exited the tree-line, a city seemingly emerged from nowhere. Wooden structures on sturdy stilts rose out of the murky water. The buildings were stacked on top of one another, increasing in height the further they progressed into Cheton. The ferry eased into the city, gently bumping against the wooden dock before coming to a stop. Everyone exited in an orderly manner, leaving Melea as the last to depart as she led Ranna down the ramp onto a narrow stone walkway.

Smooth stone paths ran alongside a network of canals, while stone bridges constructed of cut blocks arched overtop. In the distance stood large stone structures. Melea wondered if these stone buildings actually floated, the way the legends claimed. All of the structures in the vicinity were supported by stilts and made of wood. So far, Melea was not overly impressed. Standing above the water and floating were two different things.

She noted that the walkways seemed to be designated for pedestrians only. Rope bridges criss-crossed overhead from seemingly every structure, so that people could traverse a city without land. People embraced the unique habitat, choosing to use the man made rivers that penetrated the breadth of the city. Skiffs and canoes glided through a nearby canal, poling or paddling themselves along.

Supports creaked overhead as rope bridges swayed from foot traffic. Women carried items on their heads with one hand up for support and the other running along the handrail for balance. Curses and shouting came from the busy canal as men jockeyed for the fastest lanes. Melea lacked a boat, and Ranna would be unable to use the rope bridges, so she started down what appeared to be a main street.

The walkway was narrow and people passing by shot angry glances at Melea as they squeezed past Ranna. She glared at them, but quickly gave up as there were too many people. Many of the women wore flowers in their hair, the stems elaborately woven into the designs, which tended to be styled into long braids. The men had flowers pinned to the collars of their tunics. Melea was barely out of the docking station and had already passed two vendors selling flowers, oils, and perfumes. She wondered what the obsession with flowers was in Cheton, she'd never heard of this strange custom. Melea was passing yet another flower stand when a stern faced man approached to stand directly in her line of travel. The thin line of his mustache made his lips appear equally thin.

"May I see your permit for that animal?" he asked in a clipped tone customary to minor officials.

His attire was not fancy enough to be called ostentatious but Melea thought it looked as though he took great care in getting dressed. He wore dark grey breeches and a cream colored doublet, with a silver bee shaped broach that was clearly emblazoned on a wide lapel. Pinned beside the bee was a careful arrangement of multi-colored begonias.

"Permit? What permit?"

"You need a street conveyance permit to transport live animals by walkway."

"Oh, I don't have one, I just arrived."

The official pursed his lips, making them near invisible. "Then use the canals like everyone else. I'll let you off without a fine this time because you're new here. You'll have to pay for transportation or rent a skiff, otherwise the animal will have to be impounded."

"Where can I find someone to take me and my horse?"

Judging by the official's irritated look Melea surmised that giving directions was not part of his job. "Take the next right, cross the bridge, then take a left."

The official left her as soon as he finished speaking, no doubt off to complete other important duties. Melea followed his directions to the water taxi. A wrinkled man sat on a skiff, he turned a wizened face to Melea as she approached.

"Can you take me to the palace?"

"Eh?" he yelled, holding a hand to his ear.

"Palace!" Melea shouted, while pointing to herself and Ranna. The boatman nodded and motioned for her to board his skiff.

The reason for the profusion of flowery accessories became apparent as soon as Melea entered the waterways. Every dip of the paddle stirred up a fresh gust of sewage out of the stagnant water. The locals seemed unbothered by the stench of the water, as the canals were as bustling as any street Melea had ever been on. She was starting to wish she had not dismissed the flower vendors so readily. The journey took longer than expected due to heavy traffic, but the boatman eventually docked his boat alongside dozens of identical skiffs.

"Here," he said. "Ten." He extended a hand to receive payment. The palace was nowhere to be seen, the area looked exactly the same as any of the others they had passed.

"I asked you to take me to the palace, where are we?"

"No allowed to go to palace, have to rent own boat."

He clapped his fingers against his palm impatiently. Melea was becoming frustrated with Cheton's confusing system.

"Where?" her voice gruff.

The boatman pointed to the walkway leading to the next bridge, which crossed over to the side she had started on. Melea sighed and paid the fee. While crossing the bridge she was approached by another official in an identical outfit as the previous one, differing only in choice of flowers as this official preferred yellow lilies.

"Excuse me," he started.

Melea cut him off. "I don't have a permit. I'm trying to get to the palace but apparently I have to rent a blasted boat to do it."

"Watch the attitude, or I'll have to have to impound your animal for improper documentation."

"Tell me where to rent a boat or get out of my way."

The official's eyes burned and his face went hard. He was deciding how much to punish her. After a long moment he pulled out a scrap of parchment and began writing. Melea was not going to wait around for the verdict. She pulled on Ranna's reins, heading for the next canal, causing several passers to jump out of the way. Stabling Ranna would have been more convenient but she had made it this far and she would not be stopped now.

She hurried down a short ramp to find several vacant skiffs tied to the dock below. Melea would rent one or commandeer one.

"Hey!" shouted the official in indignation. "Bring that beast to a stable immediately!"

The command stirred up a sense of defiance in Melea. Her mind was made up. There was no way she was leaving Ranna alone in Cheton. The mare had been with her for weeks now, and it was the longest continuous time Melea had ever spent with another living being. Boarding a horse in this city would likely cost an arm and a leg as well. *Chets.* These unscrupulous people were not going to get any more of Melea's coin. She would walk Ranna right into the palace if she needed to.

"Stop, or I'll have you arrested!"

Melea ignored the official. She had no time for insignificant men and their banal rules. She expected the official to give chase but he did not, apparently lacking the compunction to substantiate his threat. A woman with two bright sunflowers in her hair greeted Melea in front of the skiffs. Melea pointed to one large enough to support Ranna's weight.

"That one—how much?"

The woman smiled politely, her hands clasped in front of her waist. "Fifty," she said with a nod of the head.

Melea was appalled by the expense. "I only need to go to the palace and back."

"You must pay for the price of a full rental because we will soon close for the night. Return tomorrow morning and you will receive ten percent of your payment if the boat is undamaged."

"I don't need it for the entire night."

The woman continued to smile stupidly at her. Voices near the bridge caught Melea's attention. She saw the official speaking with two city guards and pointing in her direction.

"How do I reach the palace?"

"Long way to go—right branch off this canal, left past the terrace gardens then take another right."

Melea produced the rental fee, nearly exhausting her remaining funds. The woman handed Melea a small clay token that was to be returned with the skiff in the morning as proof of deposit. She pocketed the token without looking at the imprint on it and was paddling down the canal by the time the guards arrived on the dock.

Melea poled the skiff forward as swiftly as possible, forcing others to move around her progress, unwilling to alter from her straight path. Ranna was tied to the skiff and whinnied nervously when the boat made an unexpected movement or when catching a reflection of herself in the water. If Ranna decided to bolt it would take Melea and the skiff down with her.

"Ssh, it's alright, girl. We're almost there." The mare seemed to be soothed by Melea's tone. She had discovered that horses were quite responsive to the emotions of their rider and in turn Melea had become more aware of her moods over the past few weeks.

She followed the rental woman's instructions until arriving at a juncture where the canal narrowed before a closed gate with thick iron bars set into high walls rising out of the water. A guard in a beige uniform approached. He wore a rounded helm and carried a parchment attached to a clipboard.

"What is your business at the palace?" he demanded.

"Special envoy from the Shining Empire."

The guard was unfazed, his face a piece of granite as he checked the names on the parchment. He traced his finger down the list, tapping it against the bottom when Melea's title did not appear.

"Not on the list, move along."

"I have a message and it is for the King's eyes only."

The guard stared at Melea, irritated that she was still there. "Not on the list, so move along."

"I don't care about any stupid list, I've traveled all the way from Azra to deliver a message and your incompetence is keeping the King waiting."

The guard looked offended. "Show me this message."

Melea retrieved the scroll, making sure to flash the Emperor's seal before tucking it back into her shirt. The guard's eyes danced around as he considered how to proceed.

"The message will be delivered for you," said the guard.

Melea shook her head slowly. "That is not how this is going to work. Now run along and talk to whoever you need to, so that I can be granted access to the palace."

If the guard was not offended before, he certainly was now. Melea shooed him away with the back of her hand. "Go now, hurry up, I don't want to spend any more time in this stinking city than I have to." A crack appeared in the guard's stony expression but she cut off his retort. "Are you a soldier or a doorman? Talk to your superiors and tell them what I told you. Now."

The guard's eyes were laced with suspicion, but he left Melea to enter the quarters beyond the gate. Melea waited for a long time, idly sitting on the edge of the skiff and patting Ranna's leg when the mare skittered nervously. The guard never returned but the gates slowly opened to signal her victory.

Beyond the gates, the castle loomed large as her imagination. For the first time Melea believed in the legend of the floating city. The castle appeared to be the only structure within the fenced area and was surrounded by water on all sides. From Melea's view it seemed to sit atop the water as light as a feather, despite its enormity.

The castle stood straight and proud, its linear architecture ending in hundreds of spires adorning the roof like an army of spearmen. A central column stood out from the rest, casting a long shadow across the city. The central column was perfectly aligned so that a shadow was always cast from the movement of the sun to split the daylight into sections. Certain time markers were designated by different colored spires around the central pillar.

Melea docked amongst other skiffs like her own. Another dock, separate from the one Melea moored to, was lined with vessels of a considerably higher quality. All of the boats were grander than any she had seen on the canals and many looked as though they required oarsmen. They must have belonged to the royals, to be used when venturing out. A palace emissary and his attendant awaited Melea at the end of the dock.

"Follow me," was the emissary's only greeting. The attendant quietly saw to Ranna's tending, taking the horse from the dock to a grassy patch on the shore.

The emissary led her through a massive arched doorway. Melea was quick to notice guards stationed regularly, silently standing in the shadows. The interior of the castle felt empty, its limestone walls and high ceilings imparting a sense of vastness. Melea found the effect to be like walking inside a giant tomb, or a vault with the treasury carefully tucked away. The emissary stopped in front of a nondescript door, opening it for Melea as he stepped to the side. She entered and the door closed behind her.

The room was small, two plain chairs and a faded red table were the only furniture. A thin man with thick, shoulder length grey hair and a pointed black beard sat across a table from her. His clothing was obviously well made but the cut and fashion appeared more for function than for style. He could have been a wealthy ship captain or modest merchant. His eyes were a watery blue, and they had a quivering luminosity that caught Melea off guard at first. The man did not so much as look at her as through her.

"Sit, Melea." His voice was quiet, soft enough that Melea needed to focus on each word. His Simanu was flawless. She sat, regaining her composure even though the man continued to watch her with unblinking eyes. "I know who you are, you are the Emperor's dealer of death, some might say you are a champion—or an attack dog. His choice of sending you is both an honor and an offense."

"It matters little to me. I don't know who you are, but it wouldn't make a difference if I did," Melea replied.

The man's mouth quirked slightly. "That is no way to speak to a king, but I think you are used to speaking to men of power with such disrespect. It seems Martinus has failed to teach you manners. I am King Mattias Horvkild."

Melea shrugged. "I am neither his child nor his dog so what need have I of manners? If you are indeed the King, then my mission is complete and I can be on my way."

She produced the scroll and slid it across the table. King Horvkild took it without bothering to open the message, tucking the scroll into a breast pocket. He leaned forward, elbows on the table, bringing his pale eyes that much closer to Melea.

"You speak as one with nothing to lose, but does that mean you have all that you want? I think not. You perceive yourself as untouchable because of the Emperor's preference. This quaint fondness of his is all that sustains you, and yet, you are ignorantly unaware of how quickly it can be stripped away. In truth, you have nothing. Poor Melea, clinging to her affections like a child with a favorite toy."

Melea was not going to play his little game, not when the reason for this provocation was unknown. She knew that she should get up and leave the capricious man without giving him the satisfaction of an answer, but the smugness was infuriating.

"You speak as a man who has everything and yet is unsatisfied, as one who has a twisted need to squeeze those around him for amusement. I'd say such actions were beneath you but, nothing is beneath a slug except for its own slime."

King Horvkild's eyes never wavered, only the corners of his mouth arched in a brief closed-mouth smile. He was enjoying this. "I am not content with only squeezing those around me. You'd be amazed at what comes forth when a little pressure is applied. If slime, as you put it, is all that is beneath me then all the world is covered in it. Do not think yourself above the filth."

"The Shining Empire is not like Strakos," Melea snapped.

"Why? Because of your faith? Don't lie to me Melea. I know you are no pious believer."

The accusation stunned her. Horvkild was right. Immortality and walking the Illuminated Path were immaterial concerns; promises lapped up by the fearful. The talking points of priests, whom she always tried to avoid and now detested. But the Shining Empire was better than Strakos because it was her home. Strakos was different—most of it was underwater and the floating parts were riddled with regulations. At least the Empire acted with purpose. What did Strakos ever do besides build more banks?

"If the War of the Gods proved anything it's that divinity cannot conquer the world so stop wasting your time. You do not desire that which your master does. What does Melea the mannerless want? Hmmm?" Horvkild purred.

Melea leaned forward. "I want to ride my horse out of this city and give my report to Emperor Anathasius."

"A boring answer," King Horvkild's voice was dry and unimpressed. "Such a sense of responsibility, but would you digress from the narrow margins? What would your price be? Why run back to your golden king when another sits before you? The only difference between the Emperor and I is that I am concerned with the present. You and I do not long for immortality. We are concerned with more tangible undertakings."

Melea's defenses went up. Horvkild was playing a bold game, blatantly pushing Melea to see her response. She was not one to back down from such tactics. Bullying only insisted that she push back.

"There isn't enough gold in this empty castle. To make a deal with a Chet is to go in debt." Melea pushed her chair away from the table, the wood scraping against the floor.

"The power of gold is eternal, it will remain as long as there are humans, growing stronger as each God falls, and they all fall eventually. People will always need money. Its ability to shape the world is so much more certain than intangibles like Light or Darkness. In what shape would Melea fashion her world?"

Melea paused. "You would supply the wealth to make my dreams a reality?"

"I would." The King's voice was barely above a whisper.

"You wouldn't say that if you knew the stuff my dreams were made of."

Melea stood to leave but Horvkild's quiet voice stopped her at the door. "The Emperor always instills such loyalty in his servants. Well perhaps not all. The Tannoi, for example, and your tutor…"

Melea paused, turning to face the King. "What are you insinuating?"

Horvkild's mouth quirked again. "Amusing. You do not know."

Melea changed tactics, looking to put the King on the defensive. "I could tell the Emperor of your bribery."

"I'm willing to wager that you won't. Right now you want to out of spite, but it is something else that drives you. Like you said, you are not a lapdog desperate for a master's attention. Go now. Run, run, Melea. Master is waiting."

Melea stared hard at Horvkild for a moment, insults jumbling together in her mind.

"Cheton is descended from the destroyed empire of Le'teokan, we have been here since before the Age of Stone," said Horvkild. "I wonder how long your little empire will last? Care to place a wager?"

Melea slammed the door behind her. The emissary was waiting outside the room.

"My horse better be ready."

The emissary quickened his pace to get in front of Melea, trying to lead her even though she knew where to go. Her footsteps echoed loudly in the expanse of the halls, reverberating back to her mind. What was the King alluding to? There was no one else like her in the Emperor's service—Kachina—but she was not like him.

The emissary hurriedly opened the main doors as Melea continued without slowing. Ranna was waiting with the attendant. He promptly loaded the horse onto the skiff under his own initiative. She left the palace without looking back. All thoughts of the wondrous floating construction were drowned in King Horvkild's eyes.

Her mind swarmed like a hive of bees and before she realized it she was through the gate and past the dock where the rental was to be returned. Melea found an open space for the skiff and docked anyway. She had just taken Ranna onto the dock when a man approached.

"Grevik ca nemoir alai?"

"Whatever."

He blinked as his mind conducted the translation. "Excuse me Miss but you can't dock here after dark. This space is only available on odd numbered days between sunrise and dusk."

Rules. More rules everywhere she turned, they were more stifling than the moist air.

"This space is fine, the boat fits perfectly," said Melea.

The man gave a fake smile, trying to placate her for what he was required to say next. "Refusal to move the boat means I will have to issue you a fine."

She'd had enough. No way she was not going to pay a fine for a rental that she didn't want in the first place. "Hold on, I think I have a token for that."

She reached into her pocket and grabbed the clay deposit token. Melea flicked the token into the man's forehead, the impact making a sharp crack. The man yelped in surprise as she led Ranna past him and up to a larger walkway.

"Stop!"

Melea hopped on Ranna, kicking her forward along the walkway. She was finished with this strange city. The legends of the floating city never mentioned inane regulations, arbitrary fines, and rental fees. People scattered out of the way as Melea thundered past.

When Melea reached the edge of the city she realized no more transport would be operating until the morning. No matter. Melea promptly slashed the chain of a hanging lantern so that it dropped easily into her palm, loaded Ranna on a boat large enough for the both of them, cut the rope securing it to the dock, and started paddling out into the darkness. Part of her wished that Anathasius would change his mind and attack Strakos instead of Calanthia.

Liars. The Salero brothers had lied to Melea, using her to free Iribi so they could escape with her into the Outskirts. All three of them were probably laughing at Melea's stupidity right now. Melea was not laughing. How could she have trusted them to hold up their end of the bargain? The promise of conversing with the Chuku Bartha had clouded Melea's judgement, deluding her into believing that the brothers could be trusted.

Common sense was deserting Melea more often lately, enabling her to travel far beyond what was acceptable. A pattern in her behavior was emerging, a potentially harmful distraction stemming from one unresolved matter. The unknown of her past was no longer content to remain dormant.

Melea sat in the knee high grass, absently tearing at individual shoots while waiting for the brothers even though the arranged meeting time was passed. Ranna crunched the grass, content with the break. Melea envied the mare's ignorance. The horse was untroubled by the actions of others. Ranna would never know betrayal. Even if Melea treated Ranna poorly by cruelly riding the mare to death, the horse was unable to understand how it felt to be used. To be discarded as a mere tool was beyond the animal's comprehension—that unsavory realization was a uniquely human problem.

Ranna was incapable of feeling bitter enough to plot revenge. The horse wanted nothing more than to run, to eat sweet grass, and to know security so that she might eat and run again.

The unknown bothered Melea the most. Could the brothers actually talk to the Chuku Bartha or had that also been a lie? Had they fabricated the whole story knowing that it would be needed to turn Melea to their cause? How had they known that Marikal was not her final destination? Melea would never discover these answers. Her time was up. Anathasius waited for her arrival, as did the Chosen she was supposed to help lead into Calanthia under the banners of war.

Ranna raised her head to look north, her ears swiveling forward to catch the sound. *Does she hear it as well?* Melea gazed at the horse, wondering if the simple beast was somehow aware of the approaching future. The clamor built in intensity until it filled Melea's ears. Bloodshed and death was coming down the Serpent. Ranna would soon see her share of it as well. Melea was used to death. She only hoped the mare would be able to handle the carnage.

# Bandits

"You can stop smiling now," said Iribi.

Dacre stared at her glowing face, stupefied by her beauty. He noted every freckle, each exquisitely curled eyelash, the sweet breath from the rise and fall of her chest.

"I don't think I can," he managed. Iribi returned the smile and his heart nearly exploded. Dacre pulled her into her arms for another embrace.

"We used to have a good thing going, a real smooth system," Taisto said dryly. "That is until my partner's brain turned to mush. Poor dunce never had a chance, went out grinning like an idiot."

Dacre ignored the gibe and squeezed Iribi tighter. He was in the special space between waking and dreaming. Alert but open to drifting along wherever the river would take them, ready to give himself up to fate, now that he had her.

An entire year of secret meetings, failed plans, and bitter separation had evaporated as if it had never been. There were times when a forlorn Dacre had been so far in his cups that emotions had overwhelmed him. He was not embarrassed to admit this. That is, usually after having more than a few drinks. In such moments he nearly lost hope of being with Iribi. In the thinnest hours of the night when a man tries to drown his heart but only ends up crushing his liver and bludgeoning his head. He'd wake up the next day feeling terrible from the drink but the hangover would pass and the heartache would remain. The body could retch up the toxins, expelling what sickened it, so why would it hold onto what was most painful?

Dealing with the unanswerable felt like falling down a well, the impact of cold water a reminder that no rope would be lowered to hoist him out. Dacre had stood bedraggled and shivering at the bottom of that well for several months until a ladder, not a rope but a full ladder, was dropped over the side. His unexpected savior came in the form of a dark haired girl whose eyes were the only things fiercer than her fists. She was as attractive as she was dangerous—a combination Dacre normally would have found irresistible. Before he met Iribi. Everything had changed that day.

Now he was filled with hope for the future, for their life together.

"Hope is a prayer held in the chest, an unspoken whisper caged by doubt, weighted down by fear," so said his grandfather, the artist. "An exquisite creature restrained from flight while it nourishes the spirit, providing warmth while the chaos of uncertainty rages all around."

Some things you just knew. There were few things that Dacre was absolutely certain of: the greatest wine known to man was the flameberry red of Calcedon, debts are always repaid one way or another, a people without a home will never be at peace, and there was no feeling as good as racing across a field on horseback. The day Dacre met Iribi he needed to add another item to the list, one that superseded the others. He loved her. His understanding of this truth was unexplainable, as was its meaning or where it would lead, but he was certain of it. And now they could finally be together.

Dacre could not imagine anything better—except maybe racing on his favorite horse with Iribi's arms around his waist while he drank from a freshly opened bottle of flameberry. He released the embrace to sit back against the wall with a satisfied sigh.

"I can't take it anymore. I need to change out of this dress," Iribi stated. "Taisto, toss me that bag of clothes." Taisto obliged and Iribi ducked behind a stack of boxes filled with caged chickens that formed a semi-solid wall. "No peeking!"

Dacre tried to sneak a look but all he could glimpse through the gaps in the crates was her red hair. He squinted, hoping to spy a curve or two. Flashing blue eyes suddenly glared out of the space.

"I can see you, Dacre," said Iribi.

Dacre quickly looked away, placing his hands behind his head, slouching lower against the wall.

"That's not very nice," Iribi added as she returned from behind the crates to sit beside him, a blush rising in her cheeks. She was now wearing black trousers, a long sleeved shirt, and a leather vest. Her voluminous hair was tied in a pony tail.

"Don't know what you're talking about," said Dacre. "I was just checking to see which chicken to have for supper."

"I was thinking the same thing," Taisto remarked. "But you never know which is the plumpest without a little squeezing first."

Dacre shot a sidelong glance at Iribi. "The thought had occurred to me and—"

Iribi elbowed Dacre in the ribs and threw her discarded dress at Taisto. "You two are terrible!"

Taisto threw up his hands in mock protest, his face hidden by the dress. Iribi giggled and shook her head. "Tell me again why I ran away with you two?"

"Well, that's easy," Taisto said from under the dress. He pulled the fabric off his face, tossed it into the air, and jumped up while ripping his sword out of the sheath slung across his back. The dress split as the sword sheared through cleanly, two segments fluttered down to floor.

Taisto jabbed the point of the sword into one of them. "Because we're fun."

Iribi's face squirmed. "Do you know how expensive that dress was?"

Dacre grabbed Iribi's hands and hauled her to her feet. He faced her in the formal stance customary in paired dancing. He sang in a rhythm traditional to most festival songs. "Oh, it doesn't matter how much it cost because without you I'd be lost, hold my hand and let the Eye spin, time to let our adventure begin."

Iribi laughed as she jigged a funny dance around the cramped cabin with Dacre. The chickens squawked in protest but the dancers ignored the avian complaints. Taisto kept time by stomping his heel. The dance was ended by the entrance of the disgruntled barge captain. He wore the olive green cap of his station.

"This isn't no party boat and unless you've forgot, you're all wanted criminals. Worse even—wanted by criminals! Now cut out this racket."

"Come now, don't be such a grump," Iribi said sweetly.

"I wouldn't have agreed to this deal if I didn't have six daughters between two women to feed and clothe."

"You forgot about your boys, Dago," said Taisto, looking out at the skinny-armed young men poling the barge along.

"Them, too!"

Iribi broke from Dacre and snatched up the smuggler's hands, twirling him into the dance. Dacre stepped back to clap along. At first Dago went along with the dance out of sheer confusion but soon started to enjoy himself. A shy smile crept onto his face when he looked at Iribi. He suddenly realized what was happening and managed to regain some of his former outrage. "Enough! We have business to discuss."

"Ah yes, business, all the world must stop for business," said Taisto.

"You used to be more fun, Dago," added Dacre.

"No I didn't, I was just stupid enough to listen to you two. Nearly lost my neck a few times. Might lose it over this lot," Dago grumbled as he gestured toward Iribi.

"Excuse me?" she intoned, hands on hips.

"No offense, but this is a messy affair. Your Da is going to be looking for you. His men will search my barge, mark my words."

"My Da," Iribi whispered.

An uneasy pause filled the small room. The smell of chicken droppings and human sweat was everywhere but it still was not safe for the trio to be out on the main deck. The Saleros had worked with Dago frequently in the past. He smuggled all sorts of goods in and out of Marikal for them. He had needed some prodding for this newest venture, and more reimbursement than the brothers wanted to pay, but this shipment was worth it. Dacre and Taisto considered it to be the most important transaction they had completed to date.

"So you have the merchandise?" asked Dacre.

"Of course I do and I think you're going to like it."

Dago turned to the crates and began fumbling with the fastenings. The chickens hopped in distress but had nowhere to go. Dago tinkered with the bottom of a crate while the hen clucked angrily at him.

"There we go," he muttered. "This should do it." He rattled the cage, sending the hen into a frenzy then stepping back confused. Dago gave the side of the crate an open palm smack which caused the bottom of it to shoot forward.

He retrieved a rectangular item from the hidden compartment, a few specks of chicken shit plastered to the corner. "Clever, eh?"

"Brilliant, Dago my man," Taisto said cheerily.

Dago handed the book to Dacre. "Now, they're not all in this good of condition, some are just scrolls, but you said you wanted quantity not quality." The barge captain waved a finger at the brothers, in case they were considering arguing with his effort.

"Every crate is hiding one?" asked Dacre.

"Yessir, some are hiding more than one," Dago said seriously.

"Perfect," said Taisto as he clapped Dago on the back. "Let's get them loaded."

Dacre rubbed his fingertips across the leather surface of the cover. It was smooth but some areas had bumps from weathering. One corner was torn off and threads were starting to fray along the spine. He opened it up, savoring the smell of ink on parchment. Iribi peeked over his shoulder to read the title.

"Divine Leadership: The King as Law. Doesn't sound very entertaining."

Dacre snapped the book shut. "I love that smell."

Iribi looked perplexed. "So it smells nice. That doesn't mean it's any good."

Dacre shrugged. "Somebody thought it was important enough to put it on paper, to measure out each word to their liking. That takes a lot of effort and a lot of time to complete such a specific goal."

"Still," said Iribi, unconvinced.

"Most people can't bat their big, blue eyes and get whatever they want you know," Dacre joked.

Iribi lunged at him, trying to wrestle him to ground. Dacre lost his grip on the book as he fell over laughing.

"My partner used to be helpful," Taisto lamented. "Until his brain turned to—"

"Mush!" Dacre shouted from the floor, an instant before Iribi socked him in the gut. "Oof!"

Iribi cheered. "Alright, the fighting is over." She hopped off Dacre and skipped over to assist Taisto and Dago.

"Give me a moment," pleaded Dacre as he sat up. He shook the dust out of his hair like a dog. He was dirty, hungry, the punch hurt more than he let on, and they were being pursued by merciless killers but he was happy. Sometimes all a person needed was one part of their life to be perfect.

They continued upriver for the rest of the day and into the evening, trying to place as much distance between themselves and Marikal as possible. The water was low and slow during this part of the season so they made good time. Dago's two young sons took turns poling the barge ahead.

The light of the moon shimmered on the inky ripples left in the wake of the barge. Just before dawn Dago gave the order to angle over to the northern bank.

His older son quickly moored the barge to a small dock. The rooftops of a small village poked up in the near distance.

"Go to my cousin's house. Two horses will be waiting for you there," said Dago.

They each left the barge with a heavy sack of books slung over their shoulders. Dacre saw Taisto slip a few coins to Dago's son sitting on the dock. Taisto raised a finger to his lips and the boy quickly pocketed the secret payment. Dacre looked back for the younger sibling. He was dozing at the edge of the barge, a long pole half in the water, the upper half resting against his shoulder.

"Psst..." hissed Dacre. The boy's eyes fluttered open but he was tired from a night of hard labor. "Gregory wake up," Dacre said a little louder.

Gregory blinked the sleep out of his eyes, spotting Dacre holding a coin. Dacre flipped the coin over to the boy who reached out to catch it with a grubby hand. The coin was immediately deposited in some pocket and the boy was once again dozing as if nothing had happened.

Dago emerged from the cabin with the two sections of Iribi's dress. He ran up the dock waving them. "Take these. I'll have no evidence of your passing on my barge. Now get moving. It'll be best if no one sees you."

Dacre stuffed the cloth into his bag. They could destroy it when they made camp. Fire was the only reliable cleanser when it came to hiding one's tracks. He nodded at Dago, acknowledging his prudence, and fell in line behind Taisto and Iribi.

The village was tiny, not much more than a few hovels erected on hard-packed dirt. Calanthia was famed for the agricultural prowess enacted by their drainers but these people were obviously stuck working the land with only the strength of their backs. At the moment the village's singular street was empty but the farmers would soon be rising to begin their work for the day. Dacre was astonished that people would choose to remain in despondent poverty, imprisoned by their shanties, but he supposed that some were content to eke out a living. His people were constantly on the move, no single location in the Outskirts offered continual plenty.

They found two nags saddled and waiting behind the last shack on the edge of town. Hopefully the coin payed to Dago would bring some prosperity to this bleak little community. Dacre knew it would be more than enough to replace these two horses, but trusting the honesty of a smuggler to pay his debts was a foolhardy assumption.

Soon they were riding north, not as swiftly as Dacre would have liked, but he was worried about pushing the shaky gelding too hard. Iribi's arms felt good around his waist; if only he had a bottle of flameberry. Dacre sighed, Calcedon was in the opposite direction they were headed. He breathed in the crisp morning air. This was good enough, he could live with this.

They edged around fields, staying off the main roads, traveling as directly north as the landscape allowed. The Serpent was not yet within sight but Dacre knew it was just off to their right. Since they were not going to take the Chuku Bartha Pass, using the the Serpent was unnecessary.

A steady pace brought them near where they wanted to be as the last light dropped below the horizon. They continued on the same route for several more hours before crossing the ancient stone roadway.

"Why did we wait so long?" asked Iribi.

"Never trap yourself along the coast unless you've got a ship," answered Dacre. "We're nearly there."

Taisto and Dacre had wanted to avoid becoming pinned between the coast and the Serpent. A sense of security descended over Dacre as the wall of the Eternal Forest rose into view. The size of the initial row of trees and the density of the forest behind gave the feeling of a fortification, a barrier between the wilderness and the world of men. They pushed the horses forward at a walk. The thin beasts were tired from a long day of travel. Taisto dismounted before the first enormous fir tree to lead his horse into the forest. Dacre and Iribi followed his example and stepped into a crush of vegetation.

Taisto lit a torch so that they could find the trail markers left behind. To step off the trail was to become lost in a maze. Beasts lurked within the forest, potentially behind every corner, things that even the Chuku Bartha did their best to avoid.

Dacre's nerves were on edge but he tried to keep it from showing. To enter the Eternal Forest at night was reckless. He would almost have preferred to face Jenks' men. The only consolation was that he knew they would not be followed here. They had escaped capture. Now they just needed to find safety from the unknown dangers. Iribi felt the suffocating weight of the forest as well. She clung tight to his arm.

"I can almost feel it breathing," she whispered.

*She isn't wrong*, thought Dacre. There was no sky, no outside world, the forest was a realm unto itself.

The tightness in Dacre's chest finally let go as he spied the last trail marker in the light of Taisto's torch. Just a few more steps and then they would be protected. Fatigue from the past few days was wearing him down, tugging at his shoulders, begging that he rest. *Soon*, he thought, *we're not done yet.* Taisto had stopped, he stood statue still in the firelight. Dacre caught up to his brother and immediately noticed the cause of concern.

Several summers ago they had built a small cabin in the southern portion of the Eternal Forest. It was as unfindable and secretive of a hideout as they could think of. The cabin was wedged between two fallen pillars, huge lengths of smooth stone that once stood but now lay on the forest floor. The brothers sealed the open roof and backside with good timber, filling in the cracks with mud and rocks. The front door was built of strong wood which could be reinforced from the inside. Dacre had dared to believe that their structure was impregnable. The gaping hole in the door mocked him like a demon's smile.

"What do you think?" he whispered to Taisto, suddenly very concerned about eyes that may or may not have been on them.

"We have nowhere else to go. I'll check it out." Taisto handed his reins to Dacre and withdrew his sword.

He approached cautiously, curling to the left of the opening in case whatever had destroyed the door was still inside. Taisto waved the torch in front of the door and waited. He lowered the torch to display the door—it had been ripped to shreds. Scratch marks covered what was left of it, most of the door was now only splinters and chewed bits of wood.

"Fangeri," he said. "Looks like a whole pack of them. Their musk is all over the interior, the oil is dried and crusty so this occurred some time ago."

Two pinpricks of light reflected in the dark recesses of the cabin. Dacre tried to call out a warning. A throaty snarl cut his call short. The fangeri charged Taisto.

Taisto was knocked to the ground. The beast had the torch in its jaws, seemingly impervious to the flames. The wooden torch snapped. Dacre sprinted to Taisto's aid. His sword swept in low, striking the beast across the midsection. The fangeri was thrown off of Taisto, but scrambled back to its feet to charge again.

Dacre had both blades out. The fangeri never hesitated. Its sinuous body slipping between his defenses. The fangeri latched onto one sword and wrenched it to the ground. Dacre slashed with the other sword, but the edge glanced off the creature's oily hide. Time seemed to slow for him, allowing him to see every aspect in perfect detail. Teeth and claws and mad eyes hurtling toward him.

The fangeri squealed. Dacre blinked and saw a sword coming out of its side. The beast squirmed on Taisto's blade, trying to pry itself free. Taisto slammed the point into the ground. Dacre brought his sword down in a two-hand chop, severing the creature's neck.

"I hate fangeri," Dacre gasped.

"Lucky there was only one," said Taisto. "A pack large enough to tear through the door would have made short work of us."

Iribi grabbed Dacre's arm.

"We'll have to abandon the horses," said Taisto.

Dacre rubbed a hand roughly over his face. "You're right. There's no way I'm bringing them inside without a door. It would be like serving ourselves up for dinner."

"We're still going inside?" squeaked Iribi.

"There's no other choice," said Dacre.

Taisto took both sets of reins from Dacre. "I'd rather have some protection than none. Take the bags inside. I'll let the horses go a little ways from here. If you hear something approaching and it isn't carrying my torch—kill it."

Dacre gave Iribi one of his swords and brought her to the section farthest from the door. At least the entryway was small enough that the larger carnivores could not fit through. The beasts of the Eternal Forest grew to monstrous sizes but rarely left the protection of the trees.

The smell of the fangeri was still potent. It was like urine with a dash of rotting food. Taisto's torch suddenly appeared in the doorway. He snuffed it out on the dirt floor.

"I'll take first watch. Try to get some sleep if you can," said Taisto.

"I'll go next," said Iribi. She tried to sound brave but could not keep the quaver out of her voice.

"Get some sleep," Dacre said softly. "I'll wake you when it's your turn."

She handed back his sword and slumped to the ground. Dacre sat down beside her so she could place her head on his shoulder. She was asleep in moments. Dacre wished sleep came to him as easily. He would need it. A long night loomed ahead, his turn came after Taisto, and he would make sure that Iribi's turn never came.

Dacre must have drifted off at some point as he was woken by the shriek of a big cat. The scream of one of their horses instantly followed. The sound of the kill was far off but not as far as Dacre would have liked.

"How long has it been?" he asked Taisto.

"Not quite yet your turn," said his brother, eyes fixed on the open doorway.

"Might as well switch now, I won't be going back to sleep after that."

Taisto accepted the offer, promptly laying down with his back to the opening. The message was clear if unintentional—your turn to protect us. Dacre gently urged Iribi over so that he sat in the center of the room, giving him a clear view into the forest.

The pitch black canceled out his range of vision. Dacre's mind tried to piece fragments of the darkness together, forming them into eyes, then into faces that gazed back at him. The impressions made Dacre feel anxious, so he opted to rely on his hearing.

Visibility returned with the dawn, the light filtering slowly through the trees. Dacre's breath caught in his throat as a large, dark animal walked into his line of sight. Then he recognized Taisto's horse as it calmly nibbled grass some distance away from the cabin. Dacre was considering whether to chase the horse away or retrieve it when a black form slipped into the clearing. Dacre blinked his sleepy eyes, thinking his imagination was playing tricks again.

The horse turned its neck to look at something. A black hand reached around the horse's neck. Dacre's pulse jumped as a black arm attached to the hand came into sight. A thin black form stood parallel with the horse, looking into its face. The figure looked like a person but when it turned to face the shelter Dacre knew that it was no man.

Below the nose was a black maw, twisting and turning like a snake's attempting to swallow prey larger than itself. The eyes and features were an even darker shade of black than the semi-darkness. Dacre tapped the good luck totem on a chain beneath his shirt. The being had the same shape as a man but Dacre was convinced it was something else. Some things you just knew and evil was one of them. He would have to add that to the list.

The demon leaned in to smell the horse's neck, taking a moment afterward to contemplate the scent. The demon took the reins and led the horse out of Dacre's sight. Dacre waited as long as he could, heart pounding in his ears, before tapping Taisto on the shoulder. His brother groaned softly as he rolled over, eyes squinting in protest.

"Taisto," said Dacre, voice sounding far too loud in his own ears. *Please, don't attract the demon*, he thought. "Demon—outside—eating horse."

Taisto groaned. "Hmmrh?"

Dacre placed a palm on Taisto's chest. "Quiet, it'll hear you. We have to leave out of the back tunnel. Now."

Taisto finally recognized the fear stretched across Dacre's face. He bolted upright, staring out into the empty clearing in front of the cabin. He looked to Dacre questioningly. Dacre nodded solemnly, jabbing a thumb to the right, the direction the demon had gone. Taisto nodded his understanding. He rose gingerly and carefully began removing the covering over the escape tunnel.

Dacre turned to wake Iribi. In the night she had moved from his shoulder to curl up on the floor. He shook her shoulder and she sat up rubbing her eyes. Iribi's eyes opened wide in shock as they came into focus, a shrill scream of terror escaping her lips before she managed to stifle it with a hand. Dacre looked to the doorway to see the severed head of Taisto's horse. Blood steaming as it pooled around the neck.

Dacre leapt to his feet with a sword in each hand. No demon emerged. All he could hear was Iribi's muffled, panicked breathing. He took a step forward but Taisto stopped him from moving further.

"He's testing us."

*Right, it probably wants me to rush out so that it can gobble me up*, thought Dacre. By now Taisto had removed the cover of the tunnel. He gave Iribi one of the bags and motioned her inside. She looked to Dacre for confirmation, he nodded, trying to appear confident. Taisto grabbed another bag and followed Iribi, crawling on hands and knees.

Dacre paused, afraid to take his eyes off the doorway, to turn his back on what he knew was waiting out there. The anticipation became too intense. He quickly sheathed his swords and bent down to pick up the final bag. Dacre looped the string over his neck so that the bag hung over his back, leaving his hands free. Unable to resist a final look, Dacre peered over his shoulder at the doorway.

A thin black form stepped into opening, partially blocking out the light. The demon stared at Dacre like a bird observing an insect. All Dacre could focus on was the mouth, the horrible, evil grin of serrated fangs. Dacre was half crouched, about to enter the tunnel, but that option was no longer possible. He turned to face his visitor.

"Good morning, chuckles, you look happy to see me."

The demon crossed the distance of the cabin in an instant on its spidery limbs. Dacre barely managed to draw one sword to block the attack. A clang of metal rang out in the enclosed space. Dacre felt a sharp kick to the inside of his right knee, followed by another to his ankle. He was swept to the floor, landing hard on the bag of books. The demon raised its weapon, what Dacre thought looked like a sickle, for the killing stroke. *Run Taisto, run Iribi*, were his final thoughts.

The demon unexpectedly cocked its head to the side. Could it read his mind? It ducked and stepped to the side as an impact smashed into the wall above Dacre with a loud thwack. A Chuku Bartha spear vibrated from the impact. The demon turned and hurled the sickle out through the doorway. Dacre heard a cry of pain from the brave Chuku Bartha attempting to save him. The demon stood directly above Dacre, straddling his left leg.

Dacre kicked upward as hard as he could, feeling his shin connect with pelvic bone. The demon let out a wheeze, so Dacre kicked again for good measure. The demon collapsed to the floor. Dacre scrambled to his knees and scurried into the tunnel without looking back.

Survival was all that was on Dacre's mind as he scampered out of the tunnel. He surfaced on the far side of the clearing. Several of the massive fallen stones lay between him and the underbrush. Dacre bolted into the trees. He guessed where the others would be going. The bag bounced against his back as he sprinted through the forest, his face and forearms getting scratched from the headlong flight.

He leapt over some brambles, only to slip on the mossy footing, and fell into a patch of thorns. He lay there for a moment, afraid to move, and inflict more pain. The sound of quickly approaching footsteps made Dacre squeeze further into the thorns. He glimpsed the demon's dark figure race past.

Dacre got to his feet as quietly as he could, then started on a more northerly route. He would have to take a slight detour. Soon, the sound of the river turned him east; crossing the river would be his salvation. The sound of running water grew louder, filling his heart with hope.

The river was visible through the tree branches. Dacre slowed to push his way through, unsure of how steep the bank would be. An earsplitting crack near his head almost knocked him over. Bark exploded around him as he stumbled into the sunlight on the riverbank.

The demon stood behind Dacre wielding a whip. The weapon was made of small links of metal that curved together in unison. Each link had a thin blade attached to its side, turning the length of the whip into a razor. The demon raised his hand to snap the whip forward again. Dacre took off. The sound of the whip's impact cracked behind him as he charged downstream.

He could see the bridge that he and Taisto had built. Salvation stretched out before him. Iribi urged him across from the other side, her arms waving frantically. Taisto was seated with a leg ready to kick the release that would collapse the bridge and send it crashing into the water below.

Dacre leapt out to the third rung, the bridge sagging beneath his weight. With his arms outstretched for balance Dacre sped forward as fast he could on the balls of his feet.

The bridge sagged even further as the demon stepped on.

Iribi picked up a rock but hesitated to throw it, not wanting to hit Dacre. The far bank was within reach. A whir of ripping air signaled an impending strike from the demon's whip. There was no time and even less space to evade the deadly weapon as it snaked forward to smash into Dacre's back.

The bag ripped open, books went tumbling into the river. The force of the whip caused Dacre to lurch forward and lose his balance. He jumped with arms extended for the edge of the riverbank. Iribi hurled her rock as Taisto kicked the release mechanism. The demon howled as the rock careened into his face. The posts securing the bridge to the riverbank dropped away. Dacre clung to the top of the bank by his fingertips. Firm hands grabbed his wrists, pulling him over the lip and onto his stomach. Taisto cheered as the demon poured over the falls.

Iribi was hugging him tight enough that he had trouble breathing. He'd escaped death incarnate to enter the waiting arms of his lover. There was nothing he could not do.

Dacre sat up. "We have to leave the forest."

"I know," said Taisto.

"Our camp is indefensible, and besides, it's on the *other* side of the river, the Chuku Bartha won't allow us to stay with them, and a *demon* knows where we are. I'm ready to cut our losses and keep moving."

"I know," Taisto replied, his dark eyes scanning the ground as his thoughts considered their predicament.

"We need to go home."

"I know," Taisto repeated.

Dacre got to his feet and placed an arm around Iribi's waist, directing her into the forest. "Natalya will understand why we had to leave," he called out to his brother.

Taisto stayed on the riverbank for a moment, staring out over the rushing water of the river. "Sorry, Natalya," he said quietly before entering the forest.

## All That Shines

Lucius Vand rested comfortably in the support of the wide backed leather chair. He swirled the brandy along the rounded contours of the glass while staring into the crackling fireplace across the room. Firelight cast flickering shadows throughout the cluttered office, creating a sense of the otherworldly as it magnified shapes in the cramped space. The extended hand of a marble dancer became that of a crouching giant as it reached up to the ceiling, the gilded birdcage in the corner a device to house a mythological beast, the ox skull lengthening down to the floor to swallow the carpet in its shadowy maw.

    Vand's mind drifted as he awaited the arrival of a welcome but nonetheless unsettling guest. He would soon be able to leave this office of collected treasures and expand his operation to the breadth that his mother always knew he was capable of. His dear mother. Vand knew the rumors about his treatment of her. Let the people think what they would. A chivalrous reputation did him no favor in this line of business anyway.

    The Dirty Penny was indeed a fitting name for his establishment but was not due to selling his mother into prostitution. Vand smirked as he recalled learning the tricks of the trade from underfoot growing up in the brothel owned and operated by his mother. Lucille was a calculating and ambitious woman who was still very much alive. She had carefully worked her way up from a fresh faced beauty with a bastard child in tow to become Mistress of Marikal's most prestigious brothel, the Lost Lamb.

    Never one to be content, Lucille had extended her influence to acquire the Lamb's three main competitors. She now controlled the gossip of Marikal and beyond, she was the queen of pillow talk, able to loosen lips with the curves of feminine hips. She was also Vand's benefactor and business partner, her money fronting the startup of his fledgling underworld empire. But that was about to change. Vand was more than ready to step outside of his mother's perfumed clutch.

    Exchange was how Vand accumulated wealth, how he gained leverage over his rivals. He accepted payment in exchange for his services, great sums of it, in fact, but he preferred to acquire favors. Personal indebtedness was invaluable, able to produce real world results—there was more to having someone in your back pocket than simply having access to their reserves. People were assets in themselves and it was people who made money worth anything at all.

    Vand enjoyed the power of wealth but true power resided in owning a person, to be able to bend them to his designs when needed. Having slaves was one thing, but owning a free man was an indescribable rush. To gain leverage over someone was to have control. He was playing a dangerous game with this particular exchange but the potential benefits exceeded the risk.

He raised the glass, pausing at the slight creak of the opening office door. The darker areas of the room deepened as a shadow silently slipped into the room.

"I agree, I feel we have moved beyond the need for knocking. We're practically old business partners now," Vand said, trying to sound light and confident.

Shadows flittered across the floor as Vand's guest angled around the room, remaining out of sight. He mentally built up his confidence, feeling the slow burn of brandy in his gut. *This is what you wanted Lucius, what you planned for; there is nothing to fear.* He believed the words yet a feeling of anxiety still tingled in his chest.

Vand spoke to the shadows. "Your arrival means that my rivals have had a rather unpleasant night. As one falls another shall rise. Life from death and all that rubbish."

The shadowy movement ceased, the only sound in the room was that of the crackling firewood and Vand's breathing. The speed of his rapid inhales was alarming. Was he really breathing that loudly? *Calm yourself Lucius, take a drink and remember what he has done for you.* He sipped from the glass, swallowing more brandy than expected, coughing on the strong flavor. Through the curvature of the glass Vand saw a lithe form step in front. He lowered the glass, careful to keep it from shaking as he set it on the armrest.

"Morokko Kachina, I am glad that you have joined me on this most auspicious night. A toast to the conclusion of a successful partnership."

Vand took another drink, accidentally finishing the liquor in a gulp. He stared into Kachina's expressionless black eyes. *What is beneath that damn scarf?*

"You have obligations that remain to be fulfilled," rasped the assassin.

The assassin held a burlap sack in hand, the bottom of which was a darker shade from the dampness of its contents. He set the bag down roughly on the floor, spilling the contents on an exceptionally expensive rug.

The heads of Marikal's prominent crime-lords rolled across the floor. Vand knew them all: Bernherd the Butcher's bald head came to a stop as it bumped into the marble dancer, Jermal Kursvovic, tumbled under the unoccupied second chair, and the most powerful player in Marikal's underworld rolled directly toward Vand. The dead eyes of Fitzroy Jenks stared up at Vand, somehow still hateful even in death. Vand nudged the head away with a toe.

"Quite right," he stammered.

Vand looked at Kachina. The assassin's covered face was even more frightening than the decapitated visage of Vand's longtime nemesis. The firelight behind the assassin seemed to be swallowed by his presence, the darkness becoming solid, rising up like a demonic shroud.

"Have no doubt, all preparations will be in place for the Emperor's arrival," Vand assured the assassin.

"What of Lyrene and Qu'hraz?"

A shudder ran through Vand at the assassin's voice. He could not help himself from shrinking from the concealed menace. Kachina affected Vand like no one else he had ever encountered, making him feel small and weak, unsure if he could even raise himself from sitting. He fought back the urge to flee. He was now the undisputed criminal king of Marikal and should act accordingly.

"All taken care of. I've used my most trusted men for those assignments."

The assassin pulled down the scarf and Vand gasped. "We shall see," said Kachina.

The phrase carried an implied threat of Kachina's return if he, or his master, were not pleased with Vand. His mouth went dry. He sorely wished he had another drink. Kachina stared at him for a moment longer with eyes as dark as the empty sockets of a skull. Vand nearly pissed himself.

The assassin abruptly left and the room burst into light.

Vand rubbed his hands together, trying to shake off the chill he felt despite the heat of the fire. Bands of gold and silver inlaid with precious jewels glimmered on his stubby fingers.

"It's the shine that matters," he said softly to himself.

Those were his mother's words to him as a boy, becoming something of a personal mantra. Times were tough in those early years and some nights brought more abuse than food. Lucille carefully hoarded anything of value until she was able to provide a more stable living arrangement for the two of them. He had come a long way from the frail little boy who clung to his mother's leg out of fear of her leaving; he was now the most influential man in Marikal. The King still ruled but his reign would soon be coming to an end.

Vand felt inspired by the thought of striding across the city like a colossus, clearing the Green river in a single step as people scurried out from beneath him. He had earned this newfound status, taken chances that none other was willing to risk. Vand was a good gambler, he always had been. His gamble with Kachina was about to pay off, and all that was needed were a few small actions when the time came. He slicked back his hair and licked his lips, feeling better but still unsettled by the meeting with the assassin.

"Charmonix!"

The slave consort appeared instantly, gliding into the room almost as effortlessly as the assassin. Her entrance was accompanied by a scent of jasmine that perked up the hairs on Vand's neck in a very different way than Kachina's shadow. Charmonix gracefully slipped onto Vand's lap to stroke his chest with her elegant fingers. He wanted to take her right there but he could see a sheen from the top of the Butcher's head from the corner of his eye. He pushed Charmonix off, her affections could wait.

"Find some tobacco for me. There should be some in the desk."

Charmonix batted her almond eyes, pretending to pout. "You could put your lips to better use."

"Jenks always slathered over you—he could finally get a kiss if you're that eager."

Charmonix's eyes darted to the shape under the other chair. She went to the desk without another word. Vand tapped a hand impatiently on the armchair while he waited, eventually leaving the comfort of the chair to join Charmonix.

"It's tobacco, you remember what that looks like don't you? You said that you restocked the supply last week, it shouldn't be a struggle to remember that far back. It's not like you're trying to recall the first cock you ever saw."

Every drawer held an assortment of objects but none proved to be useful to his search.

"Hmph."

Charmonix knew better than to say I told you so. Vand rubbed his paunchy belly while recalling where he last placed the tobacco. He could not remember and come to think of it, he could use something to eat as well. The air in the office was stuffy anyway. Dried blood from the severed heads made his nose curl.

"Find me something to eat, something warm; I'm going in search of tobacco. Try to remember that first cock while you're at it," Vand ordered.

Vand grabbed his pipe and a pack of matches before ambling out of the office to head for a warehouse housing a few boxes of tobacco.

As usual, there was noise coming from the gaming room—the sounds of gain and loss—but to Vand it all sounded like clinking coins. No matter who the big winner was this evening it was he who would make the most profit. He stayed in the side hall, making his way to a hidden staircase that opened into a warehouse.

A solitary carriage sat in the room, its hulking shape intimidating in the darkness. He lit a match to avoid crashing into the stored goods. Vand quickly shook the flame out when he remembered what else was stored in the warehouse. He was left to shuffle forward with arms extended in the general direction of where he thought the tobacco might be. After bumping into several crates and opening two empty boxes Vand finally found what he was searching for. He grabbed a sheaf of tobacco leaves and exited the warehouse, unlocking the only door to the outside. The dried leaves were unprocessed so he would have to crumple them himself.

An elderly gentleman stood beneath a hanging lamp attached to an awning on the outer wall of the warehouse. The street was otherwise deserted. Vand recognized the gent as a carriage driver he hired several years back. The man puffed on a pipe, sending small plumes out into the cool night air. Moths fluttered around the lamp, the insects had not yet left for their fall migration.

Vand approached, trying to recall the man's name. Draxis? Dremo? Drahomir? That was it. The fresh air allowed the scope of Vand's accomplishment to sink in.

"Ho, old boy Drahomir! What are you still doing hanging around here at this hour?"

Drahomir slowly turned to Vand, his eyes half-hooded. He seemed to be deep in thought, taking several moments to blink himself back into awareness.

"Hmm just thinking I suppose, and having a puff while watching the moon make her way."

Vand looked into the night, unable to see any sign of the moon. Most of the sky was blocked by the building across the alleyway. He quirked an eyebrow at the old man. "I'm not sure how to tell you this, but you can't see any moon from here."

Drahomir nodded slowly while taking another puff. "You can, you can, oh yes, she's always there. Sometimes a little effort is needed for the seeing."

Vand stepped out from under the awning to look into the open air above. He turned to face the warehouse and found the moon suspended in the air on an invisible thread, huge and silver and shining. Drahomir stood directly beneath the moon, still calmly puffing on his pipe.

"It looks like the reng that the Qu'hrazi keep tied to their belts." Vand returned under the awning to stand beside Drahomir. "I never understood why they keep their coin out in plain sight like that," he said with a shake of the head. "Wouldn't happen to have some more tobacco would you?"

Drahomir wordlessly produced a small pouch from an inner pocket and handed it over. An aromatic scent wafted from the pouch, tickling Vand's nose as he opened it. He stuffed a few finger-fulls into the bowl before handing the tobacco back. The smoke hit him hard, flavorful and strong, tasting of apples and spices.

"I must be paying you too much for you to afford such quality smokeables," Vand joked. "Remind me to lower your wage, there's a war coming you know."

Drahomir smiled and then looked at Vand earnestly. "The trouble with eyes is that a sunrise and a sunset are viewed as the same, depending on where destiny has placed your feet."

Vand could already feel the potency of the tobacco. His head swam with each additional inhale. It was laced with krakoa powder, the way they smoked in Nefara. He found the sensation enjoyable, like floating in a tepid pool of water. The stress he felt from speaking with Kachina was drifting along with the smoke pouring from his lips.

"I've heard that somewhere," he said through an exhale of smoke.

"Similar adages are spoken by rustic folk around these parts," Drahomir replied. He dipped his pipe toward Vand knowingly. "I have it on good account that it's a prayer of sorts for the stargazers of Fyn, oh yes."

Vand chuckled. "You've traveled that far, old-timer?"

Drahomir cast a sidelong look at Vand. "Don't need to go everywhere when there are those who are constantly on the move, willing to impart tidbits of wisdom as they pass by."

"And who might this benevolent wanderer be?"

Drahomir removed the pipe from his mouth, using it to point at the space where the moon sat above their heads, hidden by the awning. "The moon told me, she says a great many things."

Vand laughed, coughing on smoke. Drahomir laughed along with him. Perhaps it was his lightheadedness or the serious look on the old man's face but after the laughter Vand attempted to listen for the moon's voice. He strained his ears into the silence. There was the distant bustle of traffic on the street, the noise of ships moving along the river nearby and, after a moment's consideration, what he was convinced was the meaty thuds of prostitution in action. The latter was the sound of money in his pocket—Vand took a cut from all the whores in this district.

No feminine voice appeared to impart wisdom. Drahomir watched openly while Vand listened, simply shrugging when he gave up.

"She didn't speak to me, but I still like the quiet gal," said Vand. "I know she's on my side despite the silence."

"Hmm how do you figure?"

"Because she shines."

Vand dumped the burnt contents of the bowl on the ground and shoved the pipe into a breast pocket. "Thanks for the smoke, old boy. Now I'm off to find a whore or three, and drink myself silly. I suggest you do the same, this city will be bloedeth to the balls when the Shining Empire tears down the front door."

Drahomir just hummed an unfamiliar tune.

Vand stopped with his hand on the door. The noise down the alleyway reached a hasty crescendo before lapsing into silence. The world was full of people screwing each other one way or another. The smart ones learned how to profit from it.

Drahomir's humming floated as softly as the moths tapping against the lamp. Persistent fools. The shine of the lamp was obvious but its visibility did not make it more attainable. Vand understood that one needed to bring themselves closer to pure darkness in order to obtain the light that dreams were made of.

## Driftwood

The Captain of the palace guard met Melea as she entered the Palace of Light.

"I trust you traveled well?" asked the Captain.

"Quite," said Melea. "Where is Mandrikos?"

A shadow crept over the Captain's face. "Something I'd very much like to know."

"Goldwin then," Melea spat. "Where is he?"

"In his office, I believe."

Melea strode past the Captain and up the stairs in search of the master of maps. She pushed open the door and barged into the room. Goldwin sat at his desk, slumped over a disordered scattering of maps.

"Where is your friend Mandrikos? I have a few questions for the bald weasel."

Goldwin's gaze remained downcast, staring at his massive forearms. "So do I."

"That's it?" No lecture about the cross-breeding of weasels or something?"

Goldwin turned to look at Melea, his face covered in purple bruises, his bottom lip split.

"Who did this to you?"

Goldwin's gaze returned to the desk. "No more interrogations."

"He's gone, isn't he?"

Goldwin nodded.

"The bastard betrayed the Empire and they think you knew about it, right?"

Goldwin was silent. She almost wanted to ask a question regarding geography that Goldwin could ramble on about. Almost. Instead, she left the man alone with his pain, slamming the door behind her.

Melea started back towards the main entryway. The Captain of the guard was waiting for her at the bottom of the stairs.

"Darkness has twisted your former tutor," said the Captain. "Which leads me to wonder if his corruption has infected his pupil."

"Get out of my way."

The Captain blocked Melea's path. "I can have you retained for questioning."

She moved a hand to the hilt of her sword. "I can run my sword through your chest."

The Captain stepped aside and Melea exited the palace. She crossed the courtyard and kept going. She needed to think. To be alone.

Buzzing insects hovered over the shattered debris of Stone Park. Melea watched the birds hop along the twisted branches of the blasted elm. They occasionally left their perch to displace hazy pockets of black flies. Only the hungry birds and unmindful insects disturbed the unofficial tomb—nothing else moved in the final remains of Cambor.

One had dared to roam this area, claiming it as his own, but he was not buried in his kingdom. Melea guessed his fate had been to become another set of sun bleached bones beneath the scrabbling legs of hungry crabs. The priests of the Sanctuary did not seem like the forgiving kind.

Melea wondered if anyone could survive the heartbreak she'd witnessed in the thief's eyes. Gerboa had worked with absolute dedication to save his sister, his only family in the world, and yet was rebuffed at the pivotal moment. She had seen something fracture inside of the boy. One could not set a heart in plaster like a broken arm.

Movement across the debris scattered the birds. A boy made his way over the stones, moving confidently as if he were on a well-traveled route. The glare of the sun made it difficult to make out his features. He moved toward Melea, stopping when he noticed that she was watching. The boy hopped on an upward jutting chunk of stone to raise a wooden sword into the air.

"Stay where you are maiden so fair. The Forever Boy will soon be there!"

Melea watched the rascal scamper closer, slipping several times before finally jumping down beside her. He huffed from the effort of traversing Stone Park, grinning proudly at the accomplishment. The wooden sword was tucked behind a tattered rope serving as the boy's belt. His clothes were little more than rags covered in various stains.

Melea wore a green shirt with the sleeves rolled to the elbows, black trousers, and her leather boots. She was supposed to be at the palace preparing to depart, but found the idea of going to war with Calanthia less than thrilling.

The Forever Boy stood with hands on hips, staring up at Melea with a knowing expression. "So the hero has returned only to depart once more, but this time the hero leaves to start a war."

"I'm a hero now, am I? Last time I saw you I was accused of being a thief and a villain."

The Forever Boy shrugged. "Anyone can change, it's not so strange, I'll show you how, a dog that barks may even meow."

Melea groaned, she had forgotten the boy's unusual way of speaking. "Alright, it's about time I get going, besides, I can't take anymore of your terrible rhymes."

The boy's laughter was light as the chirping birdsong. He dropped to a knee, placing one hand to his chest and raising the other palm up to Melea. "I will not waste your time with another silly rhyme, stay as my reward, I promise you will not be bored."

"Again with the rhyming," Melea sighed. "Do you even notice you're doing it?"

"Please," said the Forever Boy, his dark eyes twinkling in the sunlight.

"Fine, I'll sit with you for a bit but one more rhyme and I'm gone."

The Forever Boy smiled and sat down on a flat stone, patting the spot beside him. Melea sat beside the boy, uncomfortable by their closeness. He gave her a goofy grin and she responded with a pinched smile. The boy clapped his hands together, his face becoming serious.

"Would you like to hear a story? One about a real hero?"

Melea skipped a pebble across the ground, watching it bounce into the dirt. "No, not really."

"Hmm, perhaps you'd prefer a tale about the magical power of love?"

"Nope."

"So fussy. Those are always the best stories but let's see if I can find something to match your surliness."

Melea watched the clouds glide across the sky, getting lost in the effortless movement they used to travel great distances. If only she could make herself light enough to join them, to drift away and leave her worries behind as another stone in the abandoned park. Heaviest of her concerns was what would soon be expected of her from the Chosen.

The Forever Boy snapped his fingers. "I've got it!"

Melea thought he seemed overly thrilled to tell her some stupid story.

"This is an account of the world before it became the Rua that you know, a time when the Age of Stone gave way to the power of blood."

The boy's solemn tone piqued Melea's interest. It was as if he were giving a eulogy.

"This is only the most recent collapse, the latest upheaval to contribute to the ruinous destiny of this world."

"Destiny, right," Melea muttered.

"Out of desperation they turned to the wisest of the time. To this single man they entrusted a ritual beyond their understanding. He failed them in this task, passing on the knowledge to another. A grave mistake."

"Ease up on the dramatics," said Melea. "Who are *they*?"

"The Stonemen," the Forever Boy whispered.

"And who are they exactly?"

The Forever Boy ignored her, eyes focused on the sand. With a finger he traced a crude outline of Rua in the dirt, except that the borders were much larger than any Melea recalled seeing on maps. Land extended far to the east, tripling in size as Strakos, Nefara and Fyn conjoined into one landmass. The area around the Eternal Forest protruded out into what was now ocean.

"Destruction came from above to match that which was wrought below. The land was forever altered by these changes, a fresh wound was opened, unable to heal properly. Those who were lucky enough to avoid the worst of the devastation hid from this snarling new world."

He tossed a handful of stones onto the area east of Strakos, the force of their impact burying them into the dirt. He washed out the borders with a palm until they resembled those Melea was familiar with.

"What else was destroyed?" asked Melea.

"Much." The Forever Boy stared into the dirt, eyes searching. "Connection to the past. The last memories of the Green Time faded into myth. Purpose was scattered to the four corners."

The Forever Boy smeared the map after completing his story. Melea watched him intently, wondering how a street child could learn such an account. He was a strange boy, seemingly barely in touch with reality. He was consumed with stories and myths, lost in his fantasies, attempting to bring them to life with a wooden sword. An innocent spirit struggling to escape from the confines of his small world through imagined adventures. Melea pitied him.

One aspect of the story stuck with her. *Stonemen*. The Saleros had said that the Chuku Bartha spoke this name after sensing her power.

"Where did you hear this story?" she asked.

"The best stories are never told," he replied with a wink.

"What do you mean?"

He stood up, raising his height to slightly higher than Melea's. "Stories come and stories go but they're always there for those who know, all are lived, others told, the truth in them is worth more than gold."

"Rhyming!"

The Forever Boy grinned, kicked up his heels and darted away. Melea reached for a rock to throw after him. She found a palm sized stone and raised it overhead but then slowly lowered her arm in confusion. The boy was gone, disappeared into the debris, another spirit to haunt the lost memories of a forgotten place. A cool wind picked up as clouds settled in front of the sunlight.

Melea found it remarkable that something as malleable and ephemeral as a cloud could curtail the power of the sun. The delicate interplay of these distant forms brought goosebumps to her skin. She shrugged on her cloak, leaving the ghosts to the birds hopping along the blasted elm.

The uniform hung from a stand at the foot of Melea's bed. The dark blue material was crisp and smooth. Black buttons separated the uniform from thigh to the high collar. Pressed trousers hung on a lower rack. Cumbersome looking black boots sat beneath the rack like a pair of tortoises. Melea's lip curled in disgust.

Everything else was packed, all she needed to do was change into the uniform and join the Emperor.

She ran her fingers across the plain material. The seamstress thankfully had obliged her by keeping the uniform free of insignia denoting her as an officer. Melea did not want to lead men, to give orders, to direct the Chosen.

They were not her Chosen. She was not one of them, or at least that was how it used to be.

The presence of the uniform caused Melea to doubt previous conceptions about her status in the Shining Empire. Anger percolated the longer she looked at uniform. She was trained as a warrior, fought for Anathasius, and completed missions that often required killing, but always separately, as an individual unrestrained by orders. Her function was specific, unique, leaving her outside of the control of others. The uniform might as well be a set of shackles. She imagined iron bonds cinching around her chest with the clasp of each button.

Melea removed the uniform from the stand, carefully folding it, then placing it inside a traveling trunk. She did the same with the trousers, smoothing the creases before closing the lid. Melea left the boots, deeming them unworthy for packing. As strongly as she disliked the uniform she could not bring herself to leave it behind, something about the act felt disloyal to Anathasius. She sat on the edge of the bed while staring into space.

Her world was changing. She was now only one part of something bigger, one small contributing member of an organized unit. Each member was expected to give their all toward the same goal. To give their life if necessary and for many it would be. She would live with this group—eat the same food, walk the same steps, sleep the same hours, breathe the same air.

The thought was overwhelming, it towered over her. She stared up, waiting for the crash. Melea felt like a piece of driftwood on a rising wave, following the current but unable to see over the froth of the whitecap. Others floated with her, each being directed by the same unstoppable force. The arc of the wave hid the future from sight but Melea knew that rocks waited on the other side, prepared for impact, fortified by years of immobility.

A soft rap on the door preceded the entry of a guard. "Emperor Anathasius sends for you."

"Have this loaded," she said, gesturing to the traveling trunk.

The guard tried lifting the trunk but quickly left to get help when he felt the weight of it. In his absence she walked to the mirror, staring at her appearance. Knee high leather boots, well worn but meticulously oiled so that some of their shine remained. The leather was like a second skin it fit so snugly to the contours of her feet. Black trousers supported by a simple brown belt. The long-sleeved shirt was open at the collar to display the softness of Melea's neck. Dark hair reached past her shoulders, framed in by the collar of a long black cloak. Green eyes stared questioningly at Melea, but the significance of the question eluded understanding. The eyes looked disappointed.

*What do you want?* The reflection silently shouted at her, demanding an answer she could not give. A patronizing look flicked across the green eyes. *Stupid, dull girl, how could I expect you to answer?*

The knife was in her hand and hurtling toward the mirror before she realized what was happening. Her features, distorted in anger, splintered into hundreds of tiny reflections when the knife made contact. Slivers of glass cascaded to the floor as Melea stood there dumbfounded.

Heavy footsteps marked the return of the guards. Melea stepped away from the shattered mirror as they hoisted the trunk off the ground to carry it out of the room. Melea followed slowly behind, glancing back once more at what remained of the cracked glass surface before leaving the room behind. She counted each step along the hall, aware that they might be the last she would ever take in the Palace of Light.

The noise of the army traveled down the hall through the main doors. Soon, this was followed by the musky aroma of so many men and horses cramped together in close proximity. She stepped into the sunlight to look upon a sea of Chosen. The soldiers were organized in neat rows that stretched from the bottom of the palace stairs past the walls surrounding the palace. Melea only had a few moments to survey the organization of the soldiers before a Chosen leading Ranna approached. The mare was saddled and ready to ride, wearing a blanket the same blue as the uniforms.

Melea saddled-up, spinning Ranna in a tight circle before kicking her into a trot beside the rows of Chosen. The lines of men stretched out further than she could see; the head of the line constantly extending as she traveled. Eventually, she spotted a color other than blue, signaling the front of the army. Anathasius sat atop a grey stallion in the finest white robes Melea had ever seen. The cloth looked as though it was made of snowflakes infused with sunlight. She brought Ranna beside the Emperor. He looked her over once, no reaction on his handsome face.

"You will be wearing a uniform the next time I see you." The order was polite, calm, firm.

"I brought it," Melea replied meekly.

Anathasius stared straight ahead, his calm voice carrying lightly for Melea's ears only. "You will lead the Chosen even if you do not yet believe it. The men will follow you Melea. Over time this will become evident. All that is needed is experience."

He started forward and she followed. The long procession marched toward the eastern gate. The closer they came to the gate the greater the number of common folk there were lining the streets, until they had become a cheering mass of people pressed against the inside of the outer walls.

Melea heard the booming voice of the Beacon in the background but his words did not register in her mind. The chanting of the people was a droning that neither stirred Melea's heart nor motivated her spirit. She kept her eyes focused on the stones of the street, mind on the feel of Ranna's steady stride, only looking up when the road's construction changed. The Serpent stretched out into the distance, becoming hazy against the horizon. The road she had traveled barely a month before now seemed foreign. Melea patted Ranna's neck a few times, feeling the strength of the mare's muscle.

Leaving Azra felt different this time. There would be no galloping into the unknown together this day. Blaring horns and the cheering of the crowd followed the procession for hours as the Chosen slowly filtered out of the city.

## Rising to the Challenge

A tightness squeezed Ritika's chest, disappointment, the type that accompanies unfulfilled expectations. The emotion pulled taut, invisible strings. She had been given an unexpected gift, one promising rare entertainment, and then it had been snatched away. Well, it had been altered. Ritika had allowed Jai Alvarros to compete against the Champions to infuriate her nobles, to rub their noses in the fact that she had absolute control of Rhezaria, even during its most important symbolic event. But the opposite was occurring. The nobles were enjoying the sport and growing louder by the moment.

She pushed aside the distracting thoughts, but a chant of "Six Isles! Six Isles!" bubbled in her mind. *Focus.* Ritika centered her awareness on breathing, feeling the influx of air flow through her lungs and into her movements. She stood in a half crouch, barefoot on a circle of cool green grass in the private garden at the rear of the castle.

Warm sunlight tickled her face as bees and hummingbirds flittered amongst the rows of flowers filling the garden. The sky was occupied with massive, puffy clouds slowly shifting into unrecognizable forms while peacefully gliding overhead until out of sight. Ritika tried to mimic the clouds, she wanted to flow effortlessly, to let the separate energies of her body merge into one before returning to their centers of localization.

Ritika practiced the Infinite Stream, a set of motions designed to bring balance to the body, mind, and spirit. She finished the final movements and took a moment to appreciate the stillness of the garden, knowing that the apparent stillness was only an illusion.

The hummingbirds and bees continued on their hunt for the sweet things in life without regard for Ritika's concerns. She savored the sense of invisibility in the center of bustling, interconnected activity. Ritika had nothing that the winged creatures wanted and so was rendered as unimportant as a pebble.

She basked in the solitude, her mind free of concern about the future for a few fleeting moments. The temporary peace was disturbed by the pounding of drums coming from the stadium. A new chant accompanied the drums, a surreal outcry to match her imagination.

"Six Isles! Six Isles! Six Isles!

Draggar held a bottle of Six Isle Red by the curve of the neck. He tilted the gifted wine and took a swig straight from the bottle, his lips smacking in appreciation.

"Tasty stuff, this," he said. "He's doing well, better than you'd fare my plump friend." Draggar laughed and smacked a short Six Isle noble on the back. The force of the impact made the noble's spectacles bounce.

Ritika reminded herself that the term 'noble' was incorrect. The envoy from the Republic preferred the title *politician*. The little man, Ritika could not recall his name, Grimbly or something like that, adjusted his spectacles and grinned sheepishly.

"Chancellor Alvarros is cut from a different cloth. He is the youngest to attain the position."

"Well then he has something in common with our beloved Queen," Draggar hooted.

Ritika fixed Grimbly with a dry look. "Ever, as in one hundred years?"

Grimbly coughed into his hand. "The Six Isle Republic was founded eighty six years ago, it is but a child compared to Rhezaria in terms of years, but we have made significant strides in our brief history."

"I'm sure you have," said Ritika, her disinterest clear. "And General Vol, your statement is incorrect. Blame it on your burgeoning senility or increasing drunkenness, but I am not the youngest leader in Rhezaria's history. That honor goes to Vergoth the Boy King who ruled as a thirteen year old before dying in battle at the ripe age of fifteen."

Draggar roared. "Sometimes I forget that you were nearly High Priestess. I'm not used to following such a learned leader." He took another swig from the bottle. "Your father didn't give a rat's ass about history, always looking toward the future. He had big ambitions. Him and I spent many a night planning the future of Rhezaria."

Her father's ambition had passed onto his son who had turned those big plans into a premature death. Now she sat on the Hezrakaa throne, watching a lunatic outsider compete in the Games so that he might win her affections.

The absurdity of the situation was not lost on Ritika. There was a time when she was a healer in training, when she had just met a handsome young Garrett Tumino; the only man who could match her proficiency in Batanray. Soon after that initial encounter their arms were wrapped around one another in quite a different activity.

Ritika had envisioned the two of them living out the rest of their lives comfortably. He would become a decorated soldier and she would be a High Priestess like her grandmother. They could have children who would get the best out of life while remaining just outside the pressure of royal responsibilities. The dreams of a foolish young girl in love for the first time. Responsibility and duty now dictated the course of Ritika's future.

Garrett was a soldier, a Champion, pride of the Rhezi, and more than good enough to marry nearly any woman. But not a queen. A queen made a king and would birth future kings. The history of Ritika's lineage weighed down her spirit. She held the key to what would become of the Dracarion's. Her choices would send them down a new, irreversible path.

She looked out at Garret, calm and composed as always, weights hanging perfectly still as if they were floating on air. A sheen of sweat covered his smooth black skin, clean shaven and untroubled. The Chancellor's arms were beginning to tremble, he would not hold much longer. Perhaps that was why she was allowing this farce to happen. The Chancellor presented a new route, an unforeseen alternative, his proclamation throwing a kink into the political posturing of the Clans. He offered a brief reprieve from the propositions of hopeful Remori, bitter Nataga, and resentful relatives. At the very least, the Clans would have to formulate new strategies about how to place their particular representative at Ritika's side after the Six Isle entertainment faded away.

Ritika had placed the Chancellor against Garrett in the Standing Prayer for his first trial. Veins bulged in Jai's neck and he bared his teeth in determination. Sweat poured down his face, muscles straining to keep his arms extended.

"Come on, you book reader!" someone shouted below.

The anticipation built in the crowd as they sensed the end of the competition coming. The Chancellor's left knee buckled and his left shoulder finally gave out. Ritika felt a childlike sense of satisfaction as she watched the weight drop, but the fleeting feeling of gratification vanished when the weight made impact with the stadium sand. The crowd erupted into a mix of cheers and jeers. Ritika saw coin being exchanged over lost wagers. Someone was always willing to bet on a long shot no matter the odds.

"Not bad, not bad," commented Draggar. "I can't wait for the next one, when is that?"

"The Pursuit begins at noon but the Chancellor will have to be escorted out to the starting point now so there will be enough time to prepare for the final competition."

Draggar shook his head in disbelief. "Facing three Champions in one day, you are a cruel gamesmaster, my Queen. Have to admit that I am entertained though."

Ritika raised her hands in supplication. "Chancellor Alvarros did not leave me much time to prepare; such is the case with unexpected arrivals."

Draggar winked at Ritika. "What do you think, Grimbles? Think your man is up to the challenge?"

The politician tried his best to look confident. "Chancellor Alvarros will compete to the best of his abilities. He is honored to be given this opportunity, Queen Dracarion."

Ritika kept her tone even. "We shall see how honored he feels after this next event. I doubt there is anything like it in your land."

The mighty horn bellowed out a baleful call as a chariot pulled by four magnificent black horses entered the ring. Jai Alvarros managed to make his way down from the pillar and enter the chariot. Garrett remained atop his perch, waving his arms to work the cheering crowd into a frenzy. Ritika had never seen him act so pridefully—he was not behaving this way for the crowd. He was sending Ritika a message: *Don't waste your time on this fool from the*

*Republic, I am right here in front of you.* Ritika sighed, if only things were that easy. Once, maybe, but not anymore.

She motioned for a tray of fruit to be brought over. Ritika ate to distract herself while waiting for the Pursuit to commence. A team of men on the ground worked to widen the side entryway of the stadium so those within could watch the final leg of the competition. The opening was directly across from the royal section, affording Ritika the best view in the place.

"Grimbles, what is your role within the Republic and how is it that you and the Chancellor speak the royal language of Rhezaria?" asked Ritika.

"Advisor to the Chancellor, former senator Grimbaldi at your service, Queen Dracarion. The Republic is home to some exceptional linguists who helped prepare the Chancellor and I before the voyage."

Ritika silently cursed her Remori lout of a general. Of course the politician's name was not Grimbles. Not for the first time she wondered how long the Republic had been preparing for this voyage. "What is a senator?"

"A senator is a member of the senate, which is a group of men and woman who are elected by the people to represent them in the capital. As a senator I spoke for the people of my district, similar to that of the Chiefs here in Rhezaria, except that others could lobby for the position, and could replace me from the position every five years, if I did not receive enough votes of confidence."

Ritika assessed the description, comparing it to Rhezaria's form of hereditary leadership. "A very civilized process. You must think us to be violent brutes."

"I do not judge you or your people, Queen Dracarion. Our system is far from perfect: it produces good leaders as well as bad." Grimbaldi looked uncomfortable for a moment. "I respect the candidness of your system here. There can be distasteful actions committed by senators, and potential senators alike, in order to sway public opinion for votes."

"Thank you for your honesty, Grimbaldi. Your Chancellor is undertaking a different form of election but he is seeking only one vote." Ritika left it at that, letting the reality of the situation sink in.

She was in control and her decision at the end of the competitions would decide the fates of Alvarros and Grimbaldi as well as that of the Six Isles. Ritika wondered if she would still be sitting on the Hezrakaa throne if Rhezarian leadership was put to a vote of confidence. She doubted that the Clans would be able to restrain themselves long enough to let the process run its course. She glanced over at her general—Draggar Vol had an ability for speaking, was experienced, and used to commanding respect—he would likely receive many more votes than she would. Ritika had no doubt that Rhezarian elections would be rife with backstabbing, bribery, coercion, and assassination. The thought led her to wonder.

"Grimbaldi, how long were you a senator?"

"Thirty five years."

"And were you ever outvoted or removed from the position?"

"No, I was lucky enough to have the majority of votes in my district for the entirety of my tenure."

*Luck*, mused Ritika, she did not believe in luck. "You must have been very diligent at your post. Besides the honor of serving your people, what other benefits does a senator enjoy?"

Grimbaldi appeared calm but Ritika noticed the shuffling of his small feet. Draggar watched him closely as well.

"Most senators live in an appointed estate and are exempt from taxes."

Grimbaldi was maneuvering cleverly around answering completely, but he had told Ritika enough. Senators were wealthy, they lorded over those who elected them. They had direct influence on how the nation was organized. They had power. In Ritika's experience, those with power did not give it up.

This plump little foreigner held onto his elevated status for longer than she had been alive and now he sat on the Chancellor's shoulder, no longer a representative and therefore able to operate without restriction. Ritika wondered what *distasteful actions* Grimbaldi was associated with. He was not much to look at, but Ritika was beginning to think that the politician would have fit in just fine in Rhezaria, had he been born here.

"A pity that your Republic is so far away, I would like to see this system in action," said Ritika.

Grimbaldi nodded gravely. "If I could have envisioned how far it truly is I might have reconsidered volunteering for this journey. No offense intended, but I am no sailor and there were several points when I forgot that there was an environment not composed of ocean and sky."

Draggar barked a loud chuckle. "Us Remori have saltwater in our veins, the taste of ocean spray is as natural to us as mother's milk. In the Southern Ocean, a squall can arise out of the clear blue—red clouds at sunset are the only forewarning. In my youth I was in the midst of a furious storm and shipwrecked on the western shores of Strakos. Luckily, those merchant folk are nearly as skilled ship-builders as the Remori. Got to see the floating city of Cheton while waiting for the repairs. The place is an engineering wonder, haven't seen anything like it since."

Ritika rolled her eyes, she had heard this tale countless times in her childhood. The floating city lost its wonder somewhere around the tenth telling. "When was the last time you set foot on a ship, let alone the ocean?"

Draggar gestured at her, sloshing wine onto the floor, forgetting that he gripped a bottle in his hand. "Too long! Been too busy helping you run this kingdom."

Ritika raised an eyebrow. "If you're unhappy with your role perhaps Grimbaldi could be persuaded to replace you. A senator must surely be as good as a general."

Draggar gave Ritika an annoyed look. Grimbaldi looked from one to the other, choosing silence over offending either party. Draggar wrapped an arm across his shoulders, dwarfing the man in the process. "Come on, Grimbles, help me find some more of this stuff."

Draggar led the Chancellor's advisor away in search of more wine. Ritika laughed quietly to herself. Her general was particularly easy to tease when he was drinking. She leaned back in the uncomfortable seat, enjoying the temporary quiet. The peace was promptly interrupted by a long yawn.

Ritika looked over to see two lounging hounds. The gift Alvarros had given Abi'Ragaz, which in turn had been given to her. The two beasts followed her wherever she went. They did not complain, and generally followed all of her commands. They were rapidly becoming her favorite subjects. Ritika understood that these hunting dogs were bred to listen to commands and had been selected to do so for generations, but that did not explain everything. How did that schemer manage to train them to recognize her? They should have been trained to obey her uncle. Ritika pondered this while watching the dogs.

They looked up at her with searching eyes, muzzles flat on the ground and seemingly idle, but Ritika knew they would jump to attention if given the word. She tossed an apple on the floor, causing a mad scramble for the prize. The tan hound snatched up the piece of fruit and happily crunched it into pulp. The black one gazed longingly at its companion with the unselfconscious yearning unique to dogs.

"Here you go, you big baby," Ritika said as she tossed an apple to the black hound. The hound looked pleased with the snack, devouring it in two bites. There was something beautiful in the simplicity of dogs, in how every instance was a fundamental truth, an opportunity that arrived unquestioned.

She should probably name them. That is, if she kept them. It was still too early to decide on anything yet. Despite the line of reasoning, Ritika found herself rolling potential names over in her mind until a rumble stirring through the crowd caught her attention.

The competitors were approaching, word of their impending arrival reaching the waiting crowd before they appeared, as it always inexplicably did. Ritika looked through the widened entryway and saw a thin form crest a small rise in the distance. The smooth stride signified that it was To'kal. Ritika was surprised to see another form come into view right behind the Sando Champion.

Jai Alvarros lurched over the rise, arms and legs pumping wildly as he fought to catch his competitor. The two men raced along an open stretch of flat land leading into the stadium. Murmuring of new wagers rippled amongst the spectators even though most could not even see To'kal and the Chancellor yet. Three hunters were in hot pursuit, appearing to gain ground with every stride.

Jai suddenly surged forward with arms pumping vigorously as he tried to close the gap between himself and To'kal. A spear flew over his shoulder and bounced harmlessly off the ground. The crowd cheered in excitement. Ritika leaned forward—this was going to be a close finish.

Judging from the Chancellor's actions he should have careened past To'kal—his motions making it appear as though he were running as hard as any man who had ever ran. To'kal looked like he was giving his best effort but the fluidity of his strides portrayed a sense of ease that made the Chancellor seem comical by comparison. Chants of, "Six Isles!" were countered by the odd whistling of the Sando. Jai heard the noise of the crowd and made a final push.

Ritika watched in amazement as the Chancellor gained several strides on the Sando Champion. *He just might do it.* Ritika gripped the oak armrests of the throne as she leaned forward. But the brief impression of an upset was stunted by a scene of pure misfortune, or perhaps it was the only logical outcome—an inevitable result stemming from all that had led to this exact instance.

The Chancellor went down in a heap, his arms spread out before him, unable to slow momentum as he skidded into the dirt. The hunters were on him in an instant, tossing nets and delivering several whacks with wooden spears. The actions of the hunters were unnecessary as it was obvious that the Chancellor could not move even if he wanted to. To'kal sprinted into the stadium to be greeted by an exuberant ovation, one that exceeded his previous victory. Draggar suddenly appeared at Ritika's side.

"We missed it! Damn you, Grimbles!"

Grimbaldi stuttered out an explanation but Draggar was unconcerned with what the man had to say, instead he looked to Ritika. "He nearly did it, didn't he?"

Ritika nodded. "I've never seen a finish this close."

Draggar grunted before taking a swig from a freshly opened bottle. "Well, he missed his chance. The poor sap is doomed in the next one."

Ritika looked down the length of the dais, spotting two hulking forms. Reyner Vol cracked his knuckles as he said something to Luka O'kanhana'etim. Draggar leaned over the railing, gazing at Jai's prone form on the ground just outside of the stadium.

"He looks dead," said the General. "Reyner is going to make sure of it."

Ritika knew Draggar was right. Reyner was going to murder the Chancellor in front of thousands of cheering spectators. Death would be unfortunate—that had not been her intention by putting all three events in one day, although a dead suitor would solve some problems. But it might create worse. Reyner would become even more puffed up on his own reputation and his bragging father would be unbearable to be around. *Please Mar' Edo Kon, do not let Reyner Vol kill the Chancellor, I ask this of you as your most humble servant.* Ritika hoped that God was listening.

The horn sounded again, temporarily deafening all nearby. Tehlos rushed out to the Chancellor to perform rituals that would drastically improve his current physical condition. Rhezaria had the best healers in all of Rua and they guarded the secret of their rituals more closely than any other.

A healer knelt down to assess the extent of the injuries but the Chancellor raised a hand to stop him. Jai raised himself to his hands and knees, then to a crouch with his palms on thighs, and then slowly to his feet. He said something to the healer who shrugged and walked away. Jai walked steadily but slowly, before disappearing into the underground section of the stadium that had been designated for his use. Ritika stared hard at the space where he had lain.

"Kholar," Koacachoa muttered nearby.

The interlude between events passed as a blur in Ritika's mind. More food was passed out but she only picked at it absently. The realization of what she had set in motion by allowing the Chancellor to compete against her Champions was starting to sink in. It was madness.

The banter between Draggar and Grimbaldi snapped Ritika out of her reverie.

"Listen to this, my Queen," said Draggar, holding a new bottle of Six Isle Red. "Grimbles thinks his man actually has a chance against Reyner; against my son!"

Grimbaldi held a bottle of his own. "I do, I really do."

Draggar took a long swig and Grimbaldi did the same.

"Care to make a wager?" asked Draggar. "The Chancellor scores a single point by knocking Reyner out of the ring, and I'll take you on a traditional Rhezarian hunt."

"And if he doesn't?" asked Grimbaldi.

"Well, then he isn't much of a man, is he? Then he drops his claim for Queen Dracarion's hand in marriage and leaves Rhezaria."

Ritika turned to Draggar. "Excuse me? You forget your place, General Vol. My hand, as you put it, is not under your authority."

"In that case, let's raise the stakes," Draggar purred. "If Reyner trounces the Chancellor, that being a consummate victory, then he is clearly a much better suitor and his request should replace the Chancellor's."

"And if the Chancellor wins?" asked Ritika.

Draggar chuckled. "Then I forever withdraw Reyner's request and cease all attempts at matchmaking under penalty of death."

Ritika did not like the Chancellor's odds at victory but the wager did present an opportunity to quiet Draggar once and for all. Besides, in the outcome of Reyner's victory, she could court the young Champion for a single day and then end the courtship, silencing Draggar.

"We have a deal," said Ritika.

Draggar raised the bottle and whooped.

"Might I interject?" asked Grimbaldi.

Ritika had forgotten the small man was there. "Yes?"

"Ahem, well...in regards to the wager between General Vol and Queen Dracarion...uh—"

"Out with it," said Draggar.

"In the case that Chancellor Alvarros is victorious, I would like to speak on his behalf and ask that Queen Dracarion calls an official council of Chiefs on the subject of going to war with the Shining Empire."

"Bold of you, Grimbaldi" said Ritika. "You ask that I put forward the desire to enter a war that is not our own."

"But it is," said Grimbaldi. "Or soon will be when the Shining Empire comes over the Kon mountains with the added strength of Calanthia's slave army and Ba-rük priests."

"Enough," Draggar snapped.

"Continue," said Ritika, sensing there was more the Chancellor's advisor wished to say.

"The Shining Empire sacked the Republic's great library in search of a specific item, a book of great power. This book is a compendium of rituals that I fear would make the Emperor invincible if they were to fall into his hands."

"Where is this book?" asked Ritika.

"Missing," Grimbaldi shifted uncomfortably. "Disappeared some years ago, which is why the Empire left the Republic empty handed."

"You expect Rhezaria to right the Republic's carelessness?" asked Ritika.

"That the book was misplaced is fortuitous twist of luck which has kept it out of the Emperor's possession. This is the pivotal moment to engage the Empire, while the Pillar still stands. Crush the Emperor between the forces of Rhezaria and Marikal."

For the first time since the Chancellor's arrival Ritika seriously considered the Shining Empire as a threat. She did not like the thought of the Emperor controlling the vast armies of Calanthia.

"What if the Chancellor is defeated in the ring?" asked Ritika.

The corner of Grimbaldi's mouth twitched in a brief smirk. "Then I must find a different way to raise this debate."

Ritika saw the passion in the advisor's eyes. This politician was more tenacious than he let on.

"We have deal, former senator Grimbaldi."

Draggar stepped forward. "My Queen—"

"That will be all, General" Ritika ordered. "One more word and I nullify all wagers."

Draggar stepped back, taking another pull from the bottle. Ritika looked out to the packed stadium. The crowd cheered madly as the competitors entered Verangor's Ring.

Reyner Vol and Jai Alvarros stood opposite of each other, awaiting the signal of the official. Reyner stripped off his shirt and Jai rolled his sleeves to the elbow. The official gave the signal to commence the fight.

Ritika could barely hear herself think, she could not recall the stadium being this loud before. The energy of the crowd was like lightning as they shouted, sang, stomped, and clapped. The Chancellor raised his fists before his chin as Reyner advanced confidently. Jai moved sideways with the Remori Champion, lashing out with a few quick jabs. Reyner swatted them aside as he tried to grab hold of the leader of the Republic.

The Chancellor had traveled across Rua to warn of impending war and proclaim his love, only to die in combat over honor. Against her will, Ritika found the thought to be strangely romantic. The Chancellor was confident, she had to give him that. Reyner rushed in and Jai landed a few ineffectual body shots before dancing away. The crowd whooped at this.

"Six Isles! Six Isles!"

Reyner smirked and threw up his hands as if to agree with the crowd. He adopted a fighting stance similar to that of the Chancellor and squared off with his opponent. The Remori threw a combination of heavy punches, one connecting with the Chancellor's jaw that sent Jai staggering. Reyner advanced swiftly but Jai righted himself even quicker.

The Chancellor delivered a sweeping haymaker that somehow made it past Reyner's defenses, landing squarely against the Remori's jaw. Reyner's head snapped back and the crowd gasped in shock. He stumbled backwards for several steps and dropped to one knee. Jai looked unsure of what to do.

"Attack, you fool," Ritika whispered.

The big Remori gathered himself and advanced once more—Jai Alvarros had missed his chance. Reyner caught one of Jai's fists and then the other. The Chancellor was pinned even though he stood. Reyner bent Jai's arms in on themselves, closing the separation between them, and then hammered his forehead into Jai's face. He smashed his forehead into Jai's face twice more until Reyner's strength was the only thing keeping the Chancellor vertical. Reyner placed his left hand on top of Jai's head and swung upward with his right, launching Jai skyward with a devastating uppercut. The Chancellor landed limply and lay still. Ritika prayed. *God, why have you forsaken me?* She was sure the Chancellor was dead.

Reyner turned his back on his defeated adversary, arms spread wide to soak up the adoration of the exultant crowd. And then, all of the thousands within the stadium witnessed a miracle. Jai Alvarros got up and brushed the sand off his shirt. Reyner sensed the change in the crowd and turned to find the hunched form of the Chancellor waiting for him. Reyner smiled a cold, hard smile—a mirthless expression promising pain. He shook his head and advanced again, raising his right fist to finish the fight.

Jai's hands hung at his sides, incapable of protecting his face any further. His face was a bloody ruin in any case. Ritika heard the death song of last rites play louder in her head with each of Reyner's footsteps. He raised a fist to deliver the finishing blow but never got to throw the final punch. Jai suddenly kicked straight up with his right leg, his heel slamming into Reyner's jaw.

No one expected the Chancellor to be capable of such an attack, especially Reyner. The Remori Champion keeled over, face planting into the sand. All of the air was sucked out of the stadium as everyone held their breath. Complete silence enveloped the spectators as they looked on in shock. Jai took one step and then collapsed beside his adversary.

The stunned silence continued. Sure, some had cheered for the Chancellor but nobody had actually thought this outcome to be possible.

"Six Isles, Six Isles, Six Isles." The chant started out quietly and then began to build in intensity. Ritika looked to the far right of the dais to find the speaker. She saw who had started the chant. *Mar' Edo Kon be merciful.*

Chief Soren Daro continued to chant and soon many more joined him. The words were repeated over and over as many of the spectators showed their respect for the Chancellor. A bottle smashed next to Ritika, a look was not required to know how it happened.

"Touch him and I'll demote you," Ritika warned.

"I don't care," said Draggar. "I have to kill him."

"I'll send you as my diplomat to the Six Isles and you'll waste the rest of your days surrounded by intellectuals and historians."

"You wouldn't dare." Draggar moved to push past the Hezrakaa throne.

"Try me."

Ritika did not want to follow through with her threat, but she would and Draggar knew it. Draggar fixed Ritika with a look of unfiltered rage, sizing her up with calculating eyes. Ritika held his gaze, unflinching and resolute. Draggar stormed past her, shoving Koacachoa aside as the Uzanaki tried to intercede. Draggar disappeared from sight as Daro finished chanting. Ritika was relieved that she would not have to exile her most trusted advisor and oldest friend.

She nodded to Grimbaldi, who bowed in respect then exited the dais.

The nobles were buzzing with activity, they no longer knew what to think of the visitor from the Republic. Ritika sat back, feeling the uncomfortable angle of the hard throne. She absently scratched the head of one of the dogs with her fingers. A thin smile formed on her lips. She had gotten what she wanted. That was, indeed, entertaining.

## Beast of War

A line of soldiers in olive and silver livery barred entry to the gate of Asyrith, immobile as pieces on a cüthril board. A single figure approached through the open gate on a white horse. He wore a fine uniform emblazoned with a roaring lion above crossed swords. Golden shoulder pads made his thin form appear larger.

The sky was overcast and a chill wind blew from the east; the first hint of autumn decay on the breeze for those who knew to look for it. Melea glanced over her shoulder at the unending line of Chosen and would not have been surprised if their length exceeded that of Asyrith's wall. The great barrier extended from either side of the gate as far as she could see. Duke Karracus nudged his horse forward to meet the army of the Shining Empire.

The Duke wore a patch over his left eye. Skin of a sickly pallor stretched over noticeably protruding cheekbones. Melea had seen men with eyepatches before and they tended to be grizzled veterans with a dangerous aura about them. Duke Karracus was not one of these. He appeared feeble, as if he might collapse into the hole where his eye once rested.

"Emperor Anathasius," the Duke's tone was reverent as he bowed. "The road to Marikal is yours, Shining Lord."

"That it is," said Anathasius. "I trust that half of your army waits on the other side of the wall."

Karracus kept his eyes on the Emperor's grey stallion, a meter from eye level with Anathasius himself. "Of course, they will fight bravely for the Shining Empire as a testament to Asyrith's faith in your divinity."

Melea watched the Duke's face closely, his discomfort was obvious. The man was spooked, frightened for his life. His right eye wanted to twitch to the corners, to see what might be lurking in the shadows.

"Join us Duke Karracus, and travel with us to encourage the men," said Anathasius.

"Yes, my Lord."

The Duke spun his horse around, waiting for Anathasius and Melea to pass by before falling in behind. They rode through the gate without having to pay the toll. Melea thought the Saleros would be jealous. They were always looking for a way to fulfill their needs at the expense of others.

An armed legion adorned with shining armor waited silently inside the Asyrith border. They smashed armored fists to breastplates in unison to acknowledge the Emperor's arrival.

"Duke Karracus." Anathasius called back. "Ride to the fore and show the men that it is they who will lead us into Calanthia. Onward to Ryakesh."

The Duke moved to the front, looking sicker than when speaking to Anathasius. He tried to sound brave but his voice faltered, coming out meek. "Fall in, men!"

The soldiers obeyed, moving into formation behind their Duke. Anathasius waited until the new additions were progressing in an orderly manner down the road. Melea looked to Anathasius, confused as to why he would let the Duke lead the way. He seemed to understand the look in her eyes.

"Once a betrayer, always a betrayer," said Anathasius. "Never leave one at your back long enough for them to commit the act again. A section of the dukedom of Bromaleigh lies between us and the first great battle in Carnot. The soldiers of Asyrith will serve their purpose on the way to Ryakesh before their courage fades."

"The frail Duke's heart will stop at the sight of battle," said Melea. "He won't live to see the Carnot border."

"You're learning." Anathasius encouraged the stallion forward and Melea followed on Ranna.

Two days later they crossed into Bromaleigh and another passed before they saw combat. The soldiers from Asyrith fought well against the purple and red of Bromaleigh, overwhelming the forces of their neighborly rivals. Duke Karracus managed to survive, along with approximately twenty percent of his men. Around half of the Duke's remaining soldiers fell in further skirmishes along the way to Carnot. The Duke beat the odds and made it all the way to Ryakesh. He looked beyond grateful when Anathasius sent him and his remaining men home.

Melea watched Karracus scamper away with the bedraggled survivors. "Why let him live?"

Anathasius kept his eyes focused on the black smudge of Ryakesh in the distance, not bothering to watch the Duke depart. "He is suitable enough to remain in Ishtanvor for now. Some men lash out in fear, while others shrivel—Karracus is the latter. We will finish Bromaleigh after Ryakesh, as Carnot is the stronger of the two. They think themselves well defended behind their legendary wall but their history is weak. It cannot stand against the future of the Shining Empire."

The unique aspect of Ryakesh soon became apparent. An intimidating blackthorn wall surrounded the city, giving the appearance of a city hunkered down like a snarling beast in its burrow. The outline of the Kon mountains filled the skyline in the distance. On the other side of the mountains lay Rhezaria. Melea looked across the grassy hillside in front of the moat at the base of the giant thorns. The only bridge into the city had been shattered by the hands of its own citizens in preparation of a siege.

In the morning, she would get her first taste of battle. A siege was not what she had expected but she supposed that easing into the mayhem of war was an acceptable opportunity. The Chosen were going about their business by efficiently setting up camp. Melea joined in, raising her own tent on the edge of boundary separating officers and soldiers.

She woke to the sound of screaming. Terrified shrieks pierced the night air, jolting her out of a deep sleep. Men were dying in agony. Heavy footfalls raced past her tent, moving swiftly away from the screams. The wailing intensified as more voices rang out. Melea grabbed her sword and burst through the open tent flap.

A young Chosen was coming her way at a full sprint. His face was a frozen mask of fear. Except for his eyes, the eyes were wide open. The soldier seemed unable to blink, his mind trapped in the scene of what he had just witnessed. His arms pumped and air steamed from his flared nostrils. Melea stepped to the side to let him pass; he was incapable of acknowledging anyone around him.

A tent near the edge of camp, closest to the walls of Ryakesh, burst into flame. The stink of burning canvas prompted Melea into action. She started toward the fire, quickly but cautiously, checking lane ways between the rows of tents as she went.

Multiple sections were engulfed in flames when she arrived. Soldiers raced everywhere—some in the direction of flames, but the majority fled. Those who hurried away bore similar expressions to the first soldier she had encountered. The cause for the alarm was not apparent as no enemy soldiers appeared. Screaming continued to pierce the cool night air.

Melea paused, trying to sense where the danger was coming from. Ash floated against a backdrop of sky painted the deepest black, no moon or stars showing through. A surprised scream exploded to her left. The sound quickly transforming into one of pain.

She turned to see a Chosen writhing on the ground, his limbs making spastic motions as his eyes rolled back to display only whites. She spied the cause of his torment—a thick cord nearly as dark as the night sky was wrapped around his ankle. A slick sheen on the cord was the only way Melea could separate it from the darkness. Her mouth went dry as the cord pull its way up the soldier's leg before constricting around his waist. The cord moved with an intelligence, there was purpose behind its progress. In the firelight she saw its length stretch back towards Ryakesh, disappearing along the fringe of light. It was alive.

The soldier's screaming stopped and the tentacle disengaged, waving in a sideways motion to display wicked barbs dripping with fresh blood. A thicker, black substance oozed as well. The tentacle returned to ground, slithering toward Melea like an eyeless serpent. She recognized what this was, even though the tentacle belonged to a creature that was not supposed to exist. Ryakesh had a Night Creeper.

Without thinking, Melea pounced forward and sliced off the barbed end of the tentacle. The severed chunk spasmed momentarily then lay still. The rest of the tentacle withdrew but three more rapidly converged on her location. She stepped lightly, making sure to avoid contact with any portion of the tentacles as she severed the encroaching barbs. More tentacles slithered out of the darkness towards her. She could sense the anger in their movements. They came from all sides and Melea had to be careful not to remain focused on a single one for too long. She suspected that the barbs held a toxin which immobilized the victims. One miscue and she would be lending her voice to the tortured symphony reverberating around her.

She didn't feel like singing; slicing another tentacle as it slithered toward her. This one had taken four swings, the thick skin was dulling her blade at a worrying rate.

The ground was slick from the dark blood leaking out of the tentacles. She slipped, stepping back from a squirming tentacle and a hooked barb dug into the ground next to her foot. Melea never regained her balance as she leapt out of range, falling to the ground with a thump. A tentacle shot straight toward the noise of her fall. The appendage raised itself high off the ground, intending to smash down on top her. Melea grabbed her sword with both hands, hacking wildly at the tentacle until it keeled over, mostly sawed through.

She left the sword, retreating to a quieter area away from the flames and blood. A better weapon was needed, if she was going to continue. It sounded as though one section to her right was having moderate success as battle cries roared from an area near a fresh burst of flames.

Melea angled back to her tent, hopping over waving tentacles as she ran, flames reflecting off the spattered blood on her face. There seemed to be no end to the squirming limbs. The beast lived up to the horrifying legends used to scare children into obeying tired parents.

No one, Melea included, thought any Night Creepers still existed. The beast must have been hidden in the moat surrounding Ryakesh, raised to exact its terrible wrath in a moment like this. The Calanthians must have a shaman of substantial power in their service to control such a large beast. Kerak's stoic visage rose in her mind. The Calanthians, like the Frozen Tribe's before them, were pulling out their most dangerous tricks right out of the gate.

Her tent was undamaged and Melea strode toward the chest of supplies she had requested before leaving Azra. She opened the chest, not needing any light to find what she sought. Melea had carefully packed each object herself. On top was her gauntlet and its new counterpart fashioned by Barroc Wicket. The poison darts likely would not be of much use but the iron offered protection against the toxic barbs jutting from the end of the tentacles. She slid the gauntlets onto each arm before hefting out the heavy bag they sat on.

She ripped open the top of the bag and stuck her hand into the fine white sand within. Energy coursed down her arm, sparking from her fingertips as the sand shifted and hardened into a sword. Melea pulled the razor sharp blade from the bag and set it beside her. She repeated this process four more times until the bag was empty. She had packed enough sand to make at least double as many swords but figured the severity of this situation necessitated prudence. One misstep and there would not be a next time. These swords were stronger and longer than any she had previously created: large, curved blades designed to maximize each slash.

Next, she removed a smaller bag and dumped the contents onto the ground. Ten bronze rings spilled out, which she placed on all of her fingers. Lastly, she removed a metal rod slightly longer than the length of her forearm and nearly as thick—another request she had made of craftsmen Wicket. Melea slung a shimmering glass sword on each hip and one between her shoulder blades. She placed the metal rod between her teeth and stalked out of the tent with a shimmering sword in each hand.

More tents were ablaze but to her amazement there seemed to be some semblance of order taking place. A battalion of men covered head to toe in bronze armor marched forward at a steady pace in a wedge formation. A lieutenant on horseback raced up and down their length shouting orders while waving his sword. Melea supposed he meant to be inspiring, but she gave his words no heed and guessed that most of the men did the same. They marched with harsh purpose, doing what they had been trained to do.

A monstrous beast of legend was decimating their comrades and they now marched toward this bringer of death. The time for contemplation and rousing of spirits had ended. Flames danced on the bronze soldiers, making them the brightest object in the starless night, sculpting them into a living torch. Melea followed the battalion into the dark that held a waiting nightmare.

She stayed near the back of the line but still felt the shudder that went through the soldiers when the front of the wedge made contact with the Night Creeper. The force of the impact rippled through the formation like a wave, forcing the line back a step before they dug their heels in and pushed back.

Yelps punctuated the air above Melea. Soldiers floated overhead, limbs flailing, before landing with a sickening crunch. She saw bulks of armor lying in tangled heaps where the Chosen landed, heavy objects meant to be immovable as a group. No aspect of their design was ever intended to fly. She was shocked to see more than a few of the heaps raise themselves up on unsteady legs and seamlessly merge their way back into the formation. Men were crazy things beyond Melea's understanding.

The wedge struggled to remain intact—its strength was in its continuity. The Chosen knew they were doomed if they became scattered. She could not see or hear the beast and found this invisibility unsettling. The beast had to be massive but it somehow managed to remain silent. From Melea's vantage point, the men in front were smashing themselves into darkness only to be hurled back by the nothingness. She spotted the mounted lieutenant charging along the right side, hollering orders at the top of his lungs. Melea broke from behind the wedge over to the left side. Best to avoid such an obvious target like the lieutenant.

She ran swiftly, avoiding the tentacles that swept inward toward the mass of men to her right. She could have sliced tentacles as she went but Melea recalled how quickly they converged on her before. Melea did not want the beast's attention just yet. She came round to the front, parallel with the poor bastards trying to hold the line against the serpentine onslaught. The cloud cover cracked, a sliver of moonlight cascaded through the opening and illuminated the beast. Melea nearly dropped the iron rod in shock.

The Night Creeper towered above her, the size of a castle yet capable of moving, its body spreading out wider than the battalion of Chosen. Her eyes were drawn to the gaping maw full of jagged teeth that opened and closed in a silent roar. The teeth were not pointed fangs like in the stories. They resembled the grinding mandibles of a human.

Occasionally, a soldier would be tossed between the jaws and limbs and armor would dribble down the beast's body in chunks. Above the jaws sat one huge, spherical eye that rolled lazily from side to side. The eye was glazed over with a blueish film, the iris shining yellow out of the center. Melea stared into the eyeball, feeling energy burst to life in her chest, the rush flooding her entire body, removing any fear from her mind.

Her vision became sharper, making individual tentacles apparent in the darkness. A sickly, sour smell emanated from the oozing poison held in the barbs of the Night Creeper. Melea realized this was a better way of detecting the approaching tentacles rather than just relying on sight alone. Her limbs felt strong but weightless, capable of executing any action demanded of them.

The ring of the moat was some distance behind the beast. Apparently it could move across the land. She doubted that it could move quickly so her plan was simple: plunge her way into the eye and keep digging until the beast stopped moving. The clouds shifted again, the moonlight lost to shadows once more. She tracked the path in her mind and set off toward the beast with clear intention.

Melea sliced through tentacles as she ran. Speed was of the essence—she could not afford to stop and see if the tentacle was completely severed. Her newly crafted swords worked well. The tentacles were becoming shorter and thicker the closer she got. These limbs had many more barbs and lacked the distinctive odor of those dripping toxin.

A large tentacle swung toward her at a sharper angle than she expected and its barbs punctured a sword, ripping it from her right hand. She sidestepped the tentacle while grabbing another sword from her hip. The sword in her left hand became wedged in the thick meat of another limb so she discarded that one as well, replacing it with the other sword on her hip.

As she neared the body of the beast, a wide tentacle rose up in front of her, attempting to flatten Melea beneath its weight. She raised both swords overheard and split the tentacle in two. She jumped through the gap and onto the monster.

The skin beneath her feet was firm but slick, like hard packed dirt that has not quite solidified after a heavy rain. Melea saw the big eye fixed on her position; emotion undetectable in its alien gaze. A noxious odor surfaced from behind, warning Melea to turn in time to slash through a tentacle bending back to her position. Toxin dripped down around Melea as if from a malevolent raincloud. Melea scrabbled sideways across the beast as more tentacles bent her way.

A long tentacle rapidly descended toward Melea so she swung upwards to meet it at the peak of her reach. The sword became wedged halfway into the tentacle, causing the limb to reflexively retract. Melea clung to the handle, letting herself be lifted into the air. When the tentacle reached the pinnacle of its arc it paused as the beast realized what was happening. Melea rocked herself forward with her legs to gain momentum and let go of the sword.

She fell toward the beast's neck, if it could be said to have a neck, and plunged a sword deep into the meat. She hung parallel to the black hole of a mouth, just out of range of the man-sized teeth. Melea retrieved the final sword from between her shoulders, preparing to stab into the beasts flesh and climb her way past the mouth.

The half severed tentacle arched toward her, intent on finishing its task. She hung from her sword like a parasite on a hair waiting to be plucked and flicked away. She hefted the sword in her right hand, gauging the speed of the incoming attack. The sword flashed once brilliantly in the moonlight before separating the upper half of the tentacle and disappearing below. Melea had now exhausted her sword supply. Sweat poured down her face, matting hair to her forehead. The iron remained clenched between her teeth, giving her saliva a metallic tang. Melea placed both hands on the sword handle and closed her eyes, drawing in focused lungfuls of air.

The ten bronze rings on her fingers illuminated in her mind's eye. The rings glowed faintly in her mind, as though the barrier of her eyelids added more light to her sight rather than closing it off completely. Melea pushed all of her focus, all of the coursing energy within, toward the rings. The metal vibrated and bounced in place, glowing brighter as energy washed over the rings. She drew a deep breath in through her nose and held it. The flow of energy into her hands stopped. The bronze softened as Melea breathed out, the metal extending toward her fingertips at the same rate as her exhale. Her fingers became fully encased as the last of the oxygen was released from her lungs.

Melea opened her eyes to see ten bronze claws attached to her hands. The crash of the melee below rushed back to her. She carved her right hand into the

Night Creeper's flesh, finding that she could dig deep enough to support her weight. Melea left the sword and began to climb hand over hand toward the ridge between the staring eye and crashing jaws.

A few more handholds and Melea climbed up and over the teeth, hauling herself triumphantly to her feet atop the separating ridge to stare directly into the monstrous orb. She released the bronze on her right hand, letting it slide off like liquid. Melea grabbed the iron rod, twisting it in the center to release the interlocking chambers within. Barroc Wicket had cleverly designed the rod to be filled with four levels of hollow iron. A quick snap of the wrist made the extra iron shoot out from inside, immediately tripling the spear in length. Melea twisted the center to lock it in place.

She plunged the spear straight through the center of the monstrous eye. The Night Creeper shuddered, the movement like a small earthquake, nearly tossing Melea off her perch. Melea yanked the spear out only to stab it in even deeper. The beast still made no sound but the outpouring of gale-force air below signified its distress. She pulled the spear out again to continue the grisly excavation.

Fluid poured out of wound, washing across Melea's shins and causing her to slip, then fall to her stomach. She dug in with the talons on her left hand but continued to slide. The spear became unwieldy and impossible from the slime coating her hand. The iron spear fell away and Melea slid inevitably after it. There was a moment of free-fall as the beast's gullet rushed up at her.

Her back bounced off the teeth of the upper jaw and momentum carried Melea toward the interior of the lower jaw. She hooked her right arm into a gap between the teeth and hung on for her life. The stench was unbearable as the debris of half chewed Chosen clattered around her. A bronze plated shin smacked off her forehead, weakening her precarious hold. She now dangled above the shaking chasm only by the strength of her right hand.

Melea channeled energy into the bronze on her left hand, fusing the metal together into one large hook. Her arm shot forward, driving the hook into the tooth, puncturing the hard material to secure her hold. She would not fall into the Night Creeper's innards but as soon as the beast righted itself she would be flipped forward into gnashing teeth that stood like crooked tombstones above her.

She was out of ideas. Escaping had never been her strength, anyway.

A foul wheeze rushed up from the beast's gullet and she could not fight back the urge to retch. She vomited down into a bottomless pit. The beast's nasty wheeze altered into a defeated groan, which was followed by a massive slump somewhere beneath her.

To Melea, it felt as if the world was being flipped end over end. She had burrowed into a mountain and now a giant was capsizing it like a plaything he had become bored with. A scent of the foulest origin enveloped her. She could taste the raw acidity of stomach juices and the sickly tang of fresh blood.

Gurgling liquid pooled below as she peered through the narrowing gap of teeth. The jaws closed completely, plunging Melea into utter darkness.

The Night Creeper fell sideways, which way was impossible to tell, and it hit the ground with a massive thud. The tooth Melea was attached to shattered and she tumbled out through the opening. A torrent of vomit poured out after her, drenching Melea in the beast's stomach contents. She was surrounded by the stench of death and flesh.

Melea gasped the putrid air in shallow, panicked breaths; her brain ricocheting against her skull. There was no time to savor the realization of being alive—her body screamed for movement. To remain still was certain death.

*Move or die*, she repeated the phrase like a mantra. Crawl. She had to crawl. Melea inched forward on hands and knees through the slime, feelings of claustrophobia tightening her chest as she pushed against the heavy flesh with her back. How far she crawled was uncertain. Time was the most valuable commodity, an asset that could only be counted in rapidly decreasing heartbeats.

Without warning, she slid out from under a flap of slippery flesh and was free of the crushing weight of the Night Creeper. Melea collapsed on her back, still gasping irregular pulls of air. The bronze on her left hand dribbled off her fingers to solidify in the dirt.

Her chest slowly stabilized to a regular rhythm as she looked up at the dark outline of the Night Creeper's corpse against the sky. The clouds were not as thick as before, a few stars hung in the open spaces, and the hazy outline of the moon squinted like an eye with cataracts. Melea thought her eyes were playing tricks on her.

A thin shape was moving on the Night Creeper. The dark outline was climbing down from the back of the beast and soon she could make out arms and legs. The spidery movement of these limbs informed Melea of who approached. Morokko Kachina slid across the last crest on his heels and hopped down beside Melea. His dark eyes surveyed her disheveled form like a predator calculating a strike.

"Silly little cohiko," he rasped from behind a black mask.

Her mind was too hazy to give a retort, her throat raw and gummy.

Kachina's mask twisted into a grotesque smile. "Charging straight into the fangs like always, you're nothing but blunted talent."

He dropped an object to his feet and kicked it toward Melea. She caught it, gripping a handful of coarse hair. Melea looked into the sightless eyes of a severed head for an instant before tossing it away.

"The shaman controlling the beast. He was riding near the back," said Kachina.

Melea spat. "Bloedeth. Go away and die."

"Don't go getting mashed up just yet; you are now in my debt."

Melea sat up but the assassin had already moved past her, slinking away into the night. She forced herself to her feet, unable to stand the smell any longer. The area around her was a disaster—limbs from man and beast were strewn everywhere.

Torches lined the the top of the city walls above the vicious tangle of thorns. The people of Ryakesh would go sleepless tonight. They had just thrown their biggest punch in the hope of landing a knockout but the Shining Empire proved to be too resilient to be taken down this early in the fight.

A bitter taste started in Melea's mouth as she walked through the carnage wrought by the Night Creeper. A great deal of men had lost their lives this night. Pitched battle was a new undertaking for Melea, she had not been needed in any battles up until this point. She found that the sensation did not agree with her.

A hard pit formed in the center of her ribcage, agitating her insides. This sensation was more foul than the acrid taste in her mouth, more repulsive than the goo matting her hair. The new gauntlet was shredded beyond repair, torn back to bend at an acute angle. Melea could not recall when that happened. She pulled off the broken gauntlet, leaving it on the ground with the rest of the broken things.

She had gotten lucky tonight, mere heartbeats away from certain death. A realization dawned on her as she walked through a sea of the dead and dying. She did not like this war.

Her mood darkened, her resolve becoming as hard as the jagged pit in her chest. The next battle would be ended as quickly as possible—she would make sure of it. Death would be involved but she wished to never see it on this scale ever again. Melea would use her abilities to end the fighting before it was allowed to rage to extremes.

Melea left the field of death behind, a field where nothing could hope to grow despite the magnitude of sacrifice. For once, she wondered what the priests might say. The men and women who claimed sacrifice was the key to life.

She returned to her tent, which now made up the new edge of camp. Inside was a wash basin filled with clean water which she used to clean herself. The stench of half digested Chosen clung to her. She scrubbed with soap until her skin felt raw but the smell of death remained. Melea realized that the smell was within her, not on her skin but underneath. Inside. She wondered if it was rising to the surface or seeping in.

Melea had bathed in a level of mass murder and wanton destruction that no amount of soap could wash away. This development gave her pause; *she had been killing for nearly half of her life, it was her way of life, so why would this event bother her? Those missions had been the same, only on a smaller scale, hadn't they?*

Sixthrok's words echoed in her mind. *You have taken much from us but not all, not yet.* The look in Dacre's eyes when he saw Iribi. Lastly, and most painfully, Gerboa's strained face appeared. Melea dealt out death as her vocation but the time for deciding to who and when had arrived.

The bitterness in her mouth eventually dissipated as she mechanically ate, refueling her body for what was to come. When dawn's first light crested the horizon the stench still remained but unlike other foul smells it was not one that she could get used to with time. The stirrings inside only subsided once she resolved to do battle on her own terms.

Melea exited the tent when the morning light filtered through the opening. She stepped on the light, distorting it beneath the crunch of a boot still covered in flecks of gore. The buffed sheen was gone from the leather, leaving the much traveled boots looking faded and worn.

## A New Master

His existence was one of harsh routine, each day filled with the same basic activities, the same absence of hope. The same abuse. Lately, even the weather had been unchanging. Daymon was having difficultly recalling a day without the scorching sun directly overhead. The sun was a merciless master that sapped Daymon's strength and injured his skin but at least it was consistent. His other master was far less so.

Scars perforated Daymon's back from shoulders to waist. A testament to the cruelty of the man who ruled this ship as a tyrant. Zheng Ja'hoth captained the Blind Lady, a pirate ship that prowled the waters of the Sunken Coast. Daymon could not surmise a good estimate as to how great of a distance he had helped propel the moving prison he called home.

Training in the Sanctuary and his responsibilities at the Pompae estate did more to prepare Daymon for life at sea as a slave than he could ever acknowledge. A spark remained in his husk of a body, existence bereft of the Emperor's Gift, forever craving what was lost. He could not quit. Not while there was a master to follow.

The slight curve of his seat and the worn handle of his oar were Daymon's world. Gone was the ritual knife he had carefully honed each night before bed. The white robe of his order never made it off the estate. Neither did his tongue.

A thick beard covered Daymon's face, helping to hide the burnt remnants of his bottom lip. Daymon would not have spoken even if the ability was still available to him. Speaking accomplished nothing but a brutal beating. The other slaves rarely spoke either; the new ones quickly learned that their life was over.

His forced muteness was not unique, Daymon knew there were others aboard the ship who were like him. Former priests sold into slavery. He could tell by the state of their silence. Each had the same faraway look, their eyes unable to find the location of the power they once knew. Most carried the marks of disease called blood pox by the pirates. Daymon's own arms were covered in rusty splotches, red protrusions that spread from the remnants of self-inflicted scars.

Daymon sat idly, the handle of the oar resting across his lap. He found no comfort in the brief interlude between Zheng Ja'hoth's changes of direction. The pirate captain was constantly altering his decisions while combing the coast for unwary prey. Daymon's mind was as blank as that of the barnacles clinging to the outer hull.

Only Daymon's arms and back were needed anymore and they were not his to command. They would stir to motion with the kick of a boot or the lash of the whip. One day they would not respond and then Daymon would no longer be of use. Two slaves on Daymon's right and three to his left had been tossed to the sharks when their usefulness had ceased. If Daymon were more aware he might have noticed that he was now the longest serving member in his row.

Excited voices chattered at the front of the ship. Ja'hoth joined his men who were pointing into the distance. A ship had been sighted. The crew argued over the sensibleness of attacking it.

"It's too large," said Jingo as he lowered the spyglass.

"Shut yer mouth, that's not for you to decide," spat Ka'phal, second in command.

"A Republic cargo ship in these waters," Ja'hoth said appraisingly. He stroked his curly goatee while mulling the possibilities of where it could be going.

The Six Isle Republic primarily traded with Nefara and Fyn. The desert star gazers on the island of Fyn had little wealth to offer, usually not enough for Ja'hoth to risk his life. Nefaran traders had been much more active than usual lately, they were increasingly becoming bigger buyers and sellers. Nefara had wealth worth killing for. Ja'hoth was willing to wager that the Republic trader was en route to Nefara, loaded with goods for the suddenly affluent jungle dwellers.

"Ka'phal, ready the ship," Ja'hoth ordered.

"All hands to their stations," bellowed the second in command.

The sound of whip snap on flesh stirred Daymon into action. His arms moved rhythmically in time with those around him. He wondered how many strokes of the oar remained in his arms. The thought was a passing notion, the answer did not much matter either way. His body would stop when it would and that would be it. A failure of Daymon's magnitude deserved punishment. Death could only come too soon to curtail his shortcomings.

Daymon broke his oath to Kronus Pompae when he was desperate enough to believe in Big Bo's offer of being given a new meaning for his life. The reality of the priest's unfaithfulness to the Shining Empire became evident the moment the Emperor's Gift had deserted him. Daymon must have been unworthy to the Emperor in some way. Now it was only a matter of time until his body betrayed him to Zheng Ja'hoth. Daymon was doomed to disappoint all of his masters.

The speck of the Republic ship grew larger—it could not outrun them along the coast where the winds often stalled for days at a time. People aboard the ship shouted when they heard the noise of the bells clanging against the prow of the Blind Lady. Many had learned to fear the sound of those bells but Daymon hardly noticed them.

"Faster! Together now!'" shouted Ka'phal with another crack of the whip. Daymon knew this part though—they were going to ram the ship from the Six Isles.

Daymon pulled in his oar moments before the iron battering ram on the prow smashed into the Republic ship. The impact shuddered through the Blind

Lady, jolting Daymon out of his seat. Jingo and others twirled grappling hooks, tossing them across to climb the short distance over to the larger ship. The harsh clang of swords rang out as pirates swarmed the Republic traders. Daymon returned to his seat in time to see Zheng Ja'hoth leap from the rail into the melee.

The noise above changed—things were not going as planned. "Retreat!" bellowed Ja'hoth.

Pirates scrambled back down the ropes. Less than half returned.

"Oars in the water! Backward!"

Daymon followed the command as did the other slaves. The Blind Lady disengaged from the other ship and was in the process of turning to flee when something crashed down on the main deck. Another object hurtled into the prow, shattering in an explosion of clay. A strange scent was released from the clay containers, one Daymon did not recognize. A lone flaming arrow arched gracefully from the Republic ship to stick into prow, right beneath the iron battering ram.

Flames erupted to life, roaring and crackling with intensity. Fire raced across the Blind Lady, engulfing the entire front half of the ship in an instant. The crew hurled buckets of water on the fire but the liquid did nothing to dampen the flames. Another clay container crashed down amongst the slaves opposite to Daymon. He watched as the oily substance within the container coated everything within the vicinity of its impact.

A length of burning rope dropped into a pool of oil. Flames rippled across the surface, spreading to everything touched by the vile substance. Daymon turned away from the stench of roasting flesh but the screams of those who burned still scorched his ears. Ka'phal staggered past, completely covered by fire, still gripping the whip which thrashed like a snake trying to escape its captor.

The resin coated wood of the ship burned as black smoke swirled above like a funeral pyre. Tortured screams and flames surrounded Daymon. Men jumped overboard hoping that the ocean would save them but the burning continued. The heat against Daymon's face promised that his voice would soon be added to theirs. Daymon realized that he wanted to live.

He staggered from his seat, aiming for a section of railing that was still clear of flames. He only managed two steps before the chain around his ankle anchored him in place. Daymon had forgotten about the chain—restraints were unnecessary when one had no desire to be free. Daymon pulled at his leg, causing the chain to rub and tear at the flesh of his bony ankle. He clawed at the chain but could not tear it from the bindings.

"Over here!"

Daymon spun to see Zheng Ja'hoth pinned beneath a section of the mast. He threw his sword to Daymon. The sword slid across the deck, bumping into

Daymon's foot. He used it to hack at the wood and chain with both hands. The wood splintered and Daymon pulled the chain loose.

"Save me!" called Ja'hoth.

Daymon glanced at the trapped pirate then at the opening, his only chance of freedom from the burning deathtrap. He started toward the railing.

"I am your master! I order you to help me!"

The command stopped Daymon in his tracks. He could not resist the undeviating authority in Ja'hoth's voice. The ability to perfectly obey each and every command given by his master had long been Daymon's greatest trait. He sprinted over to his master, hopping arching rivulets of flame.

"Lift this off me," Ja'hoth instructed.

Daymon squatted low, placing his palms beneath the burning chunk of mast. He strained to lift the obstacle, but he was so weak, he lacked the strength.

"Lift, you useless wretch!" Ja'hoth cursed.

Daymon put everything he had into moving the piece of timber. His body felt like it was going to snap in two. The mast shifted a little, then he managed to raise it slightly, just enough for Ja'hoth to slide out from underneath. Daymon released the wood, his hands charred from the heat of holding it. His duty was completed so he loped over to the railing and fell into the water. A second splash announced Ja'hoth's plunge.

The two men flailed and kicked as they tried to distance themselves from the inferno. They found a plank of floating wood, each man scrabbling for purchase on the makeshift raft. Ja'hoth watched the Blind Lady crumble, the debris burning down to nothing on the surface of the water. Daymon stared at Ja'hoth, thankful to remain with his master. Life could continue as long as there were commands.

The current slowly brought Daymon and Ja'hoth toward the coast. They floated into a tangled maze of mangrove roots. Small islands dotted the marshy landscape.

Slimy weeds brushed against Daymon's feet as they pressed down into the muddy soil. Unseen crustaceans scuttled out from under his intrusion. Daymon pulled the wood plank and Ja'hoth toward the shore, sinking past his ankles into the mud with each step.

"We need to find dry land," said Ja'hoth. "I dislike the look of our companions." Ja'hoth nodded at the sunning reptiles as two slid into the water, only their unreadable black eyes remained above the surface.

Daymon waded through the weeds lugging the plank behind him. A large turtle startled at his approach, propelling itself into the murky depths. The footing felt firmer near the shore as it became sandier. Daymon assisted his master to the shore. Ja'hoth's left foot and arm were both partially crushed from being pinned beneath the mast. They continued walking but the water still reached to their knees. What appeared to be solid ground was only vegetation that could not support their weight. Daymon struggled to keep them upright as they entered into the flooded forest.

Progress was slow going but eventually Ja'hoth gestured over to an area. "There, head for high ground."

Snaking vines and hanging mosses forced the shipwrecked pair to take a more circuitous route. The fibrous nature of the vines was far too durable for Daymon to tear through with his hands. Both men were exhausted and gasping when they finally stepped onto firm ground.

"Up there," stated Ja'hoth, before Daymon could sit to rest.

The former priest carried the pirate captain to the top of the small hill. He set Ja'hoth down roughly, too weak to lift him any further. Ja'hoth did not seem to care, he was weary as well. "Good dog. Find something dry to burn. We'll die without a fire."

Daymon slumped further, his thin frame feeling impossibly heavy, but he obeyed. He crested the hill and started down a vague animal trail. The contours of the trail followed the rare dry paths of earth as it wound deeper into the trees. Daymon forgot why he was walking. He was simply lifting one foot and then the other. He shuffled along until tripping over an upturned root. The ground rushed up to meet him. He lay huffing on the ground, breathing in the loam and fallen leaves.

Rest. He should rest. Daymon closed his eyes, relaxing into the debris on the forest floor.

His eyes shot open, stark white with realization. Daymon felt a familiar warmth flowing through the ground beneath him. A discreet, crackling energy buzzed like static in his mind. The sensation pricked his skin, giving Daymon goosebumps. The form of the energy was sluggish from disuse, but it was alive. Daymon lay stock still, trying to deny the sensation coursing through him. Not here. Not in this distant place.

Daymon raised his head so that his chin rested on the ground. He gazed forward to see a lone cypress tree. The scalelike leaves fanning out over a moss covered boulder. Roots snugged tightly around the rock before descending into the earth. The sounds of the swamp continued, unimpressed with Daymon or his discovery.

The former priest forced through his exhaustion, hoisting himself upright. He staggered forward to stand under the cypress tree, placing both palms against the soft moss covering the stone.

Energy thrummed through him, instantly transmitting through the new connection. The marks of blood pox on his forearms began to sizzle. They seared and scratched but he was unable to remove his hands from the stone. He felt the energy building inside of him, potent and powerful, and out of his control. This power was different than the Emperor's Gift—wilder and without direction.

Tiny seedlings sprouted from the center of each pox mark. Daymon watched, horrified, as the sprouts became tendrils that stretched across his arms, slowly constricting the skin. The tendrils continued over his elbows, progressing to his shoulders and beyond. He felt a squirming in his mouth that he knew could not be his tongue.

A white bell shaped flower popped out of his mouth, rising above his beard to open toward the sky. Daymon was terrified but he felt no pain. In fact he felt wonderful, better than he had felt in a long time. The transformation continued until Daymon was completely consumed by the sprouting vegetation.

Daymon tried to remove his hands from the stone but they were no longer hands. The thick vines that were once his hands wrapped around the stone and would not come free. He found this predicament strange but was untroubled by it.

He turned his attention to the other direction. An offshoot emerged from his back like a new appendage. Daymon concentrated on this offshoot and discovered that he could control it. He wiggled the shoot up and down, his mind incapable of fully accepting what was happening. Only one thought still rattled around in his head. The gnawing duty to his master. Ja'hoth would die because of Daymon's truancy. He focused again on the new appendage.

The offshoot was pliable, almost seeming like it wanted to move. Daymon pushed it forward, astonished as he watched the plant appendage extend. The shoot hung limply when he stopped focusing on direction. He pushed again and it extended further. The required force was draining. The energy in his hands burned so he opened himself up to it, letting the source of power flow throughout his body.

The shoot extended rapidly, following the trail that Daymon had taken. He found he could sense objects around him through the offshoot. He could not see them but could guess their approximate size and shape. Living things gave off a small sparking field.

He recognized Ja'hoth's field, noting the discrepancies within its makeup where his master was injured. He thought of turning the offshoot into the shape of his face so that his master might recognize him. Daymon realized that he could heal Ja'hoth as the energy had healed him.

He extended the offshoot to connect with Ja'hoth's injured left side. For an instant he was conscious of the other's thoughts. The only word to make it through the connection was "Letokanzhi."

Daymon finished his task and withdrew the offshoot to its original position, satisfied that he could be of use.

## Color of Change

*Breathe in, breathe out.* Feel the air flow into the nostrils to enter the lungs and disperse throughout the rest of the body. Belenus concentrated, eyes closed, focusing his breathing with the deftness of control executed by a master swordsman practicing choreographed movements. The movements were well known to Belenus, but still necessary to attune his body so that it might enact the Emperor's Gift. A fundamental lesson from his training at the Sanctuary ordained that to control your mind you must first control your breath.

Belenus was as experienced as any priest in the Shining Empire, yet he had never felt the desire to teach others his method—it felt wrong to tell others how to understand the mysteries of the Gift. Those who chose to enter the priesthood should experience the joy of discovering their own unique connection to the supreme power made possible by Rua's one true God.

The priest sensed the energy floating in his veins, drifting to the edges of his body to push gently against the inside of his skin, searching for an exit to return to its natural environment. The air became one with Belenus as he drew it in, becoming part of his being and leaving altered. A mixing of forces occurred as the air combined with warm blood. Belenus reduced his focus to one task, closing off the rest of the world, occupied only by the image frozen on the backs of his eyelids. He knew the cut across his thumb bled but the sensation was irrelevant. Singular concentration enveloped his entirety.

The image of a white tulip in bloom blazed in the mind of the priest. He could feel the satin soft curve of its petals, see individual specks of yellow pollen dotting the smooth surface, smell the delicate aroma of its perfume. The moment had arrived.

He released the air from his lungs, blowing softly against the petals. The contents of the exhale were different than the air surrounding him. Belenus sniffed the crackling energy of the Emperor's Gift. He slowly opened his eyes, hoping to see the image of his meditation.

Belenus watched as his breath washed over the tulip, rustling the wilting petals that drooped limply toward the floor. The stem retained a greenness that implied health but it was clear that the flower was near death. As the last of the air left the Beacon's lips something miraculous happened. The tulip moved ever so slightly, jumping up in the vase as if flicked by a finger. Strength returned to the petals as they regained firmness and purity of color. Belenus thought he caught the scent of pollen waft toward him as the tulip opened. He smiled, ecstatic beyond words. He had transferred life into the dying.

The corners of his mouth fell as the petals lost the imparted strength. They curled in on themselves, darkening into dried husks before falling to the floor. The greenness of the stem withered, turning sickly and slumping over the edge of the vase.

For the first time, Belenus became aware of a throbbing in his thumb. A thin stream of blood coursed out as steady as the Choisis river. Belenus jammed the bleeding appendage into his mouth, his brows furrowed in frustration. The taste of the blood reminded him of the scent in the air at Barroc's massive forge—iron, smoke, sweat, and fire.

"So close," he mumbled with the thumb still in his mouth.

Belenus had tinkered with this variation for many years and this was the best outcome to date. He knew that the Gift could bring life. The actions of Emperor Anathasius were evidence of this fact. The Beacon was not asking for that much power. He only needed enough to help those that he could, to aid the sick and wounded like the young Martinus Anathasius from the stories.

At a moment's notice, Belenus could recall the heat on his face emanating from the Emperor's hands as Anathasius healed the pox ridden boy on the Ascending Stairs. Life was returned to that child, certain death was forced to move aside as it was eradicated by the Emperor's will. Belenus wanted to be able to do the same—it was his greatest desire and only ambition in the past few years. Such an ability would be more beneficial than ever with the war going on.

Thoughts of war inevitably brought Belenus round to his current situation and to the fact that Kronus Pompae was in Azra acting on behalf of the Emperor.

"Bloedeth." The swear was garbled by the intruding thumb.

He was late for his meeting with Pompae. Belenus looked down at the dead flower, feeling remorseful about the failed attempt. He wanted to apologize, to promise that he would do better next time, but as one grew older one learned that more often than not there were no second chances. Belenus raised himself from the floor and exited his chambers.

A guard down the hall gave him an odd look which made Belenus realize he was still sucking on his thumb. He removed it to find it was still bleeding, not as vigorously as before but the flow was quite steady. Belenus stuck the thumb back in his mouth, careful to remove it before approaching the stationary guards and then returning it when the coast was clear.

*Important*, Pompae had said, *don't be late*. Belenus scoffed at the words, he could be late if he pleased. He lived in the palace whereas Pompae was only a temporary guest.

Pompae had found a seldom used room in the uppermost level of the palace, choosing to use it as his quarters. Belenus considered this act a direct slight to his status as Beacon. At the moment his knees felt more outraged than his pride, giving Belenus half a mind to protest on their behalf. Step after step he climbed, hot breath gusting onto the back of his hand as Belenus sucked on his thumb. At the final step he pushed off an aching thigh, leaving a red speck on the white of the robe.

The doorway was free of guards, though they would not have stopped Belenus anyway. He pushed into Pompae's room to find the acting leader of Azra standing on a small balcony to the left with his back to the entryway. Pompae's robes looked blood red in the light of the setting sun reflecting off the domed rooftop. As Belenus approached he saw that the color was not a trick of the light; Pompae's robe was indeed a dark red.

"What is the meaning of this?" Belenus demanded.

Pompae continued to look out over the city. "The view is quite nice. The Sanctuary is distinctly lacking in balconies."

"The robes are white, not red. You look like a hot pepper."

Pompae grimaced at the comparison. "That will be changing but don't fret, you may keep your whites if they're that important to you. Old dogs and new tricks and all that. Old dogs also have the sense to wander off and die instead of making a fuss about it."

Belenus was incensed. Pompae's arrogance piqued his ire like nothing else. "You do not have the authority to make such a change to the order. This is Azra, not your father's estate."

Pompae finally turned to face Belenus, he seemed amused, as if he were privy to an inside joke. "I'm glad that at your age you're still able to recognize your surroundings but you are incorrect about the extent of my authority. My station as leader of the Sanctuary does in fact grant me the ability to alter something as trivial as the color of priestly attire. I could make each priest walk around with a monkey on their shoulder if I wanted."

"A monkey! Dealing with a hairy imbecile would be an improvement over you, but you've gone too far, Pompae. I should have been consulted."

Pompae was unbothered by the outburst. "You are being consulted right now. Your outrage about the change is the best endorsement I could have asked for. Change is in the air, Wicket, and you'd sense it if you ever left the musty confines of your den. More is coming, which is why I have asked you here—at least attempt to be civil while I explain."

Belenus raised his finger, hand shaking in outrage. "You little...I should...If you..."

The Beacon stammered on each threat until they suffocated him into a disgruntled silence. Pompae seized this moment to continue.

"The people of the Shining Empire are blessed. They are given a life like none other in Rua, but is it because of their own doing? Who makes it all possible? The obvious answer is Emperor Anathasius, which is undoubtedly true, but who enacts his Gift? The priests do. We are the ones who strengthen foundations to withstand the elements, make multiple harvests possible, keep the animals healthy, keep hearts free from Darkness. Our sacrifices bestow the Emperor's vision to the world.

"I ask you, Wicket, what do we get for our sacrifice? Where is the honor in being considered an outsider by the common folk? The people do not treat us with the respect we deserve, taking our sacrifices for granted."

Pompae stared at Belenus, face intense as he awaited an answer. Belenus matched the expression. He kept his voice calm and even.

"We get to glimpse a power that is not of this world, to use our own hearts to create prosperity for those who cannot do so for themselves. To enact the Emperor's Gift is an extreme honor, one that all would be so lucky to have. You would do well to remember this humility."

Pompae's lips curled in disgust. "You're naive, lost in musings that have no import on the real world. If the Shining Empire is going to complete its destiny, it will be through the sacrifices of the priests and the Chosen. The soldiers are called the Chosen because their service is recognized, they are given a place of honor in the minds of the people. It is time for the priests to stand beside them as equals."

Belenus jabbed a finger at Pompae. "The Chosen deal in death, that is their burden to bear, their choice to make, but the priests aid life. Both actions are important aspects of a singular process. Peace cannot be carried on the blade of a sword or wielded in the battle against Darkness. Peace must reside in the hearts of the priests until it is our turn to bring new life."

Pompae sneered, giving his face a feral appearance. "They are not so different than you think, Wicket. You have grown too comfortable here in the palace. The world is passing you by, the people are not the same as you remember them. My responsibility is to keep them on the path set out by Emperor Anathasius and this is yours as well—keep that in mind while I explain." Pompae cleared his throat. "The ranks of the Chosen swell while that of our order dwindles. Too few think to enter the priesthood. How many potential vessels waste their lives? You have done well to include fellow priests in the marches through the streets and your speeches have helped remind the people that priests have a significant role in their daily lives. Now is the moment to capitalize on this visibility, to keep the actions of the priests in the forefront so that our value is known."

Belenus scoffed. "And red robes are going to do this? A little change of color and everyone will run off to the Sanctuary?"

Pompae glanced over the railing before turning to Belenus. "Priests will become a presence in the daily lives of the people, and their value will be made explicit. Before children reach their teenage years they will be tested and those displaying certain abilities will be sorted accordingly—to the Sanctuary first and foremost—then to the Chosen—then the unskilled others to whatever vocation they are able to accomplish."

"Those who wish to enter the Chosen or the Sanctuary should do so of their own volition. They make their own choice as we did," Belenus said in a reverent tone.

Pompae smiled a heartless smile, a look soured long ago by the humor that inspired it. "The people are weak. They are a mindless herd in need of direction. You know this; you speak to them often enough. Your assistance is required in this task. The flock will follow where the Beacon leads."

Belenus did not like how Pompae said *Beacon*. He made the title sound prestigious but meaningless at the same time. The people would follow Belenus, they trusted him, because he had spent years in Azra cultivating their spirits so they could bloom. Pompae was requesting that Belenus actively separate the wheat from the chaff.

Belenus imagined himself as a shepherd deciding which lambs would be sent to slaughter and which would be sent to the barn. He stood between the two lines as they diverted around his presence to go in opposite directions. A group of confused lambs hesitated before him, unsure of where to go. These individuals were not destined for either path, theirs was a less definite future.

"What of those who are not suitable to become priests or soldiers?" asked Belenus.

"Someone must continue with the menial tasks."

"What of their honor? Will they receive the same respect?"

"They will live because of the sacrifice of others and through this sacrifice, all may one day walk the Illuminated Path of eternal life."

Belenus shook his head, upset with the disdain in Pompae's voice. The leader of the Sanctuary had the unenviable trait of saying the proper words but having them sound undesirable. "I fear the distances that might open up between people because of their status."

Pompae waved his hand. "Open your eyes! You would see that the world is already so. We would simply be refining the process for the aid of the Shining Empire."

The fight had been taken out of Belenus, he was left with a lonely sadness arising from unpleasant truths. Maybe he was just getting old. He could recall a time when he would have yelled his retorts back at Pompae, convincing him with an unrivaled passion. The image of the wilted tulip flashed in his mind. Was the fate of his people to be the same?

He was a master cultivator but perhaps this situation was beyond his understanding. The thought injured his spirit and he could not be sure if this was because the words were spoken by Pompae.

"I will think on this, and we can speak again tomorrow."

Pompae nodded, and Belenus left. He walked slowly down the stairs as thoughts tumbled around in his head. A chill in the air caused Belenus to take in his surroundings. He stood on the platform leading to the dungeon. He had walked from the top of the palace to the bottom without realizing it. He was at first impressed with his stamina, and then embarrassed by his inattentiveness.

"Well," he said to himself. "I'm already here." Belenus sighed and started across the platform, winking at the jailor as he passed.

He snatched a torch off the wall and made his way to Kerak's cell. The shaman was standing against the bars, alerted to Belenus' approach by the light of the torch. Belenus gasped when he caught sight of Kerak. The man was in tatters, his clothes were mere rags clinging to his body. A certain strength remained in the shaman's pose but his once strong body was thin and hunched. Belenus could see the bumps of ribs through a hole in Kerak's shirt. The man was not as weak as one might have guessed by his overall appearance, though. That was clear as soon as Belenus saw Kerak's eyes. The shaman peered at him with the same determination as the first time they met.

"Don't weep for me yet Beacon. I still live."

"Ha! I wouldn't shed a tear for the likes of you, but you could stand to eat a little more."

"I cannot eat what they do not feed me."

"You know what," said Belenus, as he wagged a finger. "I'm going to find some seal meat, there must be someone in the bazaar with access to it."

Kerak smiled, displaying dirty teeth. Belenus shuddered to think of the meals fed in the dungeon.

"That would be a most appreciated gift," said the shaman.

A thought occurred to Belenus, one that would likely be scrutinized, but he was the Beacon after all and this title afforded special authority. The meeting with Pompae made it abundantly clear how easy it was for one to use their authority to make changes.

"These conditions are deplorable," said Belenus. He was getting animated and waved the torch as he spoke. "This cell is not fit for a greasy rat let alone a shaman of the Frozen Tribes. I have the sudden inclination to see that you are given more hospitable conditions."

Kerak nodded solemnly. "I would accept this decision."

"But," the word was uttered like an ultimatum as Belenus jabbed the torch toward the bars. "You would have to give me your word that you won't attempt anything like that day on the Skar. No rituals, no escapes, no trickery of any kind."

Belenus cocked his head to the side, squinting as he studied the shaman's body language. Kerak sighed and his shoulders seemed to slump a little lower. He tried to straighten but they could not reach their former stature. Flames shimmered over Kerak's eyes as he looked to Belenus.

"You have my word."

"Not good enough, I don't trust you that much. Swear on something to prove to me that you'll honor your word."

"I swear on Cynaal, the song of my ancestors that contains the wisdom of the dead and allows the living to continue. This is the wellspring of my power and the source of my faith."

Belenus chewed on his bottom lip as he considered the oath. "That's pretty good. It seems like something a sensible person would want to uphold, but we both know that you aren't right in the head, probably boiled your blood away with all of those tainted rituals, but I suppose no one wants to run afoul of their ancestors."

Kerak looked on impassively. "I would swear on my life but it means less to me than Cynaal."

"I may regret this later but I believe you shaman. I'm going to get you out of this dungeon."

Kerak nodded. Belenus was impressed with the man's forbearance; he would have jumped at any opportunity to be released from the dank and dark of the dungeon. Belenus chuckled. When did he become such a coward? He was not that far removed from the brave young priest who spoke with the great chief of the Uzanaki, who left with his head and a sign of their respect. The vivid red markings of the tattoo had faded over time but the experience retained its vitality. Honor surged beneath the priest's ribs with the recollection of receiving the tattoo, a sensation that made him feel youthful again.

"I might not be able to breathe life but I can help to sustain it. I feel as if leaving you to rot down here would be the same as killing you," said Belenus.

Kerak quirked his head to the side as if suddenly struck by an odd notion. He stood quietly for several moments, looking into the shadows behind Belenus. "Are you familiar with the final words of Wasi Bhodispraiya?"

Belenus shook his head.

"He said: Death comes for us all. Dried leaves crunch underfoot like the bones of fallen warriors. Symbols of life are made brittle by the passing of time and nature's unrelenting need to consume. The permanent becomes temporary as it crumbles into dust, so that new forms may be realized. All is shown to be transitory beneath an unblinking eye, giving shape to energy and establishing foundation in the pursuit of permanence. The abuse of power makes a mockery of death as it vainly devours life."

Belenus scratched his forehead as he considered the words. "Hmm. He must have had some time to get that out, probably wasn't about to be mauled by a bear, was he?"

Kerak laughed and Belenus joined in. For a moment each forgot their surroundings and the actions that brought them to where they stood. A tortured shriek from down the hall ended their enjoyment. The flame flickered, nearly sputtering out, regaining only a portion of its former intensity. The reality of the situation was renewed.

Belenus looked into cold corner of the cell. "I'll speak with who needs to be spoken to. Let's see if we can have you in a bed tonight."

"What has changed?"

"Nothing—maybe everything—I haven't decided yet." Belenus began to walk away, already dreading the climb to his room.

"My thanks, Beacon."

Belenus stopped in his tracks. "There's one more condition. You need to have a bath if you're going to be around civilized folk again. You smell worse than a barge rat. I wouldn't be surprised if vermin were living in that tangled mess of hair."

"What do you think I've been eating?"

Belenus jerked his head back to see if Kerak was jesting. Malnourishment caused the shaman's face to become more angular, giving him a wolfish appearance. He definitely looked hungry. Belenus shook his head. "Barbarians."

He was going to have to figure out a way to clip this crow's wings. Removing Kerak from the dungeon was one thing, having him run amok was quite another. Things were changing, Belenus could feel it. He had felt the stirring for some time, and he could no longer ignore the truth.

Kerak had been in Azra long enough now that he could be considered a constant, a figure visited often enough by Belenus to merit easing the strain of their meetings. His creaky knees would appreciate avoiding the stress of climbing the stairs. The wiry legs still had plenty of strength left in them but were no longer as inexhaustible as in their youth.

Belenus rolled up his sleeve to look at the red swirls of the tattoo, mentally tracing their pattern with the route of his former journeys. An old yearning swelled in his chest, an urge to set out with his faith as a shield against the obstacles of the world. Belenus was not finished his work yet. He did not need to go anywhere, the mission had come to him. The streets would be filled with priests in red when he lacked the strength to speak for Azra, and that was not this day.

# Serpent of Ryakesh

The famed outer wall surrounding the city of Ryakesh bristled like a porcupine. The blackthorn barricade was said to be impenetrable as no army had ever successfully breached the in-grown fortification. Needle sharp thorns up to the length of a man's arm protruded menacingly. The thorn wall was impervious to fire and its twisting branches were stronger than iron. Scaling the wall might have been possible if not for the wide, deep moat ringing it.

Supreme confidence in their defenses had kept the Ryakesh army from rushing out to attack the Chosen in the aftermath of the battle with the Night Creeper. Melea considered the defensive act a foolish decision; Ryakesh should have attacked. They would not get another chance.

Located near the mouth of the Green river as it poured out of the Kon mountains, Ryakesh sat directly between Draccar and Marikal. Ryakesh, capital of the dukedom of Carnot, had long weathered the strife between Rhezaria and Calanthia. Extreme defenses were necessary, and consequently the city became home to a battle hardened people who adhered to their own beliefs.

Melea watched Anathasius walk toward Ryakesh alone. She stood in line with the rest of the army, prepared to follow the command of their supreme leader. She was dressed in full uniform for the first time, and the blue cloth felt unnatural, as did the weight of the armor and helmet.

Anathasius reached the moat, stepping aboard a small raft constructed in the night by the Chosen. He glided gracefully across the water that had housed the Night Creeper. The stinking corpse of the monster remained where it had fallen, a rotting mass covered in squawking gulls and screeching crows.

The Emperor stepped off the raft to stand below the tangled thorns. His white robe shone magnificently against the black wall. Soldiers along the wall looked down in confusion but did not call out. Neither did they fire upon the Emperor of the Shining Empire. Melea knew that boiling cauldrons of oil lined the top of the wall, she could smell their roiling contents on the wind. The Chosen were silent as the Emperor placed his hands against the thorns.

Melea felt the change immediately, the very air itself tingling with energy. Those around her gradually became aware of the difference as well. The sentries on the wall suddenly became much more concerned with the presence of Emperor Anathasius. Frantic yelling was followed by stern commands calling for order. Melea could feel unseen movement in the air, the material of the invisible becoming agitated. Energy built, growing larger out of nothing, like a thundercloud in a sealed room. The air smelled burnt. *Here it comes*, she thought.

The water of the moat behind Anathasius stirred, waves surging out of nowhere. Rocks jumped and hopped around his feet as the grass was pushed flat. A voice called out. Anathasius continued, lowering his stance as if bracing himself for contact. The order to fire was given. A hail of arrows rained down on the unarmed and unarmored Emperor.

Anathasius did not move a muscle, remaining completely focused on his task. Each arrow disintegrated before making contact with his body. A second round of arrows were loosed but they encountered the same fate as the first. The soldiers atop the wall rolled two cauldrons of boiling oil above the Emperor. The scalding liquid poured over the edge of the wall like a grotesque waterfall. Anathasius was temporarily hidden behind a veil of oil turned into hissing steam as it evaporated.

The Chosen cheered when the steam dissipated to leave their Emperor standing in the same position as before. Melea concentrated on Anathasius, watching for any sign of movement. She saw him lean forward, forcefully pushing his palms into the thorns.

Melea choked as the air was sucked out of her lungs. For an instant everything felt thinner, less substantial than it should have. A resounding crack shook the thorn wall. Men ran from their posts as others yelled for them to remain in place. A blinding arc of light erupted out of the thorns, shearing through the wall renowned for its indestructibility. She kept her gaze on Anathasius as he pushed his palms into the wall again and again. Arcing beams of light shattered huge sections of the wall on either side. No debris or men rained down from the destruction—there was simply nothing left once it was touched by the light.

The display of power made Melea dizzy. The energy at Anathasius' disposal was incredible. Her skin felt itchy from the heat even at this distance. She had always sensed the immense power within Anathasius but never imagined it to be like this. In Melea's mind the mural in the Shining Palace of the Emperor vanquishing the Steward's army by himself had always been an embellished story, not an eyewitness account.

Her body shook with an involuntary shiver, skin clammy from a cold sweat. She found herself taking rapid breaths—the air was thin as if at a high altitude. Anathasius stepped back from the wall, or where the wall had been. The entire front section of the thorn wall, along with the men who had been on it, was completely gone. He raised his right hand, signaling the Chosen to advance.

The force of men behind Melea left her no choice but to run with them. She tried to shake off her uneasiness but was unable to dislodge a sickening feeling of dread. Four teams of men emerged from the group to place four massive lengths of cut timber on the ground. They pushed the wood steadily, holding onto chiseled handholds, forcing the planks across the water to the other side. Soldiers streamed across the makeshift bridge, continuing past the Emperor as he pointed onward into the undefended city.

Anathasius stood serenely in his white robes as the army flowed around him. His calm presence after such an unbelievable display gave the Chosen a feeling of invincibility. They had beaten the Night Creeper and shattered the thorn wall. Ryakesh was theirs for the taking.

The Ryakesh army regrouped as well as it could. Soldiers in shiny black armor hurried to meet the onrushing Chosen. Melea thought the warriors looked like human-sized beetles. Their helmets even had twin spikes that could have been antennae.

For once, she was wearing armor. She had felt uncomfortable with the cumbersome breastplate so she had opted for chain mail beneath boiled leather. The helmet was the most unusual addition. She thought that the crosspiece hanging over her nose would be distracting but it went unnoticed now that the battle had started. The helmet and armor had a function, they could easily save her life, but the uniform still felt unnecessary. Melea detested the blue colors she was forced to wear, marking her as one more soldier amongst the horde.

She was not like them. This was her chance to enact her oath, to put an end to the fighting before all of the blood was spilled. Orders were for the Chosen and she was not one of them, despite the color of her uniform. Melea had her own plan: subdue the Duke of Carnot to force surrender. The man was a warrior of some renown and in the prime of life. He would be fighting today. All she needed to do was find him. Lop the head off the snake and the body would stop squirming.

There was a solid crunch as soldiers from the two lines crashed into each other. Melea hacked and slashed at multiple opponents, never staying in one place for long. She was hunting and therefore subduing each and every foe was not her main concern. An older commander wearing armor with a greenish tinge caught her eye.

The commander led a regiment of spearmen that were attempting to move to the forefront of the fighting. Melea guessed that the Duke would be heavily guarded as part of the cavalry. The horsemen would be waiting in the rear until the foot soldiers established a hold on the area near the gate or until they lost what little ground remained.

The Ryakesh spearmen were fighting valiantly, straining to remain a cohesive unit against the unrelenting surge of Chosen. Their only hope was to hold the line so that the Chosen were unable to flank them. Melea noticed that the commander was frequently sending more men to the right side in an effort to prevent the Shining Empire from swinging in and surrounding his men. The right side of the battlefield was more open as sections of the adjoining structures had been destroyed along with the thorn wall. She needed to weaken that side so that the cavalry would be forced to enter the fray.

Melea angled as far right as she could until the press of bodies became too thick to continue. The savage vibration of battle registered in her bones. The clang of weapons, the shouting of commanders, battle cries of the victorious, and shrieks of the wounded rent the air.

The backs of hundreds of Chosen stood between her and where she wanted to be. She smacked the flat of her blade against a small exposed area on the rear of a Chosen's leg. The soldier grunted in pain as his leg buckled from the unexpected attack. Melea sheathed her sword, grabbed the man's shoulders, stepping off his hip and onto his helmet.

On quick feet she stepped across to the shoulders of the next Chosen. She skipped on tip-toes across the jostling mass of soldiers, using their broad armor as stepping stones. There was more movement in the front lines so Melea increased her pace, lunging from shoulder to shoulder until there were no more Chosen in front of her. She kicked off the final soldier, launching herself over the front line of the Ryakesh infantry, landing in a crouch and coming up spinning, her blade a whirling arc of death.

The front line of black clad soldiers could not turn their attention to Melea, so she slashed out several legs before the next line of Ryakesh beetle soldiers could step forward to crush her. A gap opened up as three of the soldiers in black armor went down at once. The Chosen pressed forward into the gap to split the line. Melea stood at the front of the wedge, cutting down any who came within range of her sword.

The bronze armbands on her left arm burned as they started to expand. The success of using bronze rings on her fingers had inspired Melea to extend the concept. Her left arm became encased in bronze, turning it into a shield and sledge hammer. Melea ducked under a spear point, lunging upward to impale her sword through the soldier's chin deep enough to knock his helmet off.

She threw out her bronze arm, feeling armor and ribs crack against it. Her sword was pure motion, moving faster than the forest of spears around her. Spear shafts shattered against her bronze arm as Melea sprang forward to send three more warriors to the dirt. More Chosen were filling the spaces around her. They were gaining ground.

The old commander pushed his way towards Melea. He wasted no motion as he dropped two Chosen along the way. His spear lunged out, feinting high, then low, in rapid succession, feeling out her defenses. He spun expertly on his heel, bringing the spearpoint slicing down at Melea's head. She sidestepped the attack only to realize that it was setup for the commander's next maneuver. His spear swept low to take out her legs as he finished the spin. She barely jumped the spear and was caught flat footed as the commander advanced to ram the spearpoint into her chest. The force of the strike was enough to pierce through the boiled leather and chain mail but something stopped the point from plunging between her ribs.

Melea's eyes snapped onto her left arm, which was now bare of iron. The commander pulled his spear back in revulsion, watching the iron flow like liquid from Melea's chest to solidify over her arm once again. Both combatants were still for a moment as they tried to understand what had just occurred.

The commander was on her in an instant, forcing her into a desperate defense. Her bronze arm turned aside two lunges targeting her throat. Melea tried to out maneuver the commander but his footwork was superb and there was not enough space in the compacted fighting. Another strike came her way and this time she was ready. She allowed the spear to make contact with her bronze shoulder, consciously opening a space in the metal so that the spear could pass through. Melea solidified the bronze when the spearpoint made contact with the links of chain mail underneath. The spear remained attached when the commander tried to pull it back.

She sliced through the wooden shaft and released the spearpoint from the bronze to let it drop harmlessly to the ground. She moved quickly toward the weaponless commander. He raised an armored forearm to block her sword, but could not stop her bronze fist. The metal encasing her hand smashed down onto his collarbone, forcing him to lurch forward. Melea executed her own spin to deliver a backhand slash to the commander's throat. Scarlet blood spurted onto Melea's blue uniform. She stepped over the greenish tinged armor toward the next black clad soldier.

"Fall back!"

Horns blared as the foot soldiers retreated from the death of their commander. Melea and the Chosen hacked down the remaining spearmen as the others hustled into Ryakesh. A roar of victory sounded behind Melea. She wiped flecks of the commander's blood off her chin with the back of her sleeve.

She loped away, leaving the Chosen behind as she chased the scurrying beetles. The cheering stopped as the Chosen obediently followed her lead. Anathasius told Melea that he had envisioned her leading the Chosen and she had scoffed at this prediction. Why would they ever follow her? What she really wanted to say was that she didn't care about them enough to be their leader. She was not one of them, she was no soldier.

No commands were issued but the Chosen followed regardless. *Let them follow, they will have their usefulness*, she thought. But she was the only one who could end this battle without razing all of Ryakesh.

The beetle soldiers could not escape, they were not fast enough. Melea chased after them as they entered a large market square. A metallic taste laced her tongue. Melea spat out a nasty brownish glob. The bronze on her arm was starting to have an effect on her body. The spreading influence had to be overlooked for now; she would need the advantage of the temporary strength for a little longer.

The streets were empty of civilians. Only the clamor of thousands of heavy footfalls occupied the streets, a noise that made it impossible to differentiate between defender and invader. A unit of spearmen stopped at the end of the square. Melea slowed to wait for the Chosen. The hair on her neck pricked up, something was wrong. She scanned the square but the danger remained hidden from sight. The Chosen grouped in formation around Melea as they advanced across the square.

Was the enemy just buying time so that the others could escape? She could push through these few soldiers to find the Duke but the scent of a trap was in the air. She caught the eyes of several Chosen looking to her for direction, expecting a command. An officer barged into the space beside Melea, deliberately ignoring her presence.

"To me, men! Spear formation!"

Melea drifted to the back as the Chosen obeyed the officer's order. *Good, follow your own.* Something in the stance of the Ryakesh soldiers bothered her, and she did not want to be the first to engage them. The sense of unease intensified as the two groups of warriors squared off. Melea worked her way to the rear of the formation, nearer to the left side. From this vantage point she was able to survey the buildings around the square.

Soldiers blocked one exit and the other was now some distance behind the Chosen. A temple stood to Melea's immediate left, the stone facade decorated with thousands of colorful snake carvings. Wide buildings squatted on each side of the exit in front of her. The clash of battle resumed up ahead.

The Chosen were scoring a decisive victory in this skirmish, the beetle soldiers being greatly outnumbered. Melea spotted movement on the wide rooftops above the fighting. She glimpsed black armor and the scent of noxious fumes. She backpedaled, keeping her eyes on the activity on the rooftops.

"Now!" came the shout from the rooftop.

Boiling oil poured over the fighting on the ground. Black and bronze armor alike seared as the oil washed over the soldiers. Men screamed, trapped in their armor like rats in a furnace. Some tried to shed their burning helmets and breastplates. Archers appeared on the rooftops and loosed a wave of arrows. Melea turned to find cover, sprinting to the nearest building.

She flew up the stairs of the snake temple, lowering her bronze shoulder into the center of the door, crashing through the barricade, headlong momentum carrying her stumbling down the stairs. A stunned acolyte yelled out in shock as he swung a long candle holder at Melea that pinged off her helmet. Her ears rang from the impact as she was knocked off balance.

A narrow walkway separated the temple floor, lined by two long pits on either side. The dark floor of the pits moved. Melea tumbled headfirst into the pit on the left. A series of angry hisses surrounded Melea as she crashed to the floor. Snakes slithered in all directions, agitated by her sudden arrival.

The ting of forceful contact on metal alerted Melea's dazed awareness. She swiveled into position to see a large cobra rise up with hood extended, ready to strike her bronze arm again. Curved fangs clanged against the bronze to leave twin streams of deadly venom dripping down to her elbow.

Melea locked eyes with the enraged serpent. An idea formed, a crazy, desperate notion. Only one opportunity would be afforded. The cobra snapped forward again. She caught the snake just below the neck with her bronze hand. The cobra was incensed, thrashing wildly at its capture.

She let the bronze melt off her arm, the metal sliding down like a sheet of water, immediately solidifying into warped spheres as it touched the stone floor. Warm scales pressed against her palm. Melea focused on the sensation. Along with the warmth, there was the snake's heartbeat and the taste of its blood. Her sight became unfocused as all thought traveled to her fingertips.

The snake calmed in her grasp. She pulled the long body through her grip until she was only holding it by the tail. Her palm burned with a searing heat that was painful yet strangely enjoyable. The separation between her skin and the snake's scales became irrelevant as the flesh became one. The cobra now extended out of Melea's palm, as securely attached as any other appendage. Her right hand burned as well, the heat intense, hungry, seeking to be released. She reached out to snag the tail of another cobra as it tried to slither away. The snake stilled as it fused into Melea's palm.

Melea stood. The other snakes were giving a wide berth. She felt tireless—ecstatic and invigorated and anxious. The options were limitless.

Disjointed thoughts raced faster than the manic pounding of her heart. *Breathe.* She inhaled slowly and deeply for several moments, drawing focus back to herself. Her mind and body wanted to go in different directions, in all directions. They would pull her apart at the seams if she let them. *Just breathe, there is a task to accomplish.*

The pit was without stairs or a ramp. Melea crouched low, springing out of the pit to land flat footed on the walkway. The jump felt effortless. Melea's body desired more. The temple acolyte gasped as Melea walked past him with long serpent bodies trailing on the floor behind her.

"Demon," whispered the acolyte.

Melea stopped. She flicked her wrists and the cobras responded. They snapped upright, raising upward out of her palms. Their sinewy bodies curved back toward her as forked tongues flicked out. An intense double pulse flowed throughout Melea and the snakes. They were hers to control. Melea walked up the stairs and exited the temple as the acolyte fell to the floor sobbing.

The square was littered with bronze and black bodies perforated with arrows. The air stank of charred flesh. Nothing alive stirred on the streets, the fighting had moved elsewhere. Melea knew it continued even though she could not see or hear the battle—she could feel it. Small rumbles flittered in the air and trembled along the ground, providing a sense of direction to the activity. The vibrations entered her body, giving a vague scope of the battle. Indistinct shadows were given momentary shape before blending into one another as they moved.

She took off in the direction of the vibrations, her feet pounding against the stone. Soon, she picked up a scent on the air, distinct from the blood and sweat of men. Horses. Quick, heavy footsteps sent out thundering vibrations. The cavalry had arrived.

Melea increased her pace. She wanted to end this battle. She felt incredible, her body thrumming with energy. The sensation reminded her of a head rush from drinking wine, but this feeling was infinitely more intense. Her senses were crystal clear, demanding movement and action. Stimulus was needed, an outlet to release the energy.

Traversing the winding streets of Ryakesh was taking too long, Melea could practically see the heat emanating off her body as she ran. More than a few frightened faces peeked out of windows, people who were unable or unwilling to flee. The entire population was likely still hunkered down, expecting a long siege, never dreaming that the thorn wall could come down in an instant.

The clash of conflict echoed through a narrow side street so she turned in that direction. She emerged on another empty street but the commotion was growing louder. Melea kicked open the door of a house, startling the family inside as she sprinted through the main room and out the back door. The battle was near, only one more row of buildings stood between her and the Duke. Melea could see the towers of a sizable structure. The fighting had moved all the way to Duke's own home.

The buildings in front of her had the feel of government to them—overly large, elaborate, and protected. Thick bars with heavy locks barricaded the doors. If she could not go around or through then she would go over. At the very least, she would get a clear view of what was happening. Melea leapt toward the nearest wall, quickly springing from crevice to crevice, using any available edge as a foothold. She raced up the side of the building with feline grace. With a final powerful leap she vaulted to the tiled rooftop.

A maelstrom of violence dominated the scene below. Armies raged against one another in fierce combat across the Duke's palatial gardens. Melea spotted the Duke straightaway. There was no mistaking his magnificent armor—the black material gleaming like obsidian jewelry in the sunlight. He was leading charges against the Empire's cavalry, clashing and then wheeling around to strike again. Melea charted a route to her target then scurried down the backside of the building—hopping, climbing, and running down the wall like a lizard until she reached the ground.

The cobras hissed aggressively, sensing the hostility around them. Two soldiers charged at her with swords upraised. She lashed out with both hands, the cobras snapping forward like whips. Fangs sank into the soldier's faces and they cried out. A surge passed from Melea through the snakes and into the men. A dark, sickening sensation made her want to retch. The soldiers convulsed and dropped to the ground.

Melea's mouth was wet with a sticky acidic liquid that she spat on the ground. Her spit was black and viscous.

"Demon!" The accusation went up from those who had witnessed the attack.

Shock turned to rage as a horde of black armored soldiers descended on her. Cobra strikes and spinning kicks lashed out in a flurry of motion, leaving Melea standing in a circle of motionless bodies. She dashed toward the action involving the cavalry as the Duke began to lead another charge.

Horses barreled into a group of Chosen in front of her. Men were crushed beneath hooves, leaving them maimed or dead. She pounced through a gap and into the center of the attack.

The horses were moving much faster than the men, but Melea was faster still. She ran alongside them as she maneuvered nearer to the Duke. His back was to her as his sword sliced down. A Chosen's head was released from his shoulders with one powerful swing of the Duke's broadsword. The Duke plunged his mount into the line of Chosen, opening a space for his soldiers to follow.

The well-trained warhorses panicked when they caught sight of Melea. She slid underneath one horse, causing it to rear up in fright and toss its rider.

A sword arced down at her neck. She dodged to the side while snapping out with a cobra. Her attacker dropped from the saddle to lie still on the ground. Melea stepped into the stirrup, and then to the saddle to launch herself at the Duke. She planted two feet into the center of his back, knocking him from the horse. The frightened horse reared and kicked out, a glancing blow from a wide hoof knocking off Melea's helmet.

The cobras hissed and snapped at anything within reach. The Duke stood to face Melea, his hard blue eyes without fear. He gripped the broadsword with both hands.

The Snake Lord of Carnot struck swiftly as he swung the wide blade in fluid, sweeping motions. With a vicious forehand to backhand combination he attempted to sever the snakes from Melea and Melea's abdomen from her waist. He was skilled but her speed was unmatched. She dodged and ducked the attack, all the while moving closer.

The cobras lashed out, fangs embedding into the Duke's wrists. He held tight to his sword so Melea sent a surge through the snakes. The sword dropped and the Duke collapsed to the ground as poison entered his bloodstream. Melea disengaged the cobras, redirecting one to bite deep into the Duke's hip and the other between his shoulder blades. Melea's face was a grim mask of hard lines. Her green eyes floated like the last bits of mold on blackened rot.

Black venom gushed out of Melea's mouth, splattering against her feet and shins. The vomiting was uncontrollable. The snakes convulsed as Melea altered the course of the venom. Her arms spasmed as she lifted the Duke into the air, hoisting him up with the clamped jaws of the cobras. He hung limply, head and feet dangling.

The fighting around Melea stopped. An eerie hush fell over the battle.

"Enough!" The force of the scream tore at her throat.

Her nostrils stuck together as if they were crusted with blood, and her tongue felt raw. The Duke groaned in pain when he tried to raise a hand. A soldier stepped forward to disembowel Melea and release his master. She sent a jolt of energy into the Duke.

"Stop!" he cried out. The command spread out over the battlefield like a stone dropped into still water. "Stop, stop, please," the Duke pleaded.

Melea was not finished yet. The energy still churned inside of her, waiting to be released. Her chest filled as she sucked in a lungful of air.

"This battle is over. You are defeated Ryakesh. Throw down your weapons or watch as I take you down one by one like your Duke. Surrender and I will let you live."

The silence was absolute. No one dared to move. Melea saw shock, fear, disgust, and hate directed at her. This was meaningless. All that mattered was that the soldiers yielded.

"Sire?" asked the soldier nearest to Melea.

"Do it," croaked the Duke.

The soldier cast Melea a hateful look. He stared down at his hand for a moment as he considered disobeying the Duke's response. The soldier's mouth flattened into a thin line and he looked away. The clattering of his sword on the ground broke the silence. Weapons fell like raindrops as others followed along. The dam broke as all of the black-clad warriors threw their weapons aside.

Melea summoned the last of the power within to give her voice the required authority. "Chosen! These men are now prisoners of war and they are to be treated as such. Any of you who choose to harm my prisoners will be shown no mercy."

She lowered the Duke to the ground. The snakes detached their fangs and raised themselves upright. Melea glared at all of the Chosen in eyesight. She dipped the head of a cobra at a Chosen commander. "Come here."

The commander approached stiffly. He stood before her and then awkwardly knelt on one knee. She smiled when she recognized the man. He gulped nervously.

"Osgood, you are in charge of overseeing the detainment of the prisoners. You will be my next meal if you fail."

"Yes, your Excellence, er uh...your Grace."

Melea's fingers had gone cold, numb like being out in winter wind without gloves. The seemingly limitless energy was now quickly departing. The snakes were moving sluggishly. Melea concentrated on where the snakes contacted her skin, controlling her breathing to an even in and out rhythm. *Release.* She repeated the word in her mind. Melea wanted to push the serpents out of her palms but they seemed to be resisting. They almost seemed to be pushing back, attempting to take more of her hand than she was willing to give. She considered ripping them out, but would it work? The violence might devastate her hands.

Instead, she channeled what was left of the energy into the two cobras, blocking it off so that the flow could not return into her hands. The snakes hissed and shook wildly. They burned from the inside, giving off an appalling reek. Osgood looked away. The snakes dropped from Melea's hands; two charred lengths of meat prematurely stopped in the final motion of their writhing. Soldiers stepped aside for her, clearing a direct pathway off the battlefield.

She tasted poison. Her limbs were beginning to cramp. But she walked straight and proud. These men needed to respect her, or fear her, it did not matter which. She wanted them to know deep down in the core of their being that disobeying her commands would result in a fate worse than death. She needed them to think she was invincible. So, Melea gritted her teeth and put one foot in front of the other, keeping her eyes level while stars danced around her vision.

She made it all the way to the camp before collapsing. She wanted to make it to her tent to lie down, or to die, in privacy. Her insides felt like a jumble of razor blades. The fire was gone, and she was only ash inside. Anathasius approached, tall and magnificent as he looked down on Melea.

"You led the Chosen and gave them orders. I told you this was your destiny," said the Emperor.

Melea could not respond, she merely blinked a few times.

"You've done well Melea but you overstepped your bounds. I decide who is to become a prisoner. Come, I want to show you something."

Anathasius strolled away, stopping to look over his shoulder as Melea struggled to rise. Somehow she got herself upright, finding the strength to stagger after him. The Emperor led her a short distance to where a trebuchet stood. The siege weapon stood silently, an engineering marvel that was not needed because of the Emperor's involvement. Melea half noticed that the Chosen were hurrying out of Ryakesh. *Where were the prisoners?* Her muddled mind drifted back to Anathasius as he spoke.

"You tried to send a message today and I think I received it correctly. Your abilities are progressing but you need to be reminded that they are not yours to use as you wish. Individuals, cities, and nations are all subject to my judgement. As are you, Melea."

Anathasius stepped aside as four soldiers loaded a large clay ball into the sling of the trebuchet. The ball reached the Emperor's shoulder and was as wide as a man is tall. A familiar odor clung to it but Melea could not place the scent. Anathasius set his hands on the ball and concentrated for a moment. Melea sensed a crackle of energy activate, a buzzing as if the ball was filled with thousands of bees.

Anathasius stepped back and the trebuchet released. The whirling creak of its action sent the ball hurtling into Ryakesh. An explosion of dust and blue lightning shot out in all directions from the impact. Melea heard screaming.

"You see," said Anathasius as he placed his hands on another clay ball. The trebuchet whirled again. More screams. "Life and death are in my hands."

Anathasius placed his hands on another of the clay balls as Melea looked on dumbfounded. She followed the graceful arc all the way to the incendiary impact. Dust slowly filtered above the city. Streaks of shooting lightning danced along the dust, sizzling with intensity. The city was screaming as one. Melea saw a man, a civilian, running for the edge of the city to escape the dust. The smothering cloud caught him with an effortlessly consuming pace.

A blue flash ripped through his chest, lifting him off his feet as it coursed through his body. The lifeless man dropped when the lightning dissipated. Melea looked to Anathasius for an explanation. She knew that death was part of war, but this? *Why?*

"I also know how to send a message," said Anathasius.

He turned his golden eyes to Melea. They seemed so big, so full of a light that she was only barely capable of reflecting.

## The Shining Lord

Anathasius looked upon the ruin of Ryakesh and savored the momentous victory. This day would become legend. Rua was given a glimpse of what he was capable of. His power was irrefutable and word of this truth would range far and wide as news of Ryakesh made its way across the countryside. The Chosen were coming—the level of destruction now depended on the choices made by those who stood in the way. Anathasius suspected that most would surrender in fear of becoming the next Ryakesh. But Marikal would not, they would stubbornly fight to the bitter end.

Calanthia's utilization of sacrifices was juvenile compared to that of the Shining Empire; meager understanding applied by marginal skill. The savages of Rhezaria were even less adept, wasting sacrifices on who could swing a club the hardest. Reckoning would come for the combative Clans and their Queen in due time. Calanthia would fall first, the inevitable defeat spreading outwards from Ryakesh like a debilitating sickness. Every individual in every town now understood the alternative to submission.

Understanding—that is what Anathasius delivered to Rua. He was imparting a truth the masses could comprehend. The common person need not be involved with the full scale of his plan or the intricacies of his goals. People were his to move about like pieces on a cüthril board. The Emperor was a being of power exceeding the imagination of the game's creators.

*We must speak.* The words whispered in the Emperor's mind, brittle as dried leaves scraping across stone. The request elicited immediate outrage. Anathasius had no patience for the one who called to him. The obligation was an infuriating nuisance. Generally, Anathasius was beyond such trivialities but he could not ignore this summons.

"General Cathair," called Anathasius. The soldier approached swiftly, bowing deeply in respect. "I am going for a short walk in the forest to the west of the encampment and do not wish to be disturbed. See that this is taken care of."

"Of course your highness," said Cathair.

Anathasius left the General and made for the outer ring of the camp. Dust from the final attack still hung over Ryakesh, the shifting clouds disrupted by intermittent fingers of lightning. He was pleased with the effectiveness of the weapon. The lethality was greater than expected.

He stalked over to a copse of cedar. The tall trees grew in bunches on this side of the mountains, standing out from the rest of pines and poplars. Anathasius moved well away from the camp, still fuming at the unexpected demand for his presence. *How dare he be called away during the middle of the campaign!* The Emperor did not bother to look behind him as he entered the trees. No one would defy his command. At least his Chosen knew how to follow orders.

Anathasius peered about the shadowy space, unable to see the other who had called him to this meeting. He could feel the unmistakable aura of the other.

The presence stood before him, centered in the darkest section of the grove. Anathasius stopped at the edge of the darkness. "This had better be important," the words hissed out in a controlled shout.

Silence emanated from the darkness. Anathasius sought to extinguish his flaring frustration. It would do him no benefit to be put off balance here.

After several long moments, a grating voice spoke, deep as though from the bottom of a well. "You are angry. Anger disrupts thought and instigates unnecessary action." The words were halting and forced, as if needing to be pushed into existence.

Anathasius expected such a response but it still rankled. He composed himself. He would be in control of this conversation, not the other way round. "I am in the middle of something vital and your request came at a particularly sensitive juncture. What pressing matter do we need to discuss?"

Silence again, this time nearly interminably long. "Your actions are exceedingly close to breaching the bonds of the agreement," said the hidden speaker with a voice like rough stone.

"The agreement also stated that I was the one, the only one I remind you, capable of undertaking this task. I believe I am granted liberty in deciding how best to achieve our mutual goal."

The emotionless voice responded quicker this time. "You were given this opportunity to accomplish our goal. There cannot be any deviation from the agreement."

Anathasius seethed. "I was not given anything—you need me. The agreement falls apart without my involvement."

"Do not hide behind veiled threats. You are not so near to completion as you think. You would do well to accept guidance," the voice now swirled like storm clouds.

"If I make a threat you will know it—trust in that. You need me more than I need you." Anathasius stared hard into the blackness. "And I do not appreciate being told how to direct my campaign."

The voice responded in a near whisper, Anathasius strained to catch the words. "Arrogance is not confidence. There is much you have not seen. You were once the only candidate but now that may not be so."

Anathasius was dumbfounded by the words, taking a moment for them to fully register. He opened his mouth to speak but shut it in silence. He hated the Bloodless. Anathasius turned away and walked out of woods. His mind was so consumed with the message that the shadowy figure slipping amongst the trees went unnoticed.

An even line of soldiers stood at the edge of the encampment, their backs to Anathasius. General Cathair stood amongst them, barring anyone from accidentally making their way out of camp toward the area occupied by the Emperor.

"At ease, General," said Anathasius.

The Emperor strolled past the line of soldiers, continuing to his personal caravan. The caravan for his attendants sat nearby. A substantial distance separated these camps and the rest, and none but Anathasius and his attendants had reason to cross the open space. The number of attendants brought for this campaign necessitated their own caravan. Anathasius wanted these specialized servants separated from the main body of the army.

Before the attack on Ryakesh, he had ordered two of them to wait in his caravan for his return. He opened the door and a cursory glance provided no sign of the attendants.

A buzz in his mind turned Anathasius around. The fragment from the Skar sat in the corner of the room. He sensed the powerful energy within the black stone. Such a rare and valuable resource that he was still deciding how to best use.

He made his way through several rooms before finding the two Flames. One girl slept, curled on a cushion. The other, a boy, was idly playing with a thin ceremonial blade. He tried to stash the knife as Anathasius entered the room. A boy, that was surprising, they were usually less sensitive and therefore unable to become Flames.

"No need to put the knife away," Anathasius said gently. "You'll soon be using it."

The boy placed the knife on the table and sat up straight, ready to obediently follow orders. Anathasius smiled. Such a good child.

"Wake her, gently now."

The boy tapped his sleeping comrade on the shoulder. She shook herself awake, embarrassed by her inattentiveness. She sat up straight, blinking the sleep out of her eyes.

Anathasius gave a beatific smile. "It is good that you are well rested, your strength is needed."

"I won't have it," Belenus said for the fourth time.

He had been summoned to the grand conclave once again, now seated in a wide chair covered in teal fabric. Belenus remained steadfast in the fury of the storm that was Kronus Pompae.

The interim leader of Azra smashed a fist against the armrest then pointed his finger menacingly at the Beacon. "Get it through your thick skull, this is the way of the future; a development needed to support the pillars of our faith."

"You keep saying that," Belenus mused.

His hands were folded comfortably on the lap of his white robe. He would not get drawn into Pompae's vortex of anger and neither would he submit. Pompae also wore a white robe—he was not brave enough to wear the red in public yet. Belenus stifled a smile. Pompae seethed like a petulant child used to getting what he wanted, and bullied those who dared to stand up to him. *Not this time*, Belenus thought.

Pompae took a deep breath, his hand still squeezed in a tight fist. "There are too many different versions of worship in the city, and that's not even considering the rest of the Empire. It's only a matter of time until one of these, or several for that matter, break away to create their own doctrine. The people need to have consistency in their faith, they need organization directed by the priests. The fact that the priesthood is not managing this more closely is a travesty."

A direct shot at Belenus' leadership, which he ignored. Belenus gave his most condescending sigh. "You're still young. Surely you remember your lessons? What is the primary task required of all priests?"

Pompae did not answer, unless the grinding of his teeth qualified as a response. Belenus could practically see the steam shooting out from the flared nostrils. Most enjoyable.

"Hmm? Well, then let me remind you." Belenus cleared his throat before quoting the first lessons taught to him at the Sanctuary. "Central to the responsibilities of the priesthood is the banishment of Darkness in all its forms. This crucial task is to be enacted by aiding the Shining Empire through the use of the Emperor's Gift—"

"Enough," Pompae snapped. "I know the lessons as well as you do."

"Could have spoken up sooner, although I am always happy to discuss matters of faith." Belenus tilted his head slightly. "So, tell me again why Azra needs a temple? Or as you put it: a series of magnificent works covering the entirety of the Shining Empire."

Pompae looked as though he might leap up and strike Belenus. *Do it, hit an old man, you little worm.* Evidence of Pompae attacking Belenus would go a long way in removing Pompae from the palace and maybe even from the priesthood altogether. The leader of the Sanctuary composed himself, smoothing the creases on his forehead to attain an appearance more befitting a man of his position.

"Each temple will be an impressive structure that inspires awe in the viewer, with the grandest of all situated here in Azra. They will serve as a representation of the Emperor's stability as well as communal meeting areas for all matters of faith," Pompae reiterated.

Belenus clucked his tongue. "Sounds an awful lot like Calanthia. In some cities they have more temples than bakers."

"This is different," said Pompae, his voice as tight as an overwound lute string. "Those heathens erect temples to every beast that slithers or crawls across the earth. The temples of the Shining Empire would be unified under a common system."

"And priests would orate to the congregations within these temples?"

"Yes."

"These specialized priests would be trained in the Sanctuary on what matters of faith and divinity to proclaim?"

"Yes."

"I'm guessing that the congregations would be organized on some form of set schedule?"

"Correct."

Belenus tapped his fingers together as he contemplated this scenario. "I fail to see why this shift is needed. Emperor Anathasius is Rua's only living God and his support of the people is unquestioned. They know it by *his* words and by *his* acts, even if those acts are performed by the priesthood, as we enact— I may remind you—the *Emperor's* Gift. I speak to the people on his behalf as that is how the Emperor's Gift has manifested in me, and when I am gone another will stand as Beacon. To have other priests distort the use of the Gift by delivering sermons would be an un-truth. The people do not need to be addressed on a regular schedule like inattentive children, particularly by individuals who themselves have been told what to say."

Pompae appeared to calm somewhat while Belenus spoke, his fist unclenching and his voice losing its edge. "The priesthood is being underutilized. The Sanctuary can be of much greater use to the Empire."

"Because it will be flooded by the new recruits you want to force to enter."

"They will serving in the best interests of the Shining Empire."

"So you say." Belenus appraised Pompae's crisp white robe. "I'm starting to think that you were just pulling my leg with all that red robe nonsense. A little color is nothing compared to these other sweeping changes."

"What you call change, I call progress. The Shining Empire must advance if Darkness is to be defeated."

"Through the growth of the priesthood as little versions of the Sanctuary arising in the heart of every community."

Pompae leaned forward. "Our blood moves this Empire and it is time we direct the flow of the current. Emperor Anathasius has practically said as much by placing me—us—in charge while he is away."

Belenus unclasped his hands, using them to aid with emphasis. "Can you not see the option of choice is being taken away from the people? Faith comes from within and cannot be forced from the outside, no matter how good the intention. The Chosen are breaking through the established religions of Calanthia so that choice will be once again made available for the people there. They will be able to see the truth with uncensored eyes and then can chose where to place their faith. Our duty is to aid during this time of transition in order to prevent Darkness from seizing hearts in their moment of weakness."

Pompae groaned, his expression pained. He rubbed his face roughly and Belenus was surprised when Pompae didn't cut his hand on the knife-like nose.

"You have my answer," Belenus said politely. "Only direct endorsement from Emperor Anathasius will change my stance on this matter. Now if you don't mind, and even if you do, I must take my leave as I have somewhere else to be."

Pompae was incredulous. "A meeting more important than this?"

"Yes, one that is long overdue."

"Could I get you anything else, Beacon? Another piece of pie or some tea?"

Belenus slapped his protruding belly and waved Mariam off with his other hand. "No, thank you, I couldn't eat another morsel. Everything was delicious, and please call me Belenus."

Mariam blushed and cleared the dirty plates from the table. "I'm sorry, it's just that I've listened to your speeches since I was a girl."

"No need to apologize and careful with that kind of talk. It's liable to make me feel more ancient than I really am."

Belenus leaned back in his chair and marveled again at how much the young Hentavio took after Barroc. The boy fidgeted with the edge of the table, clearly ready to run off and use up his youthful energy.

"Father, may I be excused?"

"Sure, but be back before nightfall."

The boy bolted from the table and out the door, off to some minor adventure. Belenus wistfully recalled that time of life when everything from the incredibly small to the staggering large was fascinating. His childhood was a series of self-contained stories where his imagination meshed with the world around him.

"What are you thinking about?" Barroc grumbled. "I can see the gears working in that head of yours, which is the only place you could ever keep any machinery from falling apart."

"Oh just wondering if little Hentavio will grow into his nose. The poor boy looks like he's been a hard drinker for forty years."

Barroc folded his arms over his broad chest as he stared down his older brother. "That nose is as much of a Wicket legacy as the business. It seems that they come in tandem."

Belenus tapped his own smaller nose. "I suppose I never had a choice, after all."

"Eh, maybe not. That was a lifetime ago at any rate."

Belenus glanced around the dining room, noting the quality craftsmanship of the mahogany furniture. "You have built a fine life here and I thank you for including me in it."

Barroc looked around the room without responding. He sat so heavily in his chair that he seemed part of its structure. Janna skipped into the room and hopped onto Belenus' lap to squeeze him with a hug.

"Nice to meet you Uncle, come back and visit." She released Belenus from her tiny arms and punched him on the shoulder, staring him straight in the eye. "I mean it." Janna hopped down and skipped away while humming.

Belenus chuckled and rubbed his arm where she'd hit him as Elowen carefully crossed the room. She looked down nervously at the floor then up at Belenus through her bangs. Belenus opened his arms wide and leaned forward.

"One hug is all I ask."

Elowen obliged, giving a quick squeeze before silently leaving. Mariam smiled at Belenus as she stood behind Barroc with her hands on his shoulders.

"Elowen likes you. She couldn't stop talking about you in the other room. She's just shy. I'll leave you boys be, and let you catch up in peace." Mariam departed leaving the brothers alone.

Barroc stood and turned his back to Belenus as he rummaged through a large cupboard in the corner of the room. He returned with two black ceramic mugs and a bottle filled with liquid the color of burnt caramel. A sweet scent tinged with alcohol filled the room as soon as Barroc removed the stopper from the bottle. Belenus watched his brother fill the two mugs—a common action from their childhood performed by their father. Barroc slid a mug across the smooth surface of the table and sat down heavily in his chair.

"To our father," said Belenus as he raised the mug. "May he have found a peace in the next life that he never could in this one."

Barroc raised his mug as well and the brothers drank in unison. Belenus coughed on the strong liquor. The drink started rough but was rounded off with some sweetness and a light smokiness—like drinking burnt coal dusted with cane sugar.

Barroc smiled at his older brother's coughing. "They don't allow liquor up there on the hill?"

Belenus pounded the side of his fist against his chest, face flushed from the warmth of the alcohol. "If this is what you consider alcohol, then no, there isn't anything like this in the palace."

Barroc took another sip which Belenus imitated, albeit taking a smaller swig this time. "You are more practiced than I."

Barroc shook his head as though the comment pained him. "Nah, I hardly drink the stuff, just seemed fitting is all. Must be getting sentimental in my old age."

"Well you handle the stuff well then," complimented Belenus.

Barroc swirled the black mug, looking into the dark liquid inside, the knuckles on his big hand were dried and cracked. "Maybe I've just seen rougher stuff than you have. Things that make this drink seem downright sweet."

Belenus leaned forward, placing his palms on the table. "What kind of things? I can help. Removing Darkness is what I do, after all." For a moment Belenus thought Barroc would tell him as their eyes met, but Barroc just sighed and looked away.

"Isn't nothing I haven't done to myself," he said as he looked into the mug again.

"There is always time for redemption. One can let go of the mistakes of the past by placing their faith in the future, by trusting in the vision of Emperor Anathasius."

Barroc looked up from under his brows. "Remember how Father refused to go anywhere in the city with you, because you insisted on stopping at every shrine we passed?"

"Well, they're all different and offer a unique display of faith, like the many cut sides of a glittering jewel, each reflecting the light from its own angle."

Barroc smacked the table with his palm. "That's what you said to him! He got so mad, his face turned into a giant beet but he couldn't yell at you, because he knew, because we all knew."

"Knew what?"

"That you were different, that this was not the life for you. I was surprised it took you so long to tell him that you wanted to enter the priesthood."

It was Belenus' turn to look into the darkness within the mug. "Father was an intimidating man."

"And a frog bumps his ass when he hops."

Belenus quirked his head. "What?"

Barroc chuckled. "I thought we were stating the obvious."

Belenus laughed and raised his mug to take another swig. The liquor burned just as strongly as before but this time he was prepared. He could already feel a buzz behind his eyes from the alcohol. A few more drinks and he might start enjoying the taste. Barroc emptied his mug so Belenus did the same.

"The taste doesn't get better the more you drink," said Barroc as he replenished the mugs. "Maybe that's why this was father's drink of choice; a reminder of the truth of the world."

"Hmm and what's that?" Belenus blinked a few times, his eyes feeling wider than usual.

"Well, the world is rough, but swallowing some of its blackness puts fire in your belly, and hardens you against the worst bits."

"I disagree. To drink is to forget, to drift off and ignore how the world really is," Belenus countered.

Barroc gestured at the two of them. "Look at us; we're drinking and we're remembering our father. Are you saying that our memories aren't how he really was?"

Belenus thought back to the shape of his father slouched low in a chair at a table just like this one, with a bottle on its way to being emptied. Hentavio's eyes drooped, his mouth covered by his mustache, as dead to the world as a stone. The posture held a profound sadness, a look of defeat, and what Belenus had always thought was an unstated desire to escape from present surroundings. Stillness was a permanent condition for a stone but only temporary for Hentavio. He would be up earlier than his two boys, already at work before their mother was finished making breakfast.

"I think he was both," said Belenus as he stared at the wood grain of the tabletop.

"Are you saying I'm right?"

"As right as I am," said Belenus.

"Well, that's a first." Barroc raised his mug for another toast.

The brothers drank into the night, trading stories as they emptied cup after cup until the bottle was empty.

Barroc shook the last few drops onto the table. "I guess that's it. Didn't think we could do it."

"We're the Wicket brothers," Belenus said with satisfaction, as if that was explanation enough. He moved to stand and stumbled, needing to grab the edge of the table for balance.

"Can you make it back up the hill? I could hear those knees of yours cracking from two blocks away, before supper."

Belenus waved his hand dismissively and stood straight. He slowly started to lean right, having to step forward to stop from falling, his hip popping loudly.

"I'll be alright. I'm the Beacon of Azra after all. This is my city."

"Ya well, you're also as old as dirt."

Belenus started walking, trying to keep as straight of a line as possible to prove his sobriety to Barroc. A loud hiccup caught him off guard, causing him to stumble.

"I haven't been this drunk since I got this," Belenus said, waving his right hand. The red markings of the tattoo emerged from beneath his sleeve.

"I should try my hand at tattooing, it can't be more difficult than making an interlocking iron whip," Barroc mused.

Belenus paused. "A what? Who would want one of those?"

"Never mind," Barroc said with a wave of his hand. "Come on, let's get you home."

Barroc shrugged on a jacket and pushed Belenus through the door into the street. Gern and Ryndell silently fell in behind the brothers.

Belenus took in the night air, tilting his head upward but the stars were obscured by a veil of clouds and the glare from the well-lit street. His brother had done well for himself, having a good sized home in an affluent neighborhood. Barroc clapped an arm across Belenus' shoulders, the brothers swaying slightly from one edge of the street to the other as they walked.

"What's in the back room of the factory?" asked Belenus.

Barroc kept walking and Belenus thought he hadn't heard the question. He let it go, more focused on putting one foot in front of the other.

"Bad things," Barroc said a few minutes later. "Things that kill people."

"Weapons?"

"The term weapon implies that they can be defended against and I don't see how anyone is going to be stopping these things."

"Why make them?" Belenus felt as though he should know the answer but his brain would not work like it was supposed to. His thoughts were slow and rarely finished a complete route. "Why do what you do?"

Barroc spoke in a low timbre, almost singing. "Taken apart by the sound of a drum, slow, steady, unstoppable—bang, bang, bang. The space between the notes a warning, the impact a promise. Structures shake from the rumble, men shudder at the force. Inevitability brought forth from the immaterial. Lay low all who hear this sound, for men come to tear creation asunder."

The weaponsmaker looked at his brother the priest, eyes expectant. "Heard that from a Nefaran trader. We've paved the war path. All that is needed is for us to bang the drums."

Belenus stopped in his tracks causing Barroc to do a pirouette as he grasped onto Belenus' shoulder.

"Don't do that!"

"Shh!"

Belenus stared into one yellow eye laying on the side of the street. The mangy tomcat glared directly at him, both recognizing the other at the same time. *You.* The cat's chest was rising and falling in quick breaths. Belenus let go of Barroc and stumbled closer to the cat who gave a half-hearted hiss.

"Not so tough now, are ya?"

The cat glared fiercely, but remained stuck to the ground. Belenus noticed the animal's back legs were broken. All animosity he held toward the creature melted away. The cat seemed to sense the shift, dropping the aggressiveness from its one good eye. It looked frail and hungry and scared.

"Must have been hit by a carriage," Barroc muttered as he approached.

"I can't leave it here," said Belenus. "I have to help it."

"Don't touch the dirty thing. It's probably diseased."

Belenus ignored his brother and crouched down to pick up the cat, nearly falling over in the process.

"Oh, stop already, you'll just drop it with your fumbly fingers."

Barroc pushed past Belenus to gently scoop up the cat in his rough hands. Belenus was shocked by the display of tenderness.

"Here. Be careful."

Barroc slowly lowered the cat into Belenus' outstretched arms. The cat squirmed slightly and then lay still, accepting the embrace.

"Thank you, Barroc, I think I can make my way from here." Belenus turned to his personal guard. "Two carriages; one for me and the other to take my brother home."

Ryndell jumped into action, giving a sharp whistle and motioning at a queue of street carriages.

"Are you sure?" asked Barroc.

"Yeah yeah, you'll just have further to go if you accompany me. Get back to your young wife and make me an uncle for the fourth time."

"Ha! Not likely. I'm going to pass out the moment my head touches the pillow."

"Poor Mariam," Belenus chided. "Or maybe it's actually a blessing for her to avoid your awkward gropings."

"Watch it," Barroc growled.

For a moment, the lateness of the hour evaporated along with the ache in his bones, leaving Belenus with the sensation of being a boy again. He looked at young Barroc with his big nose, who blushed when any girl smiled at him. They used to run around the streets together on imagined adventures before Barroc began training to take over the business, before Belenus used to stop at every shrine he passed. So long ago that it seemed less real than the dreams which forced Belenus to take a special tonic to allow sleep. The cat mewled softly, stirring Belenus from his reverie.

"Thanks for dinner. Give Mariam my regards."

"I will." Barroc looked as though he might say something more but the words died in his mouth. Two carriages approached—Barroc climbed into his and Belenus did the same.

The palace stood on the hill like an image from a dream, the curves of its many arches illuminated by the light of the city to imbue the massive structure with an unearthly grace. The cat groaned with every bump. Belenus lost all sense of time until he reached the wide stairs leading into the Palace of Light. A guard approached.

"Here, take this to my room. And be careful. It's legs are broken."

The guard accepted the strange order without question, hustling off with the cat.

"Gern, Ryndell, you are dismissed for the evening. My thanks for your company."

He let out a large exhale, his back hunching from the weight of the night as he started the final climb to his room. His chest and sleeves were smeared from carrying the cat. Belenus did not want to contemplate the contents of the grime.

When he finally entered his room he was greeted by the flickering light of a large bedside candle. At the edge of the light's reach, Belenus found the cat spread out across a desk. The creature howled in pain, likely from being placed down too roughly. Belenus tried to recall the guard's face so that he could reprimand him tomorrow but the image was blurred beyond recognition.

On the desk behind the cat was a clay bowl with a small spoon. The bowl was filled with the prepared ingredients required to make the sleeping tonic. A half-filled pitcher of water sat beside the bowl. Belenus dumped the water into the bowl, spilling half of it. He used the spoon to mix the concoction until all of it was dissolved.

"Here, drink this, it will help you sleep."

Belenus placed the bowl near the cat's mouth. It sniffed the rim experimentally then flicked out its tongue several times to lap up the tonic. The cat stilled and was soon sleeping soundly.

"There, that's better."

Belenus sat down on the edge of the bed, absently watching the rise and fall of the cat's chest. The poor thing would never be the same as it was, its days of prowling the streets were over. Maybe it could survive if Belenus fed it and it might even heal to a degree. The odds were slim, but there was still a chance for life. Belenus wished he could increase the odds by breathing life into the cat's wounds so they could heal properly. He could practically feel the bones and tendons stitching themselves back together.

A wilted flower slumped over the edge of a vase on the floor near the desk, left as a dried out husk after the last time Belenus tried to save the dying. He was mystified at how the heart could want something so badly, and still be unable to make it so. The sensation diffused into a sad form of frustration, making his heart heavy with words unspoken. Sleep was kept at bay even though exhaustion wanted to claim his aching body. He got up off the bed and exited the room.

He did not have far to go, stopping in front of the room directly across the hall. Two large guards barred entry, their serious expressions turning to confusion as they appraised the smears on the white fabric of the priestly robe. Belenus produced a key from an inner pocket, waggling it in the air as he approached.

"Out of the way gentlemen, this won't take long, just need to have a chat with our guest."

The guards hesitated, casting a look at one another as though they were telepathically reviewing their orders. They reached the same conclusion and stepped aside to allow Belenus to fiddle with the lock set into the frame of the door.

"Don't worry. I'm not planning on taking him anywhere so if you see the shaman exit you better stop him."

He opened the door into a dark room, closing it softly behind him, hearing it lock automatically. Pale moonlight slid through a small round window on the far wall to create a miniature version of the moon on the floor in the center of the room. Belenus grabbed a chair, dragging it to the edge of the circle of reflected light and sat down with a huff. Movement came from the dark reaches of the room as Kerak shifted his weight to sit on the edge of the bed.

"Darkness is a real thing, a living entity that threatens all of existence. It swallows Light like a void. But Darkness is not empty, it grows in size with the addition of those it devours," said Belenus.

The shaman was so quiet that he felt as though he were ranting at the moon.

"You have been drinking, Beacon. Despair does not suit you."

"I'm not despairing," Belenus grumped. "What's your opinion on Darkness? What does wise Cynaal have to say in these matters?"

Another pause as Kerak contemplated the request. Belenus felt his head nodding, the weight of it slowly pulling him closer to the glowing orb on the floor.

"Snowflakes know only to fall," Kerak stated.

"Eh? What's that?"

"They understand that movement does not always require force, that the temporary may appear permanent, that it is alright to be aware of spring, yet unconcerned with thaw."

Belenus recalled the last winter in Azra: how the first snowfall came down in wide, delicate flakes to coat the arches of the palace in a crystal embrace. He had walked along the gardens of the upper terrace, creating fresh footprints on a path hidden beneath a soft blanket of snow. Steps that would soon be filled in to conceal all visibility of his progress. He had paused to inhale the crisp air and to wonder at the meaning of a liquid capable of turning into a solid so that it might travel along invisible air currents and then flow onward as it melted.

"So things are as they are, is that it? Darkness only does at it must, to fulfill the only duty that it understands?"

"Something like that," said Kerak. "Snow will fall, but that does not mean I must freeze to death. Not if I learn how to create my own warmth."

"That's what I'm trying to do," Belenus said desperately. "I'm trying to teach the people of Azra how to find their own warmth. I'd give them my own if I could but the Gift will not let me. I feel a change in the air, a cold coming on that I fear we are not prepared for. Perhaps that is why you are here. You're a man who knows more about the cold than any other I've ever met."

Belenus stared into the light of the moon on the floor, imagining his father sitting in his chair with an empty bottle as snowflakes fell around him, slowly piling on his head and shoulders. His father had never found warmth and now Belenus worried that his brother might encounter the same fate.

"I fear my knowledge is lacking," Kerak said softly. "The wisdom of my ancestors is not enough. You are right. Something new is coming and it will steal the warmth from within unless we discover a new method for creating heat."

"Despair does not suit you either, shaman."

Kerak gave a tired laugh which Belenus echoed. They sat in silence for a moment as their worries about the future filled the room. Belenus slapped a palm on his thigh and stood up on creaky knees. "Sorry for waking you. I need to get to bed."

"Anytime. My thanks for the relocation."

"This was nothing. You just wait until I find some seal meat for you."

"Do you even know what a seal is?"

Belenus shrugged, one hand holding the open door. "A big fish?"

The priest exited the room, the guards silent as he fumbled with the lock, eventually remembering that it locked automatically. He shuffled across the short distance to his room, closing the door and collapsing on top of the covers. The soft rustling of the cat's snoring was the last sound he heard before sleep finally claimed him.

A pounding headache greeted the Beacon upon waking. His hangover was exuberant about starting the day. As far as he could tell, this headache was not from any vivid dream. His tongue felt as though it had sprouted a thick coat of hair, and his throat was parched. Belenus wondered if Barroc felt the same. His ornery brother would never show it, even if he felt twice as bad as Belenus. He rolled over on his side, slowly raising himself to vertical.

The cat was spread out on the desk, too calm to be breathing. Belenus rushed over to inspect the state of the rescued animal.

Sticky saliva pooled below the cat's open mouth, glinting off needle sharp fangs. The one eye was open in a blind stare, gazing past Belenus into another world. The cat was dead. Had the internal injuries been too severe? Had the journey to the palace placed too much stress on the cat? Belenus didn't think so but his memories of the trip and the initial condition of the cat were hazy. Maybe the animal simply did not want to live, knowing that it would never again prowl the streets it was birthed in. Maybe it was something else that killed the cat.

Belenus chewed his bottom lip as he looked at the nearby bowl of sleeping tonic. Was the color different? A little darker perhaps? He wasn't sure. A sniff of the liquid did not offer any notable differences, either. Belenus bumped something with his foot. He looked down at the spilled contents of the vase, the dried petals disintegrating as they touched the hardness of the floor.

## Battle of Choker Pass

As the army traveled through Carnot they passed a string of deserted cities, the inhabitants losing confidence in their defenses after the obliteration of the thorn wall of Ryakesh. The only residents left were those incapable of leaving due to infirmity.

Items of daily life were scattered in the barren streets. Children's toys lay strewn outside of homes, stray dogs picked their way through rubbish, and thieving opportunists skulked around the movement of the army as they waited to take anything of value left behind.

After Ryakesh, Melea found herself compulsively touching the hidden seed inside of her shirt pocket. At first she was unaware of the action. Her fingers would make their way to her chest, stopping just below the collar bone to brush up against the indent of the seed. The motion became habitual as they traveled, she would have one hand on the reins and another on the seed. Her mind wandered during these times. The presence of the seed provided a calming effect.

She realized the habit was forming when General Cathair commented on her peculiar riding style. His penetrating eyes gave the impression that he was calculating possibilities rather than simply noting features. She made up a quick lie about having a rash and being unable to resist scratching it. Cathair recommended a certain ointment, whose name she immediately forgot. Afterwards, she was much more aware of herself in public. The army was a sea of eyes and she wanted to keep her secret. She did not need Cathair telling Anathasius about any strange behavior.

Lubanos, the capital of Bromaleigh, surrendered without a fight. The Duke was slain while sitting on his throne and his family was killed in their chambers. The acolytes of the city's bull cult chanted in the streets, calling on Ziya'Sybel to take the form of a giant bull and trample the army of the Shining Empire. The God remained absent, despite the fervency of their prayers—the only thing to arise from the devoutness of the acolytes was further punishment.

On seeing the large herd of ceremonial bulls penned within Lubanos, Melea remarked that the acolytes did not need their God to trample the army as they already had enough animals to do so. The Emperor had then ordered the streets surrounding the penned bulls to be closed off and the acolytes rounded up, placing them in front of the waiting animals. The Chosen then riled the bulls up before releasing them and the acolytes ran for their lives. One by one the acolytes fell beneath crashing hooves and snorting breath as the symbols of their God ran from the jeering Chosen. Melea decided to keep further comments to herself.

With crushing victories in Carnot and Bromaleigh and the subservience of Asyrith, the Shining Empire now controlled half of Calanthia. Radiant sun disks, smaller versions of the golden sun watching over the ironwood grove in the Palace of Light, were established in each new city. Every sizable community in the Empire was given a sun disk, a feature that Emperor Anathasius said helped to connect the network of faith.

To the south of the Green river lay the unspoiled orchards of Lyrene and terraced rice paddies of Qu'hraz. The path traveled by the army was far from pristine. Tens of thousands of men and animals had left a trail of upturned earth. Pillars of smoke dotted the landscape of scorched farmland as the army burnt while it went. Melea understood that men must eat but she had never anticipated the unrelenting hunger of an army on the move. Locusts were a small concern compared to the appetite of soldiers.

On several occasions advance scouts returned in a hurry to proclaim that an army waited further up the road but each time the enemy had departed before the Chosen arrived. Bromaleigh's spirit seemed to have been whipped into submission by their previous defeats. Melea wondered why a people would continue to run. Surely not all could be terrified into inaction by the destruction of Ryakesh? The soldiers of the Shining Empire casually proceeded across rolling hills deserted of people until reaching the border of Bromaleigh and Calanthe. Melea then understood why the enemy was content to retreat.

The terrain changed dramatically as they neared the border. Narrow green mountains appeared—the mountains were not overly large and all were covered in thick vegetation. Scattered pockets of red and orange stood out as emblems of seasonal change. The forested mountains seemed almost delicate when compared to the indomitable snow capped peaks of the Kon mountain range to the west. She could see why these mountains were referred to as the Petals.

Birdsong and other sounds of nature continued unimpeded as the Chosen traveled along a road that mirrored the curves of the Green river as it wound through the Petals. Only one road led west-east through the mountains to Marikal: the next nearest route was far to the South. Anathasius wanted to avoid entering the southern dukedoms for now, as the watery terrain of Qu'hraz might present problems for such a large force. It was a well-known fact that the army of Lyrene was the weakest in Calanthia and a defeated Marikal would seal the fate of the South. The two remaining dukedoms might even surrender peacefully if the great golden city fell.

The road was starting to rise, moving further from the steepening banks above the brown water of the river. Melea rode in the center of the line alongside Anathasius and General Cathair.

"This is where the Calanthian forces will make their first strike," said Cathair. He pointed to some unseen distance further in the Petals. "Two days ride from here the road narrows considerably between the mountains and the river. A place called Choker Pass. They'll be waiting there, hoping to cut us down when we get bottlenecked and unable to turn around. There are fortifications along each side of the road where their archers will be able to fire down at leisure."

"So we're walking into a trap," said Melea.

Cathair turned Melea, looking confident. "Yes, but I think it is the Calanthians who will be surprised."

He looked back to the plodding bulls a dozen rows of men behind them. Tails flicked at flies as the ornery animals were herded along. Cathair had ordered the bulls to be rounded up after the events in Lubanos. Until now, Melea had thought they were just additional meat to feed the army.

"The leaders of Calanthe will discover that their perversions of the natural world cannot create warriors equal of the Chosen," said Anathasius.

"What do you mean?" asked Melea.

"You shall see that it takes more than fierceness and weaponry to create a warrior."

"My Lord," said Cathair.

'Go."

Cathair stopped his horse, allowing the men to move around him. Melea and Anathasius continued forward at a trot. She swiveled in the saddle to see Cathair approach the soldiers charged with herding the bulls. He seemed to be setting his unstated plan in motion.

"So the soldiers of Calanthe are not like us?"

Anathasius kept his eyes on the road. "Those that are men are barely even that. They will fight to the death but they do not fight with courage. They fight out of obligation."

Melea thought back to the streets of Marikal, recalling all of the capless heads that kept the city functioning. Slaves were the underlying force of Marikal's power, working tirelessly for their masters. An discomfort stirred in her gut at the thought of slavery. Seeing them move around the city beneath whips and curses was one thing but striking them down in battle was something different altogether. For a brief moment Melea pondered whether the slaves wanted to be soldiers or if they would rather be at home. Did slaves have homes? What, if anything, did slaves even want? She did not know and supposed that it did not matter. Warfare was an unwieldy sphere for contemplation.

The Shining Empire was on an unavoidable collision course with the waiting slave army of Calanthe and there was no sense in questioning certainty. Men would die, but not all, and victory would decide what mattered. Victory by the Shining Empire would show the ineffectiveness of slavery, and victory by Calanthe would reinforce the current system of forced servitude.

"Well, I hope you and Cathair have more up your sleeves than ill-tempered cattle because I don't like the sound of becoming a pin cushion from a hailstorm of arrows," said Melea.

Anathasius smiled with his golden eyes as sunlight danced across his face. The sheen of his long-sleeved shirt was pure white, unmarred from travel. Even the soft gold of his cloak was free of dust. Melea on the other hand, was coated by a layer of grime. Her back and armpits were stained with sweat from constantly being on the move.

"You know as well as I do that Morokko Kachina is at his most dangerous when unseen," said the Emperor.

Melea had noticed that he was notoriously absent within the ranks of the army. She doubted his skills would be best served in pitched battle but there certainly was use for him in warfare. Melea would never be able to like the man, but she would appreciate avoiding a storm of arrows raining down from the mountainside. Let him skulk in the shadows if it aided her survival in the upcoming battle.

A creeping nervousness settled inside of her; not fear but a close relative. She stopped her hand from making its way to the seed. Melea had faced death too many times to fear it anymore, having resolved long ago that fate was outside of her control. All she could do was fight to the best of her abilities in order to survive. Fate spins, as the saying went. One could only hope to be in a fortuitous location when the spinning top pointed in their direction.

A sense of nagging doubt troubled her.

Previous missions always served a purpose, a straightforward sequence of cause and effect. Overarching meaning and motivation were inconsequential. Melea did what she was told without question, without thought, without feeling. Life had been simple in the time before Gerboa, before the deal with the Saleros, before King Horvkild's acidic insinuations. Before Ryakesh.

The blood soaked hooves of Lubanos were still fresh in Melea's mind even though they were now covered in dust from the road. A probing question worked its way throughout Melea like a root squirming through hard clay. *Why?*

They were at war with Calanthia, but why? Because it would save everyone from Darkness. Somehow. At least that was the answer provided by the Beacon and Anathasius. Immortal life for all who chose to walk the Illuminated Path. Why didn't Melea care about that? The men fought for this goal. She overhead them speaking at night, talking of how the defeat of Calanthia would be a deathblow to Darkness. Why didn't she believe it? Maybe she was defective, damaged internally in a way that was unable to be fixed. This impairment would explain why her mind often drifted to the Saleros, why she wondered what they were doing. Why she did not hate them even though she should.

She wanted to touch the seed, to rub it between her forefinger and thumb. The urge was like an itch one could not scratch, gnawing at her attention, returning with insistence as soon as questions formed in her mind. *To doubt the divine vision is to give in to weakness and start the decline into Darkness.* A tenet of the Binding Doctrine that offered no solace for Melea's worries. The line of soldiers came to a halt. Nightfall came sooner here in the mountains. They would establish a camp while they still had the light.

"I know you do not like it," said Anathasius.

Melea's heart jumped. Had she spoken out loud? She could not have stated her doubts to Anathasius.

"Before we reach Choker Pass I recommend that you don full armor. You are experienced but the ferocity of the upcoming battle will exceed anything you have previously encountered."

"I will be ready."

She needed to be fully prepared to face the fury of Calanthe. Putting more distance between her hands and the seed would also help her mind. Perhaps the added strength of the armor would quiet the questions within, muffle them enough for her to fight with clarity.

At its narrowest, Choker Pass came to a width of eight men lined shoulder to shoulder. Calanthia was waiting with a wall of flesh and iron, to barricade the Pass at this juncture.

Melea rode Ranna at a walk in the pre-dawn dimness. She had taken Anathasius' advice and wore full armor. A chinstrap secured a rounded helmet darker than the blue of her uniform. Beneath a gleaming bronzed breastplate she wore a long-sleeved coat of chain mail that hung over her thighs. Her hands were protected by thick leather gloves with metal rings sewn into the back of them. Ranna was also covered in metal—the horse wore a coat of scale mail, protecting the mare from head to tail. Melea was armed with three long spears, a cavalry sword, and a long-handled mace.

She was at the head of the heavy cavalry that would smash through the enemy line. Rows of spears held aloft behind her appeared as a dead forest that would bring more death.

Melea would charge but she would not lead. It was up to the others if they decided to follow. Leave the organization and ordering of men to the officers in the rear. No orders would be given by her.

Anathasius had asked her to be the fulcrum of the attack and she had accepted. Some might take the position as an honor, others would view it as a suicide mission, but for her it was neither. The direct order from Anathasius provided the greatest probability for victory. Her attempt to shorten the fighting at Ryakesh had been successful—until Anathasius overruled Melea's victory—but this was another opportunity. She could punch through the line and keep it open long enough for the Chosen to follow, which would bring a faster solution than a drawn-out battle.

These were the things she told herself while riding alone in front of the army. *Who was she fooling?* Melea did not believe the daydream she was attempting to sell to herself. Her solitary position spoke volumes, as did the accompanying danger. Anathasius was giving her a message. He was in control and she had to obey. She'd made an independent decision in Ryakesh, one that he disagreed with and had immediately overruled. He had made it clear that he was directing this campaign. This was a test. Would she defy the order, request a different position, or remove herself from the vanguard?

Derclerq sidled up beside her, a big white feather attached to the top of his helmet. His long mustache bounced as he rode, hanging beneath his upturned nose like twin tails.

"How do you plan on making it out of this one, wonderchild? It'll take more than a girl who wants to be a man," said the swordmaster.

"Fight like me and you might survive as well."

"I'll be well back of your precarious position. You might be dead before I even enter the fray. I'll ride right over your body, too late to give the advice that would have saved your life."

Melea glanced at the swordsman, but he was careful to stare straight ahead at the road. "It's almost as if you're concerned about my well-being—don't go soft on me now you old cur."

Derclerq turned in the saddle to face Melea, adopting a fatherly expression for an instant. "I loathe to waste all of the hours spent on you, particularly when you still need to learn the maneuvers that have made me the greatest swordsman in Rua."

"You've been holding out on me?"

"I was waiting to see if you were worthy."

"What changed?"

Derclerq sat comfortably in the saddle, his shoulders back and hands loose on the reins. After a few moments he looked Melea up and down, inspecting her, but not in his typical lewd fashion. "Ryakesh. Never seen anything like that before. Not sure what to think of it either, but when you fight, I want men to say that Andran Derclerq trained that warrior. That can't happen if you get yourself killed today."

"I intend to survive." She meant it. She would do everything within her power to look down at Anathasius from a pile of corpses so that her worth was indisputable. "Derclerq, I—"

"Keep your womanly sentiments out of this and I'll see you on the other side." Derclerq spun his horse around to leave Melea alone at the head of the army.

Flags bearing the insignia of the royal house of Calanthe and that of the kingdom of Calanthia came into view: a streaking silver falcon on a grass-green background tinged with burnt orange, and the ominous man-shaped shadow emerging from a stand of dark pines backed by a sandy brown field, respectively.

Melea stopped and the others did as well. The road narrowed significantly at a wall ahead. Each plank in the wall was an entire tree. Calanthia's flags flapped in the breeze from the top of the barricade, but the peaceful sway of their movement could not hide the fact that the fighting would be thickest directly on the other side.

A cloudless sky was starting to lighten, illuminating a clear blue background for what looked to become idyllic summer weather. Rushing water sounded off to the right, far below. All birdsong had ended. Only the buzzing flies were unperturbed. They had adapted to the sordid actions of human kind, learning to flock toward groups of humanity during their foulest moments.

There was movement high up along the stone bordering each side of the wall. Archers were tucked into the hollowed-out mountain, waiting for the Shining Empire to come within range. The rest of the army waited behind the wall, relying on the barrier to slow the Chosen while the archers did their work. Anathasius appeared beside Melea, looking as clean as if he had just bathed.

He turned the grey stallion to face the army. "This is the first real test for you, my Chosen warriors. The minions of Darkness who stand behind this wall are prepared to take the Light from your eyes. Do not fear. I will protect you." His voice rang out clear, loud enough that the enemy must have been able to hear him as well.

Anathasius clapped his hands together, the impact echoing louder than it should have. He dismounted and walked toward Melea. She could feel a crackling energy in the air, similar to that felt before the thorn wall of Ryakesh. Anathasius reached out to gently touch her leg. A bolt of energy jolted through her, rocking her in the saddle. She smelled burning but there was no flame. A soft glow surrounded her body, bright enough to be visible in the dim light. She watched the glow extending to Ranna as well, but the mare seemed unaware of this newly acquired luminescence.

The Emperor strolled through the heavy cavalry, touching each soldier as he passed. They and their mounts acquired the same glow. When he was finished Anathasius returned to the stallion and climbed into the saddle. The sun crested the mountains to match the glow of the vanguard.

"Fight without fear—you cannot be harmed while under my protection. You are warriors of Light. Each death you claim banishes Darkness. Be brave my Chosen as you fight for immortality!" The Emperor's voice ricocheted off the mountains, as loud as shouting in a narrow hallway.

The army erupted into battle cries. Melea remained silent. She was looking past Anathasius to movement along a natural ledge near the outcropping housing the archers, movement that could have just been a shadow cast by the dawn. Anathasius spun his horse to face the wall, making it rear up on its hind feet. The army became even louder but their impassioned bellowing was suddenly swallowed up by a deafening explosion.

Rock and dust was thrown into the air near where Melea had been looking. An archer fortification collapsed, sending dozens of men spilling out. Another explosion ripped apart the wooden wall. A huge section of the wall was gone and the rest of the timber was badly splintered, looking as though it could fall apart at any moment. A third boom sent more rock and dust into the air as the other archer fortification met the same fate as its counterpart. The screams of men pierced the muffled silence after the explosions. The Chosen cheered at the destruction.

"Victory!" Anathasius called out, his voice rising over the noise of the explosions.

Melea kicked Ranna into a gallop. Horns bugled in triumphant bursts, and pounding drums drowned out all other sound. She sped past Anathasius, ears ringing from the explosions, and feeling the thundering hooves beneath her. The Emperor's words hung overhead, the power of his voice still tangible, as though he was directing her progress.

Dust and bits of debris blocked her view as she charged into the opening created by the destruction of the wall. She felt as though she were passing through a threshold separating worlds, a mythical fog that could transport her to an entirely new plane of existence. She had one moment to glimpse the army of Calanthia as she exited the dust and immediately disliked the world that awaited her.

A line of men stretched as far as she could see—an endless supply of green and tan uniforms. Their horns added to the din as they caught sight of Melea.

Soldiers clapped spears against tall, rectangular shields. The first row were lined eight across, supported by the combined bulk of thousands behind. Melea leveled her spear and braced for impact. She was going to win this battle single-handedly if need be. Anathasius would have to acknowledge her value when she rubbed this victory in his face.

The foot soldiers stood bravely before the charging vanguard of the Chosen, even though they were clearly shocked at the sight of glowing soldiers in heavy armor materializing out of the smoke. The Calanthian line did not move aside or run but they should have. Melea pinned the spear against her body, aiming for the paleness of a face amidst the row of armor. Her spear made contact an instant before Ranna smashed into the line of men, tossing soldiers aside as Melea raised the spear to skewer another face. The spear shattered after the second impact so she retrieved one of the spares.

The presence of the foot soldiers hardly slowed the pace of the vanguard. Melea sliced through the lines like a shark fin through the surf. The protection given by the Emperor was showing its value as each impact was felt only as a dull thud. Blade and soldier alike bounced off the protective barrier of light. She was invincible, a luminous arrow shot directly into the heart of Calanthia. Geography dictated that this was the area where the fighting was supposed to be most compacted, most impassable, but that was rendered irrelevant by the power bestowed by the Emperor.

Cries of victory broke out behind her as the Chosen reveled in their invulnerability. They battered down everything in front of them, trampling the enemy beneath the feet of galloping warhorses like children stomping on sand castles on the beach. The soldiers of Calanthia struck back, attempting to split the vanguard from each side but to no avail.

The narrow walls of the Pass made retreat impossible, so the foot soldiers had no choice but to stand their ground until Melea crushed them with unstoppable momentum.

She struck again and again with her spear, piercing through armor and flesh, shattering bone with ruthless efficiency until this spear shattered, too. She grabbed the final spear. Her only thoughts were on striking down the next target and to keep moving forward. Always forward. She needed to bring the attack just a little further so that General Cathair would be able to implement the next phase. She spotted an opening ahead on the right: a large gap along the side of the road that plunged down to the river far below.

The foot soldiers were carefully keeping their distance from the precipice. She looked again at the soldiers near the gap. There was something odd in their stance, a strangeness to their movements. A spear glanced off the scale mail protecting Ranna's neck to deflect up at Melea's face, bouncing harmlessly off her shoulder. She plunged her spear down into the attacking soldier and rode on, adding his crumpled body to the many others left in her wake.

More soldiers fell as the vanguard advanced. Melea was still able to proceed with ease, but the impacts were starting to feel more pronounced. Ranna seemed to notice a difference, whinnying in distress when a spear shaft splintered against her chest. An instinctive ripple of caution pierced the euphoria of invincibility clouding Melea's mind. Was the glow surrounding her and Ranna dimming? She was unable to tell for certain, and there was no time to think about it. A new line of men stood defiantly in front of her. She ran them over like all the rest, breaking her spear in the process, to emerge in an opening between lines.

The road was wider here. Lieutenants on either side of her called out for the heavy cavalry to regroup. For a moment she stood in an island of calm, able to catch her breath in a brief reprieve from violence. The gap leading down to the river was just ahead on the right—where the vanguard was supposed to wait.

"Come on, Cathair, move your ass." Melea stared across the opening to a group of bizarre soldiers who had no intention of waiting.

What ran toward Melea in a shambling gait were not men. They were Chuku Bartha, or once had been. The ape men of the Eternal Forest enlisted by the Calanthian army were hardly recognizable to those who worked with the Salero brothers. Blocks of irregular metal were strapped to skin the color of scummy pond water. Fur grew in ragged patches between the armor if it grew at all, and some of the warriors were completely hairless.

She noticed the eyes most of all. These were not the deep set black eyes full of intelligence she had seen in the Chuku Bartha Pass. These eyes were opened wide with a yellow stain where the whites should have been. She doubted any thought was occurring behind the expressionless stares. As the Chuku Bartha advanced, a captain called out to Melea's left, directing with his sword in hand.

"Lines! Forward on my command!"

Melea angled Ranna into a line of fifteen spread out across the road. She ripped the sword out of the sheath, the beauty of its curve accentuating the deadliness of its function.

"Charge!"

She kicked Ranna into motion along with the others to meet the Chuku Bartha head-on. The mare did not like the look of the ape men either or maybe it was the smell. A foul stink emanated from the Chuku Bartha. Instead of rushing forward howling, they shuffled quickly and silently in a herky-jerky fashion while holding straight blades in hand.

She plunged the tip of the sword into the mouth of the first Chuku Bartha, severing the bottom jaw from its head as she withdrew the blade. She turned her focus to the next, slicing through its shoulder and nearly cutting the arm clean off. Ranna reared to strike with her front feet, bringing wide hooves down on the skull of a Chuku Bartha. The ape men fought differently than the slave soldiers. They skittered around, hopping from side to side as they attempted to encircle her.

A quick charge sent three more to the dirt and gave Melea a little more space. The rest of the vanguard fought with the ape men, cheering wildly as they faced this new foe. Melea spun back, she was getting too far ahead, moving dangerously near the area designated by Cathair. A horde of Chuku Bartha occupied the space; the General should strike now, this was his opportunity.

A hard impact to Melea's shoulder forced her to spin back. A jawless Chuku Bartha raised his sword to swing again. *How could it still fight?* Melea had thought this one already dead. She swung through its neck, sending it to the ground without a head. The ape man lay still for a moment before rising up again. She stabbed it again, this time through the chest. It fell and lay still.

Another Chuku Bartha approached her, one arm dangling uselessly as it slunk nearer. Melea rammed Ranna into it, trampling the ape man into the ground. Two swords slashed at her, one making contact with her thigh, causing her to curse in pain.

The wielder of the blades had no head or so little of one that it should not have been able to fight. A few jagged teeth jutted out from what was left of a bottom jaw. She slashed at the Chuku Bartha, wheeling back to slash again, dropping the enemy to the ground.

Melea sliced anything and everything within her vicinity. Dismembered Chuku Bartha surrounded her, able to fight despite horrendous injuries. She hacked at them each time they returned but they would not stay down. Grunts of frustration were accompanied by shouted curses as the rest of the Chosen encountered the same dilemma.

Arrows whizzed passed her, fired from archers of the Shining Empire who had nearly caught up to the vanguard. The archers were even less effective than the cavalry. Cathair was supposed to be here by now. The Chuku Bartha fought on, their numbers apparently the same as before. Hundreds more waited just ahead, ready to take the place of those who fell.

A sound like thunder announced Cathair's arrival, shaking the very earth with its intensity. The rumbling was accompanied by a bellowing that rolled overtop of the shaking. Terrified cries filled the air, pouring down toward the road from the mountainside. The scent of smoke filled Melea's nostrils.

"Fall back!"

Sharp trumpet blasts split the noise to order the cavalry. Melea and the others wheeled back the way they come.

An avalanche of noise, fire, and death streamed down the mountainside. The bulls of Lubanos raced down the incline, their horns ablaze, driving them into panic. Cathair had ordered wicker baskets tied to the beast's horns before taking them off the main road two days ago, following a goatherd trail to bring them to this location. The terrified animals were now descending with frightening velocity.

The bulls obliterated the mass of undying Chuku Bartha. Even with their ability to sustain injury, the ape men could not stand against the bulls cutting a swath of devastation across the Pass. Archers from the Shining Empire sent black shafts into any bulls that came too close to their own forces. A single arrow was enough to drop the animals. Cathair had ordered the arrows to be dipped in the toxin of the Night Creeper before leaving Ryakesh. The poison worked fast. A bull skidded to a halt near Melea with an arrow in its neck, its horns still engulfed by flame, a thick tongue lolling out of its open mouth.

Some of the bulls plunged through the gap in the mountains, tumbling over the ledge into the water of the Green river to be washed away. Melea watched as the majority of the bulls turned toward the forces of Calanthia, causing mayhem as they hurtled into the Chuku Bartha. The bulls continued until they were finally cut down, leaving a field of crawling ape men who still tried to rise despite the severity of their injuries. Some were aflame and still moved.

Officers ordered the men while the enemy was occupied with the bulls. Cathair appeared beside Melea, as a mass of foot soldiers moved into formation behind them. Archers moved behind the foot soldiers. She was surprised with how many of the horsemen still survived. The casualties of Calanthia drastically outnumbered that of the Shining Empire. A glow still enveloped the soldiers and their horses but now she needed to squint to detect it.

"About time you got here," she said.

"Organizing a herd of bulls on a narrow mountain pass and then lighting them on fire is more difficult than one might expect."

"Fate spins. But I can't argue with the results. Those ape men wouldn't die."

Cathair looked at Melea, his face calm, showing no signs of battle thrill. "That's because they're already dead. Calanthia knows well how to manipulate Darkness to its own devices."

"Already dead, huh? So what's next?"

Cathair looked toward the enemy. "More beasts of Darkness."

Melea followed his gaze to see shaggy animals being released by their handlers. The animals were not quite as large as the bulls but were just as stocky. They were covered in coarse brown fur and squealed constantly. The high-pitched frequency burrowed into her ears. Long white tusks jutted out of the animal's mouths and looked as lethal as knives. Thick horns curved down from the temple to spiral around beady red eyes. The animals were a disgusting mix between a boar and a ram, creating a perverse hybrid.

"Cavalry! Line formation!" Cathair called out the order, pointing with his sword, and the men responded by organizing into orderly lines in front of him and Melea until the two became part of the last line, ten rows back from the front. "Cavalry attack!"

Horns blared as the mounted force of the Shining Empire rushed out to meet the beasts. Angry squeals grew louder as the animals closed the distance. They trampled the bodies of the Chuku Bartha as they went, tossing any that moved into the air with their snouts.

"Archers!"

A hail of arrows arched over the cavalry to descend on the squealing brutes. Any that were even nicked by a poisoned tip keeled over to spasm and die.

As the horsemen made contact with beasts it became clear why they had been released. They were fast, able to quickly change direction and slip between the mounted men. Shorter than the horses, their heads were beneath the protective armor. Razor-sharp tusks and battering-ram horns were thrust into the horses with incredible power.

Shrieks of pain filled the air as horses were gutted. Some collapsed from broken legs to pin their riders underneath. Those hit straight on were knocked over by the strength of the stocky animals. Man and horse screamed in agony in front of Melea and for the first time it was from the side of the Shining Empire. The protection placed on them by the Emperor was gone.

A squealing beast charged at Melea, so she slashed down across its neck. Bright red droplets splattered her right side as the beast skidded into the ground. They could bleed and that meant they could die. Melea was able to detect the faintest aura of light around her sword arm as she cut down another beast. The energy placed on her by Anathasius still remained, but for how much longer or if it was enough to stop another impact was unknown.

Melea saw a big beast barreling toward Cathair, who was busy directing combat. The General was unaware of being targeted. She turned Ranna, intending to cut off the animal before it hammered into Cathair. Froth bubbled from the its gaping mouth as it ran. Ranna's long strides closed the distance. Melea was going to arrive in time to save Cathair.

She raised her sword, coming alongside so that she could cut down at it and avoid running into the General, who was still facing the wrong direction. The beast abruptly altered direction, springing toward Melea with a powerful lunge. Ranna cried out as the wicked tusks gouged into the mare's stomach. Melea was tossed from the saddle as the mare fell, both landing heavily.

The back of her head cracked off the ground as she bounced. She wheezed, the wind knocked out of her, and her vision swimming as she looked up into the open sky. Warfare raged all around but it seemed so distant, as if Melea was removed from the conflict. Hooves punctuated her vision as they pumped down to kick up dirt. All she could smell was blood and sweat. The sounds around her were a strange symphony: the drumming of crashing hooves, a chorus of shouting men, thrumming bowstrings, tinny squealing beasts, and the sad death screams of wounded horses.

Her body felt heavy, like the sky was pushing down with all its weight. Rising seemed like an impossibility. *How could one push away the sky?* A particular note pierced Melea's awareness, a wail she recognized within the discordance. Ranna was in pain. Sensation returned to Melea's hands as she wiggled her fingers. Her toes also responded to movement. Melea grunted as she sat upright to search for the source of the death song.

Ranna lay on her side several meters away with her back to Melea. The mare swung her head wildly but was unable rise, thick neck muscles bulging in distress. Melea stood, her body stiff as she bent to pick up her sword.

The mare was surrounded by a pool of blood. Pale intestines spilled out of the gash in the mare's underbelly, fragile braided flesh, not meant to be exposed to the open air. Melea crouched near the horse's head, gently stroking clumps of dirt out of the mane. Ranna's frightened eyes were glazed over, she was no longer aware of anything but pain. Her back legs kicked out, spilling more of her insides onto the ground.

"Rannakitch, my girl Ranna."

She took her sword in both hands and drew it across the mare's throat. Ranna's movements stopped. Dark blood stained the sword. Melea stood in front of the mare's body protectively. A beast darted between horses, sending up dirt as it charged in Melea's direction.

Melea gripped her sword in both hands. An arrow suddenly appeared in the animal's side and it fell over to lash out with sharp black hooves. She pounced on the body, hacking and slashing until it was a bloody mess. A horn bugled, calling the remaining cavalry to return.

Cathair approached Melea, who still stood atop the mangled hybrid corpse, blue uniform covered in gore. Soldiers marched past to prepare for the next attack.

"Fall back. You need to regain your strength."

Melea spat. "Are they all dead?"

"Are what?"

Melea pointed at the corpse of boar beast with her sword. The area around them was now full of Chosen and the distinctive squealing had gone silent.

Cathair looked at her with calculating eyes. "You need to rest. This battle is far from over and your strength will be needed later on."

Melea stared at the Emperor's General. "Are. They. All. Dead."

"I slew the final beast myself."

Melea stepped off the corpse and started walking with the procession of infantry. The blaring of horns and issuing of orders flowed all around. Drums pounded in a steady tempo, a heartbeat of the battle demanding further action.

The Chosen were silent as they marched, stepping over and around piles of corpses. Melea thought she saw a one-armed Chuku Bartha torso dragging itself across the ground but lost sight of it amongst the legs of the soldiers. Her body felt full of energy, seemingly unaffected from the fighting. Her mind was as barren as a desert at night. Warmth spread across Melea's ribs like molten ore running downhill, liquid heat sure of its progress.

She marched forward with sword in hand, leaving the battle behind. The handle of the mace bumped against her thigh with each step, its weight implying the crushing force it was capable of. The heat inside of Melea solidified, strengthening her movements so that she no longer felt the weight of the mace. Melea could hardly feel anything at all. Arrows whistled overhead and Melea turned up her eyes to watch the gracefully arcing projectiles as they sped toward her.

"Tortoise shell!"

Wide oval shields were raised overhead to create a cohesive defense against the incoming arrows. Melea was the only one within the group without a shield.

Energy burned in her chest, the solid warmth transforming into a cold burn like that of freezing metal on wet skin. She felt the energy seep out of her skin to dance between the rings of her chain mail, infusing the two with the same force.

The woven iron rings merged with Melea's skin to harden everything on her outer surface. Everything except for her eyes. She kept them open as the arrows rained down; two green pin pricks staring out of a dome of golden shields. A man next to her fell as an arrow found its way through a tiny gap in the shield wall produced by the absence of her shield. She watched several sharp points bounce harmlessly off her hardened skin. One stabbed into her breastplate and stuck firm, so she snapped the shaft off.

"Forward!"

Shields swung down, secured to forearms. The Chosen disengaged the tortoise shell to advance at a brisk jog. Another volley of arrows forced them to hastily re-establish the protective formation before they were able to cross the open space. The Calanthians broke rank to attack and the two sides clashed together in a press of iron.

These were more slave soldiers, men forced into combat by the order of King Monchiet. She wondered how many had been farmers or rickshaw drivers only a few weeks ago. This was the first opportunity for her to get a good look at the slaves—she had been moving too fast when leading the charge. Inside the green and tan uniforms were men of every color and size, ranging in age from just past boyhood to the verge of elderly. She cut them down, shoulder to shoulder with Chosen. A shrill whistle blew and a new line of shieldbearing Chosen stepped forward to replace Melea's line.

Her line caught their breath while the others fought. Another whistle and Melea's line moved back to the front. More hacking until her hand was slick with blood. Two Chosen on her right fell and were replaced from behind. The whistle came again and the whole line stepped back.

The slave soldiers fought hard, as all men fighting for their lives will, but they could not match the trained cohesion of the Chosen. Calanthian soldiers fought to not die, whereas the Chosen fought for immortality. Having superior weaponry and training also went a long way towards victory. Melea noticed these martial differences most of all.

She fought as part of group, or rather was forced to, because of the compacted space. Melea retained the chain mail skin because she was unsure of what would happen if she released it. Her movements were slower and stiffer than usual but were still fast enough to fight the slave soldiers. The whistle came and she stepped forward.

A dark-skinned man came screaming towards her, his eyes wild with terror fueled fervor. Melea sidestepped the wide arc of his swing to ram her sword into his sternum, quickly removing the blade and taking his sword from his hand as he fell. She hacked down two more slaves.

Three soldiers burst out from the right and attacked as a group. Melea ducked a spearpoint, disemboweling one of the men as she rose. She spun and slashed out the thigh of a spearman who dropped to the ground. The third soldier lunged at her but she was quicker, and her borrowed sword connected with his throat hard enough to lift him off the ground. The sword got wedged in the man's neck and went down with him.

A stray arrow deflected off her chest and shattered. Archers were moving in from the left, weakening the lines of Chosen as they picked them off. Three men beside her fell to arrows. Foot soldiers swarmed into the opening. Melea fought madly but was forced to fall back. Whistles blasted in quick succession as the lines attempted to regroup. A captain with a pointed helm and equally sharp beard stepped in to stem the disarray.

"Stack left side! Shield wall!"

Chosen formed up around the Captain, planting their shields down like fence posts as arrows clattered against them. The second row angled their shields over top the first to deflect descending arrows. She was stuck outside the protective wall of shields, further to the right where the line was struggling to maintain order. A screaming mass of Calanthians rushed into the opening between Melea and the shield wall.

She brushed aside a spear to slash at the man behind. A pockmark faced man delivered a vicious two-handed chop to Melea's left shoulder. The force of the impact sent her reeling. She stumbled sideways, slipping in the blood-soaked mud. She bounced into the shield of a Chosen, surging back to cut down her attacker. The man fell with a burst of red spurting from his chest. Melea lashed out with a backhand slash but the sword never reached its target as a spearpoint caught her under her sword arm, jabbing into her armpit to raise her into the air. Her sword dropped from numb fingers and she tumbled to the ground.

The spearman pounced. She watched the dark shape of the spearpoint rapidly grow in size as it plunged down at her face.

The point made contact with her cheekbone, screeching as it scraped sideways across her cheek and down to her jaw before sliding into the ground.

Melea blinked, shocked to still be alive. She looked up at her attacker, his thick black eyebrows furrowed in confusion, he too thought she should have been killed. He raised the spear to try again but stalled with his hands raised overhead as a sword appeared out of his chest. A gurgle escaped the soldier's mouth as his eyes rolled back and he collapsed beside Melea.

Men jostled all around, each focused on their own struggles. Melea raised a gloved hand to where the spear-point made contact. The cheekbone felt hard hard as iron. Her skin was still protected by the layer of chain mail. Melea stood, grabbed her sword and rushed to join the nearest line of Chosen. Lines were crumbling all around; Calanthia was pushing the Shining Empire back.

She hacked and slashed, using her left arm to block incoming attacks in place of a shield. The men around her fought hard but they were still losing ground. Two more slave soldiers seemed to appear whenever one fell. They were able to use their advantage in numbers now that the lines of Chosen were beyond saving.

A big brute charged into her, knocking the sword from her hand. He bashed his shield across Melea's head making her helmet ring. She lost her balance, falling face first into the mud. Heavy feet stomped across her shoulders as the fighting continued. At one point, five men stood across Melea's back and hip. Heavy boots stomped against her hardened skin.

With a gasp, Melea pulled her face out of the mud, sucking in air as she looked around in a daze. The captain with the pointed helm was holding down the left side but the right was in shambles. Chosen were facing down the enemy, outnumbered three to one. There was no way Melea would be able to make it over to the protection of the shield wall. Even then, it was only a matter of time until the Chosen there were crushed under the weight of Calanthia's overwhelming numbers. Melea lay gasping in the mud, surrounded by the dead, temporarily thought to be one of their number, and therefore unnoticed.

Another horn blew—different than any of the previous commands—a long, low rattling note that instilled a sense of dread. She knew something bad was coming. The pointed helmed captain also recognized the meaning of the call.

"Fall back! Fall back!"

Melea was trapped between the retreating Chosen and onrushing slave soldiers. She raised her arms over her head and braced for impact as boots crunched overtop. The constant stream of men pushed Melea deeper into the mud, the weight on her back crushed her ribs and forced the air out of her lungs.

The strength of her hardened skin was cracking. She could feel it flaking off like dried plaster. Overhead, there came a sound like a giant exhale, then a scorching heat followed by screaming. Another exhale followed by more screams.

The stream of men running over her stopped and some tried to return the way they had come but they were too packed together to escape. She could hear big gasps of air followed by agonizing screams. The scent of burning was cloying even from her position against the mud. Suddenly, there was no more weight on her back, but the screaming continued.

The heat above was roasting her. She needed to move. She rolled around onto her shoulders, eyes closed, until the burning was eased by the mud. Hesitant blinks proved her incredulous survival; the world was temporarily calm in her tiny window of vision. The clamor all around made a mockery of the perceived calm, forcing Melea to lift her chin and check the surroundings.

Three lines of Chosen were advancing, one was almost on top of her. Each line pushed a large cylindrical object forward. The objects rested on wheels but still required ten men to move them. In the center of the cylinder was a black opening, sculpted to look like the gaping maw of a roaring giant.

Melea stared into the hateful eyes above the dark space of the mouth, listening for the now unmistakable exhale. She slammed her head into the mud as a torrent of flames erupted out of the opening. Tremendous heat passed overhead, becoming so intense that there was no telling where her body ended and the fire began.

Chosen walked all around her, following the path created by the flame scorchers. Melea's uniform was singed. Smoke trailed from her in thin wisps. She sat up, shaking uncontrollably. Something hard and grey bumped into her face. A strand of hair dangled down from beneath the brim of the helmet, bouncing against her cheekbone, solid as a rock. The chain mail was thoroughly enmeshed with her and the parts that had not flaked off were becoming even harder. She was being baked into an iron casing. Melea's heart thumped crazily. She was on the verge of an all-consuming panic, numbly watching those who passed by as if they were figures far removed from her position.

All Melea wanted was to breathe. She needed to pull air into her lungs but could not get her chest and brain to coordinate.

Charred corpses littered the ground all around, some of the bodies were completely reduced to ash. The air was thick with smoke, a shifting wall blocking the combat ahead. A man dismounted and squatted down beside her. General Cathair looked into her eyes.

"Melea."

She did not respond. He placed both hands on her shoulders, gently rocking her forward. Melea blinked and focused on Cathair for the first time.

"You are alive," said the General.

She understood the words but their meaning was lost on her.

"Watch me. In and out, in and out."

Cathair took exaggerated breaths and Melea copied the motion. Slowly, she felt air filtering into her lungs. Her mind started to disentangle and establish coherent thoughts. She kept breathing, gradually becoming more aware of her surroundings.

"Cathair," she said.

"Yes, I am here. You look like you've been chewed up and spit out."

Melea believed it. She felt even worse. She felt as stiff as a corpse, a sensation she knew all too well. Her eyes went to the piece of cement that used to be her hair, dangling from beneath the helmet. The chain mail needed to be removed, Melea could feel its pressure squeezing her ribcage.

"Give me a moment," she told Cathair.

He stepped back as she tried to ease the foreign material out, pushing the iron away so that it would drip off like water. The process was overwhelming her system, forcing her into a hacking cough that tore up her chest. Iron rolled down from beneath the helmet to stream off her nose. Iron droplets fell like tears onto the shredded ground. Her coughing slowed as the tightness around her chest lessened. She felt incredibly light after dispelling the chain mail but the lightness came with a sense of vulnerability, a realization brought on by the wind against her bare cheek.

Cathair watched her intently. Melea felt the squeezing pressure diminish until it finally left altogether. She stood, stretching her arms and legs to limber them up. Sensation was still deadened, she could not feel much of anything. The demands of her body returned, and a throat like sandpaper told her she was painfully thirsty.

"Water, if you have some," she rasped.

The General reached for a wineskin slung to his saddle and passed it over. Melea squeezed it in a stream, guzzling every drop of the bittersweet red liquid. She handed back the empty container, feeling immensely better.

"What's the status?"

Cathair watched her curiously. "We're advancing. The scorchers will soon be spent and we will be back to hand to hand combat."

Melea nodded. She should return to the front, to where the fighting was. But her legs felt so weak. She took a step and wobbled, nearly collapsing.

"Head to the back and rest, you're done for today."

She shook her head. Cathair frowned.

"That's an order."

Melea sat down. Cathair looked ahead to the fighting, noting something of significance.

"Stay here then."

He raced off, leaving her sitting alone. Lines of men marched past without paying her any attention. She took the time to focus on breathing, slowly calming herself, bringing about a feeling of stasis. Images of Ranna bleeding and of men on fire flashed in her mind every time she closed her eyes, so Melea sat there attempting not to think.

A guttural roar stirred Melea from her reverie. The sound was that of a carnivore, an animal that was fearless and confident in its strength. The roar held a resonance that made death real, able to be felt in the bones, a sensation that makes humans huddle closer to a campfire for safety.

Melea got up and started walking toward the noise. Little thought and even less intention inspired her motion, but she was driven by an underlying sense of purpose. A detached calm settled over her as if she were somehow distanced from certain aspects of herself. A yelp like that made by a kicked dog made her look up. A Chosen soared through the air, arms and legs flailing until he landed on his neck with a crunch. More men were sent hurtling airborne from the front line.

The Chosen retreated from this new attacker, forming a semi-circle, none wanting to get too close. The animal was fast, whatever it was. Soldiers screamed as it charged into another line. The rest of the Chosen ran to escape—most in fear, but a composed few to organize a new plan of attack. Cathair wheeled about on his mount bellowing orders. Melea was left standing alone as soldiers hurried past her. The beast roared again, the sound so close she thought she could feel the warmth of its breath.

The ground shook as a massive black haired creature chased after the men. The creature ran in a loping motion, its front legs—all four of them—were much longer than the two hind legs. It caught the last fleeing soldier, flattening him to the ground underneath a wide paw. The beast was huge, easily three times Melea's height.

She crouched down beside a quiver of arrows; the mace unnoticed on her hip. The bow was missing and to make matters worse these arrows were Calanthian, which meant they were not coated with toxin. Melea kept her eyes on the back of the beast while it casually tore apart the captured soldier.

The beast raised its shaggy head and slowly turned to face her. Savage black eyes glared out from below a pronounced brow, its snubbed snout opened wide to display two long yellow canines. Heavily muscled shoulders rounded into humps that made the beast slump forward. The front legs looked more like arms by the way they hung down from the body, each of the four ending in enormous paws with curved black claws. At first she thought the beast was a gigantic bear, but the arms reminded her of an ape. The beast snorted and tossed away the dismembered soldier, charging toward Melea, covering the distance with shocking speed.

The beast was an amalgamation of raw power, a tower of strength covered in thick black fur. It reached out for Melea with a hand as big as she was. A searing heat jolted Melea, pulsing against the inside of her ribs. The quiver of arrows emptied into her burning palms as the projectiles were absorbed by the ravenous energy being emitted. She rolled underneath jagged claws as the beast's momentum carried it past.

Melea looked to the Chosen who stood ringed a short distance away. "A sword!" None moved. "Throw me a sword!"

This time two Chosen understood and tossed their swords towards Melea. One of them was Andran Derclerq, who whipped his sword at Melea as if he were trying to impale her. The other sword barely made it half the distance. Melea snatched Derclerq's sword out of the air on the run as the beast charged again. The beast was fast but she was faster, moving with pure motion.

Heat steamed off Melea—if the beast was strength incarnate, then she would be speed. She guessed that the animal never needed to do anything other than barrel into its prey. Predictable. She moved beneath the beast's paws and struck with precision. Fingers and claws dropped to the ground like a handful of rotten bananas as the sword sliced through them.

Melea curled around behind the beast, forcing it to slow down and follow. It looked at the two injured paws on its left side, apparently surprised that she was able to dodge the attack. The beast roared and charged again. She was expecting another headlong assault so she positioned herself on the right side of the beast this time. Another slash lopped off more fingers and claws. The sword became lodged in the thick flesh so Melea let it go.

The beast spun, whirling its bleeding paws at Melea to crush her. She stepped in close, rolling between the two back feet, and pouncing at the nearest leg as the beast tried to find her beneath its bulk. An arrow emerged from her palm which she rammed into the back hinge of the beast's knee. She danced around the stumbling tree trunk legs to sink two more arrows into the back of the other knee joint.

The beast thrashed and fell as one leg spasmed. Melea sprang onto its back, grabbing a handful of fur as she climbed to stand on its shoulders, stabbing three arrows into the back of its neck. The beast reared, throwing maimed paws at Melea to knock her off. She leapt down and backed up a short distance as the beast continued to reach for her. She jogged over to the other sword thrown by the Chosen. Eventually, the beast realized she was no longer on its back and turned to face her. There was rage in it eyes but also fear.

This time Melea brought the attack, sprinting toward the beast with her sword low at her side. Spittle flew from the beast's mouth as it roared in fury. Melea produced an arrow from her open palm. A flick of the wrist snapped the arrow into the open jaws. The arrow sunk into the soft flesh of the beast's mouth, causing it to throw its head back in surprise.

The beast stumbled, its injured legs struggling to hold up the weight of its huge upper body. Melea rammed the sword up into its abdomen, tearing sideways as she pulled the blade free. A curtain of blood gushed out of the wound. Melea hacked out an ankle before jumping out of range of the falling giant. The beast landed with a resounding crash.

Melea moved around the beast, careful to stay outside of the thrashing arms. The massive head swiveled, trying to dislodge the arrow from inside its mouth. Melea stood behind the beast's head, looking down at its struggles. Finally, one paw managed to pull out the arrow. In one swift motion Melea lunged forward to sink the length of the sword into the left eye of the beast. It flinched once and stopped.

The Chosen gathered around Melea, cautiously creeping closer to the body of the beast, still wary of movement. She looked down the Pass, a force of Calanthians were approaching. Heat continued to build inside her body, the activity inside her mind was rapid, demanding action. Victory was at hand, she could taste it. Melea tossed the sword to Derclerq then sprinted at the enemy. Horns and whistles alternated as orders were given. Cathair and his cavalry passed Melea to clash with that of Calanthia.

She smashed into a wave of slave soldiers, wielding the mace with bone crushing force. The enemy was moving too slowly to have any hope of stopping her; their actions seemed delayed and sluggish. She stepped amongst them as if they were living statues, replicas of warriors placed in a mock battle scene. Again and again the mace descended to pulverize everything within reach. She lost herself to the motion.

Thought was overshadowed by the sensational speed. She was exhilarated by the strength flowing out of her, by experiencing the unstoppable force moving her. She breathed in power, feeling it wash over her as warriors in her path fell.

Time became meaningless to her. The fighting went back and forth, first one side would make a push then the other would retaliate and take back the same patch of land. She lost herself to the repetitiveness of combat. Her world became a series of faceless figures that differed only by the color of their uniforms. Green and tan smudges emerged to be felled, while blue smears jostled around her. All were stained with red.

Finally, there was no one else around Melea. The mace fell from limp fingers. A shadow passed overhead; Melea watched a large figure pass beneath the setting sun. The enormous black bird screeched as it floated above a scene of fierce combat. The sun hung just above the mountaintops on the last stage of its daily descent.

The Chosen were struggling to withstand the combined attack of three large beasts. Somehow, Melea had missed this entire section of fighting. She had been so consumed by what was directly in front of her that the rest of the world was blocked out completely. The sounds of fighting seemed so far away, much further than the actual distance.

The beasts battling against the Chosen resembled the four-armed creature she had killed, but these beasts fought as a unit and fought well. As Melea approached she noticed several differences. The beasts held weapons in their four paws, massive spears and swords that were wreaking havoc against the smaller Chosen. They had armor to protect key areas, but there was a more visceral difference, one that brought bile to her throat.

They had more faces than they should. Strange human-like features stared out from unnatural locations in the necks of the creatures.

A cold energy swallowed Melea, a different sensation than before. This power brought no joy, only a ravenous hunger. As she ran toward the closest of the beasts one of the faces turned slightly to look at her, alerting the creature to her presence. A piercing wail came from the smacking lips of the face, a disturbing sound that nearly unnerved her.

The shriek stopped as the beast removed itself from the group to face the new threat. Another disgusting face blinked at her from its fixed angle. She was surprised to see that what should have been the main eyes were covered with a milky film—the beast was blind.

Energy pulsed inside of Melea, licking hungrily at her like flames on dry kindling. She could feel the energy stretch out toward the beast, wanting it, desiring to take over the creature as its own. This sensation was at once frightening and thrilling.

The last light of the sun caused the beast's shadow to reach up to her feet. *Take it. It is yours. Everything is yours.* The whisper was almost inaudible. She reached down to touch the beast's shadow at her feet and was unsurprised when it responded to her contact. Being able to influence the shadow felt right.

She grabbed the shadow and lifted it off the ground. It stayed together in one piece like a cloak. Melea pulled it into herself, drawing the beast closer as if it were attached to a chain. The beast clawed at its shadow in panic.

Slowly and inexorably, the shadow disappeared into Melea. She felt strange but in no particular way. A numbness settled over her to replace the feel of the breeze and the scent of sweat and blood. Melea heard the wailing of three separate anguished cries. The beast.

There were different aspects of the beast and each of them was in pain. Two were Chuku Bartha. Melea could feel the distinct presences of the ape men caught up in the mass of the body. The beast itself was the majority of the mass and it was dreadfully unhappy with its predicament—consumed by a mindless anger built on powerlessness. The Chuku Bartha were filled with sorrow, yet the ape men retained a spark of intelligence, their minds still functioning on some level. Melea realized they must be the ones controlling the beast.

She wanted something else. Sensing the separateness of the three beings merged into the singular body awakened something within her. Subtle variations indicated the synthesis was incomplete, that it could be altered. Melea pushed into these borders, prying them apart with her fingers. They resisted. Melea pushed harder, digging in with her nails as she used all the strength at her disposal. The wailing intensified, filling Melea's awareness, then it abruptly stopped.

There was nothing. Not emptiness or quiet but nothing. Melea moved toward the next creature.

She pounced on the shadow like a lion on a lamb, her vision dimming as more of it entered her body. The sky became colorless. Everything turned a duller shade as numbness settled deeper into her bones. More wailing echoed in her mind. Three Chuku Bartha this time, screaming as one. Melea pulled them apart, stepping through each created opening. Her eyes were already scanning for the next silhouette as she discarded the spent shadow. One more was out there and she wanted it.

This beast fled from Melea's approach. She was confused—*why would it flee if it was in pain?* She would release it from anguish. She leapt on the shadow, pinning it beneath her foot to stop the beast in its tracks. An emptiness rumbled inside, an insatiable desire, something greater than hunger. Consumption.

She raised the shadow and shoved it into her mouth, gnashing the insubstantial into bits between her teeth. She found that breaking it into smaller pieces somewhat quieted the wailing, making it easier to separate. As she swallowed the last of the shadow she turned to find another one, even though she knew this had been the last of the beasts. She scanned the area, frustrated.

The shadows of the Chosen were small and weak, hardly more than a snack. Out of the corner of her eye she spotted something more appetizing. A large form moved toward her when all the rest hurried in the opposite direction. A miniature eclipse; absolute blackness ringed by blinding blood orange. Melea lunged toward the figure, intent on taking it as well. She only recognized the form at the last moment and by then it was too late to stop.

Emperor Anathasius stood calmly before her. His only sign of distress was a slight crease between the eyes. His shadow retreated into his feet to disappear completely. Melea chased after it like a fish after lure. He raised his right hand and backhanded her across the face. She went sprawling into the dirt to lay still. The numbness slowly lifted off her body as the energy inside of Melea steamed away.

Her skin felt like it was boiling off, like it would burn until there was nothing left of her. An irrepressible itch started behind her eyes and encompassed her entire body. She convulsed uncontrollably on the ground as she tried to escape from the sensation of herself. She screamed, her mind pulling in opposite directions; she could feel everything and it was too much to bear.

She tore at her clothes and skin, her hand brushing against a familiar bump in a hidden pocket. Dim recognition stirred inside, bringing Melea outside of herself for the briefest of instances. The break in sensation was enough for a single thought to enter Melea's mind. No. She held onto the word like a life-raft in a maelstrom, repeating it louder and with more conviction. No.

No.

No.

NO.

NO!

The burning left her, disappearing as if it had never even been there. Melea opened her eyes, needing to shade them. The sun dipped below the Petals and in the hazy light she could make out a white robe standing in front of the Chosen. Anathasius was speaking to the soldiers but his words were rendered silent by of a dull ringing in her ears.

The sight of Anathasius filled her with anger. He said he would protect them; it was his fault Ranna was dead. Melea got up and shambled over to him, noting the shocked looks on the faces of the soldiers.

Anathasius addressed the victorious army. "Darkness has been dealt an insurmountable blow this day by you, my Chosen. It retreats further into Calanthia to hole up in its lair but we will not let it rest or lick its wounds, we march to Marikal to finish it off."

The Emperor's words drifted back to Melea as she continued to shuffle along slowly. *The Chosen won this battle?* Maybe. At least they played a part. *Where was Anathasius during the fighting? Where was he when she slew beast after beast? Where was his protection when it was most needed?* She wanted to ask these questions but doubted her exhausted body had the strength. Anathasius turned, his golden eyes searching her disheveled figure.

"Are you returned?" He spoke quietly so that only the two of them could hear, his voice at once comforting and carrying the most severe judgment.

She lifted her arms to gesture at the destruction around them. "For you, I did this for you."

Anathasius looked her over. "You have done well Melea but you need more control."

She stopped next to Anathasius, carefully memorizing the expressions of fear and disgust in the eyes of the soldiers. To them she was just a weapon, a monster like the beasts of Calanthia. Even Cathair eyed her with suspicion. Derclerq would not look at her.

"The battle of Choker Pass will go down in history as the day the Shining Empire embraced the gift of Light. The moment of proof that Light will triumph against all obstacles. We will conquer Darkness, we will be victorious!"

The soldiers cheered, whooping and yelling, exhilarated to be alive, gazing upon their God in admiration. They marveled at his power and at the strength of his subordinate. The cheering had no effect on Melea, she felt no warmth or pride.

A single thought reverberated in her mind, one that grew louder as the soldiers continued. No.

## Howl of the Wolf Brothers

The sound of chanting was now a commonplace occurrence outside the walls of Cuelocano. Strange proclamations uttered by foreign tongues floated along the air like poisonous pollen. The drifting yellow clouds allowed the hardy plants of the tundra to survive, which in turn kept the animals and the people alive, marking the few weeks of pungent debris in the air as a sign of the area's health. The pollen was only given two weeks in spring to ride the wind; the priests showed no signs of stopping.

Sixthrok grimaced as hard pebbles were blown into his face. The wind was angry—the chanting priests of the Shining Empire had not consulted with Iglyl about spreading their words. Their claims of everlasting life gusted toward him on a wind whispering of vengeance.

He stood on top of the glacial wall, rubbing his hands together, trying to force some warmth into them, and to keep himself separate from a wind that was intent on taking. The spirit cast more stones in his direction, laughing cruelly at his distress. *Would Iglyl side with the southerners because of his failure?* The capricious spirit always had a taste for death, one that was matched by these followers of the Emperor.

Sixthrok ran his fingers over each other, finding that he needed to keep his hands moving or else they would be constantly clenched in rage, becoming two useless stumps. His brother's hands urged to hold weapons, to kill the priests and end the chanting. Sixthrok knew the current leader of the Tribes would strangle the spirit of the wind if it were possible.

Dozens of priests moved about on the plain beneath the ice wall, chanting another monotonous hymn. Sixthrok thought their droning sounded like mosquitos. Their thick grey jackets helped fend off the wind but also made them resemble the bloodsucking insects. Mosquitos could be a menace even this far north, rising in huge swarms, seemingly out of nowhere. Wherever there was blood, they were sure to follow.

Sixthrok had seen them drive the migrating rangif herds mad, unlucky individuals running in distress until collapsing in exhaustion, will power defeated. The size of the animal and its thick hide were a meager defense against the constant biting of a voracious swarm. The mosquito could be a nearly insurmountable foe as the violent death of its comrades did not deter it in the slightest. The bloodsuckers only understood one way of propagation. These priests were just as zealous. Sixthrok shrugged off the wind in his rangif hide jacket, feeling a nagging itch between his shoulders.

Dawn was fast approaching, the black sky turning into softer purple in advance of the rising sun. A large form silently moved next to Sixthrok. Katano's shaggy black hair hung over his face but could not hide the crookedness of his nose—a remnant of his battle with the Emperor's girl. He wore the great white bear hide overtop of his own rangif jacket.

"I hate them," Katano growled.

"The wolves would make a feast of their flesh if we had more warriors."

"I could devour them. Every last one."

Sixthrok glanced at his brother, looking for a physical change to match that inside. Katano was becoming darker, colder, more savage and Sixthrok didn't know how to stop the progression.

"The soldiers of the Shining Empire outnumber our warriors three to one," Sixthrok stated.

Sixthrok knew Katano was furious with this arrangement, growing more volatile each day they were forced to look out at the Emperor's army.

Sixthrok would have been content to wait for the winter to remove the soldiers for them but the long lasting standoff had created another issue, one that he was wary of discussing with Katano. They were nearly out of food and the sea behind the fortress had been unkind to the fishermen. The Tribes needed to move, to find a new source of food, but there were too few boats to move everyone, and the soldiers blocked escape by land.

The ladder behind Sixthrok and Katano bounced against the wall as a boy rushed up to reach them. He was gasping and his eyes held the guilt of having to relay terrible news. He looked too nervous to speak.

"What is it, Joval?" asked Sixthrok.

He acknowledged Sixthrok first. "*Ta-kal*...I mean, Sixthrok." He said with a nod of respect. Joval gulped as he turned to look up at Katano. "Chief, I went to help give out rations this morning and all the food is gone."

"What do you mean gone?" Katano's rumbling voice made Joval retreat a half step.

"Everything is gone, the storage is completely empty, and..." Joval stopped.

"What?" Katano demanded.

Joval glanced around even though only the three of them stood on the wall. "Rumor is five families from the west stole it, that they took the boats and fled."

"Qotoryl." Katano spoke the name of the western tribe like a curse.

Joval looked down at his feet. "I went to see. The boats are gone too."

"No," said Sixthrok, grabbing Joval by the shoulders. "They couldn't be so foolish."

The boy's face blanched as he swayed under Sixthrok's grip. Katano stepped toward the ladder, shoving the other two into the wall. Sixthrok followed his brother, he could sense the bloodlust stirring in him. *Keep the people together*. Kerak's words echoed in Sixthrok's head. The leader of the Tribes could not kill his own people, no matter how grievous their mistake turned out to be. Sixthrok could not let the Katano's rage destroy the unity within Cuelocano, not while the Emperor's soldiers waited outside the wall.

People shuffled around outside of their shelters despite the wind—they were hungry. Day after day of short rations left everyone feeling empty and frustrated. They stepped aside as Katano stormed past. He moved swiftly but with a slight limp, another reminder of his battle with the green-eyed cunt. Sixthrok caught up to Katano, intent on calming him before someone took the brunt of the chief's anger.

"Be wise, brother," said Sixthrok. "Do not do something that cannot be undone."

Katano ignored him, heading straight for the mud brick hut where the food was stored. A small congregation had formed around the open door. The interim chief barged through the crowd to see the empty shelves for himself. Sixthrok moved to block the entryway, turning to face the gawkers. If he could not stop Katano, then he would prevent anyone from coming into contact with him.

"Everyone get back! Now!" The crowd hopped away from Sixthrok's snarl.

One small girl started to cry, her mother making consoling noises as she led the tearful child away. An earsplitting roar was followed by a violent crash. Several people in the crowd flinched and more mothers escorted their children home. Katano ripped shelves off the wall, smashed empty barrels, and tore empty baskets to shreds.

"Out of my way, Ta-kal," Katano commanded.

Sixthrok stood firm. "Calm yourself, or I will calm you."

The hut shook as Katano smashed into a side wall. Katano burst through the wall, sending debris scattering all around him. The hut sagged to the verge of collapse. Gasps escaped from the crowd and several frightened onlookers fled.

A woman approached, striding straight toward the enraged giant, a person Sixthrok could not stop. Their mother, Nal-Farrah, looked into her eldest's eyes, causing him to pause. Her oval face was smooth and inexpressive. She reached up and slapped Katano across the face.

"Be a leader." Her voice was firm and authoritative.

She was as respected by the Tribes as her husband, renowned for her careful reasoning. Secretly revered because of her legendary entry into the Frozen Tribes. None spoke the word aloud in her company but all used it to refer to the wife of Kerak—syla.

Katano's eyes dropped in shame. Bits of wreckage fell from his hair as he started toward the small sea harbor. Sixthrok once again hurried to catch up.

"Think brother, this is the time to come up with a new strategy. The people will be looking to you for guidance."

Katano ignored him again, shouldering into an unobservant person, sending the man sprawling to the dirt. Sixthrok placed a hand on Katano's shoulder but was brusquely brushed off. They continued in silence until Katano stopped at the edge of the beach, the cold water lapping against his boots. All of the boats were gone. Katano stared out into endless blue as the sun made its first appearance over the horizon. No black specks on the surface.

"They will have gone to the western hunting grounds, hoping to find enough game to survive the winter," said Sixthrok.

Katano continued to stare out over the water. "They think I am unfit to lead. They would rather steal from their own people than follow me."

Sixthrok understood the unsaid portion of his brother's words. Katano thought this travesty would have been avoided if their father was still leader of the Tribes. The people trusted Kerak, believed in his ability to always provide for them, to get them through the lean times. Katano had been placed in a difficult position that left no room for error. He was charged with directing the future of the Tribes at the most critical moment of their history. Katano was a great warrior, an unstoppable force on the battlefield, and a hunter capable of returning from inhospitable conditions with meat for the people. He was also blunt with his words, prone to making rash decisions, and dangerous as a wounded bear. Many of the people feared him. Since the siege started, there had been a growing mistrust of the wolf brothers.

"We will find a way. Cynaal sings through us as long as we draw breath," said Sixthrok.

The assertion sounded confident but Sixthrok knew Katano's mind. How much longer would they be able to draw breath with no food?

"We will fight our way out," said Katano.

"The men are brave. They will follow you to their deaths."

A gust of wind pushed Katano's hair out behind him. He knew they were too greatly outnumbered to hope for victory. Sixthrok stepped beside Katano, the icy water wetting his boots, looking out to where the sky met the sea to become something eternal. He wondered whether their father still lived, why the wisest man amongst the Tribes chose to become imprisoned by their enemy. Kerak had only done so because he trusted the judgement of his sons.

He had told Sixthrok that he believed the future of the Tribes lay in the Shining Empire, that they would need to bend to the Emperor's will for the time being. But they could not break. Sixthrok was charged with keeping the lifesong in the hearts of their people. Cynaal, the spirit of life, would not abandon the Tribes and neither had Kerak, each working in ways not often understood by mortals. Sixthrok had faith in his father's conviction, he and Katano would see the people through this greatest of challenges. The only remaining decision was a loathsome one. Sixthrok knew that Katano would not be the one to offer it.

"We must speak with the priests," he said quietly, disgusted at hearing the words out loud. "They claim to be willing to provide food for the Tribes and able to care for the sick and wounded."

Katano stared straight ahead, unwilling to make eye contact. His mouth squirmed, twisting in rage as he bit back his words. Finally, he could not hold back any longer. A primal scream tore out of Katano's lungs, racing over the water after the thieves. Sixthrok saw the bear's spirit inside of his brother emerge, roaring along with Katano. The ghostly blue apparition gave him chills in a way that went beyond coldness.

Katano hurled stones into the water until he was panting from the effort. He stalked off without responding to Sixthrok but the younger brother understood that the new leader of the Frozen Tribes agreed with his counsel.

Sixthrok watched the sun rise over the water, feeling the warmth on his face. The heat was lessening, becoming thinner as autumn advanced. Surviving a northern winter demanded sacrifice, but Sixthrok hoped the people would not have to offer up more than they could give.

Sixthrok's stomach felt as tight as seal skin stretched across the rim of a drum. And just as hollow. Gone were the disgruntled noises of hunger. His body had decided that the effort was unnecessary as it needed to conserve every scrap of remaining energy. He sat in Katano's lodge two and half days after discovering that Cuelocano was out of food. Three priests sat across from him and his brother, each party with ten warriors behind them. They were seated around a small fire, thin wisps of smoke drifting upward toward the curved ceiling. Sixthrok worried that their warriors might pass out from hunger.

The Empire's soldiers looked tense, ready to attack at a moment's notice. They wore the same long grey coats as the priests. Katano seemed unaffected by going without food, his eyes sparking with a fierceness that Sixthrok tried to match.

The priests sat bundled in their thick coats, even in the warmth of lodge. They did not even know what cold was, they had no idea what the endless night of winter was like. Maybe they simply wanted to end the meeting quickly and could not be bothered to remove their outerwear. Sixthrok wanted this meeting to end as soon as possible. He did not want to be sitting around discussing matters with the enemy while women and children were starving just outside the walls of the lodge.

Nal-Farrah had given her counsel when informed of the decision to bring the priests into Cuelocano. "Be wary of any deals with these leeches in men's skin, they do not know how to listen. All they hear is their own thoughts."

This advice echoed in Sixthrok's mind as he looked over the fire to the priests.

"Terms," said Katano.

The priests were confused as to whether the leader of the Frozen Tribes had asked a question. They looked at each other and reached an unspoken agreement. The middle priest spoke. He was a middle-aged man with curly brown hair. He looked healthy and comfortable. Sixthrok instantly hated him.

"We will provide food for the people of the Frozen Tribes and will tend to the sick and wounded," said the priest. "The Shining Empire has a bounty of resources that you are now entitled to."

"What about them?" Katano jutted his chin toward the soldiers.

The priest clasped his hands together on his lap. "The Chosen will remain to keep the peace and help to make sure that aid is properly administered."

Katano grunted acknowledgment. The priest continued, a flicker of anxiety passing over his features before he spoke. Sixthrok flinched inside, knowing the restrictions were now to be voiced.

"Of course, all weapons must be turned in to the Chosen before aid can be administered. For the safety of everyone involved."

Katano bristled but was able to control his temper. "What else?"

The priest's smile faltered, then dropped away. "The Frozen Tribes will be eased into the embrace of the Shining Empire as its newest disciples. You will be moved from this place when the needs of the people have been seen to."

"Cuelocano. This place has a name and it is Cuelocano," said Sixthrok. The priests looked unsettled by the gravel in Sixthrok's tone.

Sixthrok was unsurprised that the priests had not bothered to learn the name. Cuelocano was not of the Shining Empire so what did it matter? Except that now Cuelocano was under the Emperor's control. The Tribes were also under his control. His disciples, whatever that meant. A trickling dread slivered through him, Nal-Farrah's words were beginning to feel more foreboding. Her counsel often gathered momentum the more one considered it, an effect of being a syla perhaps. A returned spirit knew things that those in their first life couldn't understand.

"And then?" the rage in Katano's voice was thinly masked.

*Careful, brother*, thought Sixthrok, *we do not want to start a fight we cannot win.* But that was exactly what Katano wanted. What Sixthrok also wanted. It was not what the people wanted. The brothers had addressed the people, giving them the authority to decide the fate of Cuelocano.

*Cynaal, please give us the strength to accept this disgrace so that we may take revenge later*, Sixthrok prayed. Kerak had chosen his sons to keep the people together. They could not follow his wishes if they were slain in his own lodge.

The priest offered another smile, this one lasting slightly longer before wilting. "You will be shown how to walk the Illuminated Path so that you may be granted eternal life, a right bestowed upon the people of the Shining Empire by Emperor Anathasius."

Katano was silent. Sixthrok's tired mind muddled over the priest's words. The lifesong beat strong in his chest. Cynaal was responding to the lies of these deceivers. *Play their game if you must*—Kerak's request proved to be premonitory. Sixthrok had relayed their father's message to Katano on his return from Azra.

"You said you would return with him, Ta-kal," had been Katano's only response.

The nickname burned with embarrassment at that moment. Ta-kal meant Little Chief, a title given to Sixthrok as a boy since he followed Kerak around wherever the shaman went. Sixthrok constantly nipped at his father's heels, copying his gestures and way of speaking. Others would laugh when he mimicked Kerak's cool air of authority. He had been called Ta-kal for as long as he could remember. Only Katano still called Sixthrok by that title.

While checking the perimeter one evening, Sixthrok had stumbled across a group huddled in the northeastern corner of the fortress. They spoke in hushed tones, but their frustration was clear and unconcealed.

"Our blood will drip from the jaws of these wolf brothers; they keep us penned up like rangif ready for slaughter."

"I hear that their own people receive larger rations."

"The wolves probably get the most, they hardly look like they've lost any weight since the siege started."

Grunts of agreement followed. Sixthrok was astounded by what he was hearing, his own people, those that he abandoned his father to protect, were accusing him and Katano of taking more food. Everyone got the same amount, it was the only fair way.

"Kerak was an experienced leader, he had power to protect the Tribes. What do these boys have? Katano failed against the daughter of death and Ta-kal couldn't bring Kerak back."

"They do not want him back, they can only rule without the interference of a shaman. Why do you think they call the younger one Ta-kal?"

Sixthrok had heard enough. A hushed silence swept over the group as he stepped into view; six grown men paused like children caught stealing sweets. A collective look passed between them as they tried to guess how much Sixthrok overheard. The main speaker stepped forward, he was an older man named Elia, a fisherman and seal hunter from the west.

"Now, Ta-kal," said Elia.

"Shut up. Say that name again and I will rip out your tongue and toss it to the gulls."

Everyone flinched as Sixthrok took a step closer. Elia remained where he was. In a flash Sixthrok had Elia by the throat and was hoisting him off the ground.

"I should feed your ungrateful heart to the Tribes but a meal that bitter wouldn't stay down," said Sixthrok.

Another man stepped forward to intervene, so Sixthrok lashed out with a palm to smack him to the ground. The others shouted angrily, but stopped when they saw the knife in Sixthrok's hand. He brought the knife up so Elia could see it as well. The fisherman choked against Sixthrok's grip as he struggled to escape. Sixthrok slammed Elia to the ground, bringing the knife down beside the man's head. Elia's eyes were fixed on the knife planted in the dirt a hair's breadth from his temple.

"Cuelocano is still free because of my brother and I, we are the reason that traitorous cowards like you are given an equal share of food every day. Nobody wishes Kerak were here more than I, but he is not. Who joined me when I went into the Emperor's lair to retrieve him? It wasn't you, Elia." Sixthrok looked around at the other men. "None of you spoke up then."

He cracked his knuckles while the others stayed frozen in place. "You stayed silent because you wanted to live, and you will learn to use silence again if you wish to continue living."

Elia and the others had rushed off and that was the last of the rumors Sixthrok overheard. He wondered now if they would be in this situation if he had heard more. His actions that night might have been the impetus which scared some of the Tribe to commit an unthinkable act, to desert their own people and leave them to die. To die or make a deal with the Shining Empire. Until the deal was made it was impossible to tell which was worse.

Katano nodded and one of the priest's exhaled, visibly calmed from the non-aggressive gesture. Sixthrok turned to the warriors, motioning for them to drop their spears. The soldiers walked over to retrieve the weapons. Sixthrok watched a layer of ice glaze over Katano's features, marking each soldier for death.

"We are agreed then," stated the curly haired priest.

Katano stood and everyone followed his example. "Get the food," was all that he said before exiting.

"Of course," said the priest. "The Shining Empire gives all of its people the utmost in life."

They all exited the lodge and two of the priests hurried back over the wall. The priests were barely out of sight before soldiers clambered up the ladders. Many more streamed over the wall.

Sixthrok spoke to the ten warriors who were in the lodge during the meeting. "Go and tell the people to bring all weapons to the center of Cuelocano. Tell them that they will be able to eat if they do so."

The men hurried off and soon a pile of spears, bows, arrows, and knives were heaped on the ground. Nal-Farrah approached, worry cutting through her dark eyes, a rare expression for her, and one that made Sixthrok doubt the wisdom of dealing with the priests. Katano addressed the priest who spoke at the meeting. "Here are the weapons, now bring the food."

The priest raised a hand and the soldiers sprang into action.

The soldiers moved toward Katano instead of over the wall to retrieve food. Katano instinctively understood what was happening and met the oncoming rush head on. He pummeled into the line of soldiers, knocking several aside but was soon lost beneath a pile of grey coats. Sixthrok lunged for a spear from the pile but the path was blocked by three soldiers with their swords drawn. More circled behind and attacked as a group.

Sixthrok lashed out with fists and elbows, hearing a satisfying crack as he connected with a soldier's jaw. The sheer numbers of soldiers forced him down, the weight of multiple men pinning him to the ground. Iron shackles clasped around his wrists, their cruel bite tearing into flesh.

Sixthrok heard the protests of his fellow warriors as they struggled against the soldiers. Women screamed and tried to run. The fight was over before it even started. The cries of children and their wailing mothers pierced Sixthrok's heart.

He tilted his chin off the ground to see a procession of children being led by the priest from the meeting. Soldiers pushed the children up the ladders, forcing them to climb down on the other side of the wall. Sixthrok closed his eyes, breathing in dirt through his mouth. Strong hands forced him to his feet. He looked up to see the last child climb over the wall, tears rolling down her chubby cheeks.

Katano was also on his feet; he thrashed against the soldiers holding him and broke free. He was shackled around the wrists but was still able to rip a sword away from one of his captors. Katano slashed at the nearest soldier, bright red soaking through the jacket. He sprinted into an open space near Sixthrok. The soldier's holding Sixthrok were distracted by Katano's escape, the shift in their grip only a slight difference but it was enough.

He smashed his head into the soldier on the right and spun back to push away the other. A sword lunged at his chest but he sidestepped the strike, angling the chain binding his wrists so that it scraped against the blade until it hit the soldier's hands. Sixthrok latched onto the man's wrists and ripped the sword away. He smashed an elbow into the soldier's face, followed by a swift downward slice. More red on grey. Sixthrok ran to join Katano, with soldiers in pursuit.

The wolf brothers stood back to back, holding their swords in both hands to negate the chains as much as possible. Three soldiers rushed in and all were sent to the ground. The rest approached cautiously, trying to coordinate the next attack. Sixthrok and Katano turned slowly in a tight circle, eyes on the creeping soldiers.

The soldiers attacked as one. Sixthrok swung his blade in sweeping arcs, severing arms. Katano's deep, rumbling laugh rippled through Sixthrok's back. His brother's chuckling was terrifying and inspiring. Sixthrok lashed out with a fresh burst of energy. Blood covered them both. The ground was littered with soldiers. He swung madly, hacking at anything that moved.

Sixthrok felt dizzy, his vision blurring as his body began to shut down from lack of food and sleep. He kept the sword moving but his motions were becoming slow and sluggish.

A sharp pain flared in his hip as a sword made contact. His footing slipped out beneath him. Another searing pain opened up in his shoulder. He swung wildly without seeing. A boot kicked the sword of out his hands. Katano's chuckle escalated into a booming laugh, a sound of madness.

Katano impaled a soldier, then grasped another around the neck to strangle the life out of the southern body. Two quick slashes to the back of Katano's legs sent him sprawling to the ground. Sixthrok looked around through bleary eyes at the wall of blurry, smudged figures.

"I am sorry, brother," said Sixthrok.

He tilted his head back to look up at the blueness of the sky. The wind cupped Sixthrok's face, holding him in a suspended caress. The spirit of the wind was mocking him. *Father, forgive me, I have failed you.*

Nal-Farrah's voice called out, a high pitched wail, a prayer and a curse. She spoke to Iglyl, calling on the spirit of the wind. "Ouetza na metulo Iglyl aktil za pityl mofas allin tuqwa." *Great spirit Iglyl, impart strength to my sons so they may avenge our betrayal.*

Sixthrok heard the huffing of a bear, a savage roar, the screams of men. He saw Katano running on all fours, wearing the spirit of the bear like it were another type of jacket. Katano leapt to the wall, climbed to the top, and disappeared out of sight.

## The Emperor's Gift

Kerak leaned his head back, eyes closed as he took in the sunlight like the embrace of a long lost companion. He started down the garden path once more, his steps constricted by iron shackles around the ankles. Shackles also latched around each wrist, the short chain between them forcing his shoulders to hunch inward. The shaman's face showed no discontent with the bindings, but the Beacon's did.

"I apologize for this rough treatment, but they wouldn't allow you to leave the room without them," said Belenus.

"No bother," Kerak replied, as he smiled into the wind. More streaks of grey were apparent within the shaman's black hair, but overall he appeared to be regaining his former strength. The thinness caused by malnutrition was being replaced by a fullness, now that he was receiving regular meals.

"Come, let's sit." Belenus motioned to a wooden bench placed beside a thin stream trickling over a series of flat stones arranged in a step pattern.

Belenus had provided Kerak with a new set of clothes, the others needing to be burned because of the smell. The plain, rough spun woolen clothing was nothing fancy, but it was clean and fit well. Belenus wore the outfit that he almost always picked when formality did not require something more: a simple white robe with black sandals. The two men listened to the splashing of the stream as it made contact with each successive step.

"We have spoken before about how I worry that your impure rituals bring more Darkness into the world," said Belenus while watching the tumbling water. "Something troubles me more than this harmful effect, and that is how your rituals are able to work at all without utilizing the Emperor's Gift." Belenus looked to Kerak. "Please explain how you are capable of such power."

He did not miss the unmistakeable challenge in Kerak's eyes.

"I do not even know what the Emperor's Gift is. Perhaps I access it but call it by a different name," said Kerak. "To answer your question I first must know what makes your rituals purer than mine."

Belenus clasped his hands together on his lap while considering how to explain. "All of life needs water or else it will soon die. It will dry up and crumble into dust to be scattered by the wind. One may settle next to a river or lake or dig a well but they may run dry. One may wait for the rain but rainfall is difficult to predict. Existence becomes strenuous and brutish when the greatest needs of humanity are outside of our control. What is needed is a limitless supply." Kerak nodded his understanding so Belenus continued. "Now, imagine a massive pool of water located within a crater atop a mountain. In this crater is enough water for all of Rua for drinking, bathing, watering animals, and growing crops. There is so much life-giving water that it cannot possibly run out. Now, the people know that this crater of precious water is on the mountain but try as they might they cannot scale the hazards to reach the summit. Yet, we struggle to attain this vivifying source."

"How would one get this water off the mountain?" asked Kerak.

"I'm getting to that," said Belenus. "Some people are naturally more talented climbers so they use their skills to accomplish where others fail. They devise ways to reach the water but here they make a heartbreaking discovery— the water is undrinkable. Stagnation has tainted what was once pure and clean. Yet, a person must drink or they will surely die, so methods are devised to bring the filthy water down from the mountaintop. This process is an earnest attempt to help those in need but in actuality, anything touched by the tainted water is befouled." Belenus unclasped his hands, using them to gesticulate. "The Emperor's Gift acts as a filter which removes all the harmful components that have accrued in the water. Emperor Anathasius understands how to obtain energy from the static so that the *water* may be used for its intended purpose. His lessons are taught in the Sanctuary so that others may assist in the replenishing of the world."

Kerak looked to his new shoes and smiled. "Just because these shoes are on my feet does not mean they are mine. You access this filter shown to you by the Emperor through blood, just as I do."

"Well yes, but it's not as simple as that. Blood is not just a bodily fluid. Surely you must know this?"

"I do," Kerak said, nodding his head toward a patch of grass that still held its greenness. Most of the garden was turning brown as summer gave way to fall. "All living things have their own basic juices that are not so different than our own blood. A plant absorbs the energy of the sun and turns it into growth. We share a kinship with all beings through this similarity, an inherent connection below awareness. As you said, a human must drink. We have discovered how to manipulate our own life force to affect its mirrored image in other beings."

"Good," Belenus grumbled. "At least you know something. The crucial aspect is how one does this."

"Enlighten me."

Kerak kept his face smooth but Belenus was sure the shaman was being facetious.

"I've been waiting a long time to hear you say those words." Belenus' eyebrows wiggled like two hairy caterpillars. "That northern chill must have finally worn off. Now I can talk some sense into you."

"I implore you to save my pagan spirit." Kerak bowed his head in reverence.

"Ha! Quit it with the sarcasm you buffoon and maybe I will." Belenus leaned forward on the edge of the bench. "One cannot influence the life force of another being without first becoming intimately aware of their own life force, and this awareness can only be achieved through mental diligence. The mind directs the flow of blood throughout the body, therefore training is required so that the mind may be made to focus on becoming aware of the flow and later how to manipulate it. Oftentimes, a person is only able to detect the life force of specific beings, which only allows them to influence this distinct force. For example, priests in training at the Sanctuary are sorted into different groupings to allow them to hone a specific ability that aids the Shining Empire in a certain calling."

"What is yours?" Kerak asked.

Belenus waved his hands. "I'm an anomaly. I never really fit into any of the categories, but I didn't let that stop me." He took a moment to imagine how a fellow priest might use the Emperor's Gift to help with the harvest and drew a blank.

"Please continue," said Kerak.

"Right! Well, mental acuity is only part of the process, which is good for a couple of thick skulls like the two of us. Mental focus can only take one so far unless one knows how to breathe properly. Air is akin to the blood of the world, keeping life in motion by constantly intermingling all of the various energies. Air enters the human body through the lungs as well as through the pores of the skin and in the process lets us become aware of the energies of the wider world, which in turn mingles with our own blood. These exterior energies need to be controlled within the body so they may be directed along with the internal flow to be released by the drawing of blood. The entirety of one's mental focus is used to facilitate inner awareness. Directional flow is key. This flow merges with the energies acquired from proper breathing to be released when the blood makes contact with the outside air."

Kerak was leaning forward as well. "Where does the Emperor's Gift enter in all this?"

"The Gift is actually two-fold: the correct process is the first aspect and the second is the metaphor of the filter I made earlier. Emperor Anathasius took all of the foulness of the stagnancy into himself, acting as a purifier to clean the essential life force energy so that it may be used without causing harm. This is a task he must undertake periodically and will have to continue on with indefinitely, until Darkness is eradicated from Rua."

Kerak was quiet for a moment, staring at his hands and the cold iron squeezing his wrists. "The power is indeed dangerous. Unable to be accessed by any mortal man. A human cannot enter into this force without being destroyed."

"That proves Emperor Anathasius' divinity. He is Rua's savior." Belenus wanted to say more but held his tongue. *Do you see now?* He so badly wanted Kerak to feel the truth that he felt while speaking of the Gift, but he was not going to force his beliefs on the shaman. One needed to come to the truth of their own accord, to walk toward it with the strength of their own beliefs—anything else was false.

"The understanding of this life is distanced from eternal power for a reason, not meant to be used for our own purposes." Kerak's voice was ominous as a dark prophesy. "I fear this Gift of yours has torn an opening between our world and the essential life force energy, letting it in like a deluge. The system of exchange is broken. The ancestors whisper of our doomed fate."

"Ancestors? Are they part of Cynaal?" Belenus had a difficult time understanding how the shaman's spiritual system was organized.

Kerak shrugged. "Cynaal is the harmony of existence and is sung by the deceased. One is able to fully understand this harmony in death and rejoices in the revelation. If the living give the ancestors the respect they deserve, then the dead are willing to share what they can of the balance flowing through existence. Cynaal is the song of life and of death—it is truth incarnate that I have spent my life struggling to understand." Kerak raised a hand to rub his eyes, the chain jangling as he did so. "Sometimes, I feel as though I'm deaf and wandering through a crowded festival, trying to understand the sound of the music by half-seen glimpses of the instruments."

"So these ancestors tell you how to perform the rituals?"

"They offer their wisdom through Cynaal so that I may make the proper exchanges."

"I don't understand." Belenus was trying to follow but he could not decipher what exactly needed to be exchanged with what.

Kerak's flint hard eyes changed to a soft pewter as he gazed at the Beacon. "Each ritual is a process of give and take, an exchange of energies, as the life force of the user interacts with other forces. The ability to influence the world in a desired way has a cost. The user is forever altered, as is the object of their intention."

Belenus considered this opinion, chewing it over in his mind. He recalled the supreme sensation of loss that accompanied the severing of ties with the crowd at the end of the final march through Azra. The wilted state of the flower crumpled over the side of the vase also came to mind. Could a proper exchange have brought life to the flower? What precisely was he supposed to exchange? The act of Emperor Anathasius purifying the reservoir of energy should have established an infinite supply of life force that Belenus could draw from. Surely he could use this energy if he became skillful enough. Some aspect of Kerak's theory must be incorrect.

"What exactly do you exchange?" Belenus stressed the word *exchange* as though it was slippery on his tongue.

"Your spirit."

Belenus placed a hand to his chin, rubbing it thoughtfully. "But the Emperor's Gift is boundless if one can fully access it."

Kerak shook his head. "My rituals are stronger than any performed by you or the other priests. How do you think one man was able to keep the Empire's army at bay?"

"Stronger? How?" Belenus huffed, crossing his arms.

Kerak sat up straight and for an instant the chains binding him became invisible. "I do not draw from the same source that you do though I have sensed your source in the songs of the ancestors. I dare not touch this energy and bring it into the world of the living." A pained expression flicked across Kerak's face. "My source is that of the ice in the North. I merge my energy with that of the frozen water to influence it in ways that suit my tasks. To change the water into its various forms requires an exchange of energy each time I perform a ritual. The cost is high. I feel my bones grow heavier as the ice becomes embedded within them. One day the ice will claim me as its own."

Belenus was shocked by the sad inevitability in the shaman's voice. Kerak honestly believed what he was saying. This process of exchange, if it was even accurate, could not be stronger than the Emperor's Gift. All one had to do was look at the success of the priests to comprehend this fact. Belenus intuitively knew that the source of power made accessible by the Gift was incredibly dangerous, but the actions of Emperor Anathasius remedied this potential malady. The Emperor had perfected the process so that it could be used to destroy Darkness once and for all. Belenus had felt the power coursing through his body when he enacted a ritual and could see the direct influence it had on those around him.

"Emperor Anathasius has made it so the need for an exchange is unnecessary, if it is even needed at all," said Belenus. "He is able to draw full buckets directly from the wellspring. The priesthood can only draw a thimbleful by comparison, yet this tiny amount is pure beyond compare. We do not bring it into ourselves as you say you must but instead act as vessels to contain the energy briefly until it can be released." A thought about exchange occurred to Belenus. "You said that you draw from ice and water but what of the ritual used on your son?"

Kerak's posture drooped and he looked out into the garden that was now mostly sparse brown vegetation. "That was something different, a technique I learned in Marikal, one that none of their Ba-rük priests could accomplish. Not on men. Desperation drove me to use that ritual and what I witnessed terrifies me to this day."

"You created life, gave the bear's strength to your son." Belenus was hopeful. Maybe this technique would provide clues on how to transfer life to the sick and dying.

Kerak's eyes were haunted. "I bound the spirit of the bear to my son. I took the life force of the bear without exchange. I did not pay the cost but instead awakened something far worse." Kerak stared straight into Belenus. "I saw oblivion that day. It was hungry and will return for me."

"Darkness," whispered Belenus. "You brought Darkness into the world by using a ritual outside of the Gift."

"I took selfishly and without regard for the source as my need was so desperate. Cynaal wept as the shadow inside of me grew."

Belenus offered comfort to ease Kerak's distress. "But there was an exchange as the bear was transferred to your son?"

"The exchange was unequal as I took all and gave none. My life force screams in agony at what I have done."

Belenus spoke with passion, the fervency of his yearning to save others from Darkness being expressed in raw form. "This is why one must use the Emperor's Gift. So this cruel price does not have to be paid."

Kerak matched the Beacon's passion. "There is always a price. I wonder at the price of my decision to remain here."

"Your people are under the guidance of the priests, they are in good hands."

Kerak looked away. "I did not just leave my people. I left my wife as well, the only love I have known to match that for Cynaal."

Belenus shifted uncomfortably. "I've never had a wife but I see the...attraction."

"She is also a mother and none understand sacrifice more intimately. With her blessing I departed—it is her life that sustains my own. A *syla*, a true blessing in the world."

"Syla?" asked Belenus. "I do not know this word."

Kerak turned his gaze to the stream, vision lost in the flowing water. "A returned spirit. She emerged out of the Eternal Forest, returned from the realm of death. I thought her appearance in my life to be a sign from Cynaal, a gift, a treasure."

"Not to be rude but..." Belenus coughed nervously. "Such things do not exist. She is a woman, and I'm sure a fine woman, more than fine, but spirits do not return." The priest shook his head, clasping and unclasping his hands.

The shaman grinned. "Could you even tell the difference between a real woman and a spirit?" He gestured at the priest's groin. "Haven't used that much have you?"

Belenus huffed, eyebrows waggling. "Of course I can! Just because I don't do *that* with women doesn't mean anything is faulty."

"How can you be sure?" Kerak teased.

The men sat in silence. Eventually, they got up and started back along the path leading into the palace. The shackles binding Kerak were released before he entered his room. The Beacon, in his own quarters, was surprised by the presence of a letter on the desk, particularly by the purple seal of Emperor Anathasius.

He read the letter three times before placing it on the desk where the bowl of crushed sleeping tonic used to be. Belenus had dumped the rest of the contents out of the window after the death of the cat.

A certain nervousness was always on the edge of his periphery these days. Belenus thought he was being followed every time he left his room but was unable to prove it. He requested the company of his personal guard more than usual. Whoever was tracking him was doing so quite stealthily. If he even was being followed.

Maybe he was just overreacting from lack of sleep, seeing shadows when there weren't any. The dreams had returned without the blanketing calm of the sleeping tonic, leaving him tired in the morning.

The letter was written in the Emperor's own hand, there was no denying its authenticity. Belenus gulped down the lump in his throat. Change had arrived. He would have to concede to Pompae's ambitions. The temple was going to be built. The hundreds of personalized shrines in Azra were to be taken down. Emperor Anathasius decreed that construction should start immediately after Belenus delivered a speech to Azra explaining the need for the grandiose project.

The room felt stifling. He needed to go for a walk to consider the new development. Belenus left his room, glancing back once to see if the letter was actually there or if he had imagined it.

Kronus Pompae was strutting down the hall with his own letter in hand. He wore the red robe as an exhibition of his victory. Pompae waved the letter as he approached. "I assume you received your own version?"

There was no use fighting. Belenus could refuse the orders of Pompae but he could not deny the Emperor. He was the voice of Emperor Anathasius to the people and must fulfill his duty.

"When?" asked Belenus.

A smug sneer was etched onto Pompae's narrow face. "I've arranged for an official ceremony tomorrow on the Ascending Stairs."

Belenus nodded and continued past Pompae, who seemed confused by the absence of an angry response. Pompae hurried to catch up to Belenus.

"This is in the best interest of the Empire," said Pompae. "We will achieve an unprecedented level of unity."

"I suppose so." *But at what price?*

Pompae was thrown off by the subdued behavior of his fellow priest and turned down the first available hall. Belenus continued alone, his mind a jumble of disjointed pieces that seemed incapable of fitting together. He made his way to the main floor of the palace, stopping in front of the wide doors depicting the Emperor's victory over the Steward. Belenus used both hands to pull on the handle of a single heavy door. The scent of a forest greeted him.

He strolled through the rows of ironwoods, carefully inspecting each tree he passed. They appeared to be as healthy as the last time he had seen them and showed no sign of disease even with the Emperor's absence from the palace. The great sun disk set into the wall provided a steady glow as did the far-reaching rays arching overhead.

After Emperor Anathasius had withdrawn his protection from a single tree Kerak had asked if the trees ever bloomed. The more Belenus thought about it the more certain he was that he had never seen the trees flower and produce seeds. Belenus stopped when he found a half crumbled trunk. The tree's collapse had been averted when the Emperor restored his protection but it was clear that the tree would never regain its former health. Belenus looked into the broken gaps in the canopy created by the diseased branches that had snapped off, wondering if the absence of death equated to the gift of life.

The sky was sullen, filled with chunky clouds seeming more solid than they ought to be, as if they were made of clay. A cold wind had wrapped one of the flags around the pole to the left of the Ascending Stairs. A large crowd congregated in the square despite the dismal weather. They came to hear the Beacon of Azra speak, anxious for news about the campaign in Calanthia. Rumors abounded, as always, but they trusted Belenus Wicket to tell them the truth. Each and every individual standing in the square, huddled together against the cold, believed in their hearts that the vision of the Emperor, their God, flowed out of the Beacon.

Belenus ardently loved the people of Azra and so he hid the pain felt in his heart. He could not let them see the sorrow filling him up as each word left his body. His voice was clear as the air after a spring rain, when the greenery is reflected by innumerable delicate raindrops.

"I ask you to acknowledge moments of wrongdoings in your life, instances in which you later felt remorse," Belenus called from the podium.

The crowd below Belenus gave a steady golden glow punctuated by red pulses around the outlines of individuals. This was the strongest connection to the Emperor's Gift to date. Belenus felt as though he were an aqueduct evenly distributing the Gift to the thirsty multitude. He felt the energy synthesize with the air in his stomach, becoming refined as it sped along his veins to burst from razor slices in his hands. His voice directed the new form, coursing down the strings connecting Belenus to the crowd.

"These were moments of Darkness, the most subversive force in our lives, one that is attached to our beings from before birth. Darkness aims to pull each and every one of us down into an early death. This sensation can overwhelm a person, forcing them to commit wrongful actions as it gains hold and finally takes over completely. Darkness turns a human into a demon; an insatiable being who is compelled to destroy even at their own peril."

The crowd gasped. None wanted to believe themselves capable of turning into a demon.

Belenus belted out his oration to the far reaches of the crowd. "There is but one way to remove this Darkness from within and that is through rightful actions laid down in the Binding Doctrine. We must strive towards turning the Emperor's vision into a reality so that Darkness may be removed from all aspects to reveal the Illuminated Path of eternal salvation. You have all done well to build the foundation of faith but now is the time to take the next step." Belenus paused, making his voice transfer the strength of his certainty. "Darkness is on the run. For the first time in existence, it is possible to vanquish our eternal adversary. We may win this struggle but first we must change—changes that will make all the difference. We must organize our faith to keep steady. We must keep the pressure on this most menacing of foes, for Darkness is cunning and will try to divide us in moments of weakness. Unity of body and faith is needed to keep us strong as a community. To make us impregnable."

Red pulses flared amongst the golden crowd as the people avidly listened to the Beacon. Voices cried out in desperation. "How will we do this?" Others shouted with tears streaming from their eyes. "Tell us, Beacon!"

And so Belenus described the system of organized faith proposed by Kronus Pompae. He spoke of how the strength of the temple's stone walls was the strength of their hearts, of how the spires reaching into the sky were a testament to the reaches of their faith. Belenus assured the people that attending regular sermons would protect them against Darkness, like a shield deflecting incoming arrows. He emphasized how his fellow priests would become shepherds to keep the flock together. Lastly, he described how selecting individuals to enter the priesthood and the Chosen would create unshakeable pillars that would elevate their foundation of faith to the heights they had always known was destined for the Shining Empire.

"Darkness infiltrates during moments of weakness to expand like an unnatural growth," Belenus cautioned. "I ask you to trust in the wisdom of the priests who will lead the upcoming sermons. I ask you to heed the teachings of the Binding Doctrine, to be attentive to feelings of separateness that may arise within. Triumph will be found in unity, we must become one in the mode of our faith. Have faith that those selected to enter the priesthood and the Chosen will be fulfilling a vital responsibility to the vision of Emperor Anathasius."

Belenus would have said more but at that moment he was struck by an overwhelming disorientation. The crowd of gold and red spun before his eyes. His vision became unfocused. He was still drawing on the Emperor's Gift: the sensation of power even seemed to be increasing. Belenus knew that the energy would overflow the edges of the vessel he had turned himself into if he were to continue. His body felt weightless except for a sensation of intense gravity in his core pulling downward. The disparate forces inside of the Beacon's body were threatening to tear him apart at the seams. He was losing control of the Gift. He clung on with desperate fingernails, lest he float away into the ether or plummet into an abyss.

The crowd did not notice his distress, instead taking his silence for the conclusion of the speech. They cheered madly with many openly weeping in joy. Belenus gripped the podium with hands that had gone ice cold. The strings of energy binding him to the crowd were still attached, allowing the Emperor's Gift to flow through Belenus. He brought his mind round to his breathing, using every bit of his meticulously trained focus to sever the strings.

The Gift showed no signs of abating but its hold on Belenus waned as he cut the strings, leaving them to drop away and disintegrate. The crowd cheered, exuberant in the future triumph foretold by their Beacon.

Belenus felt a presence behind him that made the hairs on the back of his neck rise. The ominous size of the presence chilled him to the bone. He wanted to run, but knew he must look to see who stood in his shadow. Belenus half turned to stare at the black surface of the Skar. His jaw dropped as the entire mountain pulsed toward him as though aware of his recognition. The priest was struck with a fear that went beyond understanding—a sublime aura of his smallness in the face of supreme power. Belenus had never felt so alone in all his life. He wanted to shrivel into nothing and disappear. A figure in crimson strode past to address the crowd.

The crowd cheered for Kronus Pompae who shushed them with a raised hand. "Azra! Construction starts tomorrow. Come, witness the birth of your victory!" He spoke as though unaware of Belenus.

Belenus wanted to rage against the man standing only a meter in front of him but as the disorientation faded he was overcome with fatigue. Pompae descended down the ancient stairs and the crowd parted to create a clear path out of the square.

Belenus watched as the people followed Pompae down the wide street, leaving him alone atop the Ascending Stairs, still gripping the podium. The gold and red of the crowd dissipated, making colors seem bleaker than the dullness of the soggy clouds. Belenus could not muster up the courage to look at the mountain again, so he slowly walked down the stairs and followed the stragglers.

A profound sense of emptiness swirled inside of him, moving about in a way that was much more disturbing than any hollowness. Belenus tried to ignore this inner movement but his mind raced in excitement from the stimulation. The Beacon had trained for decades to attune his awareness to the tiniest fluctuations of his body and the reinforced habits would not abate despite his desire for peace. Belenus felt as though his mind was filled with brambles and he could not avoid the thorny branches. The shaman's theory about exchange cropped up in his mind, sticking in place like a bur as he sat on a bench just outside of the square for a moment's rest.

A cloaked figure approached, hunching over in front of the bench. "Beacon," rasped a voice from inside the shadow of the hood. "I must speak with you."

Gern and Ryndell stepped forward with swords in hand. The man turned to run but Ryndell caught him, tossing him to the ground.

"Enough," Belenus commanded. "Who are you?"

The man trembled. "We had lunch once after I helped you out of the water."

"Take off your hood so that I might recognize you."

"Not here." The man looked over his shoulder. "Somewhere more private."

The evasive behavior was making Belenus wary of this man's intentions, bringing to mind the feeling of being followed. He suspected his movements were being monitored for weeks now but could not find evidence to prove his suspicions. Perhaps this was the proof. The man saw the Beacon's apprehension.

"Please, I need your help," the man pleaded.

Belenus was naturally inclined to aid those in need, but the situation did not sit right with him. "Your name."

The man trembled. "I was a priest trained at the Sanctuary. My name is Arnul Aderat. I wish you no harm. Please, you must help. I don't know where else to go."

"Gern, Ryndell, please escort this man to that alleyway off the main street."

Belenus doubted that anyone would be brazen enough to kill the Beacon in broad daylight. This man seemed more like the hunted than the hunter. The guards led Aderat around a small shed in the alley.

"I must show you the truth," said the man, coughing after he spoke. The cough shook his body.

"What truth?"

The man removed the hood, causing Belenus to gasp and slam into the shed as he backed away. Gern and Ryndell stepped in front to protect the Beacon.

The young priest was indeed Arnul Aderat. He was covered in splotchy pink sores that looked to be eating away at his skin. His hair, what was left of it, grew in thin patches. Worst was a vicious burn stretching from Arnul's chin across his neck. The burn looked to be recent, charred skin still flaked from the swollen protrusion.

"Light protect us. What happened?" Belenus stared in disbelief at the state of the young priest.

"It's false, all false," said the young priest with tears welling in his eyes—eyes that looked more weary than Belenus felt. "This has happened to me because of the Emperor's Gift. At first I thought I'd done something wrong, but how could I if this is what I was trained to do at the Sanctuary?" There was a sorrowful rage in Arnul's tone as he raised his arms to display his hands. "And they call it a Gift."

Arnul's hands were covered in cuts identical to those Belenus had inflicted on himself prior to making his speech that morning except these made by the young priest were crusted over with thick black scabs. Thin red veins crisscrossed the scabs like spiderwebs. Belenus saw that the sores were not only confined to Arnul's face and neck but were on his hands and arms as well. He was willing to guess that the sores extended to the unfortunate priest's entire body.

"They tried to silence me," said Arnul, pointing to the burn mark on his neck. "But I escaped. They're following me—they'll kill me."

"Who will, son?"

"Pompae's men from the estate. It's spreading there and they don't want anyone to know."

Arnul started coughing again, this time quite violently, using the sleeve of his cloak to cover his mouth. The sleeve was covered in flecks of blood when he pulled it away.

"Why would the Sanctuary lie?" Arnul's eyes were bloodshot from coughing, his expression becoming more unhinged. "They lied to me, they used me." He stepped closer to Belenus. The Beacon tried to retreat but was only able to press harder against the wall of the shed.

"Why!?" The force of the shout ripped a sore on Arnul's cheek, causing a pink liquid to ooze out.

Belenus froze, fearing that any movement would make the other priest attack him.

"Beacon," said Gern. "We must leave."

The sores seemed to pulse on the young priests skin, Belenus could practically see them getting larger. Footsteps in the street near the mouth of the alleyway made Arnul pause. He crouched and hid. Several men held a brief exchange before moving on.

Arnul started coughing again, this time with blood gushing out his mouth. Belenus jumped out of the way to avoid the spray. Arnul crumpled to the ground. The young priest coughed and spasmed, becoming covered in his own blood. More sores opened up and pink pus seeped out of them, settling on top of the darker blood like a film.

Gern and Ryndell picked Belenus up, one under each arm, and hurried out of the alleyway. They carried him at a brisk jog until people started to look at them oddly. Ryndell flagged down a rickshaw.

"To the palace," Belenus gasped.

Gern climbed in beside Belenus. The spindly rickshaw driver bent to his task, the wheels creaking under the weight. Ryndell was close behind in his own rickshaw.

"Light protect me," Gern whispered.

Belenus inspected his clothing for any signs of Aderat's blood, his heart skipping a beat at the sight of dull red on his right forearm. He used his left hand to brush the red off but the effort was futile. Belenus scrubbed harder in panic—he did not want any of the foulness on himself.

Belenus stopped scratching at his arm when he realized why the red could not be removed. The swirls of the faded tattoo twisted around his forearm as they had for almost forty years now. The Beacon chuckled at his foolishness, thinking clearly for the first time since feeling disoriented on the Ascending Stairs.

He recalled having eaten with Arnul, remembering him as a quiet lad fresh out of the Sanctuary. The boy had mentioned he was going to an estate but had not said which. Arnul now claimed to come from the Pompae estate. Belenus was not surprised that nefarious acts would be committed in the place that produced Kronus.

The Pompaes owned most of the land to the east of Azra, separating the Eternal Forest and the southern desert of the Outskirts. More priests were sent to that area than any other in the Shining Empire, which Belenus always considered to be a result of the extreme wealth of the Pompaes and the maintenance their vast territory required.

Arnul was terrified, convinced that he was being pursued by men from the estate. Luckily for Belenus, there was a Pompae in Azra for questioning, which in Belenus' estimate was the first time Kronus had ever been useful.

The rickshaw driver huffed in exertion, digging low to pull Belenus and Gern up the hill to the palace. He brought them to the main square in front of the palace, stopping at the edge of the intricately arranged tiles as if they were a barrier he should not cross.

"I'll arrange for your payment," said Belenus.

"No payment," mumbled the rickshaw driver, his head bowed.

"Don't be absurd, of course you will be paid."

The wiry man spun his cart and took off down the hill without another word, leaving Belenus to watch in disbelief. There was nothing to be done to rectify the situation so Belenus hustled into the palace. He delayed going directly to Pompae's room on the top floor. There was someone else he needed to talk to first. The priest traveled down the hall, removing a single key from his pocket to unlock the door to Kerak's room. The room was no longer guarded, on his orders. He almost trusted the shaman.

Belenus turned to Gern and Ryndell. "No one enters this room," he said. "If they even try to enter this hall you turn them around."

The shaman sat on the floor, his back to Belenus and his face to the small open window. Belenus hurried to stand in front of the shaman, leaving the door ajar.

"You've seen the sickness?"

"Yes." Kerak raised an eyebrow at the Beacon's anxiety.

"What did it look like?"

Kerak thought this over for a moment. "A pox that covers all that it touches in sores."

Belenus slumped to the floor beside Kerak. "That's it," Belenus said blandly, his hands limp in his lap. "It's here, it's real."

Kerak leaned forward intently. "You've seen it?"

"Half an hour ago. The boy died—poor lad coughed up enough blood to drown in."

"This is bad," Kerak said gravely.

"Don't suppose Cynaal has anything to say about this?" Belenus asked, half hopeful, half sarcastic.

Kerak shook his head, long hair hanging down past his shoulders to rest against his chest. "Cynaal withholds guidance. We are on our own. That is my punishment."

"I know someone who needs punishment and I'm the one to give it." Belenus moved to the door but was blocked by Kerak, who placed both hands on the priest to stop him.

"Don't do anything rash, it's not safe here anymore."

"I know, I've had someone following me for some time now. I'll stop this before it is able to go any further—we'll talk later." He left the shaman, going in search of the palace attendant.

Belenus found Hector, or maybe Hector found him. The attendant had an uncanny knack for knowing when to make himself useful.

"Beacon Wicket, how may I be of service?'

"Is the hot pepper upstairs?"

Hector smiled. "He is rather thin and pointy, isn't he? And no, he just arrived but he is not in his chambers. He's in the grand conclave with a few guests."

"Anyone important?"

"Two men from Azra's building teams, a foreman and architect I think, and the other three are unknown to me."

Belenus thanked the attendant and made his way to the grand conclave. Pompae was always hosting in this room, using it as if it were his own private suite. Belenus barged past the guards, flinging the doors open as he stormed in, Gern and Ryndell at his heels.

Six men reclined on comfortable furniture, casually drinking liquor from crystal glasses. Three rough looking men sat on a long couch, two men dressed in the high fashion common to Azra were on wide chairs, and Pompae was seated in the center in a crimson robe. Pompae's thin lips curled in an amused sneer at the unexpected arrival of the Beacon.

"We have matters to discuss," Belenus said firmly. "Your friends can stay if you like but I don't think you'll want them to hear what I have to say."

Pompae studied Belenus. He looked about to ignore Belenus' advice, glanced at the Beacon's personal guard, and must have thought better of it. "I apologize for this intrusion. Please let my comrade and I speak in private. He's like a dog with a bone when he gets worked up about something."

The men on the couch chuckled and downed the rest of the alcohol before setting the empty glasses on a side table. The architect and foreman looked uncomfortable.

"Go," Pompae said, placating their worry. "We will finish our discussion soon."

Belenus started talking before the men were even out of the room. "I have not set foot in the Sanctuary for years, and now I think this absence has been my greatest failing as Beacon, because it has allowed you to have free rein over the instruction of the Emperor's Gift. What is happening at the Sanctuary? What malevolent methods are being used to shape the vessels of the Shining Empire?"

Pompae crossed a leg and took another sip. "I am simply doing my duty. The Empire is expanding and priests are needed to aid in this progress, so I make sure that they will be able to perform what is required of them."

"I doubt the methods are the same as when you or I attended."

"Undoubtedly, and for the better. It's called *innovation,* my daft friend. Less preparation is needed these days, the vessels are able to advance from untrained youths to full fledged priests in half the time it took you. Only a matter of time until the process is completely perfected," Pompae said smugly.

"Are you the person responsible for these *innovations*?"

Pompae raised his glass in a self toast. "I am just the man and I think it's safe to say that Emperor Anathasius has rewarded my success, don't you?" Pompae leaned back in his chair, casting his gaze around the opulent room. "I've passed you by, old man, you're stuck in your ways."

Belenus let his rival gloat for a moment. "So I suppose Emperor Anathasius also knows that these methods of yours cause vessels to become infected with weeping sores."

Pompae's sharp eyes narrowed. "What are you playing at, Wicket?"

"A fellow priest came to me today, he was in such a state, and claimed his ill health was an effect of the Emperor's Gift."

"You're lying."

"He was a nice young man. You may know him, as he was sent to your father's estate, as are a great number of priests, now that I think of it."

Pompae's face hardened. He gripped the crystal cup tighter. "What are you implying?"

Belenus shrugged, appearing nonchalant. "This poor boy vomited up blood until he died and the sores covering his body looked mightily infectious. Now, neither of those things fall under my interpretation of perfection and if they are then I will thankfully change my error-filled ways. By the boy's testimony, it was the methods of enacting the Emperor's Gift, the training he received at the Sanctuary, methods that you just boasted of inventing, which ultimately caused his gruesome death. This development makes me wonder how many other young priests on the Pompae estate have met a similar end. I would think it remiss of me to withhold a proper investigation into this matter."

"If," he stressed the word as though it were a Tenet of Faith from the Binding Doctrine, "what you are saying is true, this is the first I've heard of it."

Belenus dropped the casual tone, making sure to convey the severity of the situation. "I haven't mentioned the most curious aspect yet. The boy mentioned that this unfortunate infection of his was spreading, which in some cases is not so dangerous of a word, but I fear this is not one of those cases. This infection, or sickness as some call it, was brought about through an improper use of the Emperor's Gift, which would make his actions an impure ritual. The Binding Doctrine states that impure rituals bring Darkness into the world—now this is where the act of spreading becomes most worrying—this impure ritual was taught within the Sanctuary and enacted on your own estate. Kronus Pompae you stand accused of being an agent of Darkness."

Pompae sat stone still, staring straight through Belenus. The crystal in Pompae's hand suddenly burst from the pressure of his grip, surprising Belenus who raised a hand to cover his face and stumble backward. Pompae moved to standing, his right hand covered in jagged shards, dripping a mixture of alcohol and blood.

Gern and Ryndell moved to subdue Pompae but stopped suddenly, swords dropping from rigid fingers. Pompae called for his three comrades.

"Kill them," Pompae said, gesturing at the Beacon's personal guard. "Suffocation should do nicely, would be a pity to stain this fine room by spilling blood."

Belenus was dumbfounded, shocked into inaction. Pompae's undivided attention was on the Beacon, staring at the older priest like a wolf creeping close to an aging bull trapped in a deep snow drift.

He felt a tug at his heels, almost like a hand pulling him down. He struggled to straighten his stance as the constriction moved up to his waist. The scent of the air changed to one that Belenus intimately recognized. His eyes flashed to the blood dripping from Pompae's hand—he was using the Emperor's Gift. Belenus was numb from the waist down but his arms still worked so he flicked the razor blade from the inside pocket of his sleeve into his hand. The constriction of his body sped up to stop him from cutting into his skin to draw blood. The blade dropped from the Beacon's numb fingers.

Gern collapsed to the ground; Ryndell a moment later.

"What are you going to do? Make me become so filled with the glory of the Emperor's vision that I weep big salty tears while you escape?" Pompae taunted. "You are pitiful." He walked a slow circle around Belenus. "I am creating perfect vessels. So what if their lives are shortened because of it? The priests are precious tools designed by the Shining Empire. Their lives were forfeit to this cause from the moment they came screaming into the world. Those with power decide how tools are to be used. This is the natural order of humanity."

Belenus was completely paralyzed, all he could do was follow Pompae with his eyes until the crimson robe went beyond his vision and then wait for it to emerge on the other side.

"I am doing what I was told to do. Your usefulness has come to an end."

A crushing weight in the small of his back forced Belenus to his knees. The force traveled between his shoulder blades to push him flat against the floor. Belenus found it hard to breathe with the weight sitting on top of him.

"Pick him up," Pompae commanded.

The three men hoisted Belenus up between them. Pompae led them out of the room and the men followed with the Beacon in tow. Belenus felt his joints straining from the forced rigidity, his knee screaming in pain but the pressure on his throat stifled the outcry. Worse than the squeezing pressure inflicted by Pompae's ritual was the spirit crushing effect of being completely silenced. All of the training and passion required of Azra's Beacon was rendered heartbreakingly inadequate.

Belenus had been the Emperor's voice as well as the voice of the people for so long that he considered the core himself to be the vibrations produced inside of his body. No vibrations issued now; they were gnats flittering against the suppression of a descending wall. Belenus fought to resist but it was an impotent effort.

He was unceremoniously dropped on a hard floor. Belenus knew the location by the smell. The creak of the gate swinging shut punctuated his despair. Belenus looked around the dark confines, listening to the scurry of rats in the gloom. He found no humor in noting the parallel circumstances that brought Belenus to reside in the same dungeon cell that had once housed Kerak, shaman of the Frozen Tribes.

## Forever Boy

Nothing could catch him, he was a cat on the prowl, a bird on the wing, the wind through the leaves. The Forever Boy scrambled across rooftops still slick from the rain that morning. The air was humid and the sky overcast, harbingers of more rain to come.

He scrambled down a drainpipe, skipped across a brick wall, and hit the ground running. Time was of the essence. He could not be late. This meeting was important. He had given his word and if a hero broke their word, then what good were they?

Red robes on the street, more and more of them recently. Not sure what to make of them and their loud mouths.

"Be saved from Darkness!" they would shout. "Do not stray from the Illuminated Path! Find your salvation here!"

Bullies. He saw how they scared the people into attending their speeches, how they made the elderly tremble and the young cry. The Forever Boy had given one of them a good whack across the rump with his sword the other day. The red robe had made a little girl cry by telling her she should be ashamed for not attending temple service. The girl had giggled at the smack, gone were her bubbling tears.

He'd shouted, "Make me cry, I dare you to try!"

The red robe gave chase, but was much too fat to keep up for long. A great many of them occupied the streets, too many for the Forever Boy to spank them all, but he did what he could, helped where he may.

Everyone was where they decided to be. One way or another, a person chose to accept where they were, or moved on. Every decision made in one's life led to the exact moment of the present, transferring the momentum of past choices along with it.

Many became bogged down by indecision, eventually filling with regret over situations that never took place. There was a time when he accepted the sad state of his then current situation, unwilling to make another decision because of a great failure. He was different then. The Forever Boy was not pained by doubt or racked with guilt. He was chivalrous, pure in his actions, and steadfast in his beliefs.

He raced up a set of stairs to a pair of doors beneath faded letters. Inside, the orphanage was falling to pieces, stripped of anything of value years before. Scorch marks on the floor from cook fires had been left behind by vagrants who had lived in the husk of a building at one time. The Forever Boy drew his wooden sword at the bustle of movement.

"Appear, thy bringer of fear!"

A large rat scurried out of a hole in the floor, twitching its whiskers before disappearing into a gap in the wall. The orphanage was now only of use to ghosts, vermin, and those who wanted to conduct themselves outside of public scrutiny. The Forever Boy swished his sword as he walked, imagining that he battled a monstrous rat.

"I shall sheath those teeth! There will be applause when you lose those claws!"

He slashed across the room, stopping with the sword upraised, a plump moth balanced on the tip, wide antennae twitching like leafless branches. Moths were creatures of darkness obsessed with light, creatures of the moon unable to resist chasing after the sun. A happy old man stood in the gloom.

"Dreamer, your face never ages, stuck forever in the final stages."

The old man gave a toothless chuckle. "Oh yes, old as the hills I am, but I'm just as spritely as you are, young man."

"Forever a boy, never a man, doing only what a child can."

Dreamer raised a hand in defense. "My mistake Mr. Boy,"

A stray moth fluttered around Dreamer's head, appearing confused as it looked for a place to land. The old man opened his mouth wide and the insect flew right in. "Now then, what's to be done about these developments?"

The boy grimaced in concentration. "Fight on, until all the evil doers are gone." He slashed aggressively with the sword to emphasize his point.

"Yes, yes, the time of transition nears and he has still not appeared," said Dreamer.

"Wait, wait, until he takes the bait. Keep fishing and wishing so that lovers can keep kissing until he comes sniffing."

"Then it's agreed. Stay the course until the end, whatever that may be."

"If only the end could be seen, a gleam in a dream, flashes in a stream."

Dreamer stomped his heel on the floorboards as he sang. "The long road home trapped in stone, spilled blood brings on the flood, to learn the truth is to see the end and bring this ravaged world to mend."

The Forever Boy's face turned serious, the hardness in his eyes well beyond his youthful experience. "The gift of breath has been used for death, improper teaching and twisted preaching, four gods who are four frauds."

An echo of flapping wings filled the room as Dreamer opened his mouth wide. A swarm of moths streamed out of his mouth, dispersing into the room. The moths spiraled around him, fluttering faster until he was completely encased. The Forever Boy raised his wooden sword in salute as the swarm flew single file through a hole in the wall, leaving the Forever Boy alone with the rats and the ghosts.

The Forever Boy exited the rundown orphanage with his head hung low, eyes on his feet. Pathways continually appear and one must choose; one can only look back with clarity. Look back for guidance when deciding how to move forward.

## Fugitives

Belenus wanted to cry, to add his tears to the river of shame flowing from his actions. He had offered his poor lambs up to wolves, guided the flock right into the gaping jaws. The guilt was devastating. He sat slumped in the gloom, staring into the nothingness in front of him as memories floated by, each failure mocking his faith. Pompae now had complete control of the city and would bend the people to fit his system.

"I was wrong. Despair does suit you, Beacon." Kerak's voice. It was only fitting that the shaman should mock him as well. "I've never seen a man as wretched as you," said the shaman.

"Go away, demon," Belenus whimpered. "Leave me with my misery."

"I would like to, but you made the effort many times to visit when it was I who sat in this forlorn place."

"That was likely the only good thing I ever did and yet I still must be haunted by it! Leave me be, but know that I am sorry for your involvement in this as the real Kerak is surely dead by now, even though it was the stubborn prick's own fault."

The ghost of Kerak laughed softly in the darkness. "My leaving depends on your answers to these questions, answer them truthfully, from your heart, and then I will go."

"I don't like dead Kerak, much chattier than when he was alive," Belenus muttered.

"Do you recall the pool of water you described to me? The life giving power made available by the Emperor's Gift? Where did this water come from, or more precisely, how did it come to be atop the mountain?" The shaman's voice was so clear that Belenus almost believed Kerak sat beside him in the dark.

He humored the ghost with an explanation. "It's an allegory. There's no actual mountain with a miraculous source of water. The reservoir of energy was always there, probably since the moment of Rua's creation. It is constantly diminishing, along with the state of our world, the fate of the two are permanently intertwined. Emperor Anathasius made this connection known so that we might reverse the disintegration and save ourselves."

Belenus tasted bile in his throat, it was a bitter, darker than the lightless cell.

"Cynaal has called to me," there was excitement in the ghost's voice. "I hear whispers of this power you speak of, details that are not usually shared unless the need is extraordinary."

Belenus thought Kerak was overly chipper for a dead man. He attributed this elation to the shaman's proximity to the song of his ancestors achieved through death.

The shaman spoke in a hushed tone that barely reached Belenus. "Cynaal says water only stagnates when it is removed from the flowing stream and to think well on the source of all arisings. What say you, Beacon?"

A feeling of moisture settled on Belenus' skin, the coolness of the liquid soaking through the blanket of despair swaddling him. The glowing orb beneath the waves from his dream flashed in his mind's eye and then disappeared in an ocean spray. He could smell salt water in the dry cell. A powerful thirst grabbed hold of him, much like the day he dove into the Gateway Gulf in an attempt to cool himself.

A solid string stretched taught before Belenus, one that he was scared to pluck because from it would issue an unknown vibration. An aspect of the lessons he'd been taught so many years ago crystallized inside his chest, hardening from theory into reality.

"It exists. Cynaal knows of the source," said Belenus.

"Would you care to go find it?" asked Kerak's ghost.

"Don't tease me, phantom."

The ghost would not be deterred. "You and I could discover the truth that may yet save this world."

Belenus shook his head sadly. "My broken-down spirit cannot take anymore truths—it's known too many and all have turned to ash in my mouth."

"Then I must quest alone," said Kerak's ghost.

A sharp ping of metal on metal sounded from directly in front of Belenus. The blackness moved like a raincloud against a starless sky. Belenus squinted at the shifting form, his focus startled as a small object landed in his lap. He gripped the iron key in a sweaty palm.

"I leave you with a means for escape, which is more than you gave me," said the ghost.

"But how?"

"Some might call it theft, but I prefer to call it intuition. I had a feeling you would not be coming back to see me, so I took the key off you the last time we spoke. This key here is compliments of the jailor who is sleeping comfortably near the entrance."

"You're not dead," Belenus said flatly.

"I am not, and neither are you," Kerak said lightly. "If we want to remain that way, then we must leave now."

"I can't leave the city to Pompae," said Belenus firmly. "He will twist it into his own selfish designs."

"There is no stopping that now, but the damage may be undone if we accomplish this task."

Belenus gripped the key, feeling the teeth dig into his palm. "He is a monster, he can't be allowed to continue, I will—"

"You will what?" Kerak snapped. "What more can you do? At the moment your enemy has the advantage and will snuff you out sooner rather than later. All that can be done now is to endure so that you may return to tilt the outcome in your favor. Consider why I chose to leave the Tribes before we were defeated. There is more at stake here than the lives of your people and mine."

The priest's despondency reached a new low at the shaman's affirmation of Pompae's victory. The effort required to lift himself off the floor was akin to raising a boulder over his head and the weight did not leave him as he walked over to the bars, knees cracking with each step. He reached through the bars to fit the key into the lock and swung the door open, but was hesitant to step out into the corridor. The decision to persevere through the grief was only one step away into the chasm blackness. An unforeseen future was waiting to meet him.

"How do I know you're actually alive, and I'm not imagining all of this?"

A phantom hand smacked Belenus in the face, cracking his teeth together.

"I believe it. You're the only man alive with fingers cold as a corpse."

"I've wanted to do that for some time."

Belenus could hear the smile in Kerak's voice and he chuckled despite his dour mood. "I'd smack you back if I could see you."

Kerak's hand reached out again, gently this time, to tap against the priest's shoulder. Belenus clasped the strangely cool skin in a firm grip and Kerak pulled him out of the cell.

"Consider the favor repaid," Kerak said solemnly.

"Where did we go wrong that each of us needed to rescue the other from the same dungeon?"

The two men hustled past the unconscious jailor and guards, pausing at the stairway to their freedom. Kerak led the way, several crow feathers swinging from the staff strapped across his back.

Belenus took a sword from one of the guards and handed it to Kerak, he then grabbed a torch from the wall and pulled Kerak down the staircase, deeper into the bowels of the Palace of Light. They stopped before the secret entrance used by Sixthrok when he had taken Belenus hostage and broken into the palace. Belenus had ordered the entry to be sealed off to prevent any further intrusions and the new stones stood out starkly against the aged originals.

Belenus motioned to the seals between the new stones, sloppily adhered with mortar. "This is how your boy got in. Pry a few loose with the sword and we'll taste sunlight."

Kerak set to work, using the tip of the blade to dig at the crevices between the old stones and the new; the rushed craftsmanship of the palace guard was nothing compared to the seamless work of the original builders of the wall. Sweat poured down the shaman's face as he labored, eventually chipping away enough to cut grooves into seams.

Dust hung in the still air which Belenus cleared away by waving the torch to get a better view of Kerak's progress. Belenus was distraught, at this pace they would need a week to cut their way out. Kerak stopped his efforts and produced a water skin. Belenus thought the water was intended to wash the dust out of the shaman's throat, but instead Kerak poured the liquid into the grooves he had dug.

"Step back Beacon, you will not want to be in this confined space, it is about to get very cold."

Belenus watched Kerak use the sword to make an incision across his palm. A puff of frosty air was released by the shaman's exhale. The air within the alcove changed, tingling against the priest's skin like the first snowfall of the season. Belenus stepped into the relative safety of the stairway. The sense of cold escalated, rattling the priest's teeth. Belenus rubbed his shoulders as his breath steamed in the empty stairway. Without warning, the coldness evaporated. A tired Kerak beckoned Belenus to return.

The wall was now covered in a thin layer of pale blue ice. Belenus ran his hand over the surface, marveling at the abilities of his comrade.

"Impressive, but why?"

"Water expands when it becomes ice," said Kerak. "The wall has been made brittle by the pressure of the ice pushing against it from inside."

Belenus set the torch into a sconce, guessing what was required. Kerak stepped to the wall, pausing momentarily before smashing his shoulder into the ice.

"I wish I was younger," Belenus muttered before adding his weight to that of Kerak's.

They threw themselves against the stones again and again, each impact promising to break Belenus before the wall. After the fifth attempt there was a series of resounding cracks that spiderwebbed their way through the interior of the wall. Kerak stopped Belenus, who promptly sat down in exhaustion. The shaman used the butt of his staff to experimentally tap certain sections of the wall. Several swift strikes with the staff to key points of weakness created more cracks. Kerak threw himself against the wall once more, bringing a third of the new stones down with the impact.

"You brilliant bastard," said Belenus, astonished by the shafts of sunlight filtering in through the opening. "Help me up."

The men pushed aside loose stones and stepped into the fresh air, taking a moment to bask in their accomplishment. They were free of the palace but leaving the city would be an even more difficult endeavor.

"We need supplies," said Belenus. "You might be able to survive in the wilderness with nothing but twigs and dew but I cannot."

"Entering the city is too dangerous."

"How do you propose we make it past the guards at the gates? They'll recognize me even if I change my clothes and I'm sure that Pompae has wasted no time is alerting the city of my disgrace."

"What then?"

Belenus started down the hill, retracing the route he had taken bound and gagged by Sixthrok. "Come, I have a plan. Pompae may have outwitted me but he will not have accounted for the cleverness of the other Wicket."

They made their way carefully towards the city, taking a longer, less traveled route that brought them within the vicinity of Stone Park. The skulking around reminded Belenus of playing hide and seek with imaginary friends as a boy, except that the danger of being discovered was far too real this time. A small boy burst out of an alley, dirt smeared across his chubby cheeks. He did not look at Belenus or Kerak but withdrew a short wooden sword and jogged away down the path Belenus intended to go.

"Have no fear, my sword will keep the path clear!" proclaimed the boy in a regal voice.

The boy rushed ahead and was soon out of sight. Belenus continued in the same direction as the boy, pausing when he heard shouting.

"Get back here, you brat!"

"Stop that thief!"

Belenus saw the boy sprint down a side street being pursued by two of the city guard. Kerak looked to Belenus questioningly and the priest shrugged. They continued along the back streets of Azra until finally arriving at the business Belenus had rejected as a boy. A place he now hoped would be his haven. The shop looked as deserted as the last time Belenus visited but the door was unlocked and a light was on in the back room. They crept in quietly, startling Mariam who was hunched over a stack of papers.

"Beacon! You look terrible."

"Worse than you could imagine," said Belenus. "I need your help, Mariam, I need you to bring Barroc here."

Mariam stood, smoothing the hair along her ears, her eyes bright with alarm. "What is it?"

"I'm afraid I can't say, but it is imperative that I speak with Barroc."

Mariam's eyes flicked to Kerak, who stood silently in the shadow of the doorway.

"He's a friend," said Belenus. "Please Mariam, do this for me, and speak to no one but my brother. We must act before it is too late."

The questions were visible in Mariam's expression, but she kept them unvoiced, instead giving a slight nod of the head before exiting the shop. Belenus and Kerak sat at the desk, waiting in silence for Barroc's arrival.

The creak of the door came sooner than Belenus expected as Barroc stormed into the room, his face smeared with sweat and ash. "What is it? What's happened?" His dark eyes scanned the room, locking on Kerak. "I know who that is. What have you bungled this time, brother?"

"We are in mortal danger, Kronus Pompae is acting against the Emperor. We will be dead before the night is out if we do not escape Azra."

Barroc observed the shabbiness of the priestly robes, sensing the weariness of the man wearing them. "Priests killing priests," he mumbled.

Belenus raised his hands in defeat. "I spoke honestly as I always do but the priesthood and the palace are no longer safe places for truth. Kerak and I must leave so that our voices cannot be silenced."

Mariam emerged carrying clean clothes for Belenus. "We don't have any robes but these should fit you."

"Thank you."

Belenus shrugged out of the soiled robes and put on a blue tunic and canary yellow trousers.

Barroc's face was stern. "You get yourself into this mess, then come running to me so that I can clean it up?"

"You're all I have. Everything else has been taken from me."

Barroc grunted and sat on the last remaining chair to look at Belenus and Kerak. Mariam stood in the doorway, hands at her chest, nervously looking around the room.

"There might be a way to get you out," said Barroc. "I made a little side deal with a Nefaran trader moored off shore; the dark skinned sing-songers have been buying up weapons and iron for months now. I'd be hanged if word got out so everything is hush-hush. The delivery is set for tonight. I and two others are to row out to the ship under the cover of darkness. I could replace my men with you two and barter for your passage on the ship."

Nefara, the deep south of Rua, a land of impenetrable jungle and numerous Gods and Goddesses. As far away from Azra as one could get, surely they would be safe there, but how would they get back? That was a problem for another day, one to be solved once they were out of Pompae's reach.

"The rituals of Nefara are unlike any other, they may lead us to the truth," said Kerak.

"What's he talking about?" asked Barroc.

Belenus waived the question away. "Nothing. Thank you, Barroc, when do we leave?"

Barroc eyed the shaman distrustfully but shrugged. "Not for awhile yet. I'll return for you once everything is ready. Just stay here until then."

A thought occurred to Belenus—Barroc was taking a great risk in helping them escape but that did not explain why he had arranged this deal in the first place. "Why take such a risk by selling to Nefara? Is the extra wealth worth losing your family?"

Barroc glanced at Mariam, making it clear that they'd had a similar conversation. "I do it for my family, and your claims of Pompae's seizure of power only shows the prudence of my decision. Money always outlives Gods, it has no aims except to continue itself. When I have enough money we are going to move to Cheton to start anew. In Strakos my children will be able live without worrying about immortality. Hentavio will not have to die in Calanthia in the name of the Emperor's vision."

Barroc left to make arrangements, along with Mariam who said she would bring them something to eat, commenting that Belenus looked half starved. He felt empty but not from lack of food, even though he could not remember the last real meal he had. The stacks of neatly arranged ledgers on the shelves stared back at Belenus with the life he could have led, a life that Barroc had chosen, which oddly enough, also required leaving Azra in secret.

"I feel as though I am being pulled along, tied to a string that twists and turns, bringing me to a destination I never expected," said Belenus.

"Bolo haduok," said Kerak. "The endless fishing line."

"Exactly, the hook is stuck inside of me and I'm forced to follow as I'm reeled in."

"We must like the taste of the same bait because it appears our lines have become entangled."

"Ha! Well that's something at least. I was done for in the dungeon, was ready to be gutted, but here I am thrashing around again."

The opening of the front door signaled Mariam's return. She set out a meal of rye bread, cheese, and smoked salmon. Belenus laughed at the sight of the fish but ate it heartily, wondering at the paths of life as he chewed. Mariam produced a bottle of watered down wine and poured three glasses. Her hands trembling slightly as she held the bottle.

"Figured we could use something to take the edge off, it's been an alarming day," said Mariam.

They drank in silence. Belenus must have dozed off without realizing it because the next thing he knew he was being shaken by Barroc's rough hands.

"Time to go."

Belenus blinked to see Barroc's bulbous nose hovering in the center of his vision. He was confused for a moment until the chain of events that had brought him to be in his father's office coalesced. Kerak was already standing, looking grim in his all black attire. Mariam was nowhere to be seen, having departed while Belenus dozed. The three men passed by the dusty shelves of the shop like specters through the memory of Belenus' childhood. He snatched a small shaving blade from a shelf, flicking the edge, satisfied that it was sharp enough. The tunic he wore did not have inner pockets like the sleeves of his robe so Belenus folded the blade and held it in his hand.

A small carriage was waiting outside the shop which Barroc ushered the two fugitives into. Barroc climbed aboard the driver seat, snapping the reins to get the horses moving. Already the signs of Pompae's ambition were changing the face of Azra. Belenus peeked through the wooden slats of the door to see the rubble left behind by groups of people as they systematically went about destroying shrines. He could not fault the citizens of Azra for their actions, even though the outcome of their zeal pained him so—after all, it was Belenus who had stood before the city and convinced them that such actions were necessary.

"Even though they are lost to you, at least you know what has become of your people," said Kerak.

"I'd like to visit the Tribes once this is all over, if only to persuade them to choose someone other than you to be their leader."

Kerak grinned but the mirth faded away as he stared into the distance that awaited them beyond the confines of the carriage. "We take the long way round. We will see the ends of Rua before my homeland."

They traveled in silence after that, each man mired in his own contemplations until the noise of Barroc arguing with a guard reached them.

'Get out of the bloody way, you little pissant, I'm the head armorer for the Chosen and those duties take me outside of Azra."

"I know who you are sir, but I'm under strict orders to stop anyone trying to leave without the express consent of Master Pompae."

"Who do you think's been signing my pay since the Emperor left?" The irritation was clear in Barroc's voice but the guard would not budge.

"I'm sorry sir, perhaps if you had the proper documentation..."

Belenus could sense the anger growing inside of his brother. He felt the bellows of Barroc's lungs stoking the fire in an attempt to melt the guard's resolve. He found that he could also sense the resoluteness of the guard as capable of withstanding Barroc's fury. These sensations drifted into the carriage, carried by the voices of the arguing men, causing Belenus to tingle with energy. The vibrations of their argument resonated within him, he could feel the opposing forces swirling toward an impact like clouds before a violent storm. Belenus flicked open the razor, carefully slicing a thin red line across the meat of his thumb.

The vibrations slammed into Belenus, rocking him forward in his seat. He secured them to himself, tying them tightly around his body. He reached out experimentally, flowing along the invisible lines leading outside, finding he was able to follow their route in reverse until his awareness was outside of the cabin. The scene unfolded as though he were looking down from above. The indistinct figures were identifiable by the unique resonance of each speaker's voice.

Other figures were moving closer, coming to investigate the commotion. He needed to act quickly, before the guards opened the carriage doors and started asking questions. He teased the strands of the different voices apart, focusing on that of the guard looking up at Barroc. Belenus gripped the vibration firmly and sent his own voice traveling along the established current.

"Let us pass," he said.

The guard's head tilted in confusion as he looked for the source of the voice. Belenus felt his words ram up against a wall that stubbornly pushed back against his will. He pushed harder.

"Let us pass."

Cracks appeared in the guard's willpower. Belenus slipped between these cracks just as the water did when Kerak froze the wall. He strained against the barrier, feeling the resistance give way and then he was through. One more time.

"Let us pass."

Something changed in the guard's stance—his limbs went limp but his movement rigid. Barroc had gone silent watching this bizarre event. The other guards arrived, asking for direction.

"Let them pass," said the guard.

The others opened the gate for the carriage to carry on. Barroc flicked the reins and they were once again moving toward the secret rendezvous.

Belenus held firm to the vibration emanating from the guard, squeezing tighter as the distance between them made the incorporeal form more difficult to grasp. A rough bump underneath jolted Belenus inside the carriage and the strand slipped away in the moment of distraction. The priest's awareness returned to the interior of the cabin. Kerak was watching him intently, his eyes calculating.

"You did a bad thing," said the shaman.

"Says a pagan."

Belenus did not care to investigate how he truly felt about what he had done to the guard. He was not so sure that what he'd done was any different than what he'd been doing since becoming Beacon. Nothing was certain anymore except that they needed to escape Azra. He would have time to relive his failures on the long voyage to Nefara, but they first needed to arrive at the waiting ship.

Finally, the carriage slowed as they reached their destination. Night was complete and the stars shone prominently this far from the city in the inky sky. Belenus thought the stars looked like pin pricks in a dark canvas, letting light shine through from an unknown source. The alignment of the stars seemed foreign—too much time spent looking at his past and down at his worn feet. Belenus cursed his old age and the peculiar way it affected his gaze.

"This way." Barroc's deep voice called them towards the sound of water lapping against the shore.

Each man took a slightly different path down to the beach to find a large rowboat loaded and waiting. Belenus stubbed his toe and came hopping to meet the others.

"This is the last shipment. I can get my pay and your necks won't get stretched. With any luck we'll meet again somewhere other than Azra."

"Are there any assurances the Nefarans will not kill us?" asked Kerak.

"They aren't a bloodthirsty lot, so I doubt they'll get their hands dirty. If anything, they'll drop you overboard once they reach deep water and be done with it."

"Splendid," Belenus grumbled.

"The sharks have moved to warmer waters this time of year so you'll be all right as long as you float," said Barroc.

"Ah, well then, let's be off! You're lovely wife had the foresight to remove my heavy priestly robes so there's nothing to worry about."

Flickering torches in the distance became visible. Belenus counted eight individual flames swiftly advancing on their position. His sway over the guard must have been used up. The armed men were coming to investigate just what the head armorer of the Chosen was doing outside of city limits.

"Quickly now," Barroc said urgently.

He leaned against the hull of the boat and Belenus joined to help push it further into the water. The ship seemed impossibly heavy and the two made minuscule progress from their efforts.

"Kerak you lazy whelp, get over here and help!" Belenus shouted.

"I will lead them away," said Kerak. "Continue on without me. Listen for Cynaal and you will find your way home, Beacon."

"Kerak! You'll be killed!"

The shaman was suddenly next to Belenus, his voice barely above a whisper. "I am a ghost, remember?" There was the rustle of his steps in the sand and then just the wind and the waves.

"Put your back into it, you pansy!" Barroc commanded.

Belenus heaved his frame against the curve of the hull, straining with all his might. Barroc grunted in exertion and little by little the brothers moved the boat off the beach. An outraged shout pierced the night as Kerak made contact with the guards. The boat became buoyant when the water reached ankle height. The cold water soaked into Belenus' bones, his feet going numb. He clambered over the side to land on an oar that jabbed painfully into his ribs.

Barroc made a similarly disgraceful entry. "Start paddling," growled the younger Wicket.

"You said you'd help me escape, not force me into hard labor," Belenus wheezed as he pulled on the handle of the oar.

"Tit soft as always, eh?" said Barroc in amusement.

"Father never told you, did he? We bought you from a traveling menagerie and shaved off your fur so I'd have a little playmate. You cried and cried after he lopped off your tail."

The two found a rhythm with the oars and steadily increased their distance from the shore. They watched the torches of the guards moving further away from the water. Kerak was leading them away from the city, likely trying to keep the location of the carriage unknown.

"Brave man," Barroc said quietly.

"Maybe," Belenus replied. "He might just be a great fool."

"He saved our sorry skins and I know Mariam will be thankful for that."

"I'm proud of you for doing what you think is best for your family," said Belenus as he watched the flames disappear around a bend. They were now out in the open water and the sense of space was expansive. The horizon was hidden by the night but Belenus could feel the absence of edges blocking him in.

"Maybe we wouldn't have to leave if there were more like you in Azra," Barroc said stiffly.

"What do you mean?"

"You see the best in people and try to bring it forth for their sake, instead of using your abilities to personally benefit."

This was the nicest thing Barroc had ever told Belenus, but the priest was saddened by the compliment. "And look where that has brought us."

A warbling whistle carried over the surface of the waves causing Belenus to crane his neck around. He saw a hulking form occupying the space directly in their path. The Nefaran ship was a chunk of blackness superimposed against the cool dark of the sky, darker than the waves below. The ship seemed an embodiment of the despair threatening to smother the light inside of the former Beacon of Azra.

## Metamorphosis

A sweet aroma of fresh flowers and incense filled the massive space of the Emperor's caravan. A young girl carried a tray bearing a tea pot and two porcelain glasses. The servant was dressed in a plain brown smock. She bowed and gave a meek smile before handing Melea a glass. Melea detected herbs and a hint of honey.

The serving girl extended the second glass to the other visitor sitting in the caravan and slowly retracted the offered tea. The girl gave an almost imperceptible bow and hurried away to an adjoining room. Melea set her glass on the armrest of her chair and looked over at her companion.

Morokko Kachina glared back at her, his charcoal eyes and the bridge of a thin nose visible above a black handkerchief covering his mouth. They had been summoned by the Emperor and now waited for him to emerge from the depths of the caravan. The silence grew uncomfortable as Kachina continued to unblinkingly watch Melea.

"What?" she demanded, her tone sharp.

Melea was exhausted and her nerves were frayed. What little patience she had in the past for the assassin was gone. Her eyelids wanted to droop, to close out the light and lock down her consciousness so that she could rest. She wanted nothing more than to sleep, to silence the doubting voices inside. Harsh whispers stoked her anxiety like water coming to a boil. She kept herself upright in the chair by strength of will. Sleep was unattainable despite how badly she wanted it, as badly as she needed it. All autonomy was given up when she slept, subjugating her to the authority of the darkest regions of her mind.

The back of her eyelids became a stage where images of those who had died by her hand flashed by in their final pose as the life drained out of their eyes. The fallen forms looked to her with alternating expressions, changing from pleading for mercy to cold accusation. Worse yet was when she descended into full sleep to be tossed around like a rag doll by the mysterious force of her unconscious. Powerful dreams of strange scenes filled with unknown characters caused fitful sleep which left her feeling more tired than before. The stench of death was there to greet her when she awoke, lingering like a thick fog. Something had changed and she did not know exactly what— this unknown frightened Melea most of all.

Her life was an unrelenting struggle but she still preferred it over the numbness of being dead. The curse that took control of her and sent her into the netherworld was growing more persistent. Visions that previously only appeared on rare occasions when dead were now leaking into her dreams.

A slight hiss precipitated the assassin's voice, causing Melea to imagine the air slithering between the pointed fangs she suspected were hidden behind the cloth. "I heard what you did at Choker Pass. Tell me, what does a shadow taste like?"

"You should know."

A flicker of amusement flashed across Kachina's eyes before disappearing into their black depths. "We could compare notes on such a rare delicacy."

Melea was digging her fingers into the cushion of the chair, she smoothed them out and took a sip of tea. The hot liquid burned the tip of her tongue. Kachina sat in his chair, swathed in black like a evil spirit, intent on haunting her.

"Why do you stare at me?"

"Does it bother you? Do I frighten you, cohiko?"

"No, you're disgusting."

There was something deeply unsettling about being in Kachina's presence, a sensation that left most people feeling fearful. Melea did not fear the man. She loathed him. Being around the assassin made her feel sick, a nauseous turbulence in her stomach that, if given enough time, seemed to seep through her pores to leave an oily residue on her skin. Another sip of tea did nothing to disquiet the roiling in her stomach.

"My scared little rabbit, you look ready to bolt, but what else to expect from one who wastes such ability," Kachina mocked.

"I will rip off that stupid cloth covering your mouth and ram this wasted ability right down your throat. What are you hiding? Crooked teeth? No? Oh, I know what it is, the big bad assassin likes to play dress-up, come now, take off that shawl and show me your pretty makeup."

Kachina leaned forward. "The cohiko thinks she is a lion, look at how fierce her growl is."

Her response was silenced by the entrance of Emperor Anathasius who sat down smoothly on a luxurious leather sofa. He wore his usual white garb, which was as clean as if it had just finished being fashioned in the next room. Melea wore a new blue uniform but had somehow managed to already scuff one of the black buttons. Before the meeting she had washed the grime out of her hair, which was tied up in a bun to keep the greasy mop under her helmet for the battle later on. Kachina would not be participating in the battle. Melea wondered if Anathasius would join the fray this time. Doubtful. She almost snorted in indignation.

Anathasius looked to Melea then to Kachina, his presence filling the room, too large to be contained by his physical frame. "A God will die today. The invisible will come crashing down as the blood of believers soak into the ground."

"I thought you said Ziya'Sybel was already gone," said Melea.

Kachina gave no reaction to the Emperor's pronouncement. Anathasius clasped his hands together on his lap, looking comfortable as he spoke of deicide.

"The deity of beasts and earth has deserted the people who worship him but that does not lessen their belief in his existence. Their continued survival is used to validate his power. Only complete collapse can remove the blinders from their eyes. Today the army of Calanthia will be forced to witness their utter abandonment, and soon, when the Pillar crashes down, they will realize how small and weak humans truly are."

Melea's eyebrows quirked, causing Anathasius to smile. The expression only deepened her confusion as the source of humor was beyond her.

Anathasius looked at Melea, through her. "At the best of times humans are impulsive, selfish creatures and with the death of God they will undoubtedly slide into anarchy. The shape of their world is changed, they feel shifted out of place, and it is therefore necessary to use the forces at man's disposal to organize and acclimatize the masses to renew a sense of control. But people tend to be fearful in these instances and fearful people are dangerous, which requires the use of weapons to bring order."

Melea glanced at the assassin but his covered face rendered him expressionless. Anathasius seemed relaxed but had a faraway look in his eyes, giving the impression that he was talking to someone other than his guests. The Emperor's focus returned to the room and he looked at Melea and Kachina in turn.

"You two are my greatest weapons and your value is paramount. You will bring order to the confusion, so that the people of Calanthia may find peace within the Shining Empire."

Kachina closed his eyes, bowing his head in respect. Anathasius looked to Melea who sat rigidly, the stiffness of her body nullifying the contours of the chair. Her tongue froze, incapable of responding with something intelligible. Her insides squirmed, but differently than when speaking with the assassin, this time the sensation was sharper, almost painful. She gave a quick nod to Anathasius before lowering her eyes to the floor. Her heart thumped wildly, temporarily stalling her exhaustion from progressing.

Anathasius stood and it was as though the sun itself was in the caravan. "You two will not take part in the battle today, rather you shall watch from on high, to comprehend the benefits inherent within the sacrifice of others. The stakes are being raised. It is imperative that my weapons become more versatile; a blade with two edges cuts twice as effectively. Go now, ready yourselves."

The assassin stood and bowed again before silently leaving. Melea stood awkwardly, feeling blatantly exposed while Anathasius watched her.

"Worry not," Anathasius said, calmly. "This is the destiny you must embrace. Most people are frail things, frightened of their own shadow but you are not like them, you are beginning to understand true strength. You and Morokko are the only two capable of overcoming Darkness so that others may walk the Illuminated Path. I know the way to the eternal shining city but others are needed to pave the road through Darkness to reach the gates. You are my chosen of chosen."

Melea felt her cheeks flush. She nodded stiffly and then left the caravan. A mist had descended from the mountains like a damp curtain between the earth and sky. Vague shapes hurried about in the commotion while the army made its final preparations. Melea walked slowly to where her new, nameless horse was tethered, hand firmly clenched to her chest, holding the seed that was hidden beneath the Chosen blue.

She spotted her swordmaster nearby and called out to the man, needing to bring about a sense of normalcy. The momentum of her life was increasing without her control, spinning faster than she could handle.

"How about showing me those special moves you were bragging about?"

Derclerq paused, questioning whether to approach his pupil or continue on. He sighed, a momentary look of deflation in his puffed up chest. He walked over straight-backed, stopping in front of Melea. "There is nothing more with the sword that I can teach you."

Melea smirked. "Are you saying that the greatest swordsman in Rua is no longer the greatest? What about your legacy when others see me fight?"

Derclerq's mustache twitched as he looked over Melea's shoulder. "That wasn't fighting. What does a sword matter when a man can be torn apart by his shadow?"

The Tannoi swordmaster walked away without looking back. His words stung, hurting in a way that made Melea want to double over. She went back to her tent to stare up into nothing, letting her mind drift, actively avoiding sleep.

The armies squared off across from each other on the vast plains on the eastern side of the Petals. A wide strip of grass separated the bronze and blue lines of the Shining Empire from the green and tan of Calanthia. The purple and red of Bromaleigh took up one section and there were even a few sections occupied by the shiny black of Carnot. All surviving soldiers had merged into a single army in a final stand against the Shining Empire. Melea noticed that the olive and silver of Asyrith was missing from the ranks. Duke Karracus had made his choice: his future depended on the outcome of this battle as much as the men in the front lines.

Only the faintest breeze stirred the air, not nearly enough to disperse the fog, which created a sense of confinement in the open space. Feeble heat from the rising sun was not yet strong enough to dissipate the moisture in the air. Melea's uniform clung to her skin, making her feel clammy and anxious. She was thankful for the lack of armor as the fully geared Chosen were surely sweating profusely even though the battle was yet to begin.

A large winged creature circled over the waiting armies, occasionally screeching in impatience. Melea watched the outline of the animal against the murky sky, wondering what amalgamation of creatures the Calanthian's had used to create this monster. Smaller winged forms flittered below the larger creature, altering their course in response to its calls. These beasts had leathery wings and were covered in brown fur, and their chittering noises made them seem to be some type of massive bat.

Melea sat astride her new horse, a brown gelding that had none of Ranna's vibrancy. This beast seemed to be in a constant daze, always requiring an extra moment to react to Melea's commands. General Cathair was a short distance in front of her, surrounded with officers and other soldiers bearing horns of varying sizes for different commands. Kachina stood behind and to the left, separate from everyone else. Anathasius was in front and slightly to the right, between Melea and Cathair. Together they looked down on the plains from the last large hill with the mountains shrouded in mist behind them.

A long section of heavy infantry made up the core of the battle formation for the Shining Empire. They carried spears in their right hands and were protected by the breadth of the shields strapped to their left arms. Heavy cavalry supported the foot soldiers on their undefended right side and they were in turn supported by light infantry on the outermost section. A small squad of horsemen supported the left side of the front line. Four units of light infantry, supplemented by archers, made up the auxiliary, standing evenly spaced behind the imposing front line. The long spears of the phalanx pointed straight into the air.

In contrast, the soldiers of Calanthia were organized in two long lines placed one in front of the other, with cavalry on the fringes of the first line. They outnumbered the Chosen despite their losses in the battle of Choker Pass. Beating drums broke the silence, the sound rippling through the Chosen like a wave. Calanthia's own drums started in response and men lent their battle cries to the din. A furious, restless energy built as the two armies prepared. A haunting note stretched out across the plain, Melea was not sure who issued it.

And the battle began.

Slave soldiers raced toward the line of Chosen who resolutely stood their ground behind a wall of shields while the long spears of the second line reached forward to create an offense just ahead of the defensive stance. A wave of men crashed into the spearpoints, some managing to slip through and bash against the large oval shields but the line held. The Chosen attacked from behind their protection, careful not to advance as individuals.

Men fell in heaps as the two sides fought to control the flow of battle. A sharp whistle sounded and a new line of Chosen stepped forward to face the oncoming hoard while the surviving members of the original line stepped behind their comrades for a reprieve. Anathasius maneuvered his horse next to Melea's, his aura more confining than the fog around them.

"See how disciplined they are?" said the Emperor. "The measure of control in their actions? This is what you must master to achieve greatness. A leader cannot lead if they are the first into the fray, fighting to the beat of their own drum."

Melea said nothing, keeping her gaze on the struggle below. The Chosen moved as though they were a single entity, a gigantic armored creature equipped with vicious claws. Men screamed and died as lives and limbs were mercilessly hacked away. The Calanthian horsemen swooped in to crush the right side, attempting to weaken the Empire's cavalry enough to gain access to the shieldless side of the infantry. The rush was met head on as armored horsemen clashed with a screech of metal. Melea blinked as the crunch of the impact reached her.

Cathair gave orders to shift the main body of the phalanx to the right to keep it as close to the cavalry as possible. The secondary Calanthian horses on the left were spurred into action by this maneuver, racing forward to flank the Empire's infantry. They were met by the Empire's remaining mounted soldiers and diverted, forced into taking a wider route. Cathair called for the auxiliary to buttress the opening gap on the left side.

At this moment the bat creatures descended, swooping low to raze the Chosen with wicked talons. Men pierced upward with their spears, plucking the slower creatures out of the air. A loud screech from the giant bird called the remaining bats to return to the safety of the air.

The action was intense. Melea watched with wide eyes as men and horses were moved about like pieces on a cüthril board. General Cathair was a better strategist than his adversaries, outmaneuvering them at every turn, but Calanthia had pieces that were not customary to cüthril. A dark form descended from the sky, swooping into the mass of cavalry. The enormous bird emerged from the tangle with a flailing soldier in its talons. A stream of bats followed behind the bird's dive to clear out a grouping of men. Only half of the bats who made the direct strike returned to the air.

Melea's chest tightened as she watched the bird carry the man above the battlefield, her chest dropped along with the man as he fell, cinching up as he disappeared from view. She should be helping. The thought deflated as quickly as it ballooned. She did not want to enter the combat. Viewing the carnage was making her sick.

This sensation was new, and the strangeness of it troubled her. Violence had always been a constant in her life, an activity in which she excelled, but now it filled her with anxiety and with regret for past actions. A creeping dread of future expectations gripped her and would not let go. She was a weapon, an instrument of death to be used to accomplish the goals of the Shining Empire; Anathasius had said so. Now, she was being prepared for leadership so that she could direct how and when men died as well as slaughter them herself. All for the glory of the Shining Empire. She was to wallow in Darkness while the Emperor stayed embalmed in Light.

An equal to Morokko Kachina, the man she most despised. A comrade in arms with Darkness, expected to pave a road for the benefit of others, for the ultimate destiny of the Shining Empire. A destiny that Melea was told was her own, that she had apparently been preparing for her entire life.

A hard pit formed in her stomach, a realization that she was now grudgingly acknowledging for the first time. Anathasius did not care about her. She was just an object, a game piece like any of the men down below. The only difference was that Melea had abilities they did not, abilities that Anathasius deemed more useful to his ambitions, she was a vessel to harness Darkness so that the Emperor's vision could triumph.

*What would she gain from this sacrifice?* An image of her likeness in battle painted on a wall in the Shining Palace? Chapters in the histories to be tucked away in the library? All glory was the Emperor's, she would never be his equal, never be considered more than an object in his eyes—she saw that now. Melea refused this future, wanted to refuse her entire life until this point. *Men do not share power. They hoard it ever more or cling to what they have until they are consumed by it*—the final lesson given by her tutor, Mandrikos.

Melea felt movement coursing through her veins, something foreign and unnatural. Whispering voices trickled into her consciousness, the words indecipherable, but the intention clear. *Take—it is yours—devour.* Melea's trembling hands gripped tighter on the reins.

A bitter taste coated her mouth, the substance viscous and toxic. The reek of vomit and gore, of the Night Creeper, suddenly filled Melea's nose. There were no scorchers on the battlefield yet the screams of men on fire echoed all around her. She rocked in the saddle, blinking rapidly, teeth grinding as she attempted to remain upright. Anger surged through her chest but it was like a bellows gusting wind on an empty fireplace. She was so tired.

The Empire's heavy cavalry had crushed that of Calanthia and was driving a wedge between the enemy forces, but Melea hardly noticed. All of the bat creatures were slain and the Chosen continued to advance as an unstoppable mass.

"The Chosen are victorious," Anathasius said, with pride.

Melea looked over at the Emperor dully, blinking to focus. A maddened screech overhead shocked her into awareness. The bird was making another plunge but the giant bird of prey was targeting Anathasius this time. The officers in front were too slow in raising their spears to impale the beast. The massive wings pushed air down onto Melea, disturbing her hair so that it cascaded across her face.

The seed thumped against Melea's heart. Anathasius looked up at the bird but remained still. Melea waited for him to strike but he just sat there expressionless. Time seemed to move in slow motion as Melea turned her attention to the dark form bearing down like a shrieking harpy.

The bird was an ugly thing. Its head and neck were mostly bald and covered in folds of saggy pink flesh. Its feathers were a sooty grey and each wing three times Melea's size. Curved yellow talons extended, opening wide to rip Anathasius from the saddle. She moved by instinct as she leapt from the back of the horse. A glint of silver was in her right hand as her sword slashed down at the nearest clawed foot.

The sword cut deep into the meat of bird's footpad as she smashed into its legs. The bird shrieked in pain and Melea hung on as it stopped the dive to hover in position with gale force thrusts from the massive wings. Anathasius finally reacted, raising his hands to expel a blinding flash. The bird twisted and elevated as Melea's horse bolted.

Her vision was a wash of intense white that went black as the brightness faded. She could feel her uniform snagged in the talons as the bird moved higher into the sky. The bird traveled swiftly away but Melea was not willing to risk cutting herself out of its grasp with her vision compromised.

The wind whipped Melea's hair around as the bird fled. She was blind but could feel the strength of the bird's clutch, as well as an underlying pulse that was even more powerful. The steady thrum of the bird's wings; she could feel them above as well as through the tight grip holding her. The movement called out to her in an unexpected way, triggering something inside, akin to when she had encountered the Chuku Bartha monsters. She licked her lips, tasting the hint of a shadow. Melea kept her eyes closed as she began to pull this aspect of the bird closer.

The bird squawked in panic as it was tugged violently downward in Melea's direction, sending the bird into a tailspin. Melea opened her eyes to see mountains, stone, and the shimmer of water nearby. They landed together in a heap, a sickening crack rippling through the bird on impact; the bird on its back with Melea raised aloft, still in its grasp. Melea dropped as the foot went limp.

She rolled to her knees, head swimming as she tried to make sense of her condition. All she could sense was the rapidly disappearing shadow of the bird. She wanted it; wanted to take it as her own. The sensation of flapping wings burst into Melea's mind in an auspicious moment of clarity. She envisioned the wings as part of her own body and for an instant was overcome by an indescribable feeling of release. The wings promised weightless movement that could not be attained on the ground.

A haunting whisper emerged from the shadow, as it became paler. *Take.* Melea grasped the thinning edges of the shadow and pulled, shearing the wings cleanly from the back of the bird. The shadow dissipated and she opened her eyes to see both wings slide off the mangled corpse.

Melea gripped one wing with both hands, maneuvering it behind her so that she could slam it into her right shoulder blade. Her back arched painfully, forcing her up on tip-toes as sinewy strands ripped through the uniform to attach to the wing. Searing pain flared as her skin merged with the wing, suddenly coming to a stop as the process was completed. She shuffled over to the second wing, thrown off balance by the new appendage on her back. The pain was just as intense the second time as the strands of her skin wove themselves into that of the wing until they were one and the same.

Her awareness was chaotic. Bizarre sensations flooded her body as she adjusted to a distorted reality. The world felt unreal, as though her body was false. She had to leave, had to escape the maelstrom enveloping her. An instinctual urge to flee overpowered the accompanying distaste of cowardice. She sprinted as fast as possible with the added weight of the wings. Melea let the wings do what they wanted to, what they understood better than she could ever hope to.

The dark feathers spread out on either side and started flapping, rapidly forcing air down as Melea ran. Without quite expecting it, her feet left the gravely stone and she was thrust airborne.

She glided over the rounded green tops of the Petals, her eyes watering from the wind. At least, she thought it was from the wind. Great strength powered the wings as they beat steadily, lifting Melea higher as she sped away. She heard snatches of fighting but could not see any of the battle. Soon, she entered the clouds and could see nothing at all.

As she flew, she began to feel the alternating currents of air, the different temperatures and updrafts that aided or hindered flight. Understanding how to use the features of this foreign environment in any rational way could not register, so she relied on instinct to carry her. Landscapes changed below while she rose and fell without any apparent pattern. An endless ocean of forest appeared as the last of the daylight ebbed away. On and on, pushing herself beyond exhaustion; she could not get far enough away. The distance would not be great enough even if she crossed the entire expanse of Rua.

An excruciating pain erupted in her shoulders without warning, racing down her spine with electric fire. Her back arched as she cried out. She tried to make the wings flatten out, to catch a gust of air, but her mind was static. The bird's vengeful spirit was digging its talons into her skull and demanding that Melea pay penance for her stolen flight. The ground appeared before her, the trees were gone, having been replaced by sand dunes. There was no time to consider her location. Melea was going down.

"Flew high over the mountains until I lost sight of her in the clouds," rasped the black clad assassin.

Anathasius looked into the sky as if he could discern the flight of the bird. Nothing but a solid mass of undisturbed clouds. Melea was gone. The bird might drop Melea to her death at any moment or could devour her whole. Anathasius no longer cared. She had failed him again. She was not destined for greatness. Her fate was sealed. He licked his lips, anticipating the taste of her spirit.

Anathasius looked down at Kachina from the stallion. "Did you see which direction it went?"

The horse paced from side to side, still unnerved by the recent attack. The assassin nodded.

"Go after her. Bring her back. Despite our preparations I expect Marikal will have to be taken by siege. Return as swiftly as possible," Anathasius ordered.

"And if she's dead?"

"Bring back the body, even if there are only bits and pieces left. Bring it all."

# Appendix

## Terms
Ba-rük, blood rituals enacted in Calanthia
Batanray, martial techniques derived from the Infinite Stream
Binding Doctrine, the Tenets of Faith established by Emperor Anathasius
Chuku Bartha, ape men of the Eternal Forest
Emperor's Gift, source of the priesthood's power
Flames, attendants to Emperor Anathasius with specific ritual training
Green Time, oldest known era of human existence
Illuminated Path, system of faith in the Shining Empire; Light over Darkness
Infinite Stream, physical motions to balance body, mind, and spirit
Sickness, an encroaching decay believed to be an aspect of Darkness
Syla, a returned spirit
Tehlos, sect of healers in Rhezaria
Vessel, the act of channeling the Emperor's Gift

## Gods & Faiths
Chetaunus, believed to have founded Strakos, God of intellect and numbers
Cynaal, lifesong sung by deceased ancestors
Iglyl, spirit of the wind
Mar'Edo Kon, believed to have founded Rhezaria, God of strength and healing
Swampnakama, believed to have founded Nefara, God of dreams and art
The Eye, cosmic totem of the Outskirts
Ziya'Sybel, believed to have founded Calanthia, God of earth and justice

## Peoples
Amparo Tannoi, considered to be excellent swordsmen
Frozen Tribes, loosely affiliated groups of hunters and fishermen in the far north
Shining Empire, former domain of Cambor. Expanding through conquest

## Rhezaria: the Clans
Nataga, the oldest Clan. Fiery demeanors have them always prepared for a fight
Remori, seafaring traders with close affiliation to the Rhezi
Rhezi, the most ethnically diverse Clan. Founded by the first king, Verangor Dracarion
Sando, reclusive mountain people. Known to travel in groups of five whenever possible
Uzanaki, generally massive in size; fierce warriors covered in tattoos

## Calanthia: the Dukedoms

Asyrith, smallest dukedom. Influences trade along the Serpent with their great wall

Bromaleigh, home to the most varied temples of worship

Calanthe, the controlling dukedom. Home to Marikal, the golden city; a place of many slaves

Carnot, hardy people on the border with Rhezaria

Lyrene, producers of fine wines and ciders

Qu'hraz, masters of rice cultivation bordering the Sunken Coast

## Other Regions of Rua

Fyn, island desert dwellers and esteemed astronomers

Nefara, jungle dwellers considered to be great artists

Outskirts, nomadic bands of diverse cultures who abstain from blood rituals. Are generally disliked by the established nations

Six Isle Republic, faction that separated from Strakos. Noted scholars with an elected government

Strakos, claim lineage from the lost empire of Le'teokan. Shrewd merchants and bankers

## About the Author

Tyler lives in Alberta, Canada. He has had several short stories and poems published with Polar Expressions Publishing.

Author blog and to contact by email: www.tylersehn.com
Join me on Twitter @TySehn

Reviews are an important part of the hustle for an indie author so if you found the first installment of The Spiritbinder Saga to be anywhere on the scale of, "Hmm, better than I expected" to "Whoa! What happens next?" please take a moment to share your opinion. Goodreads.com and Amazon are great places to post a review.

I'm a big fan of talking to people in person (yes, I'm aware of what year it is) and if you are too then tell a friend about Daughter of Shadow!

Made in the USA
San Bernardino, CA
25 March 2018